HIDDEN EMBERS

A DRAGON'S HEAT NOVEL

TESSA ADAMS

HEAT

HEAT
Published by New American Library,
a division of Penguin Group (USA) Inc.,
375 Hudson Street, New York, New York 10014, USA
Penguin Group (Canada), 90 Eglinton Avenue East, Suite 700, Toronto,
Ontario M4P 2Y3, Canada (a division of Pearson Penguin Canada Inc.)
Penguin Books Ltd., 80 Strand, London WC2R 0RL, England
Penguin Ireland, 25 St. Stephen's Green, Dublin 2,
Ireland (a division of Penguin Books Ltd.)
Penguin Group (Australia), 250 Camberwell Road, Camberwell,
Victoria 3124, Australia (a division of Pearson Australia Group Pty. Ltd.)
Penguin Books India Pvt. Ltd., 11 Community Centre,
Panchsheel Park, New Delhi - 110 017, India
Penguin Group (NZ), 67 Apollo Drive, Rosedale, North Shore 0632,
New Zealand (a division of Pearson New Zealand Ltd.)
Penguin Books (South Africa) (Pty.) Ltd., 24 Sturdee Avenue,
Rosebank, Johannesburg 2196, South Africa

Penguin Books Ltd., Registered Offices:
80 Strand, London WC2R 0RL, England

First published by Heat, an imprint of New American Library,
a division of Penguin Group (USA) Inc.

First Printing, April 2011

Copyright © Tracy Deebs-Elkenaney, 2011
All rights reserved

HEAT is a trademark of Penguin Group (USA) Inc.

LIBRARY OF CONGRESS CATALOGING-IN-PUBLICATION DATA:

Adams, Tessa.
Hidden embers: a dragon's heat novel/Tessa Adams.
p.   cm—(Dragon's heat; 2)
ISBN 978-0-451-23263-2
1. Shapeshifting—Fiction.   2. New Mexico—Fiction.   I. Title.
PS3623.O57H53 2011
813'.6—dc22   2010052159

Set in Minion Pro

146122990

Praise for
Dark Embers

"Written in a compelling voice, *Dark Embers* introduces a sexy and intriguing new world. I'm looking forward to seeing where Tessa Adams takes her dragons next."

—Nalini Singh, *New York Times* bestselling author
of *Archangel's Kiss*

"*Dark Embers* is a blistering-hot, fast-paced adventure that will leave readers breathless. Dylan and Phoebe have great chemistry and a romantic story that will captivate you and keep you turning pages long into the night. I'm really looking forward to the next book in the series!"

—Anya Bast, *New York Times* bestselling author
of *Wicked Enchantment*

"This darkly seductive tale will have you longing for a dragon of your very own."   —Shiloh Walker, national bestselling author of *Broken*

"The first Dragon's Heat romantic fantasy is a wonderful shape-shifter tale. . . . Fans will enjoy soaring with dragons."

—Harriet Klausner, Genre Go Round Reviews

"*Dark Embers* is a fantastic debut to a new erotic paranormal series that will take you on a scorching-hot adventure and leave you wanting more. . . . There was even a moment I felt myself get teary eyed—in an erotica, people!"   —Among the Muses

"If you're looking for a fast paranormal read featuring suspense, hot shifters, and even hotter sex, then look no further."   —Smexy Books

ALSO BY TESSA ADAMS

Dark Embers

For Shellee Cruz and Emily McKay,
two of the best writing pals a girl could ever ask for

ACKNOWLEDGMENTS

I'd like to thank all the people at NAL who work on my books, especially the incredibly talented people in the art department, who give me such amazing covers.

My wonderful, amazing and brilliant editor, Jhanteigh Kupihea, for believing in me and the Dragonstars. She is always there to bounce ideas off and is always willing to let me try something a little different. Her enthusiasm and talent has made writing the Dragon's Heat novels an absolute joy and they are definitely better for her hard work and suggestions.

My dear friend Sherry Thomas, who always makes me laugh (and brings me chocolate cake when the situation is dire).

My fantastic agent, Emily Sylvan Kim, for everything she's done for me, and especially for putting up with endless phone calls and e-mails, so many of which begin with, "So, I have this really great idea. . . ."

My wonderful fans, whose support of and fascination with the Dragonstars I appreciate more than I can say. Your comments and e-mails make it a million times easier, and more rewarding, for me to write these books.

PROLOGUE

He was tired.

So tired that he could barely hold his head up.

So tired that he didn't have the energy to finish the chart he was working on.

So tired that even the act of breathing seemed like a chore.

Rubbing his hands over his face, Quinn Maguire tried to fight against the despair that was his constant companion.

He failed.

It weighed him down, made his movements slow and clumsy as it pressed in on him from every side. When was this going to be over? When was he finally going to be able to stop fighting?

After scrawling his initials on the line at the bottom of the chart, he shoved back from his desk and walked over to the window that stretched the length of one of his office walls.

Outside the desert was dark and peaceful, the city lights far enough away that the stars glittered against the ebony blanket of the night. The sight almost always soothed him, but tonight it wouldn't. He could feel it.

His eyesight was keen enough that he could see the night predators shadowed against the blackness, his hearing good enough that he could listen to their prey as they scrambled across the rapidly cooling sand in an effort to get away.

But there would be no escape for them. There never was. If his years on this planet had taught him nothing else, they had taught him that much. You couldn't escape your destiny.

Like him. He would be fighting forever. It was, after all, the nature of the beast.

Never in his 471 years had his nature, his abilities, his *limitations*, been so hard to accept.

Four hundred and seventy-one years. He closed his eyes, leaned his head against the cool glass. And wondered how he was supposed to survive another four hundred years. How he was supposed to survive another *day* when his every instinct demanded that he end things, now, while he still could.

Perhaps that was his destiny as well.

What did he have to live for, anyway? His lover was dead, and while he hadn't been mated with Cecily, he had cared deeply for her. Two of his three brothers were dead. Four of his closest friends were dead.

Thousands of his people were dead—a number that was growing larger with every month that passed.

And there was nothing he could do to stop it.

Nothing he could do to stop *any* of it.

All those years of training, all the time he'd spent honing his gifts—wasted. Because now, when he needed the knowledge most, it was gone. Or, worse, was so useless against this latest threat that it was as if it had never been.

He was useless, ineffectual, his power nothing but a joke in the face of the crisis ripping through his clan at an alarming rate.

Was this it, then? he wondered. Nearly half a millennium of life boiled down to nothing in a matter of months? Was illness and exhaustion and crushing disappointment all there was?

If so, what was he still doing here?

Why was he still fighting?

For the first time in centuries, he didn't have an answer.

Inside him, his beast screamed in agony. Battered at the walls he kept around it in an effort to get out. Raked sharp claws down the inside of his skin as it fought for its very survival.

It sensed what Quinn's mind was only beginning to comprehend: he had no purpose on this earth anymore, no meaning. No matter what he tried, no matter how hard he fought, no matter how many antidotes he came up with, his people were dying. And it was his fault.

He glanced over at his computer screen—at the magnified results of the latest tests he'd run. The virus was still impervious to his attempts to immunize against it. His best ideas on how to stop its spread had only multiplied the infected cells, as if whoever had designed the disease had anticipated his every attack. He didn't know why he was surprised. It wasn't as if this was the first time they'd thwarted him.

It was becoming a regular occurrence—his enemy was too determined, too insidious, too *clever*, and he was not clever enough.

Quinn deliberately turned his back on the computer and his newest research and eyed the cabinets across the room instead. Inside him, the beast roared in protest, but he shoved the thing back down. He took two halting steps across the carpet toward the built-ins.

Inside was every manner of medical device—medicines, bandages, scalpels and forceps for surgery. He imagined what it would feel like to grab a scalpel and plunge it straight into his jugular—and was vaguely surprised when the thought didn't bother him nearly as much as it should have. Yes, dragons usually healed quickly—very quickly—but would that be enough to repair a mortal wound, especially if he didn't *try* to heal it?

He was across the room, his hand reaching to open one of the cupboards, before he finally regained control, finally stopped himself as the dragon screamed inside him. He thought of Dylan and Phoebe, Gabe and Logan, Michael and Shawn and Tyler—and despised himself for even thinking of taking the coward's way out. He might have lost all hope, but his friends, his *clan mates*, hadn't. Was he really selfish enough to off himself and take even that small grain of hope away from them?

His hand fell back to his side, sharp talons poking through his fingertips before he could stop them. No, he wasn't that selfish. Wasn't that pathetic.

At least not yet.

He wouldn't kill himself and leave Dylan to clean up the mess. He owed his king far too much to take the easy way out.

And yet the despair swamped him, overwhelmed him, until all he could see or hear or feel was the utter darkness of it. Sinking to the floor, he laid his head on his knees and prayed for some idea of what he should do next. But as with so many of his prayers of late, this one went unanswered.

CHAPTER ONE

"That was the worst one yet." Quinn kept his voice level through sheer will, though everything inside him was screaming for release, for revenge.

"Each case seems to be a little worse than the one before it," agreed Phoebe Quillum, his research partner and the clan's soon-to-be-queen. Her normally clinical voice was tempered with so much sympathy, it nearly suffocated him. "As if every full-blown infection mutates the virus just enough to make the suffering worse for whoever contracts it next."

"Not surprising when you think of the bastards who created this thing. Silus probably had his mad scientists do it on purpose."

"There's no 'probably' about it, Quinn. They had to have engineered it this way. There's no other explanation for how this is happening— sure, viruses mutate, change, all the time. But this one does it in an incredibly complex pattern. Its abilities have to be manufactured, the result of genetic engineering."

He hadn't thought he could feel any worse than he already did. Trust Phoebe to change that. She always knew just what to say.

"This can't keep going on." His fist came down so hard on the crash cart that he dented the thing. "If we can't get inside its walls, then we have to find a way to immunize against it. I don't know how many more of these deaths I can sit through."

"It's far too sophisticated for a virus—even one that was manu-factured in a lab." Phoebe hadn't even heard him. She was muttering now, taking notes on the small pad of paper that went everywhere with her, and he knew she was talking as much to herself as she was to him. "It has the brutality and quickness of Ebola coupled with the sophistication of lupus. Which doesn't make sense, even after looking at it under a microscope and taking it apart for months like we have. If they could create this damn thing in a lab, we should be able to tear it apart in much the same way. I can't believe the Wyvernmoon scientists are really that much further ahead medically than we are."

Quinn didn't respond, but his entire body tightened at the men-tion of the enemy clan. For centuries the Wyvernmoons had been trying to wipe the Dragonstar clan out of existence, but it wasn't until recently—until their king had hit on this damn virus as a weapon of annihilation—that they'd had any success. Of course, Silus was dead now, killed by Phoebe a few weeks before, but the virus was stronger than ever. The Wyvernmoon council obviously wasn't letting a little thing like losing a king affect their long-term goals.

He started to apologize to Phoebe for not being able to come up with a solution, or facts that either supported or debunked her opin-ion, but, judging by her expression, she wasn't looking for a response, just someone to bounce ideas off of.

Not that he was surprised. He'd heard her express the same sen-timent a million times in the few months she'd been with his clan, and she was right. That didn't make the devastation wrought by the disease any easier to swallow.

Unable to bear a reexamination of the fucked-up state they were in, he concentrated instead on cleaning up the patient. He could do that if he thought of the man lying there as only a patient. Or at least, that's what he told himself.

The bleed-out had been quick and ugly, death coming even faster than usual. Quinn tried to tell himself that a death this fast—only eighteen hours from the onset of the symptoms—was a blessing, but he didn't really believe it. How could he when he'd seen Michael scream in agony and had been unable to do anything? Though Quinn was trying his best to compartmentalize, the wall he'd built around his emotions crumbled, leaving him feeling raw and exposed.

"I'll do it, Quinn." Phoebe's hand stroked his back gently, cutting off his self-destructive thoughts, while she removed the blood-soaked rag from his hand. She rinsed it in the basin of warm water on the table next to the bed, then reached forward to stroke the rag over his younger brother's still and bloody face.

His fingers curled into his fists, his talons poking through his fingertips and scoring his palm. He wanted to argue with her, to tell her that Michael was his responsibility and no one else's. But the beast was too close, and if he opened his mouth right now, he was certain that only a growl would come out. He wanted to lash out at something, at someone, and Phoebe was a convenient target.

As the scent of fresh blood—Michael's blood—permeated the room, Dylan stepped between the two of them. His gaze was steady but rife with warning, and it was clear he was no longer content to observe silently. "You don't have to be here. Not for this."

Again, Quinn didn't answer, and Dylan didn't push him—though his king had every right to expect an answer. They'd been friends since childhood, long before either had suspected that Dylan, a second son, would have to take up the reins of ruling their clan. But friendship— even four centuries of it—got them only so far. Especially when the king's mate was involved and the threat against her was coming from one of Dylan's sentries, who was sworn to protect her.

Instead of arguing, Quinn backed off—as much as he was able. Let his clenched hands open, forced his claws back under the surface, tried to calm his breathing. It wasn't much, but it seemed to reassure Dylan, whose shoulders relaxed even as he kept himself between his mate and his best friend.

"I'm not leaving." His voice was much harsher than usual, weighed down by too much loss and too many years of failure.

"Of course you're not," Phoebe soothed, as she rinsed out the bloody rag a second time before moving back to the body.

Back to Michael.

Quinn and Phoebe both knew the nurses could have done this—it was their job, after all. In fact, two were currently hovering at the door, waiting to be called in. Normally Samantha, the older of the two, would have come in and demanded to take over, even without Quinn's instructing her to do so. But Dylan's presence must have intimidated her because she simply watched and waited instead.

As he observed, Quinn told himself he should stop her. Phoebe administering to the body. She had a PhD in biochemistry from Yale and a medical degree from Stanford—this should have been beneath her. But she was doing it for him. Even as the rage ate him from the inside, he recognized that—and tried to keep the dragon under control. She didn't deserve to have his fury, his utter and complete hopelessness, leak onto her. Not when she was only trying to help.

Silence stretched between the three of them, tense and forbidding and overwhelming. He closed his eyes and imagined killing everyone involved in the creation of this virus, imagined ripping them open with a quick strike of his talons and then leaving them to bleed out as Michael had done.

As so many Dragonstars had done.

For years now, this virus had ravaged his people. The first case had shown up a few decades before, but it hadn't spread, and while he'd saved samples for research, Quinn and the other clan doctors had considered it nothing but a bizarre anomaly. At least until it resurfaced a decade ago, spreading and killing off clan members in larger and larger numbers. By the time they'd started to take it seriously, to understand that a disease could actually bring down the normally impervious dragons, it had been too late. The thing had gotten a stranglehold on the clan.

Even then, as he'd fought the thing day and night, Quinn hadn't realized what it had taken Phoebe only a few weeks to pick up on—that the disease had been manufactured specifically to attack the Dragonstars. That it had been created to bring the clan to its knees.

The Wyvernmoons were the likely suspects—how could they not be, as they'd spent centuries attacking the Dragonstars? A brutal clan with little money and almost no status among the four dragon communities in North America, the Wyverns wanted the land, resources and power that the Dragonstars had—badly enough to kill for it. Badly enough to die for it, as any head-on attack was met with brutal force by Dylan.

But this disease, this insidious little virus, was doing what centuries of fighting couldn't, and if it continued at this rate, their clan would be nothing more than an empty shell, one that was ripe for conquering.

The loss of his brother combined with his rage at the Wyvernmoons ate at his control, making matters worse until Phoebe finally spoke.

"I want to call someone. I have a friend who works for the CDC in the infectious diseases department and specializes in fast-working hemorrhagic viruses. I think she might be able to see something that we've missed."

Quinn stiffened as an instinctive protest rose within him. He didn't want someone else in his lab—*anyone* else, let alone another human woman. It had been hard enough for his beast to accept Phoebe's constant presence when she'd first arrived—dragons were territorial, and the lab, not to mention the health of his people, had been Quinn's exclusive responsibility for as long as he could remember.

Eventually, his dragon had accepted Phoebe because she was a brilliant scientist, and, even more important, because of her relationship with Dylan. But bringing someone else in—someone who didn't have ties to the clan—was out of the question.

He looked to Dylan for support, certain that his king would feel the same way. After all, their clan—and all the dragon shifters, for that matter—had survived for millennia by keeping their presence shrouded in secrecy. The idea that they should bring yet another human into their confidence was as laughable as it was impossible.

But Dylan didn't immediately shoot down Phoebe's suggestion. Instead, he seemed to be mulling it over, something Quinn couldn't understand.

"Are you insane?" Quinn demanded. "You want to bring the CDC in? They'll be all over this in seconds, and we'll all end up in government labs somewhere."

"I didn't say we'd bring in the entire CDC," Phoebe told him quietly. "Just Dr. Kane."

"Like that's an improvement? You bring one, you bring them all, Phoebe. You know that as well as I do."

Dylan growled low in his throat. It was a definite reprimand for how Quinn was speaking to his future queen. It was also a threat, but he was too pissed off to care. Besides, theirs wasn't a clan that stood on ceremony.

"It's a stupid idea, Dylan, and if you weren't blinded by your feelings for her, you would know that. Yes, you brought Phoebe in and it worked out pretty well, but then again, she turned out to be a dragon. How many humans are you going to let in on this? Sure, we could use a specialist in hemorrhagic viruses, but I'm learning as much as I can about them as fast as I can."

"Reading doesn't substitute for experience, Quinn." Phoebe's voice was soft and reasonable, a direct contrast to the violent emotions ripping through him. "If it did, you never would have agreed to let Dylan bring me here."

"He didn't." Dylan's voice cut through the tension. "I did it against his will, against the will of most of my sentries. Part of the reason he's arguing so hard now is because he knows that if I think it's the right thing to do, I'll do it again—with or without his approval."

"Fuck you, Dylan." The rage was a living thing inside of Quinn now, tearing into him from all directions. He focused on it, used it.

Anger was much better than the grief and helplessness that lay right beneath it. "You aren't always right—you just think you are."

Dylan's laugh was anything but amused. "How many people have you lost to this damn disease, Quinn? How much time has passed since we first found it? No matter how hard you work—how hard Phoebe works—we're still empty-handed." He paused, ran a frustrated hand through his long black hair. "I would think you, of all people, would be interested in pursuing every avenue possible. But if you've got a better suggestion, then please let me hear it."

Quinn's silence said more than he wanted, but Dylan didn't rub it in. He wasn't that kind of king—or friend. Instead, he spread his arms wide and said, "Look, we can't keep losing people, not in these numbers. Not if we want to survive. We've already tried raiding the Wyvernmoons, looking for the doctors that created this thing, but we've had no luck so far. And after we burned half the compound to get Phoebe out last month, they're locked down tighter than ever."

Dylan's voice smoldered with leftover anger that his enemies had dared take his mate in an effort to weaken him. But he didn't let it distract him—proof that he was slowly getting over the ordeal that had nearly ripped him apart a few short weeks before. Quinn could admire him for it, even as he disagreed with the decision he knew was coming.

"You and Phoebe are making advances, no doubt about it. But you're too slow."

Quinn protested, "You can't rush science, Dylan. Avenues have to be explored, hypotheses made."

"Believe me, I understand that. Which is why I think that the more people we have exploring those avenues, the better the chance we have at solving this thing."

"More isn't always better. Bringing in another human—especially one connected to the CDC—isn't the answer. Can't you both see how risky that is?"

"What's risky is allowing this to go on, Quinn." Phoebe paused from cleaning up Michael long enough to turn to him. "The clan is dying. This virus isn't picking out the weak, the sick, the submissive. It's preying on the strongest, most vital members of the community—as if it was designed to do just that. How many more people have to die before you acknowledge that we can't do this alone?"

Her words felt like fists plowing into him, but he was nowhere close to conceding defeat. "You don't know that. More hands could just ruin everything."

"I *do* know it. Because I've been in the lab with you every day since I got here. I know your strengths and weaknesses almost as well as I know my own. The way this thing changes in different people's bloodstreams is amazing, and unlike anything I've ever seen before. We need someone who knows more about blood than we do if we want to stand a chance against it."

Phoebe's face revealed her bewilderment with the disease and her determination to beat it. Quinn stared at her for long seconds, tried to remember what it felt like to be so confident, so sure of one's course of action. But Michael's death had shattered him, left him reeling and without direction. Despite that—or maybe because of it—he just couldn't see his way clear to bringing yet another scientist into his lab.

"But how do you know you can trust her?" he demanded. "I thought the CDC was bound by law and protocol to report infectious diseases?"

"Absolutely. But then, so was I, yet here we are."

"You didn't work for the Centers for Disease Control—in the infectious diseases department!" Quinn thrust a hand through his hair in frustration, felt his beast straining against the chains he bound it with. How could Phoebe—and Dylan—really be considering trusting a woman who spent her life conforming to regulations?

"You're right. But so am I. Dr. Kane is different from most scientists. She has a truly open mind and a tendency to look at rules more as suggestions—especially when they pertain to her. She gets into trouble over it pretty often."

"And yet the CDC keeps her?" Quinn had a hard time imagining that. He didn't have a lot of experience with the Atlanta-based agency, but he knew enough about them to know that they took policies and procedures very seriously.

"I told you. She's brilliant at what she does." Phoebe glanced at him appealingly, but he refused to be swayed. Not when everything he'd worked for, everything his entire clan had worked for, was at risk. "The CDC puts up with her because they don't have anyone else who can do what she can—in the most primitive conditions imaginable."

"If she disregards their rules, she's more than likely to disregard ours, as well. What's to keep her from telling the world about us?" Quinn addressed his question to Dylan, who was looking as uncomfortable as Quinn about Phoebe's defense of her friend.

"Because she's incredibly steadfast when she believes in something, and will work herself into the ground to find a solution even when no one else can. She's exactly who we need on this case, Quinn. Trust me. I promise you, she won't betray us."

Phoebe reached out a hand to touch him—to soothe him—but he shrugged her off. Arguing, he could handle. Sympathy would only make him lose control. Already he could feel the rage and pain eating away at his control. He struggled to keep it together for just a little bit longer. "It's not you I don't trust," Quinn said in a voice that was way too close to a growl. "And you can't possibly promise that. Besides, if she's as brilliant as you say she is, how is she available to do this for us?"

"She was injured during her last assignment. Badly enough that she was flown back to the States and has had four operations in the last seven weeks. She's better now—or so she says—but still on medical leave."

Quinn absorbed what Phoebe was saying—and what she wasn't—then glanced over at Michael's body before he could stop himself.

When Quinn looked at his baby brother, the last of his anger drained away, replaced by the devastation that was his constant companion these days.

It was hard to believe that his brother was gone, that *Michael* was gone. He would never crack another joke, never break another heart, never charge blindly into danger simply because he liked a good fight. He was dead—just like their parents, just like their other brothers. All killed in the fight against the Wyvernmoons. Though Michael was the only one who was a victim of the virus—all the others had died in combat, including his mother, who had been trying to heal Dylan's brother when the Wyvernmoons got her—his death was no less the result of an attack.

The Wyvernmoons had finally succeeded in wiping out his entire family. There was no one left. Quinn was suddenly, completely, and absolutely alone in the world.

Sadness swamped him. He tried to throw it off, tried to get back to the wrath that was the only thing that had kept him going for far too long. Anger was so much easier to deal with than the despair that threatened to swallow him whole.

"Come on, Quinn." Dylan's hand fell on his shoulder, almost as if the other man could see the shift in his feelings. "Come back home with me and Phoebe tonight."

"Why?" Quinn reached out a hand, ran it over Michael's hair. Part of him expected his brother to wake up, to pop off some irreverent yet accurate remark. Twenty-four hours before, they'd been having dinner together, swigging down beer while Quinn teased Michael about his sudden interest in Caitlyn, one of Dylan's female sentries.

Now he was dead—because Quinn hadn't been smart enough or fast enough to save him.

"Because you look like hell," Dylan said with his trademark bluntness. Phoebe gasped and tried to elbow her mate, but he pulled her into his arms before she could do any real damage—not that she was trying to.

"What Dylan means, Quinn, is that we're worried about you."

"Don't be. I'm fine." He pulled the sheet over Michael's head and tried not to remember all the games of peekaboo they'd played when his brother was a toddler. His brother had been nearly thirty years younger than Quinn and the responsibility for taking care of him had often fallen on Quinn's shoulders.

Those shoulders slumped abruptly, the weight of everything that had happened in the past year too much for him to handle. But he couldn't lose it yet, he told himself. Not here, in front of Dylan and Phoebe, who were already looking at him as if he would blow a gasket at any moment—or rip a helpless bystander to pieces with his talons.

"I appreciate the offer, but I think I'm going to head home. I'm tired and I want to be alone."

"That's a crappy idea and you know it," Dylan said. "Come back with us. A bunch of the others will be there, and you'll be safe."

"No one's safe, Dylan. Haven't you figured that out yet? This fucking disease is everywhere, and until we figure out how the hell to get at it, no one is ever going to be safe."

His best friend's face grew more alarmed, but Quinn just didn't have it in him anymore to care. He shrugged Dylan off and headed for the door at close to a run. "Thanks for your help, Phoebe. Tell the nurses I'll make arrangements for Michael's body tomorrow."

"I can—"

"I'll do it. He's my brother."

And then he was out of there, his long legs eating up the winding stretch of hallway that led to the front door of the clinic. *His* clinic. He'd built it from the ground up fifty years before, after spending centuries working to heal the sick and injured members of his clan. Lately, it seemed that the only time he spent there was with someone in the last stages of this damn disease—most of his time was spent at the lab sorting through notes and blood samples and journal articles, searching for a way to end this thing.

Too bad he didn't have anything to show for all that time away.

Slamming through the clinic doors as if the hounds of hell were after him, Quinn turned himself over to the night.

To the desert.

To the change that had already begun.

The streets of the sleepy little New Mexico town they inhabited were empty, but it wouldn't have mattered if they weren't. Nearly everyone in the town was a member of the Dragonstar clan and shifting was as natural as breathing to them.

As the cool night air brushed against his overheated skin, he stripped out of his clothes, then shoved them into the small pouch he was never without just as his talons burst through the ends of his fingers. He tied it clumsily around his neck, nicking himself with his claws as he did so.

He secured the knot moments before his human side lost the last vestiges of control.

His bones cracked, rearranging themselves, and his wings ripped through the muscles of his back. His skin cooled rapidly, slicked over, as fire burned along his nerve endings. It kindled a flame deep inside of him and for long moments, the agony—and ecstasy—of the change ruled him.

When it was done—when he was dragon—he launched himself straight into the air. And then he flew.

Cloaked in the invisibility every member of his race was gifted with, Quinn spun and whirled through the air. He climbed high, then shot straight down toward the ground, pulling up only at the last possible second. Did it again and again as he flew through hundreds, thousands of miles of darkness, his speed rivaling a fighter jet's. His only thoughts were of escape and freedom and fire.

The headlong rush away—from death, from failure, from himself—went on for hours. Through night, into day and back again. He soared over the beautifully barren deserts of New Mexico and West Texas, cruised over the cement jungles of Dallas and Houston before heading toward the verdant lushness of Louisiana's bayous. From there, he flew high above the wide, muddy banks of the swollen Mississippi River, following it for hours before circling back toward the Southwestern deserts that echoed with the same loneliness he felt inside himself.

When he finally returned to his senses, Quinn forced himself to land—he needed food and sleep—and the pain began all over again.

The shift from dragon to man happened much more quickly than the reverse, but it was just as painful. His talons retracted at the same time his wings did, and then he was shrinking, his bones cracking, re-forming, knitting seamlessly together. His skin was the last to change, going from green and scaly to smooth and tanned, and within a couple minutes Quinn was dressed and walking down an almost deserted street in search of distraction. He found it in the guise of a large, dilapidated bar standing in the middle of a large parking lot at the end of the street. The half-lit sign above the door proclaimed that he was entering the Lone Star, which meant he was somewhere in Texas and almost home after a flight that had taken him more than halfway across the country.

But where in Texas was anyone's guess. Navigation had been the last thing on his mind when he was flying, and now that he'd landed, the truth was he really didn't give a damn. He liked the anonymity of not knowing where he was or when he would leave, liked that there were no rules, no responsibilities, no regrets. At least not here. Not now.

Slipping silently into the bar, Quinn did something he hadn't done in at least three hundred years.

He very deliberately went looking for trouble.

CHAPTER TWO

She stood in the shadows of the clinic corridor, quietly watching. Waiting. It was far from the most glamorous place she'd ever hung out, but these days it was one of the best, especially with its easy access to the king's mate and the clan's best, most important healer.

Not that she didn't have access to them in other places—she did. But in those other places she also had responsibilities. Duties that often took her far away from where the action was. Duties that were important enough that people would notice if she wasn't performing them.

Not like here, where she could just step into the background when she wasn't working and observe the illness and pain, the desperate struggle for survival that so often gave way to resignation and death. Especially these days, when disease lingered in every hall. Murder in every examining room.

And if anyone spotted her—which was unlikely—at least she always had a valid reason for being here at this hour. A few tears for a lost clan member or a complaint about her current medication. A grumble about working overtime. All three were easily believable—and might even be true, if she bothered with her medication anymore. But she didn't, and hadn't for nearly a year now. Not since she'd met Brock.

Two orderlies came down the hallway, rolling what she could only assume was Michael's body, as it was covered with a sheet from head to toe. She watched as the men moved toward the long elevators at the end of the hall that would take them underground to the morgue.

The place used to be as dead as the people it housed, as her species had a tendency to live—if not forever, then long enough to make the distinction negligible. But lately, it had been the hottest ticket in town, thanks partly to her.

She often wondered if she should feel regret. Sadness. Horror that her clan was just one outbreak away from extinction. Guilt that by the end her role in the spread of the sickness would be completely indisputable.

Maybe she should feel that way, but the truth was she didn't. She couldn't—how could anyone really expect her to care when no one had ever cared for her? Not really. Not as she'd needed to be cared for. Not as she'd needed to be loved.

Oh, to this day they patted her on the head like a favored pet, let her close to the king. But she wasn't trusted with his most important secrets, wasn't trusted with his most complicated plans.

Not like her brother, who was one of Dylan's most faithful lapdogs. Not like her parents, who had both died in service to the Crown like the faithful subjects they were. No, she was nothing but an amusing little distraction—fun to watch but never taken seriously.

But that was their problem—and their mistake. Because these days she was no one's amusement . . . and no one's lapdog.

She felt in her pocket, a nervous gesture meant to reassure herself that the syringes were still there. Though they weren't meant for her—had in fact been very precisely calibrated for clan members living much more public lives than she—it still made her nervous to carry them around.

She'd seen Michael die; she had even been there when the king's sister had succumbed to the disease a few months before. After witnessing those deaths, she was only sure of two things—one, that she didn't ever want to piss the Wyvernmoons off enough that she made it to their hit list. And two, that when the time finally came for Brock to spring his trap, Dylan and his precious council wouldn't know what hit them.

CHAPTER THREE

This couldn't be happening to her. Not at—she glanced at the clock on her dashboard—close to midnight in the middle of the West Texas desert. But as her car shimmied and shook beneath her, the left side thumping, thumping, thumping, she knew it was indeed happening.

Cursing long and hard, Jasmine Kane pulled her '67 cherry red Mustang off the highway at the nearest exit. Once stopped, she wasted no time in climbing out of the car and heading for the trunk. As she did, she prayed that she still had a flashlight rattling around back there somewhere. The glow from the closest streetlight was dim, and without the additional boost of a hand-held light, changing the flat tire was going to be a total bitch.

But the angels must have been smiling on her because, when she popped the trunk, her long, black flashlight was laying out in the open—right between the small suitcase and the medical bag she'd placed there sixteen hours before, when she'd started this journey all the way back in Atlanta, Georgia.

She knew she should have waited a few more days, knew she should have caught a flight like a normal person. But when her closest friend had called her with the story of a strange new virus sweeping through an indigenous population of New Mexico, she hadn't been able to resist—not when she'd been sidelined from her own research for the last seven weeks because of what the disability paperwork listed as a "work-related injury."

She snorted as she pulled out the bags and started digging in the trunk for her spare tire. Work-related injury, her ass. More like getting blown to hell and back by some amateur idiot's idea of a bomb. Because of it—and the numerous surgeries she'd had to repair all the damage—she was sidelined for another four to six weeks before the CDC would even let her back in the door. And at the rate things were going, it would be at least another six months before she could even think about getting back into the field.

Being denied access to her work was as close to death as she could get and still be breathing—much worse than the car bomb that had gotten her in Sierra Leone. Which was why she'd jumped into her car and headed for New Mexico almost as soon as she'd gotten off the phone with Phoebe. She'd been too itchy to sit still for much longer.

Her arm twinged as she yanked out the tire, but she ignored it. It had only been two days since the cast had come off—of course her muscles were going to complain a little bit. It had been weeks since she'd done anything more strenuous than flipping the channel on the remote control.

But as she positioned the jack under the tire, her side did more than twinge, and she had to stop to catch her breath. When was the damn thing going to heal? Jasmine wondered as she braced her palms on her knees. When was she going to be back to normal? This whole weakness thing sucked ass.

The doctor side of her felt obligated to remember that it had only been forty-nine days since they'd pulled some heavy duty shrapnel out of her side.

It had been only forty-nine days since she'd broken four ribs, shattered an elbow, punctured a lung, cracked her ankle and sustained a pretty heavy-duty concussion.

Not to mention that it had been a whole lot less than that since the last of the surgeries to correct the muscle and ligament damage to her hip and shoulder. Maybe changing a tire *was* pushing things just a little.

The thought grated, and she blocked out the searing pain as she bent and started pumping at the jack. She'd been on her own since she had left home at sixteen, and she took pride in the fact that she was almost completely self-sufficient. She didn't need—or want—some man to take care of her, to change her tires and tell her what she could or couldn't do. She would rather eat dirt.

But self-sufficiency was one thing and stupidity another, she reminded herself as her torso caught fire. The ribs obviously weren't healing up as fast as she'd thought—and taking off the binding today had been pretty damn stupid. But the thing had chafed after a few hours of driving, and she'd slipped it off in a restroom in Mississippi. Clearly, doing so had been a bad move. Maybe there was a reason doctors weren't supposed to treat themselves, after all . . .

When the pain grew bad enough that she had trouble breathing, Jasmine stood up and leaned against her car. She gave up on changing the stupid tire by herself. Reaching into her back pocket, she pulled out her cell phone and dialed AAA. One of the things about having a classic car was that she had the auto service on speed dial.

Within minutes, she'd arranged for someone to come fix her tire, though the estimated time of arrival was about an hour and a half, which meant she had to put her plans of stopping in El Paso that night on hold. Her experience with tow trucks told her that an hour and a half was really more like two to three hours, especially after working hours, and she really didn't want to be pulling up to a motel at five or six in the morning, hoping to get a little sleep just as the sun came up.

Which meant she was stuck here in Fort Stockton for the night. *Fantastic.* She looked around the deserted street, noting lights about half a mile away, but decided she wasn't comfortable leaving her baby alone on the side of the road. So, with a disgusted sigh, she crawled back into her car, locked the doors and prepared to sleep until the tow truck finally showed up. But while her body was exhausted—nearly seventeen hours on the road could do that to a woman—her brain was wide awake. She'd spent much of the drive mulling over the information that Phoebe had given her, trying to match it up to any of the hemorrhagic viruses she'd worked with.

She'd come up empty, but it was early days yet. Besides, Phoebe hadn't given her much to go on. That could be why—

A knock on her window. Jasmine bolted upward, reaching for the can of pepper spray she kept in the console between the front seats. She had another one attached to her keys. A girl could never be too careful.

Turning on the flashlight she'd deposited on the passenger seat, she shined it out the driver's-side window—and then wished she hadn't.

Two men were standing there, and neither looked sober—or skilled—enough to change a tire. Which probably meant they weren't knocking on her car window to offer her a hand.

Her heart sped up a little and tiny frissons of fear worked their way down her spine even as her mouth tightened in annoyance. Why was it that a woman broken down on the side of the road was a beacon for every asshole in a fifty-mile radius? Normally she wouldn't have been the least bit nervous about her ability to take these guys, but as recent events had brought home, she wasn't anywhere close to her usual fighting form.

One man knocked again, and with a resigned sigh, she cracked the window. Neither looked as though they were going to go away—at least not without talking to her first. And the last thing she wanted was for one of them to get the bright idea to pick up one of the rocks by the side of the road and smash her window in an effort to get in.

"Hey, lady, do you need some help?" one asked with a drunken leer.

"Yeah. We're really good at working on cars."

Since neither looked like they knew how to bathe let alone work on a classic car, Jasmine couldn't keep the doubt from her voice as she said, "No, thanks. I appreciate the offer, but I've already called triple A. They should be here any minute."

"You don't need them," said the first guy, reaching for her door handle. "We can help you with whatever—"

Her fingers tightened on the pepper spray, and she cursed herself for leaving her gun at home in Atlanta. She usually carried it only when she was going into an area of the world a lot more dangerous than Texas. Here at home, she'd always felt able to defend herself without a weapon.

And she was able to now, Jasmine assured herself, broken body or not. These certainly weren't the first drunk guys she'd ever run across, and they probably wouldn't be the last.

"Really, guys. I'm fine. I appreciate the offer, but I'm good."

"Aww, come on now, sweetheart. Open up." The second guy went around to the passenger door and yanked at it. When she made no move to let him in, his voice turned mean. "I said, open up."

"No." Her fear was growing more pronounced, drowning out her annoyance, but she shoved it back. There was no way she had survived working in half the developing nations in the world only to fall victim to two drunk idiots on the side of the road. She wasn't sure of much anymore, but of that she was absolutely certain.

"Listen, bitch, we just want to help you out." The first one sounded a lot less drunk suddenly. Interesting, but definitely not encouraging.

"And I already told you, I don't need your kind of help."

"You could have fooled me." He kicked her front tire. "This thing is flat as a pancake."

She didn't answer, just rolled the window back up, which infuriated the two of them even more. The first one walked to the front of her car and started shoving up and down on her hood, making the Mustang bounce crazily. This really pissed her off, seeing as how she'd just had new shocks put in.

Gritting her teeth, Jasmine weighed her options. She could call the police, but who knew how long it would take them to get there?

Or she could take care of the problem herself.

As always, the second solution was the one she liked the best.

Reaching for the ignition, she turned the keys. Her engine roared to life at the same time she hit her headlights. In an instant, the two idiots were bathed in yellow light, and she took a moment to note what they looked like—just in case. Then she revved her engine once in warning.

When the jackasses didn't take the hint, she rolled her eyes and crept forward. *Bent rim, be damned*, she thought. She'd rather pay for a new tire *and* rim than deal with these assholes for one more second.

Cracking her window a second time, she snarled, "You have two choices. Get the hell out of my way, *now*, or get pancaked. And truth be told, I really don't care which one of those options you choose."

The guys glanced at each other, but they were either stupider than they looked or they must have thought she was bluffing, because neither moved. *Their loss.* Shifting the car into reverse, Jasmine rolled back about ten feet and then hit the gas, aiming straight at the two men caught in her headlights.

For one long moment they just stood there, staring at her with their mouths agape. And then they jumped out of the way. *Chickens.* But at least she had the satisfaction of knowing she'd clipped the one on the right with her bumper. If he wanted to go around hassling "helpless" women, he was going to have to get faster on the uptake— or suffer a hell of a lot of injuries.

She didn't stop the car even after the men jumped to safety. Instead she proceeded down the street toward the closest lit parking lot, her tire thumping out a warning the entire way.

She sighed in relief as she realized the lot belonged to a bar, and judging from the number of cars parked there, it was still hopping. A glance in her rearview mirror told her the idiots weren't following her; they must have decided to cut their losses. *Good.* She really didn't want to deal with them any more that night anyway.

After a quick call to the auto club informing them of her shift in location, Jasmine took a second to look around. The only people in the parking lot were the couple leaned up against the big red truck at the front of the lot, going at it for all they were worth.

Still, she didn't relinquish her hold on the pepper spray. A woman never knew when she needed the element of surprise—Jasmine had learned years ago, the hard way, never to go anywhere empty-handed. But after that last encounter, she'd decided that hanging out in the car until the tow truck arrived might not be the best idea—even in a relatively quiet little town like this.

Grabbing her purse, she climbed out of the car and headed for the bar's door at a fast clip. Her keys were in one hand, the sharp length of one jammed between her fingers as a makeshift weapon, and the pepper spray was in the other. She kept her head up, her eyes alert, and ignored the quick, staccato beat of her heart. The jerks who'd hassled her were long gone, she reminded herself, as she beat time across the parking lot. But that didn't mean there weren't more out there. She'd feel a lot better once she was inside.

She hit the door a few seconds later, read the name scrawled across the top in neon lights. The Lone Star. It sounded like her kind of place.

His beast went crazy the second she walked into the crowded bar. He wasn't facing the door, didn't even know who it was that had crossed the threshold—only that it was a woman and something about her had whipped his other half from its regular state of preternatural stillness into a near frenzy.

As the beast struggled to burst through his skin, struggled to get to her, Quinn slammed on the restraints. Held them tight even as the thing fought against the unnatural captivity. Unlike a lot of the men in his clan, he and his dragon usually existed quite peaceably together, but judging from the way it was suddenly slamming against him in its desperation to get out, it looked as if that was about to change.

He was not impressed.

Taking a deep breath to steady himself, Quinn all but roared as her scent coasted over the stale cigarette smoke and raw whisky odor of the place and sent him spinning.

She smelled rich and ripe, like blackberries in the summertime and the night-blooming jasmine that grew along the back fence at his house. His beast liked the scent, wanted to glut himself on it until he was drunk, and the man wasn't far behind.

Unable to resist, he turned toward the door, grinding his teeth together as he realized that a number of other men were doing the same thing. Not that he could blame them—she was, by far, the hottest thing in the bar, despite the fact that she looked like she'd just rolled out of bed. Or maybe because of it.

Unlike the rest of the women in the bar who were wearing tiny skirts and enough makeup to keep Maybeline in business for a long damn time, this one was dressed in a pair of black yoga pants and a matching tank top. There was no makeup on her face, at least none that he could see, but her lips were a rich, cherry red anyway, her cheeks flushed a soft, pale pink.

Her blond hair was cut short and sassy, and her eyes were big and dark and rimmed with long, sexy lashes. He was too far away to see their color in the darkened room, but what he could see of them he liked a lot.

She wasn't the kind of trouble he'd been looking for when he landed here, but as his dragon all but scrambled across the scarred wooden floor to get to her, he figured she would do.

She stood in the doorway for a few seconds, eyes narrowed and hands clenched into fists as she surveyed the room. As she did, nearly every man in the room sucked in his gut and straightened his shoulders.

She didn't even notice.

He grinned. Yes, she would do very nicely indeed.

Her gaze swept the tables first, all of which were full, before falling on the only two empty barstools in the place—which were on either side of him.

Go figure.

She headed straight toward him, her long legs eating up the floor between them in a matter of seconds. His beast tensed in anticipation—and so did he. He wanted to know what she looked like close up, wanted to know if her skin was warm and if her smell was even sweeter without an entire room between them.

But before she could get to him, some asshole grabbed her elbow and spun her around, his other hand groping for her hip as he pulled her against him.

Quinn was off his barstool before the woman had even come to a stop, more than ready to teach the guy a lesson. But before he could take a step, she'd twisted her arm out of the idiot's grasp and sent him stumbling backward with a well-placed shove to the shoulders.

The guy laughed, low and mean, and reached for her again. But there must have been something in her eyes that stopped him, as he froze, his hand halfway to her waist, and not even the threat of being embarrassed in front of all the other yahoos in the bar made him close the gap between them. Instead, he took the few steps back to his table and drank his beer like a man dying of thirst.

As she turned back to the bar, the light of battle hadn't yet faded from her eyes. She wore a smirk as big as Texas, and when her eyes met his, there wasn't an ounce of fear in their violet depths.

He grinned at her—he couldn't help himself—and lifted his glass in a quick but sincere salute before downing it. He'd never been a big fan of women who acted like they were as tough as a man, but there was something about her that made her ability to defend herself sexy as hell. Besides, he wasn't looking to marry the woman—he just wanted to feel good for a little while. Just wanted to forget, and she looked like she could help him do just that.

And when she slid onto the barstool to his right, calling out for a shot of Patrón as she did so, his dragon curled up inside of him and all but purred.

Yes, he thought as he gestured for another shot of his own. She was trouble, no doubt about it. And she would do very nicely, indeed.

CHAPTER FOUR

The bartender slapped two shots of Patrón on the bar between them, along with another shot glass full of lime slices. Jasmine reached for hers, aware that the guy sitting next to her was doing the same.

She might have thought it was lame that he ordered the same drink as her—as if that would impress her or something—but there was a line of used shot glasses in front of him, and when he turned his head to look at her his breath smelled faintly of her favorite tequila.

"What should we drink to?" he asked in a low, smoky voice that made her toes curl inside her favorite pair of Skechers.

She thought about it for a second, then remembered how good it felt to defend herself against the jerks outside. "How about to kicking a little ass?"

If she'd hoped to shock him with her response—which she was honest enough to admit she might have—she was disappointed. His only response was the lifting of one dark eyebrow and the sardonic question, "So, you like to kick ass, do you?"

"Absolutely. If the occasion warrants it, I'm all for a good ass-kicking." She raised her glass, clinked it against his. Then tossed the shot back in a hurry.

It burned all the way down, lit a fire in her stomach that worked its way through her bloodstream until every part of her was tingling and warm. Tequila didn't usually have that effect on her, but she refused to give the guy next to her the credit. No matter how hot he was.

And God, was he hot. Long and lean with heavily muscled arms and a torso so sculpted she could see the outline of his six-pack through his T-shirt. He was so sexy that she had to surreptitiously wipe her mouth to make sure she wasn't drooling.

Add in the brooding green eyes, chin-length black hair and cut-glass jaw lined with stubble, and he was every late-night fantasy she'd ever had. Even as she told herself she wasn't going to be sticking around long enough to find out if he tasted as good as he looked, a part of her was intrigued enough to turn toward him and watch as he lifted his own shot glass.

He caught her looking and grinned, a sharp, seductive expression that made her nipples tighten against the thin cotton of her tank top. She started to cross her arms over her chest, but saw that she was too late—his emerald gaze had already found the telltale peaks beneath her shirt.

"That was fast," he said with a grin. She wasn't sure if he was talking about her response to him or the way she'd downed the shot. "Can I get you another one?"

She shrugged. "Sure." It wasn't like she was going to be driving anywhere anytime soon.

He flagged down the bartender and ordered them both another shot before turning back to look at her. "So, whose ass did you kick tonight, if you don't mind me asking?"

"A couple jerks who thought a woman stuck on the side of the road with a flat tire was fair game."

The smile slid off his face and his eyes darkened dangerously. "Are they still alive?"

"Unfortunately."

He scanned the bar. "Are they here?"

"Nope. They took off once they figured out things weren't going to go the way they wanted them to. Why? You planning on coming to my defense?"

She held her breath as she waited for him to answer. She was all for a knight in shining armor, but she preferred a man who knew she could take care of herself—*and* who trusted her to do it.

"Not your defense, no. But I figure there are a bunch of women in here who wouldn't be able to handle themselves as well in a similar situation."

She melted a little at his words. Despite his very badass exterior, it sounded like he was one of the good guys. At the very least, he had more than a passing respect for women. She could totally get into that.

"They're long gone, so that's one less thing for you to worry about tonight." Even as she spoke, she couldn't believe the flirtatious tone in her voice. She never went that route, usually went out of her way to avoid sounding like some silly schoolgirl with a crush. But something about this man was really ringing her bell—in the best possible way.

"I'm glad to hear that." He spun his barstool toward her, so that his knees brushed lightly against her upper thigh. Pleasure fluttered inside her and she caught her breath, shocked that such a light touch could elicit any response from her at all, let alone one strong enough to have her libido stand up and take notice.

The sudden heat radiating from him told her she wasn't the only one whose body was just a little out of control.

"Are you? Why?"

"Because as entertaining as it would be to teach those guys a lesson, I much prefer sitting here with you."

"Really? And why is that?"

"You smell a lot better than they probably do—*and* you have excellent taste in tequila."

"Yeah, well, a girl never knows when a taste for highbrow tequila will come in handy. Speaking of which—" she said, as she reached for her second shot. "Cheers."

He inclined his head forward. "Cheers."

She downed the shot in record time, but when she slammed her glass on the counter, she realized he still hadn't taken his first shot—which was resting, neglected, between his fingers—let alone the second one that was sitting in front of him.

"Something wrong with your drink?" she asked.

"No. I just enjoy watching you indulge. Besides, I'm already a few ahead of you." He nodded to the empty shot glasses the bartender had yet to clear away.

"You are indeed. Why is that, by the way?"

This time his smile was anything but warm, and she felt the chill of it cut through the rosy tequila glow currently enveloping her. "It's been a rough year."

There was something in the way he said it, something in the sudden sadness that wrapped around him like a cloak that made her think that his "rough" was a number of shades worse than hers. And that was saying something, considering her year to date had consisted of dealing with a serious outbreak of Ebola in Congo, followed by being blown up in the third week of a research trip that had started going wrong the second she'd gotten off the airplane.

Still, no one was more surprised than she when she reached a hand out and covered his, where it rested on his knee. "I'm really sorry to hear that."

His fingers clutched at hers like a lifeline. "Don't be. You didn't have anything to do with it."

"Yeah, well, I'm having a pretty crappy year myself, so I can empathize."

"Awww, don't tell me that."

"Why not?"

"Because I wouldn't wish my luck on anyone." His thumb ran in soothing—and seductive—circles across the back of her hand. Her sex grew damp at the contact. "Look, if we're going to drown our sorrows together, we should at least exchange names. I'm Quinn."

She tightened her hold on his fingers, relishing the strength and width of the hand that held hers. "My friends call me Jazz."

"Oh, yeah? What do your enemies call you?"

"You don't want to know."

"I think you might be surprised at what I want to know about you. But for now I'll settle for your name."

He turned her hand over and glanced down at her palm before tracing one long, elegant finger over her lifeline. As he did, shivers worked their way down her spine, and for a moment Jasmine wanted nothing more than to crawl into his lap and see where this crazy attraction would take them. Normally she was a lot more cautious, but there was something about him that made her crazy. Made her want to *be* crazy.

That desire should make her nervous, Jasmine told herself firmly. If meeting a really hot, really sexy guy in a bar sounded like a fantasy, it probably was—of the nightmare variety. And yet . . . and yet part of her was in the mood for a little fantasy tonight, as long as she got to act out that fantasy with Quinn.

"Hey, Jazz. Is something wrong?" Quinn's voice broke into her reverie, and when she glanced up from their entwined fingers, she was surprised at how concerned he looked.

"No. Why?"

He shrugged. "You look a million miles away."

"No. Just a few hundred. But I'm back now."

"Are you?"

"Absolutely."

"Good. Because there's something I've been meaning to tell you."

Her stomach turned over at his words, though she did her best not to let it show. She promised herself that she would drop kick him to the door—no matter how big and hunky he was—if the next words out of his mouth included *married*, *wife* or *misunderstood*.

"What's that?" she asked, barely aware that she was holding her breath.

He reached for the salt shaker sitting next to him on the counter. "You did those last two tequila shots all wrong."

Relief flooded her, and she laughed, feeling more than a little stupid for getting so worked up. But then he was leaning toward her, and she let the thought drift away. She could examine her motives later. At the moment she just wanted to concentrate on the first thing that seemed to be going right for her tonight.

Propping her elbow on the bar, she moved forward until her chin was resting against her left palm and her breasts were only inches from the bar. By the time she was settled, she was close enough to Quinn that she could feel the sweet and spicy warmth of his breath against her forehead. "And I suppose you're going to show me how to do it right?" she asked.

"I'm going to try."

Jasmine wasn't sure what to say or how to react when he grabbed her wrist and brought it to his mouth. She did know that if any other man had tried it—flirting or no flirting—she would have decked him, no questions asked. But there was something about Quinn that made her twitch, though not in a way she minded. For that, she was willing to give him just a little bit more leeway than usual.

She told herself that she was ready for anything he could dish out. But she still wasn't prepared when his tongue darted out to trace the delicate veins right below the skin of her wrist.

Wasn't prepared for the warm, wet heat of his mouth or the flames that ripped through her belly and between her thighs.

And she sure as hell wasn't prepared for the sudden, irrational need to be alone with Quinn, naked.

His tongue swirled back and forth over the veins, then traced the slightly raised scar right at the seam where her hand met her forearm. Her knees trembled and little shocks of electricity speared through her wherever his tongue touched.

When her skin was finally as moist and hot as his mouth, he pulled back, tilted the salt shaker and sprinkled a few grains of salt on her wrist before setting it aside. Then, before she could brace herself, his mouth was back, licking, lapping, lingering over the salt—and her skin.

And he did it all without ever taking his eyes from hers.

Her pussy clenched once, twice, and for a second Jasmine couldn't help thinking that if he kept this up much longer she might actually climax right here in the middle of a crowded bar.

She didn't know if the thought horrified or intrigued her.

She never got the chance to find out because Quinn chose that moment to lift his head. He reached for the glass of limes, pulled one out and raised it to her lips. At first she kept her mouth shut—wanting to play with him a little—but the look he shot her was hot enough to melt glass. Certainly hot enough to shoot her arousal to fever pitch.

Strangely parched, she darted her tongue out to lick her suddenly dry lips. As she did, he took advantage and slipped the lime partially into her mouth, while at the same time taking one last, leisurely lick down her arm.

Then he grabbed his shot of Patrón. Slammed it back. She watched his strong throat work as he swallowed, right before he leaned forward and closed his mouth over hers.

He bit down hard on the lime she still had clenched in her teeth and Jasmine gasped as its sour-sweet juice shot straight into her mouth. That gasp was all he needed. With a couple quick flicks of his hand, he had the lime peel out of her mouth and into his discarded shot glass—right before his mouth slanted over hers for a second time.

Nothing in her life had ever felt quite so right—or so dangerous.

She told herself to pull back even as she pressed her body to his.

Told herself that they were in the middle of a bar filled with people even as her fingers tangled in all that long, silky hair.

Told herself that she didn't engage in public displays of affection even as she slid off her barstool and pressed herself between his legs.

Told herself . . . nothing as he sucked her lower lip between his teeth and bit down softly. She simply imploded.

Her hands tightened in his hair and her mouth came alive beneath his. She opened herself fully to him, gasping when his tongue darted inside her. For long moments, it tangled with her own—teasing, taunting, titillating—but then he stroked deeper. Ran his tongue over the roof of her mouth, down her cheek, between her upper lip and her teeth, where he played with her frenulum until she was utterly boneless. Utterly his.

How could she have made it through four years of medical school, and six as a doctor—thirty-two as a woman—and not know how sensitive that small bit of skin could be, she wondered. And then she ceased to think at all as he slid a hand up her cheek and around to the back of her head, pulling her closer. Pulling her under.

It was a long time before she surfaced.

CHAPTER FIVE

The second Quinn tasted Jazz, he was lost. Lust rose within him, sharp and terrible and all-consuming. It raked its talons through his belly, its heat down his dick. Got in his head and demanded that he take her. That he fuck her, again and again, until she couldn't remember her own name. Until he couldn't remember the laundry list of misery that had sent him here.

For a second—just a second—common sense tried to intrude. He slapped it back, ignored it. There would be time for everything else later—time for his anger and his pain. Time for his worry and his desperation. Right now all he wanted to think about—all he could think about—was *her*.

She nipped at him, her teeth almost drawing blood. And still he kissed her, reveling in the pain. Unwilling to give up her lips, to break the strange connection between them when the beast inside of him roared, knowing she was his for the taking.

She burrowed deeper against him, and it sent him over the edge, had him doing wild, crazy things to her mouth as he savored every gasp and moan that escaped her mouth into his.

Her fingers clamped onto his shoulders, her nails digging into his upper back. The small, sharp pain took him higher—even as it cleared his head for a moment, let him think. That moment was all it took for him to remember that they were all but eating each other alive in the middle of a crowded bar. And while the animal in him was more than willing to take her right there, in front of everyone—to claim her for all to see—the man was more cautious.

And more determined that no one see her naked but him.

Wrenching his mouth from hers, Quinn yanked out his wallet. He dropped a couple of hundred dollar bills on the counter before reaching into the well for the bottle of Patrón the bartender had parked there.

The bartender didn't even try to stop him.

"Let's get out of here," he growled, low in his throat.

Jazz nodded mutely, and he grabbed her left hand with his empty one and started cutting a path through the bodies to the front door. It only took a second, as most of the people in the place took one look at his face and got the hell out of his way. He wasn't surprised. He was so frenzied with need that he figured everyone could see it.

He didn't give a damn, would even admit to basking in the knowledge, because it told every man in the bar that she was his. That she belonged to him and that he'd kill anyone who tried to take her from him.

The last thought came from his beast, and it brought him up short. What the hell was going on? Neither he nor the dragon had ever been possessive of a would-be lover before, but as he glanced back and looked at Jazz—with her swollen lips and bright eyes, her messed-up hair and rosy cheeks—both of them wanted to rip apart every man who saw her and wanted her.

Which was absurd, especially since he was the one who had deliberately brought her to such a state in a public place.

He held her hand more tightly, pulling her closer to his body as he shoved open the front door. The cool night air hit him like a freight train, need ripping through him until his human side took a backseat to the dragon that had been aching to get out from the moment it first scented her.

Quinn tried to hold on, tried to tell himself that it was dangerous to take her without reining in the dragon first, but he was too far out of control to care. His body wasn't concerned with who was in the driver's seat—all that mattered was getting inside her as quickly as he possibly could.

He glanced around wildly, wondering where her car was, and if the shadows of the parking lot would provide them with enough privacy for him to do all the things he wanted to do to her. Or he could drag her around to the back of the bar, yank her pants down and take her up against the wall. He was about to go with option number two when his eyes fell on a motel, a couple of hundred yards across the parking lot. He pulled her toward it.

"Wait!" she said, breathlessly, trying to dig her feet into the ground. "My car."

"It'll be safe here until morning." The words came out deep and dangerous, so distorted that they barely sounded human. The dragon was even more firmly in control than he'd thought.

"It has a flat tire, remember? I'm waiting for the tow truck to show up."

Quinn nearly roared in frustration. He couldn't remember the last time he'd felt like this—couldn't remember if he'd *ever* felt like this—and she didn't seem anywhere near as affected as he was. He could barely remember his own name, and she was worried about a stupid tow truck.

His dragon sliced at him with its razored claws, telling him to hurry. Warning him that he didn't have much time before he lost the human side of himself altogether. Already, he was so frenzied he could feel the change beginning to take hold, the familiar burn that was the precursor to the shift. And wouldn't that put a crimp in his plans? Changing into a dragon right now was definitely not the way to go—unless of course he wanted to scare the hell out of her instead of fuck her near to death.

No, scaring her was definitely not on the agenda.

But how could he convince her not to worry about the tow truck?

"Don't worry about it," he finally growled, tugging at her arm until she started walking again. "I'll change your tire tomorrow morning." Had the damn motel always been this far away?

"You're just saying that," she answered breathlessly, as he propelled her across the parking lot so quickly that her feet barely touched the ground.

He shot her a look loaded with heat, which filled him to overflowing. "I'd say just about anything to get inside you right now, but I swear, I'll change the damn tire. After."

That seemed to be all the reassurance she needed because suddenly their frenetic dash across the parking lot was more about her pulling him than the other way around.

"Hurry," she gasped, waving him toward the front office as they finally made it to the motel. Then she rested her back against the closest wall as if it were the only thing keeping her standing.

The dragon and the man both seethed with excitement. She looked so damn hot leaning there, hair mussed, lips swollen, nipples tight and hard against the fabric of her little cotton tank that he almost said to hell with the hotel room—and common decency—and took her right there.

His dragon flooded him with approval at the thought. *Yes,* it seemed to say as it had back at the bar. *Take her here, now, in front of anyone who walks by, so they know she's yours.* He'd actually taken a step toward her before he could get his head back in the game, and even then it took every ounce of self-control he had to turn around and walk toward the office, away from her.

His beast didn't want to go. It snarled and clawed and snapped at him more and more frantically the farther he got from her. He tried to ignore it, but it wasn't easy—not when his hands were shaking like a junkie in desperate need of a fix.

Shocked at himself—at his behavior and his need—Quinn tried to regain a little control. But he couldn't—there was a red haze in front of his eyes and all he could think or feel or smell or taste was *her.*

Ripping out his wallet, he slapped a credit card down on the counter and growled, "I need a room. Now."

Perhaps it was Quinn's urgent tone—or maybe the clerk was just used to people coming over from the bar in a hell of a hurry—because he didn't say a word, didn't bother asking any questions. Just took the platinum card, ran it, and handed Quinn a key.

"It's number twenty-seven. At the top of the staircase to your left."

"Thanks."

Then he was outside, his entire body stretched as taut as a violin string. His dick ached from being locked inside his jeans—from being so incredibly aroused for so long—and all he could think about was the relief of plunging into Jazz's warm, willing body.

"Come on," he snapped, bent on hustling her up the stairs. But she was way ahead of him, her long legs taking the steps two at a time. He followed her, the tequila bottle still clutched in his hand, and imagined what she would taste like drenched in the spicy alcohol.

As he fumbled the key into the lock, he made a promise to himself that he would find out. Later.

After what seemed like an eternity, the lock turned and he shoved the door open. He kicked it closed with his foot, started to reach for her. But she was already on him, her arms wrapping around his neck as her mouth slammed down on his.

Jasmine was on fire, her entire body a conflagration of need and want and give-me-more as she launched herself at Quinn. He caught her— as she'd somehow known he would—and started backing her across the room while his mouth raced frantically over her face.

Over her forehead, down her cheeks, across her jaw before his lips finally found hers. When they did . . . when they did, her knees buckled and she had to twist her fingers in the soft cotton of his T-shirt to keep from falling. He was so intent on devouring her that she doubted he'd even noticed.

"I need to be inside you," he growled against her mouth, his hands slipping beneath her tank top to cup her breasts. They were full, aching, her nipples so tight it was a physical pain, and when his thumb brushed against them she didn't know whether to scream in frustration or whimper with delight.

She did both, letting out a little squeal that was as foreign to her as one-night stands in ratty motel rooms. The sound seemed to push him over the edge because suddenly her pants were around her knees and he had two long fingers buried inside her.

She did scream then, the sensation of being full with him almost more than she could bear.

"I'm sorry," he snarled, as he spun her around so that her ass rested against his upper thighs. "I can't go slow. I'll make it up to you next time."

"Just do it," she whimpered, fumbling for her purse. Whipping out a condom, she all but threw it at him before steadying her hands on the dresser and bending at the waist in open invitation.

There was one long second of silence, one long moment of agony, while he sheathed himself and then he was there, between her legs. Blunt and hard and so big and thick that her eyes nearly crossed as he probed gently at the opening of her sex.

She expected him to be rough, hurried, expected it to even hurt a little at first, and braced herself for it. It had been a long time since her last lover, after all. But now that he was so close, he didn't rush. Instead, he leaned forward until his lips were right next to her ear and whispered, "You're so beautiful. So goddamn beautiful." He ran his hand down her cheek.

The words, combined with the feel of his cock right against the heart of her, ratcheted Jasmine's need to a fever pitch. "Please," she begged. "I need—I need—"

"What?" he demanded, thrusting forward just a little, until he was buried about halfway inside her.

It wasn't enough.

"I need *you!*" she wailed, thrusting back against him in utter desperation.

He broke. She didn't know if it was her words or the feel of her pushing against him, but Quinn's control snapped like a fragile spring twig.

He slammed into her, so hard that he rocketed her up onto her toes. She was wet and hot and more than ready for him, so there was no pain—only pleasure so intense that she climaxed right there, with the first stroke of his cock deep inside her.

"Fuck!" he growled, his fingers digging into her hips as he held her in place. Again, she expected him to pound into her, was even anticipating it, but he held her—and himself—still. As if he were absorbing every clench and contraction of her body on his.

As if he were somehow absorbing her very pleasure into himself.

And then he began to move, slow, long, powerful strokes that had her clutching at the dresser as the fire reignited deep inside her. Soon—too soon—she was on the brink of coming again. But she didn't want to go over alone this time, didn't want to lose herself in the ecstasy without him.

Tightening her inner muscles in a long, slow caress, she tried to take him as high as he had taken her. He groaned, thrusting harder, so she did it again. And again. And again.

One of his hands worked its way up from her thigh to her hair and he pulled her head back sharply. She gasped, but didn't fight him, as he twisted her head to the side.

"Kiss me," he snarled, seconds before his lips came down on hers, hard.

She did, pulling his lower lip between her teeth and nipping at him. He tasted like lime and tequila and the desert on a warm summer evening and she wanted more of him. Craved more of him until he was an inferno in her blood.

She bit him again, a little harder this time, and the little shock of pain must have been what he was waiting for because he came with a roar. She followed him over the edge, her body wiging out in twenty different directions as her orgasm ripped through her like a forest fire.

There was a pain in her left side, another in her right hip—her body protesting such vigorous use after being babied for so long. She wrenched her mouth from his, gasped for breath, but Quinn wouldn't let her go. He followed her, his mouth ravenous on her own while the heat of his body seared hers wherever it touched. In moments, the pleasure overwhelmed the pain.

She gave herself to him—gave herself to his kiss and his touch and the wild, wicked need that was as much a part of him as his lopsided grin and intense, electric green eyes.

As she did, the whole crazy maelstrom started inside her all over again. She pulled him with her as she fell.

CHAPTER SIX

When it was over, Jasmine's faculties returned slowly. As the seconds crept by, she became aware that she was spread-eagled across the dresser, her stomach resting on the cool wood while her hands still gripped the sides for traction.

Her tank top was pushed up around the top of her chest and tangled with the bra that Quinn had unhooked but hadn't taken the time to remove. Her pants were still around one of her ankles and her ass was in the air—or it would have been, if Quinn hadn't been collapsed on top of her, the ragged sound of his breathing harsh in her ear.

"Can you breathe?" he asked after sucking a huge gulp of air into his lungs.

"I don't think so," she gasped.

"I'm sorry." He started to move away.

"Don't go." She moved her arms back to clutch at his hips, not wanting him to leave despite the sudden screaming of her not-quite-mended ribs.

"I'm not going anywhere." He soothed her by running one strong, smooth hand up her back, tangling it in her hair and gently massaging her scalp.

She relaxed into his touch, shocked at how soothing it was when minutes before it had been anything but.

He stroked her for a few moments, his hands leaving little trails of warmth wherever they touched, and unbelievably, she felt her body stir to life, when seconds before she would have sworn nothing short of a tornado ripping through the room could have roused her.

It wasn't the same as the first flash of desire—or even the second—that had him throwing her over the dresser, going at it like wild things. No, it was a slower burn, one that was less intense but no less powerful for its slow climb.

He was still buried inside her and she moved against him, seeking a deeper contact. He groaned, thrust more deeply into her, and then paused when he was seated to the hilt.

She concentrated on the feel of him inside her, against her. The way the smooth skin of his abdomen felt resting against her ass. The way his fingers felt as they pressed in and around her spine in a massage that made her want to curl up and purr like a cat. The way the rough denim of his jeans scraped against her upper thighs.

She liked the feel of him, liked everything about him, especially the way he responded to her, like he had been wandering in the desert and she was the only thing around that could slake his thirst.

Then he was pulling away, though he gave her plenty of time to steady herself. She wanted to complain, wanted to hold him to her again and freeze this perfect moment in her memory for all time, but she knew he was right to leave her.

Her legs were trembling from the strain, her hip screaming from the awkwardness of her position. Not for the first time, she cursed the car bomb—and its makers—that had put her here.

She wanted her old body back—unblemished, strong, capable of going for hours without complaint at whatever activity she chose. She barely recognized herself with all her aches and pains, barely knew this woman who waited for her lover to head into the bathroom before unpeeling herself—slowly and painfully—from the dresser.

What should she do now? she wondered, looking around the still-darkened motel room for the first time.

Should she give him a quick thank-you and head out to her car to see if the tow truck had arrived? Or should she stay here and make small talk with the man who had just turned her world inside out?

Neither option appealed to her as she fumbled her pants and underwear up her thighs and settled them back into place. She saw the bed—lake-sized and centrally located—and an unbearable tiredness filled her. What she wanted, it turned out, was to stretch out on the mattress and fall asleep.

But doing so would be stupid. Quinn might have just rocked her world, but that didn't mean she could trust him enough to let herself be vulnerable in front of him. Slumping against the dresser, she prayed her tired, aching body would hold up a little longer. Just long enough to get the pain under control, and then she'd be ready for whatever he threw her way.

Before she could do anything more than sigh in relief at having most of the pressure taken off her injured leg, Quinn was back.

He flipped on the bedside lamp, and though the bulb was dim, the sudden influx of light blinded her. She blinked a few times in an effort to adjust her vision and then stared across the empty room at him.

He was looking right back at her.

For the first time, she realized how big he was. He stood at least six foot six, with incredibly broad shoulders and arms that looked like they could rip a hundred-year-old tree out by the roots without so much as breaking a sweat. It was strange to realize that a man so large, so dangerous-looking, had taken her without hurting her in the slightest.

The knowledge shattered the last of the tension she was carrying—along with her renewed sense of caution—and she truly relaxed for the first time since she'd been forced to pull over to the side of the road. As soon as she did, the tiredness she'd been fighting rose up and overwhelmed her.

As if sensing her weariness, Quinn was across the room in a flash of speed that barely seemed human. He rested a hand on her lower back and propelled her toward the bed that suddenly looked as inviting as an oasis in the middle of the Sahara.

She grabbed her cell phone and made a quick call to cancel the tow truck. As she did, he yanked the comforter back and she sank down onto the cool sheets gratefully, her mind going almost completely blank before her head had even hit the pillow. Inside a little voice screamed at her to wake up, not to drop her guard no matter how good a lover Quinn had been. But it was too late, and Jasmine slid, softly and easily, into sleep for the first time in a long, long time.

Quinn stripped off his T-shirt, then settled himself on the bed next to Jazz and simply watched her sleep. Despite the seething storm of emotions he sensed right below her surface, she looked so peaceful, so calm, that he felt a little of his own tension draining away.

It wouldn't last—how could it?—but for the moment he would take the gift she had given him and savor it. Who knew how long it would be before he felt this way again?

Reaching out, he traced a finger down her still flushed cheek. The skin was so soft, so delicate that he found himself savoring the feel of it. The feel of her. He moved closer, fitting his body against hers so that her head was pillowed on his bicep and the soft ripeness of her breasts rested against his chest.

Inside him, the dragon stretched once before settling down to rest. Their frantic lovemaking had soothed his beast as well as his body. Closing his eyes, he concentrated for a moment and the light on the side of the bed winked out. It was a small power, but one he found exceedingly handy. He hadn't gotten up to turn off a light since his powers had first manifested themselves somewhere around his twenty-third birthday.

Tired from his long flight, worn out from his time with Jazz, he closed his eyes and settled down for his first sleep in three days. But the second he relaxed—the second he let his guard down— thoughts of Michael started to invade.

He saw his little brother smiling and laughing on the day Quinn had taught him how to fly, saw him dressing up for his first courtship with a girl more than four hundred years before. Saw him training patiently to be one of Dylan's sentries, though everyone—including Quinn—had thought he was too immature, too soft, to ever make it on the High Council.

Michael had proven them all wrong.

Quinn shuddered at the memories, and a cold sweat broke out all over his body. He rolled away from Jazz, ignoring the small sound of protest she made in her sleep, and swung his legs out of bed.

As he did, pain radiated through his body, so intense that it felt like every nerve ending had been dipped in acid. He lowered his head, fought the pain as he fought so much in his daily life—with as much energy and dedication as he could muster.

Part and parcel of his healing gift, the pain was the physical consequence of his race to cheat death. It was the cost for being able to manipulate the earth's energy to save—or try to save—those clan mates who were so bad off that modern medicine didn't stand a chance of helping them. Tonight's payment was going to be a bad one, as he'd given every ounce of power he had—wielded all the energy he could call up—to try to save his brother's life. He'd even gone inside his brother to try to shore up the failing cells—a healing technique that was incredibly dangerous, and it exacted a huge price. Though he hadn't been able to save his brother, he'd still have to pay the price that came with holding that much energy for that long.

The shakes started, violent shudders that wracked him from torso to toes. They were made worse by the pain that continued to invade his every pore. The vomiting would start soon—as it did with every bad attack—followed by a blackout that could last minutes or hours or even days.

He'd been a fool when he had decided that he was safe, that it wouldn't happen this time, since it had been over twenty-four hours since Michael had died and nothing had hit him. Usually, the symptoms started soon after he used his gift.

He hadn't given it much thought when he'd been flying—he'd been too wrapped up in his emotional pain to worry about the rest of the shit. But now that it was happening, now that agony was racing through his system like a Molotov cocktail on the brink of exploding, the scientist in him couldn't help wondering whether his grief had somehow managed to block the physical symptoms—or at least mask them.

If that was the case, this should have started happening hours ago—back when he'd been flirting with Jazz in the bar. Instead, it had waited until now to rear its ugly head. He couldn't help wishing that if it had waited this long, it could wait a little bit longer. Long enough, certainly, for him to see Jazz off in the morning.

He glanced around desperately, knowing he needed to get out of the damn motel room. He'd spent years keeping the side effects of his gift a secret, and though she wouldn't understand what she was seeing, he still didn't want to scare the hell out of her.

He tried to stand, but he'd waited too long. The shakes were too bad. His legs went out from under him, and he fell to the ground next to the bed. Unable to do anything else, he curled into a ball and waited for the tremors to stop.

It seemed to go on forever. On some level he was aware of time passing, but he was so locked into the pain—into the misery—that one minute bled into the next. More than once he tried to fight it, but it was the worst attack he'd ever had and his powers were useless against it. He couldn't move without feeling like he was breaking wide-open.

He'd locked his dragon deep inside of himself, so deep that he could barely sense it as it snapped and snarled at the invisible enemy. Which was good—the last thing he needed was for the dragon to be front and center when Jazz woke up. God only knew what it would do to her.

Another wave of pain swamped him, so powerful that he thought he might have passed out for a minute. When he came to, he was aware of nothing. He was blind and deaf, locked into a darkness from which there was no surcease.

He wanted to scream, but didn't have enough strength—or enough hope. He was suddenly, abruptly sure that this time he had gone too far. This time he wasn't going to make it back. His one regret was that poor Jazz would be dragged into this. She would wake up in the morning with a dead man on her carpet.

The thought galvanized him for a moment and he tried to move, tried to make it to the door and out of the room, but he only got a couple of feet. Besides, without the use of his senses, he was so turned around he wasn't even sure he could find the door.

For a second—just a second—tears welled in his eyes for the first time in over three centuries, but he refused to give in to them. Crying wouldn't bring Michael back any more than it would help Dylan save the clan. It wouldn't find a cure for the disease, and it sure as hell wouldn't make him feel any better.

In other words, it was a total waste of time.

In the end, he stopped fighting and simply yielded to the inevitable. He put his head down on the carpet and simply waited to see what would happen next.

More time passed, though he wasn't sure how much.

He did know it was long enough to count to ten thousand in his head.

Long enough to go over every joke and punch line Michael had ever told him.

More than long enough to figure out that maybe he really didn't want to die after all. At least not blind and deaf and alone on the floor of a cheap motel hundreds of miles from home.

And then suddenly, someone turned the lights back on.

CHAPTER SEVEN

One of Jazz's arms snaked around his waist, and the second she touched him, every one of Quinn's senses came flooding back with a jolt.

It was the strangest thing that had ever happened to him, and for a moment he was too stunned to do anything but lay there and absorb the sound of her breath against his ear. Then she was sliding her other arm beneath him, trying to pull him into a sitting position, and with the way she was tugging, it didn't feel like she was going to take no for an answer.

Afraid she would hurt herself trying to move him, he rolled to a sitting position, all the while bracing himself for another white-hot stream of pain. Since this thing had started, every move he'd made had been met with renewed agony.

Yet, this time nothing happened—no pain, no vomiting. Even the shudders that had all but knocked his bones together had just disappeared.

He didn't know what to make of it.

"Quinn, are you all right?" Jazz's voice was low and serious, harsher than he had heard it all night. But then again, waking up to find her lover curled on the floor in the fetal position could probably do that to a woman.

"I'm fine," he croaked, his mouth and throat so dry that he could barely form the words. And yet he took a couple seconds to take inventory of his body and realized, with a shock, that it was true. He was *fine.*

He'd been to hell and back in the past two hours, but now he was feeling better than he had any right to expect. He was still weak, but he always was after a typical one of these episodes—and what he'd just experienced had been anything but typical.

"Well, you don't look fine," she said. "To be honest, you look like hell." As he had been assessing the damage, she joined him on the floor, scooting until her legs rested on either side of his hips while her breasts pressed against his back. That's when he realized two things simultaneously. The first was that sometime during the night, she had discarded her tank top and there was nothing between them now but skin.

The second realization was that she was still holding him. Her arms were wrapped around his waist, her hands holding on to his wrists. A low-grade warmth started in his belly, and began to chase away the chills. He knew it had nothing to do with his strange and sudden recovery and everything to do with her.

Shifting a little, he tried to hold her hand but she pulled away—a low, warning sound coming from her throat.

That's when a third realization hit him—she wasn't holding his hand to give comfort, as he'd thought. She was taking his pulse. Which probably wasn't a good thing, seeing as on a normal day his heart rate was almost twice what a human's was. And at the moment he was anything but normal. She probably figured he was a walking candidate for a heart attack.

Not wanting to deal with questions—and not wanting to lie to her—he jerked his wrist out of her grasp and hoped that she hadn't gotten enough of a count to realize just how different he was from her.

He waited for her to say something, to protest his pulling away or to demand to know what the hell was wrong with him. But Jazz did neither—instead she simply sat there, the front of her body pressed against his back, and held him while he struggled to gain control of his riotous thoughts and emotions.

More than once he considered turning to look at her, but in the end he couldn't bring himself to do it. Firstly, because after waking up and finding him nearly comatose she could have run for the door but hadn't. That frightened him even as it made his dragon preen. And secondly, because he couldn't stand the thought of seeing how her opinion of him had changed—not now, when he was still so raw, his wounds so close to the surface.

Not now when he was still confused and trying to figure out what the hell had happened. He'd never had an attack that bad before, nor one that had ended so abruptly. Even while the man was grateful it was over, the scientist in him wanted to know the whys and wherefores.

Minutes passed and he braced himself for a confrontation, figuring Jasmine would start pushing him for answers. Not that he blamed her—if he'd woken up and found her in a similar situation, he would have demanded to know what the hell was wrong with her.

But she didn't do that, didn't say a word. He didn't know if it was because she'd sensed how vulnerable he felt or because she simply didn't care. But the way she was holding him—so tightly and tenderly—didn't feel like lack of caring.

As if sensing the ever-changing thoughts that were mixed up in his brain, Jazz smoothed her palms over his shoulders, down his arms and up his spine, kneading softly everywhere she touched.

It was exactly what he needed, though he hadn't had a clue, and the dragon reveled in her warmth and attention. *He* reveled in it, realizing with a shock that he was cold for the first time in recent memory. And not just any cold, but a bone-deep frigidity that went so deep he wondered if he'd somehow lost the ability to control his own body temperature. Dragons were the only animal of reptilian descent that could regulate their temperatures, due largely to the fire that burned deep inside any healthy dragon.

But now, it was like his fire had gone out. He reached for it but it wasn't there, and a low-grade panic started humming through his veins. Jazz must have realized how cold he was, too, because suddenly her arms were around his waist. She held him tightly to her while her hands chafed against the skin of his arms and her mouth skimmed over his bare back as she tried to share her body heat with him.

It was the nicest thing a woman had ever done for him. That she was doing it now, when he'd been so close to giving up hope, meant more than he would ever be able to tell her.

He wanted to explain things to her, but his normal eloquence had deserted him, and he settled instead for simply leaning into her body, concentrating on the soft, warm feel of her.

On the crazy, blackberry scent of her.

On the sweet caramel taste of her that still lingered in his mouth. It felt amazing to have his senses back, especially after spending so many minutes locked in complete and total sensory deprivation.

He focused on them—focused on her—as an excuse not to think any more about what had happened to him. It wasn't the best coping mechanism in the world, but here—in the dead of night—it was enough.

"Can I get you anything?" she finally asked tentatively.

How about a nice dose of sanity? he wanted to ask. *Forgiveness. Oblivion.* But since asking for any of those things would only make her think he was even crazier than she already did, he simply said, "I could use a drink."

"Of course." She scrambled to her feet, crossed to the bathroom and filled one of the plastic glasses with tap water.

A few seconds later she was back, the cup extended toward him. He reached to take it and suddenly there was a searing pain on his arm—it circled his bicep and shot up to his shoulder and down into his fingers. For a second Quinn was afraid that his reprieve was over, that the agony was coming back, but within seconds he realized this pain felt different. It felt hot and sharp and comforting in a way he didn't recognize and couldn't explain.

Then it was gone and he was cold again. Lonely. Desperate to connect in a way he never had been before.

"My brother died yesterday."

As soon as he said the words, he wanted to call them back. What kind of idiot blurted something like that out—especially to a woman he'd just met? It was a lot more than she'd signed on for. After all, this whole night was supposed to be about fun and games, not his complete physical and emotional collapse. But it was so much easier to show his pain to a stranger, to her, than it was to acknowledge it to his clan members.

Jazz didn't say anything at first, and he waited, expecting to hear all the meaningless platitudes that strangers voice at times like these—followed by a run for the door. But she didn't move, didn't speak. Instead, she slipped behind him again, tightened her arms around his waist and just held him for long moments, the feel of her heart beating steadily against his more soothing than anything he'd felt in a very long time.

When she finally did speak, she said the one thing he never expected to hear. "Was it your fault?"

Anger surged through him, even as he told himself he was grateful she hadn't pulled her punches. "It was completely my fault."

"Somehow I doubt that. Death is rarely anyone's fault—at least not completely," she answered. "Things happen."

"How can you say that?" He shrugged her off, got up and paced across the room on unsteady legs. "For all you know, I could have pointed a gun at him and shot him."

He whirled to face her, and if he expected her to be scared, he was disappointed. Instead, she regarded him steadily from her spot on the floor, her knees pulled to her chest like they were having the most regular conversation in the world.

"Did you?"

"Shoot him? Of course not."

"Well there goes that argument."

"You're being pretty flippant considering I just told you my brother is dead."

She didn't look as embarrassed by his observation as he'd expected her to be, only a little sad. "It seems to me that you're torturing yourself enough for both of us. Someone needs to keep a level head here."

He didn't know what to say, didn't know if there was anything he could say, as a small part of him wondered if she was right. Turning away, he faced out the window toward the parking lot where the last of the traffic from the bar was slowly working its way onto the main street. It was easier than looking at her, easier than seeing that odd understanding in her eyes.

He struggled for control, continuing to watch the mass exodus until the last car had turned out, leaving a lonely red Mustang as the lot's only occupant. "Is that your car?" he asked, at a loss for anything more meaningful to say.

She crossed the room to peer over his shoulder. "Yep."

"You want me to change the tire now?"

She wrapped her arms around his waist, skimmed her lips over the ornate lines of the dragon tattoo that covered most of his back. Her easy affection was balm to his tattered soul, even before she answered, "It'll still be there in the morning." He felt her smile against his shoulder blade and allowed himself to sink into her words. He didn't know why, but she helped keep his demons at bay, and right now he was too worn out to do anything but let her.

"Besides," she said, "I can think of a better way to spend the rest of the night."

"Oh, yeah? And what way is that?"

She leaned away from him a little and he almost protested, except her voice was light and teasing and still close when she whispered, "Guess."

He turned just in time to catch the wicked grin that flashed across her face. It aroused him all over again, and he gave himself over to the feeling. If sex was the only thing he could bring himself to share with her, then he'd settle for that. The oblivion that came with losing himself in her body sounded really good right about now. Moving toward her, he murmured, "I should probably let you know I'm a pretty good guesser."

"Now, see, that's exactly what I'm counting on."

CHAPTER EIGHT

Quinn took another step toward her and Jasmine retreated—not out of fear, but out of a need to keep the game going a little longer. As he followed her, matching each of her backward steps with a forward one of his own, he arched an eyebrow suggestively. She much preferred the wild glint in his eye to the look of complete and utter devastation that had been there just a few minutes before.

She wasn't fool enough to think that she had banished the agony she'd seen in his eyes when she'd woken up—she knew it was still there, lurking, right below the surface. But if she could give him a few minutes reprieve from whatever was hurting him, then she was all for it.

"Where are you going?" he asked, as he backed her slowly across the room. "There's no place to run."

"Who says I'm running? Maybe I'm just executing a strategic retreat."

"I'm not sure if there's anything strategic about it—seeing as how you're about to bump into the dresser."

He took another step forward, and in those moments he was all predator and she was his prey.

It was not a relationship she normally espoused, but right then, with Quinn bearing down on her, she couldn't remember ever feeling more excited.

As she continued to back up, making him work for it in an effort to keep his mind off his pain, she let her gaze sweep over him, lingering on all the parts of him she'd wanted to touch during their first lovemaking session, but had been denied.

With his shirt off and the top button of his jeans undone, he was even more gorgeous than he'd been at the bar. His too-long black hair was tousled, while his eyes gleamed electric green in the semi-darkness of the motel room.

And his chest—his chest was the stuff fantasies were made of. Her fantasies, anyway. It was smooth and broad and extremely well-muscled, and he had a complicated looking black and green tribal tattoo decorating his right pec. As for the six-pack she'd spied through his shirt earlier—it was more like an eight-pack, and it made her mouth water with the need to taste it. The only thing she wanted more was to trace her tongue down the light happy trail starting below his belly button and leading into his jeans.

Her need to touch him was so real, so powerful, that she shuddered and reached for Quinn before she even knew that she was doing it. Whether it was brought on by the fact that she couldn't be in the same room with him without wanting him, or whether it was because she needed to comfort him when his pain was so real, she didn't know. And didn't care.

But before her fingers could touch him, before they could skim down that hard, flat stomach, he took advantage of her lapse in attention and pounced on her. His hands went around her waist and then he was lifting her, plopping her down on the same dresser he'd taken her on earlier in the night.

"You have something against the bed?" she asked with a grin.

"We'll get there eventually, but right now I want to see you clearly." Before she could object, he reached behind her and switched on the lamp embedded in the dresser mirror.

Light flooded the small area and she knew she was displayed—scars and all—to his very discerning eye.

She shifted, tried to cover her nude torso with her hands, but he grabbed her wrists. Smacking her hands down on the table, one on either side of her hips, he held her pinned in place as he looked his fill.

She shuddered beneath his scrutiny, knowing what he was seeing. And while she normally wasn't self-conscious about her body, for some reason it bothered her that this beautiful man with the perfect body was looking at her odd collection of scars.

She wanted to be perfect for him, wanted him to remember her for something more than the jagged, pink lines that crisscrossed her torso from where she'd had shrapnel removed—or the surgical incisions from where they'd gone in and saved her lung and set her ribs.

She closed her eyes, waited for him to ask what had happened to her. And waited. And waited.

Finally, when she could bear the tension no longer, she opened her eyes to see what was taking him so long. But he wasn't looking at her scars. Instead he was waiting patiently for her to work up the nerve to look him in the eyes.

Hating her weakness—and the self-awareness that made her ashamed when she should be proud for surviving—Jasmine tossed her head and finally met his gaze, head-on. When she did, what she saw was nothing like what she expected.

There was no revulsion, no curiosity. Just an open, honest acceptance that humbled her even as it freed her to be herself.

Jasmine tugged at his large hands, which were still wrapped around her wrists. "I want to touch you," she demanded breathlessly, her desire back in full force now that her fears about his reaction had proved groundless.

Deep inside, she still wondered what he thought, wondered what he was feeling, but she wasn't stupid enough to let her insecurities ruin everything for them.

Quinn studied her for a second, as if trying to see inside her brain. She must not have looked like she was going to dive for cover, because he slowly freed her hands.

As soon as he let her go, she smoothed her hands over his chest, letting her thumbs linger on his nipples and flick back and forth against the sensitive buds. He groaned, low and deep, his head falling back a little as a shudder wracked his big frame.

She wondered for a moment if he was going to stop her, but in the end he didn't seem to be threatened by her wanting to take control for a little while. In fact, if the grin on his face was anything to go by, he seemed to relish it.

Which was fine with her. She'd more than enjoyed the way he took her earlier—all dominant, possessive he-man—but she liked to give as good as she got, and it was definitely her turn to drive him a little crazy.

Leaning forward, she licked a long, teasing trail across his tattoo, lingering on each twist and curlicue of ink. "Mmm, salty," she murmured.

"Sorry. I was . . . working out before I hit the bar."

"It was an observation, not a complaint," she answered, as she curled her tongue around his nipple, pausing to nibble at the hard bud. "It might even have been an endorsement. You taste delicious."

His laugh was dark and smoky. "I don't know about that."

"I do."

She reached for the bottle of tequila he'd bought at the bar and uncapped it. "Besides, I have it on the best authority that tequila tastes better after a little salt."

"Does it?"

"So I've been told. I haven't actually had a chance to test it out yet."

"Oh, well in that case, test away." He spread his arms wide, an offering if she'd ever seen one, and she wanted to devour him in a series of sharp, greedy bites.

At the same time, she didn't want it to be over so quickly. She wanted to live on this memory for a long time, and she wanted it to last and last.

Leaning forward again, she swept her tongue from his belly button to his throat, pausing to nuzzle at his collar bone for a few long, sex-drenched seconds. He groaned, and his hands clutched at her shoulders, but she pushed him away. Then she lifted the bottle of Patrón to her lips and took one long, slow swallow.

"How was it?" he asked, and a shudder worked its way through her. She loved his voice, all flash and fantasy and low, smoldering flame.

"The best I've ever had."

He closed his eyes, and when he opened them, she swore there was something in there, watching her. Something dark and dangerous and not quite human. It excited her, as did the sharp scrape of his nails against her back as his fists clenched and unclenched against her.

She held out the bottle to him. "Here. You try."

He took the bottle, his eyes darkening even more. Then he licked his lips with a slow, deliberate swipe of his tongue that had her pussy clenching and every nerve in her body quivering.

He looked her over from top to toe, as if he couldn't quite decide where to taste first. His slow regard drove her crazy; she squirmed in an effort to relieve the pain and the pleasure building slowly within her.

"Come on, Quinn," she whispered, reaching for him with unsteady hands.

"Come on what?" he answered, his lips a scant inch from her own.

She arched her back, let her head and neck fall back as she offered herself to him. "Taste me."

And he did, his mouth lowering to her breasts so slowly that she wanted to beg him to hurry. She arched again, higher this time— needing his mouth on her with a desperation she had never felt before.

Then he was there, his tongue swirling in circles over the curve of her left breast and then her right— teasing, stroking, tasting her again and again, until it was all she could do to keep from ripping off her pants and begging him to fuck her.

"You taste so good." It was a whisper, low and raspy, but she heard it over the wild, staccato beat of her heart, and her body reacted, her arousal ratcheting up another notch when she thought she couldn't go any higher.

"So do you, Quinn. I love the way you taste." She leaned forward, intending to lick her way back across his chest. But the second her mouth met his warm, resilient flesh she wanted nothing more than to mark him as hers—even if it was just temporarily.

She sank her teeth into his pec in a sharp little bite that made his hands clench in her hair, and he started to shake.

Quinn nearly lost it as Jasmine's teeth nipped at his flesh. He fought for control when all he really wanted was to rip her pants off and bury his face in her sweet pussy until she was screaming his name.

To pull her off the dresser and onto her knees so she could suck his cock until he blew straight down her throat.

To throw her on the bed and fuck her until they were both too exhausted to move.

At the same time, he didn't want it to end—not when the simple feel of her hands in his hair and her tongue on his skin brought him so much pleasure.

But when she fumbled the Patrón out of his hand, he almost lost the battle at the sight of her sweet, pink tongue licking at the rim of the bottle as she let the spicy liquor stream down her throat.

Her eyes met his, clinging for long seconds before she took one last sip of tequila. Pulling the bottle from her mouth, she leaned back until her shoulders were resting against the mirror. And then she poured a long, cool stream of tequila right onto his bare chest.

"Fuck," he said, and groaned. It was a curse and a prayer, a complaint and a plea for more, and Jazz seemed to understand that.

Hopping off the dresser, she nuzzled her way from his neck to his chest and down to his abdomen, making sure to lick up every drop of tequila she could find. He felt himself grow harder with every touch of her tongue, felt himself leak just a little as she dipped her tongue below the waistband of his jeans for one fiery, hot lick.

"Do you want some more?" she asked, her eyes glinting a sexy violet as she tried to hand him the tequila.

"I'd rather have you."

"The two aren't mutually exclusive, you know." She shimmied out of her yoga pants before settling herself on the bed and tipping the tequila bottle so that a few drops dribbled onto her breasts and down her stomach to pool in her navel and below.

The bold move shot straight through him, turning up the heat until there was a raging inferno inside of him. The chokehold he held on his beast slipped, and the dragon snapped and clawed in an effort to get out. It wanted her as badly as he did.

Jazz gasped as the cold liquid hit her, arching her back so that her nipples were only inches from his mouth. Because he was dying for another taste of her, he bent down, following the trail the alcohol had made with delicate flicks of his tongue that tormented both of them.

Then, because he couldn't resist, he tilted the bottle so that the tequila coated his index finger. He swirled it first over one of her nipples and then the other before bending his head and circling the hard buds with his tongue. He sucked until all the alcohol was gone, savoring its rich burn.

Bringing his hands to Jazz's shoulders, he pressed her back slowly until she was resting on her elbows, soft and relaxed, her beautiful body completely open to him. For a moment he couldn't move, couldn't think, could barely breathe as he was overwhelmed by the picture she made.

Her cheeks were hot and red, her eyes slumberous with desire, her lips slick from the journey she'd made down his body, a journey that had left him shaken and furiously aroused. Laid out on the hotel bed like a pagan fire goddess, her legs open and dangling over the edge, she was the most beautiful thing he'd ever seen.

"I may never drink tequila any other way." He lifted the bottle, poured a steady stream of the liquor over her stomach.

She gasped as it ran down her sides and pooled in her navel, and he bent forward, sipping from her slowly. Savoring the spicy-sweet taste of her that mingled with the smooth heat of the aged tequila.

As he drank from her, he made a point of running his tongue over her scars. Some were shallow, some were deep, but all were recent. The doctor in him recognized the sharp, thin slice of a scalpel under her right breast and over her left hip, but the other scars were less precise, more random, as if pieces of glass and metal had sliced into her body.

A car accident, he wondered, as he kissed his way over a particularly large scar on her side. Or something more treacherous, less mundane? He murmured a few words, skimmed his hands over the injury and let warmth flow from his fingertips into her. He'd seen the way she'd gingerly moved after their first round of lovemaking, favoring this side, and he couldn't stand the idea of causing her more pain than she'd already suffered.

He felt the heat spread through her, and the shadows he could sense under the wound slowly loosened up. He moved on to her hip, did the same thing. Then on to her rib cage and her elbow and the long, deep scar on her upper thigh, making sure to cover his healing with the seductive touch of sex.

As the shadows dispersed and the pain faded, Jazz moaned—a low, sweet sound that made him grateful for his gift for the first time in a long while. He might not be able to put a dent in the virus that was ravaging his people, but the fact that he could ease Jazz's pain meant something to him.

"Quinn." His name was a breathy plea on her lips and he glanced up, afraid that he had somehow given himself away.

But she only grinned, then whispered, "My turn," before grabbing his hand and sucking his tequila-coated finger into her mouth.

His knees actually shook as she twirled her tongue around his long finger, stroking it up and down in the same rhythm he wanted desperately for her to use on his cock. His heart was pounding out of control; the need to fuck her was an all-consuming ache inside of him as he sank down onto the bed beside her.

"Jasmine." He tried to retrieve his hand—along with his sanity— but she lifted her arms and curled her body around his arm, holding him like she never wanted to let him go.

The thought whipped through him, arrowing straight into the loneliness that had plagued him for too long. Even as he told himself he was being stupid, even as he listed all the reasons in his head that this could only be a one-night stand, he couldn't resist playing the what-if game.

What if she were still there in the morning?

What if she were as moved by what was happening between them as he was?

What if she wanted something more than the hottest one-night stand on record?

His dragon roared in approval, shooting his lust-crazed body into overdrive, and he clutched at Jazz, determined to give her as much pleasure as she was giving him.

But she chose that moment—when his hands were trembling and his cock was aching—to swipe her tongue around and around his finger. And then, just when he didn't think he could get any more turned on, just when his knees were locking and his cock throbbing, she bit down, hard, on the tip of his finger.

The dragon howled and Quinn lost any and all control he'd managed to hold on to.

Ripping his finger from her mouth, he took a deep breath and grabbed the tequila bottle with a hand that shook so badly it was all he could do to hold it steady as he drank his fill. When he was done, he started to hand the bottle to her, but she wouldn't take it. Instead, she hooked her fingers in the front belt loops of his jeans and tugged until the denim was in a pile on the floor.

Then she smiled and repeated his words back to him. "I'd rather have you."

The second she put her mouth on him, he knew he didn't stand a chance. Her tongue was everywhere at once. Flicking over his shoulder, sliding down his chest to play with his rib cage. Moving higher again to lick at his jaw.

"Jazz, stop." Quinn tangled his hands in her hair, tried to stop her before the beast took control. He wanted to make this good for her—needed to with an intensity that bordered on obsession—but if the dragon managed to slip through the cracks, he was desperately afraid that it would be beyond his control, that it would drive only for its own satisfaction.

But Jazz refused to heed his warning. Her hands slipped around his waist as her nails dug into the muscles of his back, directly over the dragon tattoo that was as much a part of him as the beast that lived inside.

The flickers of pain were exquisite, the feel of her clawing him so sexy he feared that he would come before he ever got inside her.

"Stop," he gasped again, but the protest was so weak that even he didn't know whether he believed it.

She lifted her head, looked at him with lust-glazed eyes. Then smiled naughtily and murmured, "Oh, I don't think so," right before she closed her hand around his throbbing, raging cock.

He groaned, then rolled over so quickly he nearly fell off the bed. Desperate to be inside of her, he pulled her on top of him so that she was straddling him, her knees on either side of his hips, her pussy resting directly over his dick.

She gasped at the first touch of his cock against her, then rocked herself over him until he slid between her labia, the tip of his cock resting directly against her clit.

It was his turn to gasp, his turn to tremble, as her warm heat closed around him like a fist. And then she was moving, her slick, hot body sliding against his cock, and he almost forgot how to breathe.

"You feel so good," he muttered, his fingers flexing against her hips as he struggled to remember not to hurt her.

"I think you have that backward." She slid her hips forward and backward slowly—so fucking slowly he wanted to beg her to end it. But she didn't look particularly merciful at the moment, and besides, this was still the most amazing feeling he'd ever had. Being in her without actually being in her, being cradled by her body without the heavy thrusting that would push him over the edge.

Jazz slid back again, until the tip of his cock was resting against her entrance, rising high on her knees to keep him from taking control. And then she slid a little ways back down so that his tip once again worked its way inside of her.

"You're killing me, Jazz."

"Again, I think it's the other way around," she gasped.

They were the words he'd been waiting for, the tacit permission he had to take them to the next level. Rolling his hips against her, he pushed himself a little deeper into her pussy.

She whimpered, arched, her eyes closing as the pleasure jolted through her, and he couldn't resist a grin. Or doing it again—this time with an added zip of heat that he knew would light her up from the inside.

Her eyes widened and her body clenched around him so tightly that he repeated the process, focusing his power and sending it directly inside of her.

Just that easily she went over the edge, her hands grabbing his and squeezing as her orgasm slammed through her.

Quinn watched her come, overwhelmed by how beautiful she was like this. If he had his choice, he would keep her like this all the time— making love to her again and again until she was so sensitive that one jolt of heat from him sent waves of ecstasy rippling through her.

He waited for her to come back down before shifting his hands so that they tangled in her short, sassy locks. Then he pulled her down so that her face was only inches from his. Her eyes were glazed and satisfied, her mouth swollen from the kisses he'd already given her.

Still, he couldn't resist her like that, so he pulled her the last couple of inches until her mouth met his in a kiss so deep he could feel his own orgasm beckoning. Desperate to be inside her every way he could, Quinn ran his tongue along the seam of her lips and nearly shouted in triumph when she opened for him.

He slipped inside, explored her. Curled his tongue around hers and sucked until she was as much a part of him as he was of her.

Jasmine moaned, her tongue tangling with Quinn's as she took her time exploring every part of his mouth. She wanted to go on kissing him forever, never wanted this moment to end as she savored the incredible taste of him. Tequila and desert and sweet, wild rain.

But he was growing desperate for his own orgasm. She could feel it in the muscles bunching under her hands, sense it in the restless movements of his hips beneath her own. So she took one more minute to taste him as he had done to her earlier, sliding her tongue over his teeth and the little piece of skin that connected his upper lip to his gums.

He jerked when she touched it, his entire body going rigid, as if electricity had shot up his spine. And perhaps it had—that piece of skin was incredibly sensitive and totally erotic.

Before she could prepare herself, long before she was ready for her exploration to end, he stood and pushed her against the dresser. Grasping her hips, he plunged upward, entering her with an urgency that had her trembling on the edge of orgasm.

"Take me," he muttered, plunging deep again and again. "Take all of me."

"God, yes." Twisting her hands in his hair, she smoothed them over his powerful chest. Clutched at the strong muscles of his back.

She wanted to touch him everywhere, wanted to feel every part of him against her as he took her higher than she'd ever gone before.

And then he was cursing, pulling her up and off of him so quickly that she had no time to prepare. She locked on to the dresser with desperate hands to keep from falling. "Why—"

He growled something unintelligible at her as he reached for his jeans. Pulling a condom out of his back pocket, he ripped it open with his teeth and started to roll it on. She stopped him.

"Let me." His eyes were blacker than she'd ever seen them as he handed her the condom, and her hands were shaking so badly she wasn't sure she'd even be able to do the job. She knew only that she wanted to touch him, to do this intimate thing for him before she took him back into her body.

So with trembling hands, she slipped the condom over his tip and stroked him—hand over hand—as she rolled it on.

"Enough," he growled, grabbing her hands and pinning them behind her back. "One more touch and I'll come before I get back inside you."

She purred, arched her back so that her nipples were in his face. Luxuriated in the feeling of being taken. Wallowed in the strength he wore so effortlessly.

Then he was leaning down, pulling one of her nipples in his mouth. Her knees buckled and she cried out, reaching for him in an effort to stay upright. He caught her easily, lifted her off the floor and continued to suck as he lowered her onto his raging-hot cock.

She bucked against him, tried to rush him, but he used his free hand to hold her hips still. "I want to touch you," she said, gasping, yanking against the tight hold he had on her wrists. Her arms were still pinned behind her and she was completely at his mercy, able to take only whatever it was he chose to give her.

"Not now. I'm too close." He buried his face in the curve of her neck, bit her shoulder in an effort to establish dominance—as if she didn't already know who was in control.

It grated on her—not the bite, but Quinn's sudden bid to control her. He was already driving her crazy, taking her higher than she'd ever dreamed possible, but that wasn't enough for her. She wanted, needed, to make him as out of control as he made her.

With that thought in mind, she pushed her knees into his sides and slowly—oh, so slowly—clenched the muscles of her sex around him. She felt his response in the jerk of his cock, saw it in the clenching of his jaw as he fought to maintain control.

She did it again, squeezing a little bit harder, a little bit longer before she released him.

"Stop it," he growled, his free hand coming down hard on her ass.

She threw her head back and laughed, even as she tightened the muscles again and again. "Make me."

"Jasmine." His voice was low, warning, more animal than human as she continued to caress him with her body. He was getting ready to lose it—she could feel it in the thighs that trembled beneath her own and the hand that clenched more firmly around her wrists.

But she didn't care. She wanted him to lose it, wanted him to plunge inside of her with all the darkness and passion and emotion he had inside of him. She wanted him as crazy as she was.

She wanted him every way she could have him.

"Come on, Quinn," she whispered tauntingly. "Fuck me like you mean it."

He released her hands with a roar, his fingers clenching on her ass to keep her in place as his hips began to piston against her. Harder, deeper than before, he pounded into her. Again and again he slammed his cock inside her, until she was overwhelmed. Surrounded. Completely taken over by him.

And still he surged inside of her. Desperately. Furiously. Each quick, hard stroke of his cock a branding that told her exactly how much he wanted to possess her.

Jasmine moaned as she wrapped her arms around him and held his shaking, furious body against her own. She'd wanted to push him, to see him without his infernal control. To show him that she could take whatever he dished out. And she was taking it, but, God, she'd never felt anything this intense before, not even the first time he'd made love to her. She was completely in his thrall.

Overwhelmed.

Taken.

Dominated.

She was lost in the fire of his possession, explosion after explosion, as the most unbelievable orgasm of her life tore through her—one that put those she'd experienced a few hours before to shame.

"Jasmine!" Quinn's groan was low, hoarse, his body jerking spasmodically against hers as he emptied himself inside of her in long, jetting streams. His shudders set off another explosion, and she was screaming, wailing, burying her face against the heavy muscles of his chest as her body spun onto a whole different plane, one where the pleasure went on and on and on.

They stayed that way for a long time, her back against the wall, Quinn's heavy body crushing hers as he leaned against her. His mouth trailed kisses down her neck, over her chest, between her breasts, little nibbles that had her shivering in reaction despite the climaxes that had just seized her.

But he couldn't seem to stop touching her, and she understood, felt the same way. Her hands smoothed over his back, down his arms. Her fingers clenched in the cool silkiness of his hair. She never wanted him to let her go, never wanted her feet to touch the floor again.

CHAPTER NINE

Quinn had disappeared. He had walked out of the clinic two days before and hadn't been heard from since. It was perfect, exquisite. The only thing that would have been better was if he was still at the clinic—as a patient. Laid up with the beginning symptoms of the disease.

Though it was more dangerous for her to be here than at the clinic, she stood in the back of Quinn's main laboratory and simply watched as things went to hell around her. Interesting, wasn't it, how the entire operation fell apart if he wasn't there to keep it running smoothly? Despite her arguments to the contrary—she hadn't wanted to give Quinn that much credit—Brock had been right all along.

He'd told her that striking at Michael was a better move than infecting Quinn—a big payoff with none of the unsightly consequences. Michael's death had gotten the healer out of the way, his feelings of grief and incompetence sending him off somewhere to lick his wounds, at least temporarily. Yet it hadn't raised Dylan's suspicions. And if the virus somehow managed to infect Quinn as well, then so much the better. At least it would have been "accidental."

If she'd infected Quinn first, as had been her original thought, she could only imagine how different things would be. His death would have struck a new kind of terror into the hearts of the entire clan, which would have jibed nicely with her agenda, but it also would have looked odd, since he'd attended so many of these deaths and had never before been infected. Like Dylan, Quinn seemed to have a natural immunity to the virus in its more basic form. Which meant that questions would have been asked, and people would have been sniffing around—two things she and Brock definitely didn't want.

Brock had warned her—the last thing any of them needed right now was for Dylan to figure out he had a traitor among his people. Security would tighten up, and the narrow windows of opportunity she had been carving out for herself would close completely. She couldn't afford that, not if she was going to accomplish what she'd told Brock she could.

At the front of the lab, Phoebe banged her hand down onto one of the marble lab tables in frustration. A couple of lab techs rushed up to her, started to soothe her, but she shooed them away and continued fumbling through the information she had in front of her.

Earlier, she had tried to get close enough to get a peek at the info Phoebe found so fascinating, but she didn't really belong in this part of the lab. Someone might notice, and though one slip-up wouldn't give her away, she didn't want to worry about anyone putting the pieces together. At least not yet. Not when Brock wasn't ready for her. Not when her job here was unfinished.

No, she would just follow the plan. Brock hadn't steered her wrong so far. He had, in fact, come up with a lot of really good ideas. Like injecting Michael.

After all, Phoebe was supposed to be some hot-shot scientist, some miracle-working doctor, and yet she was clueless in the lab without Quinn. She hadn't done anything all day but fiddle with the report she had in front of her, glance at the clock and stumble over the other employees in the lab. If Quinn didn't come back, or if Michael's death drove him away from the clan for an extended period of time, then the Dragonstars would never recover.

They would be doomed—just the way she wanted them.

CHAPTER TEN

He woke alone, sleepy and satisfied, his dragon curled up and relaxed inside of him.

It was an odd feeling, and one so unfamiliar that it took him a moment to place it. When it hit him—when he realized that he was at peace for the first time in longer than he could remember—Quinn sat up abruptly. After all, being with a woman had never made him feel like this before. He wasn't sure what to make of it. Wasn't sure what to make of *her.*

She was prickly enough to slap down an entire room full of interested men, yet had melted like warm honey the first time he'd touched her.

She was honest enough to strive for her own satisfaction, but at the same time gave so much pleasure that he had nearly drowned in it—drowned in her—throughout the long night.

She hadn't been afraid of a confrontation, hadn't been afraid to bully him out of his bad mood, but had also held him more tenderly than anyone ever had.

Jazz was a puzzle, a strange amalgamation of parts and emotions that shouldn't fit yet somehow did. Adventurous and sweet, brave and sexy, confrontational and so confident that it bordered on arrogance, she was everything and nothing like what he wanted in a woman.

Not that he was looking for a woman right now, he told himself hastily. His plate was more than full without adding the extra complication of trying to turn a one-night stand into a relationship.

And yet he wasn't quite ready to say good-bye to her, either. He wanted to take her out for breakfast and watch as she glutted herself on food that he had provided. He wanted to hold her, to kiss her, to make love to her one more time before they parted for good. And, more than anything else, he wanted to make her smile once more.

He would take that smile, hold on to it and use it to get him through the bad times that were bearing down on him—and his clan—with the power and destructive force of a twenty-foot tsunami.

As soon as that thought invaded his head, others quickly followed—ones that were nowhere near as pleasant as his fantasies about getting Jasmine naked for one last round.

Once the pain of his losses caught up to him, as well as his worries about the future of the Dragonstars, they crowded in on him, ripping away his satisfaction and replacing it with the ever-present guilt.

How could he have just flown off like that? What were they doing for Michael? Had his funeral already been arranged? As his brother, that job fell to Quinn, but it would be just like Dylan to take it on if he thought Quinn couldn't handle it.

He closed his eyes again as the reality of his brother's death hit him like a one-two punch to the gut. Instinctively, he reached across the bed, searching for Jazz, though he knew she had already gotten up. But her side of the bed was still warm and fragrant, so he rolled over onto it and tried to absorb the very essence of it—of her—into himself. He wasn't sure what that woman had done to him last night, but whatever her powers, she had turned him inside out.

Because even as the worry and the pain converged, even as he started wondering what turmoil his absence had caused back home in the lab, it was as if he were buffered. It was as if there was a barrier between him and the emotional maelstrom he'd found himself locked in these last few days, weeks. The time he'd spent with Jazz had made everything, if not all right, at least more bearable than it had been twenty-four hours before.

The mere idea that a woman—a human woman—could have such an effect on him should have set off every warning bell he had, but it didn't. Nor did the beast snoozing within him seem alarmed.

Glancing around, he noted that the door to the bathroom was closed, though there was no sign that anyone was in there. No sound, no movement, no heat signature for the dragon to pick up. The room around him was silent, the only noise the hum of the air conditioner and the steady beating of his heart. Outside he could hear the rumble of cars as they pulled out of the parking lot in a fairly steady stream.

Stretching lazily, he climbed out of bed and pulled on his jeans. He wasn't worried about waking alone. He figured Jazz had gone down to her car for some clean clothes. After all, he hadn't gotten around to changing her tire yet.

He grinned at the thought, looking forward to doing something small to pay her back for the peace she had given him. He knew under normal circumstances she would have been able to change the tire herself—probably faster than he could—but she was injured, her body healing from something that had nearly ripped her apart.

His smile faded when he realized that he still didn't know how she'd been hurt. He'd done his best to dispel the pain, to help the injuries heal more quickly, but she was human, not dragon, and he could only do so much—especially when he was still so drained from what he'd done with Michael.

As if he'd conjured it up with his thoughts, that same strange, searing pain he'd felt while making love to Jasmine the night before sizzled along his bicep. Glancing down, annoyed, he froze as he watched a tribal band magically work its way around his arm, winding its way through the other two he already possessed until it was completely joined with them—becoming as much a part of him as the other bands were.

Eyes widening with a huge, alarming heap of what-the-fuck, he prodded it with a finger, then hissed out a curse when his fingertip blistered at the first contact. Bending closer, he examined it without touching it, and what he found was far from reassuring.

This band was different from the ones he'd had since puberty. To begin with, it was much more ornate—much more feminine—than the other two, one of which joined him with Dylan, and one with the other sentries. Even more important, it wasn't black like the other two. It was a deep, dark violet almost the exact color of Jasmine's eyes.

Shock ricocheted through him as he stared at the band, telling himself that it couldn't exist. It couldn't have happened that quickly, that easily. It just wasn't possible. And it sure as hell couldn't have happened with Jasmine. She was human, for God's sake.

And yet, there it was, no mistake about it. He'd seen enough of these through the years to recognize exactly what it was. His own father had had one in gold, and now, after years of searching for a mate, Dylan finally had one in the same bright blue-violet as Phoebe's eyes.

It was a mating band—magical, pure and completely irreversible. Even death didn't make it fade. He and Jazz were now joined for eternity.

Inside him, his dragon screamed in triumph, its claws raking at him in a way that told him it had recognized her all along. That's why it had tried so hard to get out and get to her in the bar the night before, why it had been there right under the surface while the two of them had been making love. The dragon had wanted to make sure that Jazz was claimed—not just as Quinn's mate, but as its own as well.

Why the hell hadn't he recognized it? Why hadn't he figured things out before they'd ended up tied together like this?

His legs went a little gummy underneath him, and Quinn sat down on the bed, hard. What was he going to do? How was he going to explain this to Jazz without coming across like some crazy, fucked-up stalker?

He thought of the pepper spray attached to Jazz's keychain and the hard-ass look in her eyes when she'd talked about the assholes who had hassled her the night before. Yeah, he could totally see this thing going over really well, especially when he mentioned how uncomfortable it was for mates to be separated for longer than a few days.

Oh yeah, she was going to love this—probably about as much as he did. The question was, how would he tell her? He couldn't exactly blurt out the truth. She'd be gone so fast, her tires would probably smoke as she shouted over her shoulder that he needed to check himself into the nearest mental institution. And he wouldn't even blame her. It was exactly what he would do if someone came to him with the fantastical story he was about to tell her—at least, if he didn't already know the truth about the things that went bump in the night.

His heart started to beat double time, even as he told himself not to panic. He could take this slowly, not spring it on her. He could buy her breakfast, get her cell phone number, maybe date for a while before hitting her with the whole "by the way, we're bound for eternity" thing. "Sorry, I might have been able to stop it when it first started, but I didn't even see it coming. My bad."

That was going to go over really well. But he had to think of something—and quickly—because he didn't relish being the guy who lost his mate before he ever really had her. Not to mention the fact that eventually it would destroy them both if she walked away. While he was almost self-destructive enough to relish that, he couldn't stand the idea of Jasmine suffering because of him. He wasn't sure how he felt about her being his mate, but he did know he would do anything to keep her from being hurt.

It was his self-absorption that had gotten them into this mess. He was just going to have to figure out a way to get them through it.

He was so caught up in his thoughts that it didn't occur to him for another five minutes that Jasmine still wasn't back. Worried that something had happened to her, he crossed the room in a flash, throwing the door open. He stepped onto the landing in front of the room, stared at the empty expanse of the Lone Star's parking lot and instantly knew the truth.

Jazz had found someone else to fix her flat tire and, in doing so, had completely screwed them both.

Jasmine glanced in her rearview mirror just in time to see Fort Stockton disappear into the West Texas desert behind her. Her conscience dinged her, reminding her that she should have at least had the courtesy to say good-bye to Quinn. It wasn't as if he'd done anything to warrant her sneaking away as soon as dawn broke over the horizon.

But when she'd woken up that morning tucked against his chest—her arms and legs tangled with his—she'd had a moment of intense, blinding panic. Okay, a lot of moments of panic, all strung together, until it was all she could do not to bang her head against the fake wooden headboard until everything that had happened between them in the middle of the night was nothing more than a distant memory.

It wasn't the one-night stand that had freaked her out, although she'd never actually indulged in one before. Nor was it Quinn himself who had her stomach churning with acid. He'd been wonderful— caring and considerate and so sexy she'd nearly spontaneously combusted at numerous times throughout the night.

And those moments, when he had simply held her, when they had held each other, would probably always be special to her. It had been a long time—maybe forever—since she'd been held like that, or had the opportunity to hold someone like that.

No, the problem wasn't with Quinn. He'd been great. The problem was with her.

It had felt entirely too good—too natural—to be wrapped in Quinn's arms, and that had completely freaked her out. She'd had lovers through the years—not a ton, but more than a couple. And while she'd respected and liked all of them, she'd never felt the sense of rightness that she'd felt with Quinn after just one night.

How could that not scare the hell out of her?

She was a doctor, a scientist, definitely not one of those people who believed in things like connections or soul mates or any of those other weird, indefinable things people liked to ramble on about. And she wasn't going to start now, just because she'd had the best sex of her life with a truly incredible man.

He probably wasn't all that incredible, after all, she tried to convince herself. He just seemed that way because he'd given her a string of amazing orgasms. In the light of day, he probably was completely normal.

Not that she would know. She'd snuck out not long after sunrise.

Her side ached a lot, and she ran a cautious hand over it. The pain was an unpleasant surprise when, for most of the night, she'd felt so good that she'd all but forgotten the injuries were even there. But she'd aggravated her side when she'd been changing her tire, exactly what she'd hoped to avoid by calling the tow truck the night before.

She'd almost called and scheduled another one, but by the time she'd gotten dressed and snuck out of the motel room, she'd been so frantic she probably would have chewed off her own arm if it had meant freedom. A flat tire was nothing in comparison. Except that her body ached a little more with each mile she put between Quinn and herself.

Thoughts of Quinn had her glancing at her watch. It was seven thirty. Had he woken up yet? Had he figured out that she'd bailed on him? And if he had, was he upset? She hadn't wanted to hurt him, but she—

Jasmine stopped herself cold. She wasn't doing this. Not now, and not in the future. She wasn't one of those women who sat around and worried about how her guy was feeling. It was ridiculous. Besides, Quinn was a big boy—and a far cry from meaning anything to her. He could take care of himself.

Still, she was afraid her absence would hurt him, or at least give him the idea that he'd done something wrong. And she hated that. This was one of those times when "It's not you, it's me" was the truth.

But sitting here worrying about him wasn't going to change anything. No, she'd made her choice when she'd snuck out of that motel room at five thirty in the morning.

Forcing him from her mind, she focused on what lay ahead for her outside of Las Cruces. She kept driving, despite the little voice in the back of her head that told her it wasn't too late to turn around. If she was lucky, he'd still be asleep. She could crawl back into bed and—

Jasmine refused to give herself the satisfaction of finishing that thought. God only knew what might happen if she did.

Three and a half hours later, she pulled into a Starbucks in Las Cruces. Stepping out of the car, she stretched her aching muscles and ignored all the little jolts and pains that came with the movement and wondered when her body was going to get back to normal, or if it ever would.

Probably when she stopped pushing it so damn hard and actually gave it time to rest, to mend, like her doctors had ordered.

Too bad she wasn't any good at following orders, even those she knew were obviously important to her well-being. Besides, the sexual marathon she and Quinn had engaged in had been totally worth the ensuing pain this morning.

After heading inside and buying a huge coffee and a cup of fruit, she strolled back into the early morning heat and surveyed the city outskirts where she was going to be living for the next few weeks—or months.

It was a far cry from Atlanta. The buildings here were new, and the Southwestern architecture couldn't be more different from the antebellum and urban South. Most of the houses had flat roofs and light-colored stucco, meant—she was sure—to reflect the powerful rays of the desert sun.

While there were a few modern-looking buildings in the distance, which she assumed belonged to the University of New Mexico at Las Cruces, even those evoked a Native American Pueblo feeling.

At the same time, there was none of the high-society airs put on by Atlanta, or at least none that she could see. There was no historical society here preserving huge sections of the city, no business district that pretended to be more sophisticated and urbane than it really was. No huge medical complexes promising the most sophisticated version of anything . . .

Not that she was complaining. Quite the contrary. Besides, as long as there was running water, electricity, a decent hotel with air-conditioning and enough food, she was golden. Any way she cut it, it was a huge step up from the locations where she usually set up shop.

But standing here studying the city that was to be her temporary home wasn't going to get things done. With a sigh, she climbed back into the car and pulled up her GPS, programming in the address to the lab that Phoebe had given her. It was in a small town a few miles on the other side of Las Cruces, and she was more than ready to get out of this car for a while.

More than ready to get to work on this mysterious virus, whatever it was.

More than ready to forget Quinn.

The drive was short—another thirty-five minutes or so—and then she was pulling up to an ultra-modern building that was as different from what she'd seen in Las Cruces as the New Mexico desert was from the lush greenery surrounding her apartment in Atlanta.

She pulled her Mustang into the nearest parking space, then took a minute to look at the place she would be calling home for the next few weeks. If the inside was anything like the outside, she was in for a treat.

Since she spent most of her time out in the field, it was rare she got to work in the CDC facilities for any length of time. This lab might be a nice change of pace while she finished recovering. She could probably even handle having her wings clipped for a while—as long as she told herself it wasn't forever. As long as she knew the escape date was some time in the not-so-distant future.

For a second, Quinn's face floated in front of her eyes, his head tossed back, his eyes glowing a lush, verdant green as she bent her head and took him in her mouth. He'd tasted incredible, like—

She grabbed her purse and slammed the car door with a firm snap. Then headed for the laboratory's door at a fast clip in an effort to leave her memories—and Quinn—far behind.

CHAPTER ELEVEN

"So, you're really not going to tell me where you went?" Phoebe asked, as she settled herself next to him at the lab table.

"I'm really not."

"I was worried about you. I don't know what it is about you guys that makes you take off like that when you're hurting. It's really nerve-wracking for the people who care about you to be left behind."

"I keep telling you not to care about me. It would solve a lot of your problems."

"Sorry, but it's too late for that. You're my closest friend here, Quinn, and if anything happened to you, I'm not sure I would recover."

Despite the fact that he was in the mother of all bad moods—losing a brother, finding a mate and losing that mate all within forty-eight hours could do that to a guy—Quinn felt the ice wall he'd built around his heart melt a little at Phoebe's words.

He'd been suspicious as hell of her when she'd first shown up three months before, but working with her—getting to know her—had changed all that. She was an incredible doctor and a hell of a woman. Dylan was lucky to have her.

As was any dragon who found his mate. For some, it was pretty easy; they grew up within a few blocks of each other and figured things out before they were even out of high school.

But for many of the really powerful dragons, mating was a lot harder to work out. Maybe the universe figured if it gifted someone with all that power they didn't deserve to have it easy when it came to finding a mate.

God knew, Dylan had spent almost four centuries looking before he'd found Phoebe completely by accident. And as for his sentries, to date, the only one to have actually found a mate was Gabe. He had fallen completely in love with Dylan's younger sister, Marta, more than two centuries before, mated her and had a child with her.

Now Dylan's sister and niece were dead, victims of the same damned virus Quinn couldn't stop, and Gabe . . . Gabe was a complete and total disaster. When Marta died three months before—right before Phoebe had come to work on the virus—Gabe had gone completely insane. When their daughter, Lana, died a few weeks later, it was like the Gabe they knew disappeared.

He had eventually come back to the clan, but he was an automaton, completely devastated and barely able to get out of bed most mornings. He was an empty shell of a man, who lived only for the chance to avenge the deaths of his mate and daughter. Quinn was afraid—as was Dylan—that once they finally stopped the Wyvernmoons, Gabe would simply die of grief.

That kind of bonding and dependence was just one of the many reasons Quinn hadn't been in a hurry to find his own mate. His job hollowed him out enough without also having to worry about a mate. He'd seen his father—who had been a great healer—suffer for years, caught between his powers and his mate. Quinn's mother, Veronica, had never understood her husband's compulsion to heal, had never been able to deal with the consequences of using his gift. She'd been a warrior, a sentry for Dylan's father, and had no patience for weakness of any kind—especially her mate's.

In a lot of ways Jazz reminded him of his mother, one more reason the rug had been pulled out from beneath him when he'd realized what had happened that morning.

Not that he was going to have to worry about ending up beaten down and bitter like his father—his mate would have to actually stick around for that to happen. As it was, he had no clue how to find Jazz now that she had disappeared. He didn't know where she was from, didn't know where she was headed. Hell, he hadn't even caught her last name before she'd run out on him. He'd even wasted his time checking out every tow truck service in town before he'd left, but he'd had no luck finding her in Fort Stockton.

This was really bad news, considering he was already itchy and uncomfortable, though he'd only been away from her for a few hours. Or maybe it was the miles separating them. Either way, both the dragon and the man were out of sorts. They wanted their mate, and he had a feeling there was going to be hell to pay—for everyone—if he didn't figure out a way to find Jazz soon.

"Well, I'm glad you're back," Phoebe said, slipping a new slide under the microscope. "And not just because I found something new."

"Oh, yeah? What'd you find?" He shoved Jazz out of his mind and went to see what Phoebe had discovered.

"You're not going to like it." She pulled her eyes away from the microscope, gestured for him to look. "I can barely believe it myself— the stupid thing has mutated again."

"Of course it has," he said facetiously. "But come on, you don't want it to be too easy, do you? I thought you were the one who liked a challenge."

"Oh, I'm plenty challenged, thank you very much." She clicked a few buttons on the computer keyboard, and the slide popped up on the huge state-of-the-art monitor he was sitting in front of. "Here, take a look. I've never seen anything like it."

Quinn barely bit back the vilest curse he knew. While the base characteristics identified the blood sample as being infected by the same disease they'd been fighting, the outer markers had definitely changed. Phoebe was right—the thing was mutating faster than they could get a handle on it.

Goddamnit. The beast gnashed its teeth and Quinn wanted to do the same. They were fucked, totally and completely fucked, and there was nothing he could do. His failure hung heavy around his throat. He'd never failed at anything, after all, and it destroyed him that the first thing he couldn't think or fight his way around was the very thing that was threatening to totally annihilate his people.

He'd been working on finding a cure to the disease that ravaged his people for what felt like forever, and while he and Phoebe had made some huge leaps in understanding in these past few months—the least of which was the understanding that this virus was biological warfare, created by their enemies to destroy their clan—they still weren't moving nearly fast enough. For every discovery they made, the virus mutated two or three times, forcing them to constantly play catch up.

"So, what do you think?"

"You don't want to know what I think."

Phoebe blew out a gusty breath. "Yeah, that's pretty much what I figured. I don't think I had a clue what I was doing when I let Dylan talk me out of my nice, safe Harvard lab."

"Do you miss it?"

She looked at him askance. "What? Harvard?"

"Yes. No. I don't know."

"Well, that's clear."

"Sorry." He paused, tried to formulate his thoughts. "Do you miss living in a world where every decision you made wasn't the difference between life and death? Where you felt safe when you went to bed at night? Where you never had to worry about shifters or blood enemies or solving impossible, deadly puzzles?"

"How could I not miss my old life when you describe my new one so eloquently?"

"I—"

She held up a hand, cut him off. "I know what you mean. And honestly, yeah, I miss some things. I miss my apartment and the great little bakery right down the street where I'd stop every morning for a cup of coffee and a pastry. I miss my friends and my students.

"And some days—like today—I really miss the surety of my research on lupus. I miss the fact that while it's a terrible disease, it's predictable. Understandable. And it wasn't designed as a constantly changing, constantly evolving weapon. When I made a breakthrough on my lupus research, it meant something. Now I feel like I'm starting all over again every couple of days."

She shook her head. "But would I go back to that life? Would I give up Dylan? Or you? Or this high-tech lab that has everything I could ever want—including a freaking supercomputer—just so I could sleep better at night?" She laughed. "I wouldn't give up any of it. I love my life with you dragons—love my life *as* a dragon. How could I possibly have imagined three months ago that I would be able to fly? And if thoughts of the Wyvernmoons keep me up some nights, well then, I'll take it. Besides," she said with a sly grin, "Dylan knows just how to help me sleep."

It was Quinn's turn to laugh. "I bet he does."

"That's not to say I won't be damn glad when Jazz gets here. I really want her perspective—"

"Who?" Quinn demanded, cutting Phoebe off, as the dragon stirred to life within him.

"Dr. Jasmine Kane, the woman I was telling you about the other day. I know you don't want her to be involved, but I need you to give her a chance. She's the absolute best at viral-borne blood diseases—and a damn whiz when it comes to mutations. If there's anyone on earth who can help us nail this thing down, she's the one I would put my money on."

Though he'd heard everything Phoebe had said, Quinn remained stuck on the only thing that mattered. "What's her name again?" he demanded.

Phoebe gave him a strange look. "Dr. Jasmine Kane?"

"No. You called her something else. You called her—"

"Jazz?"

"That's her name?"

"Yes. That's her name. She called me from Atlanta yesterday morning before she left and told me she was hoping to make it here by tonight."

He stopped listening when the side door of the lab swung silently inward. Phoebe hadn't heard it—she hadn't been dragon long enough for her senses to be as developed as his.

He didn't turn around to see who had entered his sanctuary, but then he didn't have to. Just like at the bar, his beast smelled her before Quinn saw her. That blackberry jasmine scent of hers wound its way through the harsh antiseptic cleaners they used in the lab and wrapped itself around him.

As it did, his mind—and his beast—went nuts.

Had she known all along who he was?

But if that was the case, why had she snuck out of that stupid motel room without so much as a wham-bam-thank-you-man?

Or had she been as clueless as he about the professional relationship that was about to be thrust upon them?

Did it matter? his dragon side asked, as it strained and pulled against his control. The beast didn't care what she knew or why she had left—it only cared that she was here now. The man was much more cautious. He had to be. For better or worse, she was who fate had decreed as his mate—and it wasn't like he'd get a second shot, at least not while she was alive. He couldn't fuck things up now—no matter how angry he was.

And he was angry, he realized suddenly. Underneath the shock and bewilderment and oh-my-God-I-have-a-mate-and-she's-disappeared drama he'd been through, anger had been lurking all along.

And it was directed—almost exclusively—at Jazz. She was the one who had set this whole thing in motion, after all.

She was the one who had walked up to him at that bar.

She was the one who had given herself to him so completely that he knew no other woman would ever satisfy him the same way—even before he realized she was his mate.

And she was the one who had walked out on him without so much as a screw you, even after they'd held each other all night.

Fuck, yeah, he was angry. So angry that he didn't trust himself to turn around and greet her. He wasn't sure he could be civil.

Which was why he did his best to ignore her, when every instinct demanded that he go to her, that he confront her and get her the hell out of his lab and into his bed. The dragon growled at the thought, low and deep. For the first time in a long while, Quinn wanted to join it.

Jazz stepped into the lab, trying to get her bearings—and their attention. When neither he nor Phoebe turned around, she finally said, "Phoebe?" Her loud, clear voice rang with authority.

Phoebe whipped around at the sound of her name—and so did Quinn, positioning himself slightly in front of her. Jazz might be the mate destined for him, but he wasn't sure he trusted her. Phoebe was his king's mate. It was his duty to protect her.

Then Phoebe pushed past him, squealing with delight as she rushed across the lab—straight at the woman who had made the past few hours of his life a living hell.

"Jasmine!" she cried, wrapping her arms around Jazz—his Jazz—and pulling her in for a huge hug. "You're early! I wasn't expecting you until later this evening."

"Yeah, well, I left a little earlier than expected. I was going stir-crazy and was afraid that if I had to spend any more time staring at the walls of my apartment I was going to lose my mind. Literally." She bent down and hugged Phoebe just as fiercely in return. Then she pulled back. "You look good. The desert must be agreeing with you."

Phoebe's laugh twinkled through the room. "I'm not sure if it's the desert or Dylan, but I feel great. I love it here."

"What's not to love?" Jasmine asked, her eyes sweeping around the room as she took in the lab's setup. "This place is state of the art."

"I know, right? When I think of how hard I had to work to get my lab set up back in Cambridge, I can't believe how lucky I got when I fell into this." She pulled Jasmine forward, toward Quinn. "There's someone I want you to meet."

Balancing on the balls of his feet, his hands clenched in fists at his side, Quinn stayed where he was, waiting for them to come to him. He was spoiling for a fight, and the second his eyes met Jazz's across the shiny, well-equipped lab, he knew she was the one who would give it to him.

For a moment, just a moment, surprise registered in her violet gaze. It was followed by a brief flare of heat that had his dragon's claws coming out, raking against the inside of his skin and shredding his self-control as surely as they did the first layer of his human form. After hours of glutting its senses on her, it could scent her desire, her need, all the way across the sterile lab, and it was all he could do to hold the beast in check.

To hold the man in check, if he was honest. Part of him wanted nothing more than to close the distance between them with one, quick leap and set about devouring her in the most pleasurable way possible—Phoebe or no Phoebe.

But he was still too raw, too angry.

Besides, the look she was giving him said she knew what he was thinking, and she'd gut him if he even tried to touch her. Of course, that only made his impulse harder to control.

Despite his feelings of betrayal, Quinn had a hard time suppressing a small, unexpected spurt of amusement. There was no doubt about it—life was about to get very interesting. He had a feeling he and his mate were going to have a hell of a time before they managed to come to terms. The thought wasn't anywhere near as disappointing as he'd expected it to be.

"Quinn, I'd like you to meet the hematologist I was telling you about, Dr. Jasmine Kane." Phoebe's smile was dazzling. "Jazz, I'd like you to meet Dr. Quinn Maguire. He's an absolute genius and a joy to work with. This is his lab and his project."

"Nice to meet you, Dr. Maguire." Jazz held her hand out to him, and for a moment Quinn thought he would implode. Just go up in smoke, right there. She didn't actually think he was going to play it like that, did she?

Except, apparently she did. Her eyes were carefully blank, her smile professionally polite. It enraged the dragon and the man.

"Oh, we've met before," he said, and it was an effort to keep his voice coldly clinical as he clasped Jazz's hand in his own. It was trembling, just a little, though the look on her face was pure hard-ass. He couldn't help wondering which of the reactions was more honest.

"Have we."

It wasn't a question, but he answered anyway. "We have. Of course, I wouldn't expect you to recall it. It wasn't exactly memorable."

Her eyes turned from lavender to aubergine—from cold to boiling—in the time it took her to blink. The reaction soothed him in a way no amount of protesting—or apologizing—could. She said, "Now that you mention it, I do vaguely remember meeting you. You were drunk, weren't you?"

His grin was fierce. "Relaxed, I would say."

"Oh, right. Of course. Relaxed."

Phoebe's head had been swiveling back and forth between them, like a spectator at a boxing match, and she finally broke in, "What's going on here?"

"Nothing, Phoebe. Why?" Jazz's attention shot to her friend— a rookie mistake if ever Quinn had seen one. If she was frazzled enough to take her eyes off the ball, then she was in worse shape than he had originally believed. He took advantage of her lapse in attention to invade the personal space she set up around herself like a damn barricade.

Phoebe didn't answer for a long moment, and when she did, her voice was filled with curiosity and atypical restraint. "Never mind. I guess we'll get to that later."

"I wouldn't count on it," Quinn muttered under his breath. From the look Phoebe gave him, it was obvious both women heard what he'd said. Jazz flushed, but he couldn't bring himself to be sorry.

"Would you like to see the lab?" Phoebe asked. "We've got everything you could possibly need."

"I'd rather see this top-secret project you're working on. It's been eating at me ever since we got off the phone. A brand-new blood disease that isn't hereditary and isn't contagious. I'm dying to get a look at it."

"I never said it wasn't contagious—just that it couldn't be caught through the normal channels."

Jasmine's eyes narrowed. "What exactly does that mean?"

Phoebe looked at Quinn for help, but he just shrugged. She was the one who had wanted to bring Jasmine in, so she could deal with the . . . complications such a decision caused. There was no way he was going to waste his breath trying to convince any human that their species wasn't necessarily top of the food chain after all. Especially one who had already shown a propensity for not listening to a thing he had to say.

"It means people can't catch the disease in the usual way."

"No kidding, really?" Jazz rolled her eyes. "Come on, Phoebe. You called me, so why don't you just ante up, here? How can people contract the disease? If it isn't contagious through air or fluid contact, how does it spread?"

"That's kind of what we were hoping you would be able to tell us."

CHAPTER TWELVE

Jasmine stared at her friend and fellow scientist in complete astonishment. What the hell had happened to Phoebe? Had the desert heat fried her brain? Because this woman, with her roundabout prevarications and lack of details, wasn't the doctor Jasmine knew. She wasn't even a close facsimile.

Annoyance skittered down her spine, but Jasmine tuned it out. She could be ticked off later. For now, she needed to concentrate. Something was going on, and she suddenly wanted to know exactly what that was.

That didn't mean Phoebe needed to know how curious she was, and neither did Quinn. Thank God for her poker face, as the man watched her so intently it was a wonder she didn't melt. The last thing she had expected was to see Quinn bent over a microscope and cozied up to one of her closest friends.

Hell, the last thing she had expected was ever seeing him again at all. When she'd walked out of that hotel room, she'd been certain she was closing the door on that whole insane encounter. To find out otherwise . . . This was a real kick in the ass. And anyway, how the hell had Quinn gotten there before her when she left him naked and sound asleep back in Fort Stockton?

But she wasn't going to let him know how freaked-out she was at seeing him. If he could play it all cold and amused, so could she.

Even as she promised herself she could keep her cool, Jasmine felt her cheeks heat under Quinn's scrutiny—and memories of the night before pressed in on her from every side. Refusing to give in, she strode over to the microscope they had been looking into so intently when she first got to the lab. She'd be damned if she let him get the best of her with his little "*I don't expect you to remember*" routine. She didn't know what game he was playing, but she wasn't buying into it. Leaving him this morning had been hard enough.

"Do you mind if I take a look?"

Again, that strange look passed between them. Then Phoebe said, finally, "No, please. I'd love to hear what you think. But, be aware, there are certain anomalies . . ."

"What kind of anomalies?" she asked, as she dropped her purse on the counter.

"The DNA is a little different from what we're used to seeing. It's—" She broke off, as if struggling for words, another first for Phoebe.

"Corrupted?" Jasmine supplied. "Do you have any other samples? I'd prefer that the first time I look at this thing it not be damaged."

"It's not damaged." Quinn finally broke his silence. "It's just not what you're expecting."

She started to ask him to be more specific, but the look on his face told her that he wasn't going to say more. Perhaps his panties were still twisted because she'd run out on him earlier that morning, or perhaps he didn't want to unduly prejudice her regarding the specimen she was about to look at.

She chose to believe it was the latter, though she ached—just a little—at the thought of what he'd felt when he'd woken up alone. After the intensity of what they'd shared, she knew she would have had a hard time waking up alone.

But that wasn't important now, she told herself. The work was what mattered—only the work. Sinking into the chair in front of the computerized microscope, Jasmine looked through the lens. What she saw there was so startling, so strange, that it took her a minute to figure out what it was she was looking at. Even then, she stared at it for a long time, trying to decide if she was really seeing what she thought she was.

But it couldn't be. It didn't make sense. Not corrupted, Quinn and Phoebe both insisted. Just different. Unexpected.

That was the understatement of the decade.

Pulling back, she punched a few buttons on the computer and brought the image up on the large monitor to her right. Then she magnified it so that the cell anomalies were big enough that they couldn't be ignored.

Neither Quinn nor Phoebe said anything, and for long minutes she was so caught up in looking at the blood cells—and the virus ravaging them—that she didn't either. Behind her, she could feel Quinn and Phoebe studying the specimen as well, but she had a feeling they were looking for very different things than she was.

When she finally had a grip on what it was she thought she was seeing, she turned to the other two doctors and asked, "Does someone want to tell me what the hell is going on here? If this sample isn't corrupted, then you've dragged me down here for nothing. Because whatever this blood belongs to isn't human, and I'm not a veterinarian."

"It is human," Phoebe insisted. "That's why I didn't want to say too much at first. I wanted you to—"

She stopped abruptly as an alarm went off overhead.

Jasmine glanced up, distracted, at the bulbs lining either side of the lab. They were blinking red, in time to the god-awful sound that was grinding, on and off, through the building.

Before she could do more than wonder what was happening, she was yanked out of the stool and propelled against the wall so fast her feet barely touched the ground. Phoebe was next to her, and Quinn stood in front of them both, blocking the way with his huge shoulders and six-foot-six frame.

"Quinn?" Phoebe whispered. "What is it? Who—"

"I don't know," he said, reaching for the telephone on a nearby lab station. "Give me a minute to find out."

Jasmine didn't want to wait that long. She wasn't sure what was going on, but there was no way in hell she was going to spend the next few minutes cowering behind Quinn like some nineteenth-century heroine—and she couldn't believe Phoebe would either.

Annoyed at the entire situation, she shoved at Quinn's back, but it was like trying to move a two-ton rock with a child's shovel. It wasn't going to happen.

"Logan set off the alarm?" Quinn barked into the phone. "Why?"

The answer must have been worse than he'd expected because the look on his face changed from wary and grim to downright dangerous. The fact that she got all that from only his profile was more frightening than the alarm itself.

Jasmine shivered as she wondered what those dark green eyes of his looked like right now—and what could possibly have put that look on his face. She could almost feel sorry for this Logan person, whoever he was, if Phoebe wasn't stand next to her, trembling.

"Well get the damn thing cut off. I can barely hear myself think." He hung up the phone with a bang. Jasmine started to ask him what was happening, but he moved away from her and Phoebe so quickly that all she could do was stare at his retreating back.

He rushed across the lab, threw open a cabinet at the back and ripped out a black doctor's bag, very similar to the one currently stowed in her trunk.

"Quinn?" Phoebe's voice rang out above the alarm, sounding more frightened than Jasmine had ever heard it. "What's wrong?"

He never got the chance to answer, but then, he didn't need to. At that precise moment, two huge men came crashing through the door at the back of the lab. They were covered in blood and cuts, looking like something straight out of a horror movie. They carried a third man, who made tortured sounds as they jostled him into the room. A woman trailed behind them, her face pale as she held the injured man's hand.

As they brought him closer, Jasmine blanched at the damage that had been done to him. His stomach had been ripped open, and her first impression was that if he was still alive, it was only because his brain hadn't yet figured out that he was dead.

Shock held her immobile for precious seconds, and then her medical training kicked in. Jasmine rushed across the room for the injured man, right behind Phoebe.

"Put him down here," Quinn barked from the left side of the lab. He was standing next to a bed covered in white sheets. Jasmine blinked—how had he moved so quickly? Mere seconds before he'd been all the way across the lab, at the cabinets on the opposite end.

Phoebe gasped. "Dylan?" For one horrible second Jasmine thought the man who was so close to death was her friend's fiancé.

"He's fine," ground out the tall blond one who had helped carry the injured man in. "He wasn't with us."

That seemed to be all Phoebe needed to hear, as finally she sprang into action. "We're going to need blood." She eyed the man stretched out on the bed. "Lots of blood. There are a number of packs in the fridge, two labs over. Get one of the assistants to show you."

The second man, who was as tall and dark as Quinn, nodded and left without another word. He, too, moved so fast that Jasmine wasn't sure his feet even touched the ground.

Not that she had time to worry about that now, with an eviscerated man dying in front of her. Shoving past the blond man, she told Quinn, "We've got to stop the bleeding. Do you have a clamp in your bag until we can get him to the hospital for surgery?"

"Stay out of my way." It was a growl so menacing that it had her rearing back on her heels. But she'd never backed down in her life, and she sure as hell wasn't going to do so now.

"Don't be stupid," she snapped. "You need all the help you can get." Turning to the other man, she said, "Can you pull this bed out? I need to be on the other side of him."

He looked at Quinn for permission and her temper sparked. "Do you want your friend to live or not? Because I don't care how good a doctor you think he is, he can't do this alone."

Quinn didn't answer—he was too focused on trying to find the bleeder to pay attention to their exchange. But the guy must have taken her seriously because he leaned down and lifted the bottom half of the bed up and out.

"What the hell are you doing, Logan?" Quinn barked without looking up.

"You look like you could use all the help you could get. And Tyler doesn't have much time."

That is an understatement. Phoebe crowded in next to her, and the three of them tried to stop the blood gushing from the open wound. They'd worked together in grim silence for a little over a minute when Jasmine's fingers finally closed around the ripped vein. "I've got it," she gritted out from between clenched teeth. "Get the clamp."

Phoebe was already handing it to her. "Are there more?"

"I won't know until I've got this one cut off." She clamped the vein, trying to ignore the way her patient's body arced up off the table in silent misery as she did so.

"Do you have something here to put him out?" Jasmine demanded of Quinn.

"I need him lucid."

"That's ridiculous. He's going to go into shock, if he hasn't already—"

"Don't argue with me."

Jasmine opened her mouth to blast him, but Phoebe moved her gently aside. "Let him do his thing, Jazz. He knows what he's doing."

This was probably the most insane thing Jasmine had ever heard. Quinn might be a doctor, but he'd obviously spent far too much time in the lab. He was ignoring the most basic procedures for acute trauma.

"There's another one," Quinn said, interrupting her thoughts and pulling her back to the present crisis. "The bleeding has slowed down, but something's still leaking in there."

"Let me back in," Jasmine demanded. "My hands are smaller than yours. I'll find it."

"It's too late for that," Quinn said. He leaned over the table. "Tyler, man, look at me."

The patient's pain-filled gray eyes opened slowly and focused on Quinn.

"I need you to focus on what I'm telling you. Can you do that?"

"Yeah," he said, gasping.

"You're in bad shape, man. If you're going to make it, I'm going to need to do it the old-fashioned way. But for me to do that, I need your help. You need to lower your guards, let me in." He paused for a second, studied Tyler's face. "Do you understand what I'm telling you?"

The other man nodded, but his eyes were closing and Jasmine couldn't be sure if the other man understood Quinn's request. Not that she could blame him—she hadn't understood one word Quinn had said. But Phoebe looked totally calm, as if she knew what he was talking about and was all right with the whole thing, so Jasmine reined in the protests welling in the back of her throat.

She prayed that she wasn't condemning this Tyler person to certain death as she did so.

Quinn lowered his head and closed his eyes, his hands hovering just above the wound. Frustration snaked through Jasmine. How the hell did he think he could help a patient by just standing there? Ignoring Phoebe's protests, Jasmine shoved her aside. Maybe Phoebe had lost her mind out here in the middle of this damned desert, but Jasmine hadn't.

She didn't care what anyone said, didn't care that for a moment Quinn had seemed to know exactly what he was doing. Every ounce of medical training she had told her that Tyler was going to slip away if they didn't do something—now. The clamp she'd put on was a stopgap measure, but much more needed to happen if he was to survive.

"Let me go back in," she demanded, shoving her blood-coated hands back into the wound. "I'll find the second—"

An invisible force reached out and shoved her against the wall, held her pinned there. It hadn't pushed hard, hadn't hurt her, but it was inexorable and unrelenting. Shocked, horrified, she struggled to free herself. But there was nothing, no one to fight. The thought scared the hell out of her.

"Phoebe!"

"It's okay." Her friend reached out and grabbed her gloved hand, tugged a little. "Stop it, Quinn."

"Then keep her the hell away from me." The force holding her in place fell away, but Quinn never opened his eyes.

Then again, he didn't have to. All of the fight drained out of Jasmine as she looked around in shock. Had she entered some alternate universe when she'd driven into town, one where people could actually bend the laws of physics?

The whole thing was absurd, and yet she wasn't crazy. Something, *someone*, had held her against that wall, and judging by Phoebe's reaction, that someone was Quinn. As her panic receded and she could think again, she realized the touch had seemed familiar—and more than a little intimate.

If that was the case, it had to have been Quinn. God knew, there wasn't much he hadn't done to her in that motel room the night before.

Then, as her attention returned to her patient, she saw that Quinn was obviously doing something, despite the fact that he wasn't touching Tyler. The bleeding had completely stopped, and beneath her fascinated gaze, the veins and organs under his hand seemed to be mending themselves. They were actually putting themselves back together on their own.

It was impossible. She had a pretty open mind, had traveled enough of the world to know that there was more to healing than what she'd learned in medical school. But this—what she was seeing—was impossible. It couldn't be happening. It absolutely, positively *could not be happening.*

Yet it was.

She couldn't tear her eyes away from the patient, couldn't so much as blink for fear she would miss some part of the strange, miraculous healing going on in front of her. *He* was fixing Tyler, mending his wounds without benefit of a scalpel or any other instruments. Without so much as a painkiller for the patient. And Tyler didn't say a word, didn't even squirm as Quinn repaired the damage and moved his organs back to where they belonged.

She thought again of that force, that invisible hand, that had pinned her against the wall. Was this the same principle at work? Was Quinn somehow holding Tyler immobile while he . . . ?

Jasmine didn't complete the thought. She couldn't. She had no idea how to describe whatever it was Quinn was doing. *Worked on* hardly seemed adequate and neither did *operated on*. Maybe *healed*, but the word had such strange connotations—especially in this context—that she shied away from using it.

Then it was over, the bleeding stopped. The internal damage repaired. She glanced at Quinn, saw that he was nearly gray with exhaustion. He swayed where he stood. Prompted by some unexpected instinct, Jasmine stripped off her gloves as she moved closer to him and placed a bracing hand in the center of his back.

"You did well, Quinn," she said. "Tyler's a lot better. Let someone else take over. I can close, or Phoebe can."

He shook his head. "I'll finish."

She wanted to argue, but when he opened his eyes, the look in them was implacable. Tyler was his patient, and he wasn't going to step aside now, not when things were almost done. She would have felt exactly the same way.

So she moved back to give him room to work and started digging in his bag for the supplies he would need to sew up Tyler's wounds. She found them, raised her head, and then wondered why she'd even bothered. Under Quinn's steady hands, Tyler's wounds were slowly, carefully mending themselves—the ripped edges of skin fusing themselves back together without the benefit of stitches, until only raw, red lines existed where there had once been gaping injury.

It knocked her for a loop, even considering everything else she'd seen. Jasmine had absolutely no idea how to react.

Just then, the man who had gone in search of blood came back, his hands full of blood pouches, all of which were marked O negative— the universal blood type that could be accepted by anyone in an emergency. Behind him came a lab assistant with an IV machine, which she plugged into the nearest power source.

Figuring that she could at least do this, since Quinn had rendered all of her other efforts obsolete, Jasmine replaced the materials needed to perform stitches and pulled out an IV kit instead. Quickly and efficiently, she got it set up, and within a couple of minutes, blood was pumping from one of the pouches into Tyler's right arm. It wasn't as quick or as pretty as it would be at a hospital, but she'd spent her career working in makeshift clinics in developing nations. She'd learned long ago that things didn't have to be quick or pretty, as long as they got the job done.

She stepped back, but kept a close eye on Tyler. Already, he was looking better. Whatever Quinn had done to him had obviously worked, and with the steady influx of blood pumping through his veins, it was almost as if he'd come in with a minor injury, instead of one so life-threatening she had first placed his chances of survival at next to nothing.

Quinn wasn't so lucky. He looked like hell, and she figured it was only a matter of time before he fell down. Though she had a million questions—at least—Jasmine forced herself to wait for the answers for just a little while longer.

Grabbing one of the lab stools, she scooted it up to Quinn and then pressed on his chest. "Sit down before you fall down," she told him, in her most physician-like tone. She grabbed his wrist and surreptitiously took his pulse for the second time in less than twenty-four hours. Like before, in the hotel room, it was weak and thready and way too fast. For a moment she couldn't help wondering if Quinn had saved Tyler at the cost of himself.

"Phoebe, he needs something with sugar. Do you have a soda or something?"

"Sure." Phoebe was out of the room in a flash, and Jasmine gritted her teeth, doing her best not to notice that her friend also moved with preternatural speed.

"How are you feeling?" she asked Quinn, whose entire body was trembling.

"I'm fine." His voice was little more than a whisper, and Jasmine had to strain to hear him, a sure-fire sign that he was not doing as well as he pretended. "I need to check on Ty—"

"Ty's fine." She gestured to where Tyler was resting, his head in the lap of the woman who had trailed him into the lab. She was softly stroking his hair and murmuring to him.

She glanced around the lab, cursing as she did so. The place had everything, but that didn't help her much—not when she didn't know where anything was.

Her frustration must have showed because Logan came over to her. "What do you need?"

"Do you know if there's a blanket around here anywhere? He's freezing."

He looked at her in surprise, then crouched so that he could get a better look at Quinn's face. "Hey, man. You doing all right?"

"Just peachy." It came out as a growl, and Logan laughed and patted him on the back. "He's okay. Just a little tired."

Jasmine had to admit that Quinn did look somewhat better, but she had a strong feeling it had more to do with him not wanting to look weak in front of his friend than him actually feeling even close to okay.

God save her from cavemen who pounded their chests. Nothing annoyed her more.

Phoebe chose that moment to pop back in with a cold can of

soda. Jasmine took it from her, then sent her off again in search of a blanket. As they waited, she opened the can and handed it to Quinn. "Drink the whole thing. Fast."

"I don't want—"

It was her turn to bend down until she was eye to eye with him. "Too bad you don't get a vote. I don't know what you just did there. I'm not even sure I want to know. But it took a hell of a lot out of you. You look like shit, your pulse is weak, your system is shocked, and at the moment I'm a hell of a lot more concerned about your health than I am about his." She gestured behind her to the bed, where Tyler was resting peacefully.

Quinn looked like he wanted to argue but seemed to change his mind. With a shrug, he took a long gulp of the soda. Jasmine kept her hand on his shoulder as she watched him carefully, pleased to see a little color return to his cheeks.

Phoebe came back with the blanket, and within a couple of minutes, Quinn's shaking subsided to the occasional violent chill. His hands became a lot steadier, and even his pulse calmed down a little. It wasn't normal, but at least Jasmine wasn't worried about him dropping dead anymore. At the same time, though, he still didn't look ready to run a marathon or anything. He was a little pale, and his eyes looked absolutely exhausted.

She didn't like it—and not just from a medical standpoint. He'd pushed himself far, too far, to help Tyler. While she couldn't fault him for that, it bugged the hell out of her that she was the only one who seemed concerned about him. Everyone else seemed to take his condition in stride. Even Logan had bothered to check on him only at her urging.

It didn't seem to upset Quinn at all, though, and that bugged her even more. He didn't deserve such blatant unconcern. A part of her wanted nothing more than to get him into a bed where he could rest, and where she could curl up next to him and watch over him. It was a strange feeling, one she wasn't entirely comfortable with. But obviously he needed someone to take care of him, as he did a crappy job of watching out for himself.

She started to pull away—she wanted to get a stethoscope and listen to his heart—but his hand reached up and grabbed hers, holding it against his shoulder. "Don't go."

"I was just going to—"

"Please." His fingers tightened and something moved deep inside of her. Again, she saw him as he'd been when she'd awoken the night before, curled up on the floor, utterly vulnerable and worn out, yet determined not to bother her. It seemed this man was willing to take responsibility for everyone and everything but himself.

Which meant she was just going to have to do it for him—at least until he was back up to fighting form.

"Hey, Phoebe, is this kind of thing normal?"

Phoebe snorted. "Define normal. Nothing around here is exactly status quo."

Like she hadn't figured that out for herself? "I mean, is Quinn always like this after he does his—" She broke off, still not sure what name to put to whatever it was he had done.

"I don't know. Quinn's a really private person. I've never noticed him having a problem before."

"Is that true?" Jasmine asked, turning to Quinn. "Is this kind of reaction unusual for you?" She bent down so no one could hear what she said next. "And don't even think about lying to me. You won't like what happens if you do."

His lush lips pulled into a grim line and his eyes narrowed, but not before she saw something move in them—something that wasn't quite human. And suddenly all of the little clues fell into place.

"Oh, shit. You're—"

She didn't get a chance to finish as the side door banged open a second time. And this time, when a man so large he made Quinn, Gabe and Logan look regular-sized entered the room, Jasmine didn't even flinch.

CHAPTER THIRTEEN

"Would someone like to tell me what the hell is going on here?" The question echoed through the lab, and Quinn looked up just in time to see Dylan stride into his lab like an avenging angel on the warpath—which was pretty much what he was, if you substituted dragon wings for angel's wings. It was also exactly what Quinn didn't need right then—even if his old friend was in human form.

It was hard enough to deal with Dylan when he was like this under normal circumstances. Add in the fact that Quinn currently felt like someone had drop-kicked him from one end of New Mexico to the other—several times—and it was a guaranteed recipe for disaster.

Healing always took a lot out of him, and this time was no exception. But he couldn't complain. He'd expected the side effects to be much worse considering the episode he'd gone through the night before. And it had started out bad. He'd been concerned at first that he wouldn't be able to make it somewhere private before the effects took hold of him.

Then the strangest thing happened. The worst part of the effects had receded. His breathing had steadied, and eventually so had his pulse—and he didn't think it was because of the soda Jasmine had insisted he drink. The more he thought about it, the more he decided that his mild reaction had something to do with her.

It had happened the night before. The moment Jasmine touched him, he had started to feel better. The pain had stopped immediately and the shakes had been reduced by at least half. He'd been able to think, when normally he was completely at the mercy of his instincts when the trouble started.

She buffered him. Somehow, in some way, she stood between him and the worst effects of the healing. It didn't make sense, and if anyone else had tried to convince him such a thing was possible he would have told them they were full of shit. But there was no other explanation. No other reason that could explain what happened to him.

Maybe, if last night had never occurred, he'd be willing to write this off to something else. But it had happened, and his energy had been so low today that healing Tyler should have knocked him completely on his ass.

Tyler had been pretty far gone—so far gone that normally he wouldn't have attempted to heal him in the old ways.

To do so risked both of their lives, and he was going to suffer the consequences whether he succeeded or failed.

But he had no choice. And even if he did, he would make the same decision again. Their clan was weakening, this damn disease running rampant through its strongest members. Losing Ty would have made them even weaker, would have made Dylan and the sentries who guarded him and made up his Council more vulnerable, as Ty was one of the clan's best warriors.

That was why he'd done it, why he'd risked his life to bring Ty back when everything inside of him had warned against it. He'd owed it to Dylan, owed it to the other Dragonstars, to try.

Even as he assured himself that was the case, a small part of him knew the truth. A small part of him understood that he'd been more than willing to trade his life for Ty's. He couldn't lose one more person, couldn't fail one more time and survive. He was as sure of that as he was that Jasmine was his mate.

"Dylan." Phoebe rushed forward to greet her fiancé, and Dylan's eyes ran over her quickly, checking to make sure she was unharmed.

When he was satisfied that she was really all right, he pulled her gently against him and leveled the full strength of his glare on Logan, Gabe and Quinn.

"Well?"

"The Wyvernmoons attacked again." Gabe's voice was low and hard, his eyes glacier cold. "Eight of the bastards ambushed Ty when he was on patrol on the southern edge of our territory. He held on long enough for Logan and me to get there, but he was injured."

"And the Wyvernmoons?" Dylan's voice was silky soft and so threatening that it made nearly everyone in the room cringe. Even Quinn felt a little uneasy, and he'd been the recipient of that tone more times than he could count through the years.

"Four of them are dead. The other four, including the leader, who was using some kind of glamour by the way, took off after they realized things weren't going their way."

"Yeah, well, I don't like the odds. Eight on one pretty much sucks. It's just a matter of time before one of these battles goes their way, and I don't want to lose any more of my people." Dylan moved to Ty's side. The other dragon had slipped into a light doze as his body continued to mend itself. "How badly was he injured?"

Quinn didn't know whether the king was addressing him or Phoebe, but when she didn't immediately answer, he said, "It wasn't terrible. There was a lot of blood, but the wounds weren't as bad as they looked."

Phoebe gaped at him incredulously, then rolled her eyes. "He's totally underestimating himself again, Dylan. Ty's wounds were about as serious as they get. If anyone other than Quinn had been here, I'm almost positive we would have lost him."

At her words, Dylan turned to Quinn, eyes narrowed. He was one of the few in the clan who understood what it meant for Quinn to have brought Tyler back when he was that far gone. "Well, you're still breathing," he said, and coming from him it didn't necessarily sound like a compliment.

"Barely," Jasmine piped up for the first time. She was leaning against a lab table. "I had a few moments when I wasn't so sure he was going to make it, either. He was in bad shape for a while there. Hell, he's still in bad shape, to be honest."

Quinn ground his teeth and wondered what possible incentive he could offer Jazz to get her to shut her mouth. But one look at the other dragons' faces and he knew that train had already left the station. His mate hadn't even been around for twenty-four hours, and already she was revealing secrets he'd spent four hundred years keeping hidden.

Dylan must have reached the same conclusion because the look he shot Jazz straddled the line between respect at the way she so easily spoke up in a room full of dangerous predators and a warning not to go too far. But then, Quinn wasn't surprised that his best friend saw more in the situation than the words being exchanged. He was the shrewdest person Quinn had ever met, and he had a way of seeing every nuance in a situation, then applying just the right amount of pressure to get the best result.

"Who are *you*?" Dylan demanded.

Phoebe ripped her eyes from Quinn—thank God—and said, "This is Dr. Jasmine Kane, the hematologist I was telling you about."

"Oh. Right." His eyes narrowed. "It looks like you got one hell of a welcome to the Dragonstar clan."

Jasmine lifted one inquisitive eyebrow. "The Dragonstar . . . clan?"

"Yeah, well, we hadn't exactly gotten that far yet, Dylan," Quinn said as he pushed himself to his feet and concentrated on walking without wobbling. Without Jasmine's touch, he was suddenly a lot shakier, but he'd be damned if he let anyone see it. Jasmine's big mouth and observant eyes had caused enough problems for him without him passing out like a total candy ass in front of half the clan's High Council.

Dylan turned to his fiancée in surprise. "Exactly how far *had* you gotten?"

Phoebe grinned affectionately. "About as far as 'Here, take a look at this blood sample and tell me what you see.' You remember the drill."

"I do. And what did she see?"

"I don't think she had a clue what she was seeing."

"I never said that." Jasmine's voice was cool when she spoke. "What I said was that what I was looking at was either contaminated or not human. It looked much more reptilian in nature, if I remember my days from college biology correctly. But I guess you already knew that, didn't you, Phoebe—if you're running around with *dragons*."

The five of them gaped at her in surprise, and Quinn couldn't help wondering what game she was playing at. No one knew about dragon shifters—*no one*. It was a matter of their very survival, and they were incredibly careful about who they revealed themselves to. Though they hated to do it, once in a blue moon they actually had to alter some poor person's memories who found out about them. Not every dragon could do that, mind you. Only the very old ones, as well as Logan, who was relatively young but whose command over human and dragon minds alike often bordered on the miraculous, and frightening.

It was what Quinn had originally planned to do to Jazz when Phoebe convinced Dylan to bring in another human doctor.

"What?" Jazz demanded testily, as they continued to stare at her. "In the past hour I've looked at strange DNA that you insisted came from a human, have seen someone live through an injury that should have killed him in under two minutes, watched Quinn heal the injury using nothing but his mind and what I assume were currents of energy, and seen all of you move around here at about four times the speed of the average human. I'm not stupid, you know, and I've lived in enough cultures to understand that there is more to this world than meets the eye. After finding out you call yourselves the 'Dragonstars,' it wasn't a huge leap to go from supernatural creature of some sort to dragon. From the looks on your faces, I must've hit the nail on the head."

"So, that's it?" Logan asked her curiously. "Seriously? You're completely okay with being in a room filled with six dragons, all of whom are capable of inflicting wounds like the one you just saw with one blow?"

Jasmine grinned. "Define 'okay.' And I only see five dragons, unless Phoebe's been holding out on me for the past ten years." She glanced at her friend quizzically.

Phoebe nodded. "Everything changed for me when I met Dylan. My dragon had been latent—so latent that I hadn't known it existed until I came in contact with other dragons. It's been . . . an adjustment."

"I bet." Jasmine looked around at the mess that was Quinn's formerly pristine lab. "Now, it looks like Ty is out of danger, right?"

"He'll be fine in two to three days," Quinn acknowledged.

"All right then. I'd really like to get to work, if you don't mind. And the first thing I'm going to need is a few samples of healthy dragon blood, so that I can compare the differences." She raised her eyebrows. "Do I have any volunteers?"

After every single one of them had given blood—including Phoebe and Quinn—Dylan called an emergency meeting back at the War Room, the section of his home cave he reserved for dealing with issues concerning the clan.

This meant, much to Quinn's chagrin, that he had to go. As one of Dylan's top two ranked sentries, absence wasn't an option—no matter how much he wanted to stick around and see what Jasmine did with the blood samples. If she had a new idea about this thing, he wanted to be in the thick of it.

Then again, if they didn't find out how the Wyvernmoons were breaching the protections they had put up to keep them out, curing the virus would be meaningless. They'd have the other clan's dragons so far up their asses there wouldn't be enough Dragonstars left to stop the damn disease.

Dylan's people were better fighters, but that didn't mean much when the Wyverns had such incredible numbers—and they hadn't spent most of the last decade being ravaged by disease. Three on eight, the Dragonstars had a chance. Three on eighty . . . not so much.

With a grimace, Quinn turned off the main highway that cut through the desert and drove straight through the sand out to the caves he and his clan had inhabited for nearly a thousand years. About halfway there he ran into the invisible safeguards that had kept their homes from being discovered for centuries, and the ride got a whole lot bumpier.

Ty groaned where he was stretched out on the backseat, and Quinn cursed the fact that they'd had to drive out rather than fly. The constant bumping over the deliberately unsettled land wasn't good for Ty's injuries. Of course, neither was shifting, which was why Quinn was driving him to the caves instead of flying with the other dragons.

"Hold on, man. It's just a few minutes more."

"I'm fine," Ty answered. "Don't worry about me."

But he did worry about him. That was his job as one of the clan elders, and also as Michael's brother. Ty and Michael had been best friends since childhood, and Quinn had grown so used to seeing the two of them together through the years that seeing Ty alone now was like a red-hot knife to the gut. He could only imagine how the other man was feeling.

They slammed along in silence for the next couple of minutes, hitting what felt like every uneven spot in the damn desert. After a particularly bad dip, Quinn opened his mouth to apologize, but Ty beat him to it.

"I'm sorry I wasn't there when Michael died."

Every muscle in Quinn's body tensed to the point of pain, but then he forced himself to relax. Ty wasn't going to be the only person who wanted to talk to him about Michael in the next few weeks and months. Better to get used to it now than freak out every time it happened. But it still hurt. God, did it hurt.

"Quinn? Did you hear me?"

"I heard you." His voice came out a lot more clipped than he'd intended, and he could feel Ty wince in the backseat. Struggling for something to say, he finally came up with, "You couldn't have done anything. It was better for you to stay away instead of risking infection."

"Is that what you think?" Ty's voice was indignant.

Quinn glanced in the rearview mirror, watching as his patient struggled into a sitting position. "You should lie back down. You're not completely healed yet."

"You think I stayed away from Michael because I was scared of getting sick?"

"I think you stayed away because you couldn't stand to watch him die. I understand that, even respect it. Believe me, if I could have been anywhere else but that hospital room, I would have been." He kept his tone matter-of-fact, not wanting to antagonize Ty any further. The last thing he needed was for the guy to tear open his wounds.

"Oh." There was a long silence. "Do you mean that? That you don't blame me for not being there?"

"Why would I blame you?"

Ty shook his head, but didn't say anything else for a long while. When he finally did speak, his words were so low that they were almost inaudible—even with the dragon's superior hearing. "Because I blame myself."

"Oh, Ty, don't."

"He was my best friend for over three hundred years. We were family. Don't you think he wondered where I was? Don't you think it hurt him to realize I wasn't there?"

"Most of the time he was so out of it he didn't know who he was, let alone who I was. In the end, I don't think he even had the faculties to miss you."

There was another long silence. Then Ty said, "That's it? That's the best you've got? Don't worry about it, he was too insane to miss you, anyway? You think that's supposed to cheer me up?"

Quinn smiled a little at Ty's incredulous tone. "Why not? You said you felt bad for not being there for him. I told you he didn't even notice that you punked out."

"You know, your bedside manner sucks ass. Did anyone ever tell you that?"

"It's been mentioned a time or two."

Ty snorted. "I can only imagine."

Convinced that he'd made his point regarding Ty's guilt, Quinn didn't say anything else as the cave's entrance finally loomed in front of them.

Pulling his SUV to a stop several yards away from a small, dark hole rising out of the ground, Quinn turned off the ignition and hopped out. Before he could make it around to the passenger side back door, Logan was there to help—along with Ian and Riley, two more of Dylan's sentries.

"I'm not an invalid," Ty grumbled as he pushed himself up and out of the car. "I can get down there myself."

"Yeah, well, consider us a little extra insurance," Logan said with a grin. "You don't want to fall on your ass and mess up all of Quinn's hard work, do you?"

Ty flipped him off. "I've never fallen on my ass in my life."

"Are you kidding me? I saw you do just that a few hours ago. You fell hard enough to put a dent in your head and your ass."

"I don't think you can really blame me for that. It was kind of hard to stay upright when my internal organs were spilling out of my abdomen."

"Exactly," said Riley, as he slid one of Ty's arms around his shoulders. "And since it's only been about two hours since you nearly expired in front of poor Logan, don't you think you should cut the poor guy a break? I'm pretty sure he doesn't want to see that again."

"True that," Logan muttered, taking up a spot on Ty's other side. Riley was one of the strongest dragons in the clan, and Quinn knew he didn't need any help, but he didn't stop Logan. The look on the other man's face said clearer than words that he needed to be doing something to help, even if it was only getting Ty down into the cave. "I don't know how the hell you do what you do, Quinn. I'd lose my fucking mind—not to mention my lunch—if I had to do that every day."

"Yeah, well, what can I say? When you've got it, flaunt it."

"Hey, shouldn't that be Ty's line?" Riley joked. "He was the one playing show and tell with his intestines a little while ago."

"Shut the fuck up," Ty said, but Quinn noted that his color was a little better and that he'd stopped protesting about the help. Logan and Riley's Frick and Frack routine was obviously doing the trick, just as they'd intended.

The five of them made their way slowly into the cave that was Dylan and Phoebe's real home—despite the house they kept in town—with Quinn walking a couple of steps behind the other three in case Ty slipped.

As they wound their way through the long, dark labyrinth-like hallways, Quinn used an old incantation to light the way. Not that they needed the light—they'd all spent hundreds of years negotiating the twists and turns down here. But with Ty so badly injured, Quinn wanted to make sure none of the men got tripped up on the various stalagmites and gypsum chandeliers that lined the hallways and most of the rooms in the cave.

Thankfully, they made it to the War Room with no incidents, and the second he entered the huge cavern, Quinn felt himself relax slightly. It was the largest room in Dylan's cave, and the walls were embedded with precious jewels of sapphire and emerald, whose chemical properties lent a calming influence to everything that went on there. Throughout the room, Dylan had arranged a huge bar and lots of comfortable chairs and sofas, but true to form, most of the sentries who were already there were perched on the various rock and gypsum formations that dotted the cavern. Even in their human forms, they preferred the natural to the man-made.

Dylan himself was sitting in a huge chair at the front of the room, talking intently to Gabe, who was perched on a huge, flat stalagmite. Shawn and Caitlyn, two of the newest sentries but also two of the most powerful, were leaning against a wall and squabbling, as usual, while Travis, Paige, Jase and Shawn were deep in conversation as they lounged against a huge rock formation in the center of the room.

As they were the most tech savvy of the dragons—and the ones responsible for much of the clan's security—he imagined they were probably trying to figure out how the Wyvernmoons had managed to breach the many technical and magical security safeguards they'd put into place in order to attack Ty.

Only Callie was by herself as she squatted next to the stream that ran along the back wall, rinsing her hands and face.

Quinn helped Logan and Riley get Ty settled on a cot Dylan must have had brought in for just that purpose, then followed Ian to the bar in the center of the room. Figuring he'd had more than enough tequila the night before—and tormented by the memory of how it had tasted warm from Jazz's skin—he passed on the half-empty bottle of Patrón and went for a cold bottle of water instead.

He'd barely gotten himself settled at the front, near Dylan and Gabe, when the king's voice rang out, filling every corner of the cavern. "There's a traitor in Dragonstar."

CHAPTER FOURTEEN

Dead silence followed Dylan's announcement, which was then replaced by complete pandemonium as ten of the dragons in the room started talking at the same time.

Quinn turned in his seat so that no one could see the "what the fuck" look he shot the king. Dylan's answering smile was grim, his silver eyes ice cold. It was a look echoed on Gabe's face, and the other sentry shook his head when Quinn started to ask who the traitor was.

After a couple minutes of listening to his sentries' confusion, Dylan held up a hand. "I know that it's hard for any of you to imagine someone betraying Dragonstar. It's hard for me to imagine such a thing too. But Gabe and I have been aware of the possibility for a while. This latest incident just confirms what we already suspected."

He stood up, and walked to the center of the room. "Someone is betraying us. At the very least, this person is giving the Wyvernmoons information about us, information that is being used to infiltrate our safeguards and hurt our people. At the worst, he or she is actively conspiring to hurt us and is, in fact, acting as an agent for the Wyvernmoons. Either way, this person must be stopped."

"Do you know who it is?" demanded Jase, who looked ready and willing to be judge, jury and executioner. As the youngest sentry, he was still something of a hothead—but he was also hell on wings in a fight. More than once, he'd saved Quinn's ass when a battle went to shit.

"If we did, he'd already be dead," Gabe answered, and Quinn couldn't help admiring Dylan's shrewdness in letting Gabe be the one to make that announcement.

Kings were meant to lead and to protect. When they found the traitor, Dylan would be the one who dealt with him, but until that time was upon them, he needed to avoid speaking about the killing of one of his people so casually. Much better to let Gabe be the one to keep the idea front and foremost in the sentries' minds.

"It's someone relatively high up," Dylan said. "Someone who knows which safeguards we've used to protect ourselves—and someone who knows exactly how to break them."

"But that's impossible," protested Caitlyn. "The only people who know that information are sitting in this room. Surely you're not accusing one of us—"

"Don't be stupid," Shawn growled. "Dylan knows better than to think we would betray the clan."

"Does he?" Callie asked, jumping to her roommate's defense as she straightened from her spot near the stream. "Because from where I'm sitting, he doesn't look nearly so sure."

"Well, then, you're stupid," chimed in Ian, his gold eyes glowing brightly in the dim room. "Dylan knows other people know the safeguards. He doesn't think we would turn on him or the clan. Especially not now."

"Don't be so sure," stated Riley, his huge hands clenched into fists. "I think it makes sense for him to be suspicious. Someone is selling us out to the enemy, someone who has freedom of movement. Someone whose actions won't be called into question, even if they show up at the wrong place at the wrong time. Who else but one of us has that privilege?"

The tension in the room soared as the sentries all turned to Dylan. Quinn didn't like the looks on their faces—everything from anger to betrayal to outright disbelief that their king would think they were capable of such a thing. He wasn't crazy about the accusation himself, but he knew Dylan well enough to know that if his friend was thinking along those lines it was because he had a very good reason.

Instinctively wanting to soothe everyone before things reached the breaking point, Quinn sent out a healing wave meant to calm tempers and bring clarity. He kept it subtle—very subtle—not wanting anyone to pick up on what he was doing, but from the look Logan shot him, it was obvious his touch wasn't as light as he'd hoped.

But no one said anything, and he watched as, one by one, fists unclenched, claws retracted and tense shoulders relaxed. They were still angry, still demanding an explanation, but none of the dragons looked like they wanted blood anymore. At least not yet.

"Clan doesn't betray clan," Dylan's voice rang out. "Isn't that the code we live by? Your clan is your family. They're who you lean on, who you fight with—who you fight for. They're who has your back when no one else does."

He stood up, strode to the middle of the room, using the power of his huge frame and mighty charisma to command every eye in the place. "That's the code I stand for, the code I know you stand for as well. We've lived that way for thousands of years, and for thousands of years, it's worked.

"But just because we believe it, just because we would die to keep our clan and our people safe, doesn't mean that everyone feels the same way.

"Do you think I stand here and accuse one of my own people of being a traitor lightly? Do you think I want to even imagine that someone is working with our sworn enemies to defeat us?

"This clan is everything to me. *My people are everything to me.* I have lost my parents to the enemy. I have lost my brother, who was meant to be king before me. In the last three months I have also lost my sister, my niece and three of my sentries to this enemy.

"In the last three months," his voice boomed across the cave, bouncing off walls and filling every nook and cranny, "I have lost one hundred and twenty-seven of my people to this enemy. I know the

124 • TESSA ADAMS

names of every single one of them. I have been to each of their funerals, visited with every single one of their families. Can any of you, besides Quinn, say the same?

"Do you think, for one second, that I want to imagine that one of my own has been a party to this? That someone I have trusted, someone in whose hands I have rested my entire clan's fate, has betrayed me? Betrayed us? If you believe that, then you are not the men and women that I have worked and fought beside for centuries, and I am not the king you have chosen to serve.

"I do not appreciate the accusations, any more than I appreciate the lack of faith some of you are showing in me. So I will make this offer and I will make it only once—you know the way out. If you want, feel free to use it now."

No one spoke, no one moved, and for a few seconds, Quinn didn't think they even breathed. When no one started for the door, Dylan's eyes narrowed dangerously. "Know this, if you stay. If you listen to the evidence Gabe and I have accrued and still believe that we are wrong, you will not be allowed to leave later. Not until the traitor is caught. Not until our enemy is vanquished.

"It is my duty—and my right—to protect my people to the best of my ability. I would die for them, would die for you. I am lenient on many things, but I will not tolerate betrayal, not when it risks the very fabric of this clan. So make your decision now—get the hell out or stay and help me find the person, or people, who have sold their souls to our enemy."

When he finished speaking, Dylan waited a few moments to see if anyone was going to take him up on his offer. When no one immediately headed for the door, Dylan inclined his head, then walked through it himself.

Looks were exchanged, but no one spoke, so Quinn, as Dylan's second-in-command, stood and filled in the gaps. "We'll take a ten-minute break. If you want to take advantage of Dylan's offer, now's the time to do it. If you decide to stay, however, remember what he said. You're locked into this—whatever the outcome may be."

Then he turned and retraced Dylan's path out of the room, knowing, without looking, that Gabe was right behind him.

They were ten of the longest minutes of Quinn's life. Judging from the looks on Dylan's and Gabe's faces, the other two men felt the same, though none of them said anything about the gauntlet the king had just thrown down. Instead, they spoke of mundane business matters, things that needed to be taken care of but that no one had had time to deal with in the wake of all the death and destruction.

Finally, though, the last minute ticked away, and they headed back into the War Room. Still, Dylan didn't say anything, but Quinn could feel the tension radiating from him and could only imagine what his friend was feeling right now. Dylan had given his very soul to keep the Dragonstar clan alive through the last century, and it sucked that he was being doubted now, when he most needed his council's trust.

Unable to do much but stand next to him and offer his unwavering support, Quinn did just that, laying a hand on the king's shoulder and transferring every ounce of healing warmth he had inside him into Dylan.

Taking a deep breath, Quinn braced himself and looked out at the waiting sentries. The room was still full. None of them had left, though Callie and Caitlyn still looked doubtful. The others all seemed solid, however, which was as much as they could expect.

"All right, then. Thank you for your trust." Dylan turned to Gabe and Quinn. "Gentlemen, please fill us in on what your research has shown in the last few months."

Gabe went first, discussing each one of the breaks in the safeguards.

"As you know, each of the spells we've used to protect our

territory carries a certain magical thumbprint that reflects back on its owner. Most of our newest safeguards were done by Travis, Paige, Jase and Shawn, though Dylan, Quinn and I are responsible for the most powerful, outer layers. Their stamp is all over the safeguards.

"But what we've found in the safeguards that have been broken recently—like the one a couple months ago when Liam was killed—is that they've been ripped apart from the inside. Which means someone had to be inside our safe zone to do it."

He paused, but when no one said anything, he continued, "I haven't had the chance to examine today's break yet, but my suspicion is that we're going to see the same thing—that the safeguards were torn apart from the inside. And if that's the case, I'm going to want to compare it to the others, to see if the magical thumbprint is the same."

Shawn spoke up then. "Shouldn't you be able to trace the magic? I mean, each of our powers has a distinct signature. We know each other's, so if it's one of us, wouldn't it stand to reason that you'd be able to tell?"

"That's the weird thing. I should be able to tell, but the traces left have all been corrupted by Wyvernmoon magic. Their signature is very different from ours—darker and a lot messier—and it's completely intertwined with whatever traces we have left."

"But isn't that to be expected in a case like this?" asked Logan. "Can't you just separate them somehow? I know some of the old magic can—"

"Yes, but we're not talking just about the Wyvernmoons' magical thumbprints—we have those in abundance from each of the sites. We've managed to identify three Wyvernmoons who have come consistently through the breaks, with the others changing regularly."

"Who are the three Wyvernmoons?" demanded Paige, the quietest of the sentries, but also one of the most cunning.

"Give me one second and I'll get to that. I want to finish answering Logan's question first." Gabe turned back to the light-haired sentry. "The kind of signature I'm talking about is infused directly into the fabric of the safeguards and the magic used to tear them apart. It can only be left by the person who actually unraveled the spells, ripping them apart."

"But how can that person be both Dragonstar and Wyvernmoon?" demanded Ty. "The two are pretty much mutually exclusive. Our DNA is different, the spells we use and the powers we wield are all different—"

"Not if the person has switched allegiances. Whoever it is can't hide the fact that he or she was born Dragonstar. But now that his loyalties have shifted and he's probably taken a blood oath, much like the one you take before entering my Council, he carries the stamp of Wyvern magic as well."

"But shouldn't that make it easier to catch him, then?" asked Shawn. "We should be able to smell the Wyvernmoons on him."

"I thought the same thing," Dylan agreed. "But so far, we haven't been able to find any trace of them—at least not one that didn't come from Brock and his group being here."

"Brock?" Travis, who Quinn believed was the smartest sentry by far, leapt on the name. "Wasn't he one of Silus's guys?"

"He was," acknowledged Dylan grimly. His stance screamed aggression, and Quinn knew he was remembering how the last Wyvernmoon leader had died at his mate's hands—after putting her through hell first. "And now that we've eliminated Silus and his son the Wyvernmoons are pretty much in a civil war as different factions fight to fill the power vacuum left by their deaths."

"But that's good for us," Paige said. "If they kill each other off . . ."

"Oh yeah, that would be great," agreed Gabe. "The only problem is what they're using to jockey for position—which, it seems, is mainly us. Each group is trying to prove its leader is stronger than the others by getting in here and killing some of us."

"Which is where the traitor comes in," Dylan continued through the horrified silence. "We're pretty sure that he or she is working directly with Brock, which is why he's had so much more luck infiltrating the safeguards than the others have.

"That doesn't mean there haven't been attempts by others. You all know there have been because you've seen them, even fought in some of them, but no one else is having near the success Brock is. And we never see him coming, like we do the others. He's always in before we even have a clue that he's around. And today's incident is looking like it follows the same pattern."

The room was silent as the sentries absorbed what Gabe and Dylan were telling them. After a minute or so, Riley turned to Quinn and asked, "What else? Dylan said you had things to say, too."

"To begin with," Quinn answered, "you know from our discussion a few months ago that one of the main methods of virus transmission is actual injection with the disease. They tried it on a couple of us three months ago, and they've tried it a number of times since."

"You mean when they break in?"

"Yes, and even when they aren't here."

"What does that mean?" demanded Caitlyn, who had moved closer to the inner circle. Her mother had died of the virus a few months before.

"What I'm finding is that while not every victim has been injected with the disease—meaning there is another way of contracting it that we haven't found yet—most of the recent victims have been."

"But there's only been three or four Wyvernmoon attacks in the last couple of months," Jase objected. "Lately, people are dying almost every day."

"Oh, shit," said Shawn incredulously. "Are you telling me this traitor is actually injecting his own clan mates with that goddamned disease?"

Quinn nodded. "That's exactly what I'm saying."

The sentries went wild and Quinn knew exactly how they felt. The act of physically fighting was one thing—they could understand it, they could see it, and they knew they had a better than fifty-fifty shot at winning in battle. But biological warfare was something else entirely—it was something none of them were equipped to fight. Even worse, they'd all seen what it was like to die from this virus. The idea that one of their own was doing it was anathema to them, not to mention absolutely enraging.

"Michael?" Ty choked out, from his spot on the cot. He had pushed himself into a sitting position and his eyes were colder than Quinn had ever seen them.

"Yes, Phoebe found that Michael was injected. Which meant that someone got close enough to jam a needle in him without either him getting upset about it or reporting it. Which means he either didn't know it happened, or he trusted, implicitly, whoever injected him."

"Shit, fuck, goddamn motherfucker. Are you shitting me?" Riley was out of his seat and rocketing to the front of the room. "Are you fucking telling me that one of us—one of the *Dragonstars*—killed Michael?"

"And Marta," intoned Gabe, his face carefully blank as he said his wife's name. "And God only knows how many others. My daughter wasn't injected, at least not that we can find, which means that there's still another method of transmission that we haven't found. But overall, a lot of dragons have been given the virus that way. That's what Dylan's been trying to tell you. Things are much worse than we ever suspected."

"Well, then, the only question is, what the fuck are we going to do about it?" demanded Logan. "I'm done sitting around and waiting to die of this fucking thing."

"That's why we're having this meeting," answered Dylan. "So sit down and start talking, because we're not leaving here until we have not only a plan but a set course of action that involves more than blowing the Wyvernmoons sky high."

"Hey, I think that's a damn good course of action," insisted Jase.

"Believe me, so do I," Dylan said. "But not until we find out which Dragonstar sold out to them. I'm not putting up with a traitor in this clan one second longer."

CHAPTER FIFTEEN

A thrill of uneasiness worked its way through her. Damn, that had been close. Brock and the others had barely gotten away, and she knew he was going to be furious with her. But how could he blame her when he'd been the one who hadn't been able to take Ty down on the first shot? If he'd done that, then none of this would have happened. Ty never would have gotten a call for help out, and Brock never would have lost four of his team.

It was his fault all the way, but somehow she knew he wasn't going to see it like that.

The uneasiness became out-and-out anxiety as she paced the narrow confines of her apartment. She hated the place—would much rather be out at the caves, but she was afraid her duplicity would be written on her face. The last thing she needed was for someone to make the connection between her and Brock. Especially considering how careless she'd been lately. She'd almost been caught today. No one had questioned what she was doing there at the time of the attack, but that didn't mean they wouldn't once things calmed down. Dylan hadn't maintained control all these years by being stupid.

But how could she have known that Brock couldn't live up to his promises? How could she have known that for all his bragging and assurances, he and his group of eight sentries were no match for three Dragonstars. It didn't bode well for their plans, and if something went wrong ... if something went wrong, she was going to have to stay here and blend back into the community. She'd rather not do that in a jail cell.

She snorted. Who was she kidding? Dragons didn't believe in jail. Either you were loyal to the clan or you were dead. She shivered, thinking of the way one of Brock's soldiers had laid Ty wide-open. She hadn't expected it to be like that, had figured it would be cleaner, more honorable. Although why she'd thought that when Brock had proven himself, time and again, to be anything but honorable, she didn't know.

Then again, it took someone wily and unprincipled to run the Wyvernmoon clan. Anyone else would be bulldozed over in a matter of weeks, maybe even days. No, the Wyvernmoons weren't known for their honor.

And if a direct attack on Dylan's sentries wasn't going to work—and she had a feeling Brock wasn't stupid enough to try again after the debacle with Ty—then that meant they were going to have to stick to the viral attacks. Which meant her job was going to be a million times harder.

The phone she kept on her left hip at all times vibrated, and she pulled it out quickly, checked the caller ID. It was the call she'd been waiting for. Clicking the phone on, she listened to Brock's instructions and then hung up without saying anything but "Yes, sir."

She'd been right. He wanted DNA samples from all the sentries, and it was up to her to provide them. Lucky, lucky her.

Crossing to the small bathroom, she rummaged in the drawer until she came up with her roommate's brush. One down, twelve to go.

It was going to be a very long night.

CHAPTER SIXTEEN

After eight of the longest hours of his life, the meeting finally broke up and Quinn headed back to the lab. His dragon was itchy and out of sorts, and to be honest, so was he. No one understood more than he the necessity of what they had spent all afternoon doing, but at the same time he was desperate to see Jasmine. To talk to her without Phoebe and a bunch of other people watching them. To find out why she'd left him that morning.

Had he been too rough with her that last time they'd made love? Not rough enough? Or had his neediness in the middle of the night totally freaked her out? He could understand if it had. It had certainly freaked him out, as he'd never let anyone else see his problems. The fact that he'd done it with her hadn't made sense, at least not until he'd understood that she was his mate.

And though a large part of him wanted nothing more than to grab her and take her to bed, there was another part that just wanted to talk to her, to get to know this woman who had so captivated him that his dragon had mated with her—signed, sealed, delivered—in less than twelve hours.

As long as he was being honest with himself, he had to admit that he also just wanted to make sure that she was still there, in the lab. She'd seemed to take everything that had happened earlier that day in stride—Ty's injury, Quinn's healing ability, even the fact that they were dragon shifters—but if the previous night had taught him nothing else, it was that with Jasmine, looks could be very deceiving. After all, hadn't she looked and sounded completely normal when she'd cuddled against him after that last bout of lovemaking? Hadn't she fallen asleep in his arms and wrapped herself around him while they'd slept? And then hadn't she gotten up and walked out on him without leaving so much as her cell phone number—or last name—behind?

He didn't think he was being paranoid to worry that she might take off again. After all, the woman had just found out that she'd made love—several times—to a living, breathing dragon. It would shake anybody up. And he hadn't even brought up the fact that she was his mate . . .

As it turned out, his worries were for naught. When he got back to the lab, Jasmine was sitting at one of the lab stations, speaking into a small microphone she wore attached to a headset while her fingers flew over her laptop keyboard.

Next to her was a pile of discarded slides and a microscope, which if the desktop monitor was any indication, still had a slide under its lens. His beast wanted to bound across the lab and take her in his arms, but the scientist preferred to hang back and watch her work when she thought she was all alone.

She was fascinating to observe, especially since she appeared completely absorbed by the quest that had ruled his life for so long. When she wasn't typing what looked to be two hundred words a minute, she was tapping her thumbs against the desk in rhythm to music only she could hear. Her right leg was bouncing, and so was her head—yet she rarely stopped talking, recording any and all thoughts she was having regarding the virus.

Which, he admitted, were quite impressive and indicated she'd been working nonstop while he was gone.

He glanced around the lab, noting that Phoebe's computer was turned off and her lab station straightened up—a surefire sign that she had left for the day. Which meant that he and Jasmine were completely alone, except for the security guards stationed at either end of the building.

The thought had him skating close to the razor's edge of his control, a condition that was worsened because he hadn't given himself a chance to recharge his batteries. In the past two days he'd tried to heal Michael, given what he could to Jazz, had healed Ty, and then done his best to keep emotions and tempers under control in the War Room. He was one short slip away from grabbing Jasmine and fucking her wildly, but he wasn't certain that was the best way to convince her to stay.

What he should do, what he needed to do, was to go home. He could get something to eat, could rest, could let the weakness take him for a while in a way he hadn't allowed yet. But even as the thought formed, he knew he wasn't leaving the lab—at least not without his mate.

Which at this rate might be never, Quinn was forced to acknowledge, as Jasmine reshelved the slides she was working on and grabbed a whole new pile. He sat there, semi-patiently, while she went over each one, taking notes on her laptop and speaking key observations into her recorder. If this was any indication, she planned on catching up on four years' worth of work in one night. It was admirable—and crazy as hell.

Still, he didn't interrupt her. Instead, he continued to sit and watch her. He wished he could see more than her profile, but he didn't want to startle her, so he contented himself with watching her lips move as she spoke. He tried to guess which slide she was on, as his view of the computer monitor was impeded by her full breasts.

Time passed slowly as he watched her, and eventually his brain started replaying highlights from the night before. Even though he told himself that she'd left, that it obviously hadn't been as important to her as it had been to him, it didn't matter. The dragon remembered the pleasure—the incredible, mind-boggling pleasure—of being with her, and he wanted it again. Desperately.

He remembered what she looked like, drunk on tequila and pleasure, her cheeks flushed a rosy pink and her lips swollen with his kisses.

Thought about her breasts, with their tight, raspberry nipples and the silky softness of her skin when he'd run his lips over her stomach.

Pictured the small smattering of freckles that ran across her shoulders and the look in her eyes when he'd thrust inside her for the first time.

His dragon stretched at the memories and lazily raked its sharp talons across the inside of his skin. It was a warning—loud and clear—that his human side wasn't going to be in control much longer. Hours of fighting the pain and exhaustion were wearing on him. When he added in the fact that he was nearly desperate to figure out what had sent Jasmine running away at the first sign of dawn, he figured he was doing pretty well, especially now that he was back in the lab where he could smell her. The ripe blackberry scent of her drove him insane, as did the insatiable desire he had to touch her.

Eventually, he couldn't wait any longer without losing what small grip he had on his self-control. "How many more samples do you have to go through?" he asked in a voice husky with disuse and desire. He'd been sitting there for more than an hour.

Jasmine started a little at his voice, and for the first time he felt bad about watching her work without her knowledge. The dazed eyes she turned on him made him feel a little like a voyeur.

"I'm sorry, what?" she asked, as if trying to comprehend where he'd come from.

He repeated the question as he crossed the lab, adding, "It's getting late."

Her eyes flew to the clock on the wall and widened, as if she'd just realized that it was almost midnight. Sighing, she stretched a little before rubbing her hands over her face.

For the first time, he realized he wasn't the only tired one. Her eyes were shadowed with dark circles, the skin of her face pulled taut

136 • TESSA ADAMS

over her cheekbones. And her hands were shaking almost as badly as his own were.

He thought of the scars he'd seen on her body the night before, the way she'd refused to talk about them. Remembering what Phoebe had told him about her friend, he figured the scars were a lot more serious than Jasmine had let on.

She was on leave from the CDC in order to recover from her injuries, and he'd put her through a demanding night of sex on top of a long drive, then followed that with an emergency trauma, eight hours of work and the realization that humans weren't the baddest thing on the planet.

What a great job he and Phoebe were doing helping her get acclimated to the lab and the Dragonstars. He would have kicked his own ass if he could have reached it.

"I just need a little longer," she said. "I want to look at a few more cases and—"

"It looks like you've already examined close to a hundred. I figure the rest can wait until tomorrow morning."

"But there are so many. I can't believe how many of your clan have died from this in the last year. It's scary."

He already knew that. It *was* frightening and infuriating, and sometimes fighting it was the only thing that got him up in the mornings. But he'd been struggling with this thing long enough to know that wearing himself out over it—each day, every day—wasn't going to help. It looked like she needed to learn the same thing. "You need to rest. You're still recovering from your injuries."

Her eyes turned hot. "I told you they weren't—"

"Yes, but Phoebe told me something completely different when she first mentioned you coming to help out. In this case, I'm more inclined to believe her than you."

"It's my body."

"It is," he agreed. "But you don't seem to be taking very good care of it."

"Like you take such good care of yourself? You healed that guy today when you were already run down. It took so much out of you that I swear I really thought you were going to have a heart attack. And yet, here you are, nearly twelve hours later—still working."

"I'm waiting on you. I would have gone straight home from Dylan's, but I wanted to check and make sure you were all right."

A flicker of distress flitted across her face, but was quickly banished by indignation. "I'm not an imbecile, you know. I am perfectly capable of shutting down a lab by myself."

"Yes, but seeing as how my clan members are being attacked on a regular basis, it didn't seem smart to let you wander around on your own, unprotected. Besides, Phoebe would kill me if something happened to you."

"I'm not one of your clan. No one would bother me."

"Don't underestimate our enemies. The Wyvernmoons in particular are total bastards, and they would do whatever it takes to strike us—even if that means taking out a human doctor. Especially if it means that. They're not overly fond of humans."

"But how would they even know I'm working with you? I just got here."

"Well, that's the million-dollar question, isn't it? They're getting information from someone. How do you think they knew to take Ty when they did? Besides, in your case, they don't even need someone to tip them off. You smell like us."

"What?" She jerked in her seat, discreetly sniffed at herself. "I don't smell like anything—and neither do you."

"You smell like a lot of things. Night-blooming jasmine mixed with summer blackberries and wild, desert rainstorms."

Her eyes widened and one hand went to her throat. "I don't—"

"Oh, you do." He leaned down, putting an arm on either side of her even as he told himself he was being incredibly stupid. "Oh, you definitely do." Closing his eyes, he breathed in her scent and for a moment remembered what it was like to be between her legs with his mouth on her hot, wet pussy. She'd tasted even better than she smelled.

He grew hard at the thought, his blood running hot. A quick look at Jazz showed that she seemed as affected by him as he was by her. Her eyes were wide, the pupils dilated and her chest was moving in a rapid rise and fall that had him aching.

He was close to her, so close that their lips were only inches away, and for a moment he thought about closing the distance. Thought about what it would feel like to put his mouth on hers. Thought about what it would feel like to sink his tongue deep inside her and absorb every drop of her honeyed warmth. Only the thought of what it had felt like to wake up in that hotel room without her kept him from acting on the impulse.

He wanted her with an intensity that bordered on madness, but he wouldn't go there again, wouldn't push her if it wasn't what she wanted. He'd lost too many people to deliberately open himself up to someone he knew would walk away.

Forcing his brain away from sex with Jasmine and back to the point he'd meant to make, he said, "Besides, when I said you smelled of us, I wasn't talking of your normal scent. When he was here, Dylan extended his protection to you—the protection of the Dragonstars. With our enemies running around unchecked, he wanted to make sure you weren't completely vulnerable whenever you stepped out of the lab. But in doing that, he coated you with evidence of that protection. You can't smell it or see it, but any dragon within a hundred yards of you will sense the magic and know that you are under the protection of the king."

"King? You guys have a king?"

He almost laughed. Of course, that's what Jazz would choose to focus on. Not the fact that she needed protection from things much larger and scarier than she was, but rather the clan hierarchy. It was a much more tangible thing, and even after only knowing her a day, he'd figured out that Dr. Jasmine Kane was much more comfortable dealing with what she could see and feel.

"Of course we do," he answered. "We're a fully operating society, you know. We have a king, and he has an advisory council that helps him govern and that protects the clan."

"And Dylan—he's your king?" she asked.

"He is."

"Wow," she said softly, looking him over. "And you work for him?"

"In essence I'm a sentry, which means I'm part of his advisory council, as are the others you met today—Gabe and Logan and Ty. Even Phoebe has an advisory role now."

"Because she's engaged to Dylan?"

He nodded. "And because she's brilliant. In the many, many years Dylan's ruled the Dragonstars, he's always respected intelligence—even if it means people disagree with him. That's the reason he made the decision to bring in Phoebe—and now you—to fight this disease. He takes his responsibilities very seriously, and the fact that his people are suffering is killing him."

Jasmine nodded as if his words made perfect sense, and the look she gave him was thoughtful. "What about you?"

"What about me?"

"This lab is your baby. Your name is on a hell of a lot more of the research about this disease than Phoebe's is. How do you feel about this disease—and your inability to find a cure?"

Her matter-of-fact question hit him hard, and the dragon, already awake and interested in the conversation, took it the wrong way. Before he could stop it, before he could put a chokehold on the anger that was always too close to the surface, his talons punched right through his fingertips and the flames he kept carefully banked inside of him roared to life.

CHAPTER SEVENTEEN

Jasmine watched in fascination as Quinn's eyes caught fire, the green irises blazing so brightly that she swore just looking into them could make her burn. A quick glance down at his hands—and the claws that had punched right through the pads of his fingers—confirmed that the fire she was seeing belonged to the dragon, not the man.

Her heart rate tripled even as her breathing stopped. She told herself to hold very still, despite the fact that every instinct clamored for her to run. But she'd learned enough about wild animals to know that running only triggered their hunting instincts. The last thing she wanted was to be pursued by Quinn's dragon.

She'd tried to take the notion of shape-shifters in stride—after all, the dragons weren't the first shifters she'd ever heard about. In the course of her work, she'd heard various tribal legends of different races of shifters—particularly in Africa and South America. She'd never experienced any up close, however, and these dragons were still almost too much to wrap her mind around. Leopards and lions were real creatures, so she'd been able to believe in the existence of cat shifters in an abstract way, but dragons were mythological—weren't they?

Except that she'd stood in this room with a group of people who had seemed eminently reasonable, including a woman she trusted above all others, and they told her that dragons really did exist. And now, staring into Quinn's eyes, seeing the predator in there looking back at her, she knew what they said was true.

She started to lean back, to ease away from the power and the pull of his gaze, but Quinn was having none of it. His low, deep growl reverberated through the empty lab, telling her that much. Even after he'd managed to sheath his claws, to return his body to normal, his eyes didn't change.

What did it say about her that she wasn't sure she wanted them to? There was something exciting, something infinitely arousing, in being the focus of a stare that powerful, that intense. And even as she wondered if she had lost her mind completely, the rest of her didn't care.

She wanted to touch Quinn, wanted him to touch her. Wanted to feel again what she'd felt back in that motel room. Being with him had been the most exciting thing that had ever happened to her. It was one of the reasons she'd run—she'd been afraid of all the things he'd made her feel.

Fate had a hell of a sense of humor, for here she was again, right in Quinn's path. The look on his face said that this time he had absolutely no intention of letting her go, which was fine with her—for the short term. She'd spent the last three years in one stressful field position after another. Maybe a brief fling with a hot—make that very hot—dragon shifter was exactly what she needed.

If she got a little singed in the process, well . . . she had a feeling the pleasure would be more than worth the pain.

Reaching a hand out, she tangled her fingers in Quinn's shaggy black hair, savoring its silky softness as the strands wound themselves around her fingers. His eyes darkened to the lush, verdant green of the rain forest at twilight, and his mouth—that sensuous mouth with its full, kissable lower lip—parted on a harsh, indrawn breath.

"This isn't a good idea, Jazz." His voice was lower, harsher than she was used to—like talons scraping across velvet—and it sent shivers down her spine.

"Are you sure?" she whispered, licking her suddenly dry lips. "Because from where I'm sitting, it seems like an excellent idea."

"Yeah, well, you're the doctor who likes to play around in the world's hot spots with some of the most contagious diseases on the planet. Your sense of self-preservation is definitely not what it could be."

"And yours is?"

He started to answer, but she stopped him by laying two fingers across his mouth. "Before you answer that, remember that I saw you in action today. You're no different than I am. You just manifest it differently."

"You should probably find a better yardstick to measure yourself against. I'm not exactly sane," he said, then nipped at her fingers.

Heat shot through her, straight from her fingertips to her sex. It was an electric, incandescent feeling that lit her up like a strobe light and had her body begging. Begging for everything it knew he could give her . . . and more.

But things were getting too intense—*she* was getting too intense. Lightening things up a little, Jasmine tucked her tongue firmly in her cheek and murmured, "What if I like your yardstick?"

There was a moment of stunned silence and then Quinn cracked up. His laugh was warm and infectious and only increased the inferno blazing to life within her. This wasn't the outcome she'd been looking for, but even after only two days or so, she knew that while he could joke around, it was rare for him to truly smile. The fact that she'd made him happy—even for a moment—did something to her that she wasn't quite ready to poke at yet.

"That might very well be the worst line I have ever heard," he said, sinking to the ground, so that he was kneeling between her thighs.

"Surely not."

"I don't know. It was pretty terrible."

"Too bad I won't be sticking around all that long. I'm sure I'd be able to come up with worse."

As soon as she said the words, she knew they were the exact wrong thing to say. The amusement fled from Quinn's face as quickly as it had come, the darkness once again overtaking his expression.

This time the shiver that worked its way down her back was from nerves, not desire.

Quinn felt the last of the ties that bound the dragon to the man snap taut inside of him at Jasmine's words—a condition intensified by the dawning awareness in her eyes. She knew what she'd said, knew that she'd thrown down the gauntlet, though from the wariness in her look, it might have been unintentional.

The dragon didn't care. All it cared about was marking her all over again, punishing her for leaving him like she had and threatening to do it again.

Quinn lunged to his feet and with a growl pulled her to standing. Then he spun her around so that the front of her thighs rested against the desk where she'd been working. With one hand, he sent the papers on the right side of the desk floating to the floor while his other pressed on her lower back, bending her over the desk until her stomach and breasts were flush against the wood.

Her round, sexy ass was in the air, the threadbare seat of her jeans making it look even more inviting. There was a small hole near the pocket on her left cheek, through which he could see the black lace of her underwear.

He slowly slipped his finger into the hole, twisting it back and forth until the opening widened a little bit, and he could feel the soft warmth of the lace and the silkiness of the skin that lay beneath it.

She gasped, but this time it wasn't in fear. Or not entirely in fear, he should say. The dragon could smell her uneasiness, the nerves she was working so hard to hide. But it could also scent her desire—a hot, spicy richness that came out of her in waves and drove the beast absolutely insane.

Leaving his finger where it was, stroking the near bare skin of her ass, he leaned forward and nuzzled his way along the skin of her upper back, left bare by the fire engine red tank top she was wearing. The smooth, tanned expanse of skin had been driving him crazy from the second he'd laid eyes on her this morning, and now that he was actually touching it . . .

He sunk his teeth in, unable to resist the desire to mark her. She stiffened, moaned, then relaxed as he used his mouth to soothe the small hurt. Her body quivered against his and the warm, heady smell of her desire grew more blatant, more seductive until he wanted nothing more than to glut himself in it, in her.

"You left." The words came out unexpectedly, another window into his soul that he'd had no intention of opening. But there was something about her that made him speak without thinking first.

The accusation hung in the air between them, and for long seconds neither of them moved. The spicy scent of her arousal dimmed, and his annoyance with himself grew.

Shit. He didn't just say that, did he? Was he acting like some kind of candy ass who sat around whining because a woman wasn't interested in a second round with him? Except this one obviously was interested, so what the hell was he bitching about? He must still be suffering the ill-effects from bringing Ty back from the brink. If he'd been stronger, more himself, he never would have slipped up like that.

Jazz squirmed against him, as if she wanted him to let her up. But he didn't do that—couldn't do that, if the truth were known. Not when he was aching with the need to bury himself so deeply inside her that she could never get him out.

She settled down, as if she realized that she wasn't going anywhere until he got an answer. With a sigh, she murmured, "Phoebe said it was urgent, so I was in a hurry to get here. It isn't like I exactly knew we were heading to the same place, you know."

He could smell the lie on her and the scent of it enraged the beast. He called her on it, not understanding why it was so important to him. All he knew was that he wanted only truth between them.

Whatever it was, whatever she had to say, he didn't want her to lie to him.

"You weren't expected until tomorrow. We both know that."

"Yeah, well, I was more than ready to jump into this thing. I've been sidelined for almost two months, and if I didn't do something useful soon, I swear I was going to lose my mind. Of course, if I'd known what I was running to, I might have stuck around that motel room a little longer."

There was truth in her words, not a lot, but enough that they appeased him and the dragon. "So, you've got a thing against ancient dragon clans?" His stomach clenched as he waited for her answer.

"No. I have a thing against senseless brutality. I left Africa to escape it, and it looks like I landed myself smack dab in the center of another bloody conflict, if this afternoon is any indication. Only this one doesn't follow any of the rules I'm used to. It's . . . disconcerting."

There was nothing he could really say to that. "I'm sorry. I didn't want to bring in anyone else for that very reason. Things are becoming more and more dangerous for us with every day that passes."

"I got that impression." She shifted a little, and it rubbed her ass against his cock. His arousal roared back to life, and he pressed himself more firmly into the soft lushness of her.

She went still, the prey catching the scent of the predator, and for one never-ending moment neither of them moved. Then she arched her back, pushing her ass out. The suddenness of the move had his eyes crossing with lust.

He wanted to see her face, needed to see her eyes, had to know if she was feeling the same incredible urgency that he was. Burying his hands in her hair, he turned her head so that her right cheek lay against the desk and her eyes—a storm-tossed violet—were locked with his.

"You can still leave," he said, his voice nearly unrecognizable with desire.

She shuddered, arched against him a second time. "I don't want to go anywhere."

"Are you sure?" He thrust against her a second time, wanting to make certain she knew what he was asking of her.

Proof of her arousal flooded him, the sweet, sexy scent reaching out to him as nothing else could have. His fingers tightened in her hair, and with a roar, he lifted his torso off of hers, pulling her with him as he went.

Twisting her head even farther to the side, he slammed his mouth down on top of hers and took everything she was willing to give him and then some.

She gasped and arched her back, clutching the edge of the table as if she didn't trust her knees to hold her. As she did, he yanked her jeans and underwear down before sliding his fingers deep inside of her.

She moaned, her body running like honey around him as he rubbed against her sweet spot. She was so responsive it blew him away, so hot that he burned with the need to see just how fast he could send her up and over.

He pulled his fingers out, pinched her clit between his thumb and middle finger at the same time he sunk his teeth into her shoulder.

She jerked against him, screaming, her fingers reaching back to grab his cock through the thick material of his jeans. He groaned, thrust against her, though he knew better. His dick was on fire, burning for her, and her unexpected touch had taken him all the way to the jagged edge of his control.

She laughed, low and a little mean, as her fingers worked his zipper down. His cock leapt from between the parted denim, and she palmed him, rubbing while he thrust helplessly against her soft hand.

Shit. He was as ready to go off as a teenager with his first girl. How could she do this to him so easily? Make him lose it when he'd had four hundred years to learn the reward in taking things slow? Was it the mating connection that made him feel like this, or was it her? Did it even matter, as long as he could be inside her?

Fumbling in the back pocket of his jeans, he grabbed a condom.

Tore it open with his teeth. Rolled it on in a fever of need. Then sank into her waiting heat with a shudder of relief.

Jazz came at the first thrust of Quinn's cock inside of her. How he'd gotten her so hot so quick, she didn't know, but each stroke of his fingers had sent heat shooting through her like fireworks.

She'd wanted more time to play with him, more time to touch him, but she couldn't complain—not when he was making her feel this good.

But then he was pulling out, robbing her of the last sweet waves of her orgasm. She pressed back, tried to take him again, and he laughed darkly before pushing himself inside her, one excruciatingly slow inch at a time.

She shuddered, again tried to press back against him so she could take all of him, but he stopped her with a steady hand on the small of her back. Held her in place so that her screaming nerve endings felt every inch of his invasion.

And it was an invasion, a slow, deliberate conquering that she recognized even through the incredible pleasure. Quinn laying claim, establishing dominance, challenging her to deny his possession.

It was the last thought that had her bucking beneath him, smiling in triumph as she dislodged him. She was no man's possession— and she never would be.

"Jazz." His voice was low, warning her, as he brought both hands to her hips and pulled her sharply against him until he was as deep inside of her as he could go.

Her muscles clenched involuntarily around him, her body in thrall to his mastery even as her mind rebelled at the limits he set for her. For them. Twisting her hips, she slid away from him again, shimmied until he'd once more slipped from her body.

One of his hands grabbed her hip while the other shoved her shirt up before tangling in her hair, holding her in place. He leaned forward until he covered her, until her breasts were pushed tightly against the unforgiving marble of the lab table and her back was wedged just as tightly against his heavily muscled chest.

"Take me," he demanded, his voice low and harsh in her ear. "Take me now."

He slammed into her so hard she rocketed up onto her tiptoes. Then he was pulling out and slamming into her again and again. He was wild, out of control. She'd challenged him, defied him, pushed him past his limits until the only drive he had was to mark her. To dominate her. To show her who had the upper hand.

It was delicious, every thrust a shocking invasion. Every slam of his cock a test of her own limits as unimaginable pleasure rocketed through her.

He was moving quickly now, each thrust fast and hard. She closed her eyes, clutched the table, tried to center herself in the maelstrom he'd released. But there was no escape, no control, no salvation. Only Quinn and the wicked, inescapable, unbelievable things he was doing to her.

The pleasure rose, tingled, burned, spreading from her sex to her stomach, up through her breasts, down her arms and legs until no part of her body was unaffected. Until all that she felt, all that she was, was wrapped up in Quinn and this unbelievable moment out of time.

Another orgasm rose, sharp and undeniable, yet she tried to push it back. She didn't want this to end, wasn't ready to let this perfect moment between them slip away.

Quinn's fingers were clenching in her hair, scratching down the delicate skin of her back while his breath shuddered in and out. He was on the edge, holding on through sheer will alone, waiting for his release until he'd sent her careening into her own climax.

It was cruel to make him wait when staving off her own release was nearly killing her. But she shoved the heat down for a few more seconds, reveled in Quinn's brutal pounding, in the agony and ecstasy that came with being taken by this man.

"Come for me, Jazz." His voice was dark, distorted, and it sent shivers of electricity through her already primed body as she recognized the smoky shadows of the dragon. "Come for me now!" His teeth sunk into her shoulder, just hard enough to pin her in place and demand that she do what he asked.

And she did, her body shattering into a million pieces, flying far beyond her scope of pleasure as unimaginable ecstasy roared through her.

Quinn came a half second later, his body stiffening and jerking as he pulsed inside of her, his semen coming in forceful spurts that only intensified her own climax. His hands clenched at her hips, held her still as he poured himself into her.

"Quinn!" She sobbed his name as she went under yet again, the contractions building on themselves, over and over until it was both agony and ecstasy. Total fulfillment and complete devastation. She was laid raw and open before him.

Quinn collapsed on top of her, his big, still-clothed body rubbing against every inch of her sensitized skin. It was too much and not enough, and she went into sensory overload, her body so far beyond her control that it could have belonged to a stranger, for all the attention it paid to her.

When Quinn dragged his teeth along her back, licking his way down her spine, she somehow came one final time. Her body shooting into the stars until all that was left of her was a mindless bundle of sensations.

It took Jasmine a long time to return to her senses, even longer for her to realize that she was having trouble breathing.

She was still spread across the desk and Quinn was still on top of her—still inside her—his cock long and firm and by all appearances ready for another go-round. She might have been amenable to a second shot herself if the world around her wasn't currently tinged with gray.

She struggled against him, trying to dislodge the heavy weight of his chest upon her back, and Quinn growled. But he moved, reluctantly.

She sucked in a few good breaths then nearly whimpered in disappointment when he pulled out of her. *Don't go*, she wanted to tell him. *Don't leave me.* The feeling swept through her so completely that she nearly said the words out loud, nearly begged him to stay next to her, to keep making love to her even though she was almost half dead with exhaustion. That desire, that compulsion to keep him close scared her as nothing else could have. It was perilously close to need, and she had sworn, a long time ago, that she would never need anyone.

She turned, watching as Quinn disposed of the condom and cleaned himself up before tucking himself back into his jeans. The fact that he was fully clothed made her suddenly aware of the fact that she was naked except for the jeans and panties that were pooled around her knees.

She yanked them back into place as quickly as she could, achingly aware of Quinn watching as she did so.

What the hell had gotten into her? Jasmine wondered frantically. Since when did she mix work and pleasure like this? Since never. She'd always made sure to keep the two separated by a wide margin. Yet here she was in the middle of the lab for God's sake, recovering from yet another marathon sex session with Quinn.

Maybe that was it. Maybe her IQ dropped a little more every time Quinn made love to her. God knew, the pleasure was so intense she wouldn't be surprised to find out it melted a few brain cells along with everything else.

The whole thing was ridiculous, especially her response, but the scary part was that she had no doubt if and when he wanted her again, she would fall into bed with him. Or onto the floor. Or up against the closet wall. Wherever, whenever. She'd known him a day and already he had an incredible amount of control over her body—and her mind.

It wasn't a pleasant realization. Glancing over at Quinn, she couldn't help wondering what he was thinking, what he was feeling. His face was completely impassive as he waited for her to finish putting herself to rights. Only his eyes were alive, and they glowed so brightly that she wondered if she was looking at the man—or the dragon.

The fact that she was even wondering about it should have freaked her out, but it didn't. Just how far gone was she that it didn't even matter if she'd made love to a man or his beast? She had a feeling she would take Quinn—and the pleasure he gave her—any way that she could get him.

Which was a problem, no doubt about it.

"Did I hurt you?" he asked, and his voice was back to normal.

"No. Of course not."

"Are you sure? I was pretty rough. I'm sorry about that."

"Don't be. It's not like I was complaining." She turned, gave him a flippant smile that she was far from feeling and noticed that his eyes were no longer glowing with that strange electricity.

Well, that answered that question once and for all—as if she'd had any doubt. She'd just had sex with Quinn's dragon. Oh, he might have been in human form, but she was positive the dragon had been in control. Too bad she didn't have a clue how she felt about that.

But it explained a lot, including why Quinn was looking at her with such concern. She wondered if he even remembered what they had done together, if he remembered how he had taken her, his body pinning her down while his teeth sank into her flesh to hold her in place.

She could still feel the ache from his bite, but it was a sweet pain—unlike so many of the other aches that were currently ravaging her body. Nothing like two days of hot sex to get her injuries complaining.

"I should probably get you to Phoebe," he muttered, running an agitated hand over his hair. "Otherwise, she'll be back here in a little while, demanding to know what's taking you so long."

"Somehow, I can't see you explaining to her just what it is you've been up to."

"Yeah, well, I can't see you piping up about what got into you, either."

They grinned at each other, the terrible innuendos bridging the awkward distance that had grown between them as they'd pulled themselves together. Quinn held out a hand to her, and Jasmine shifted to take it, wincing when her sore hip protested the sudden movement.

"What's wrong?" Quinn demanded, his eyes searching her from top to bottom as if he could see straight through her clothes and skin to the muscles and bones beneath. Which, now that she thought about it, he might actually be able to do. He was a healer after all—and how cool would that be? The doctor in her thrilled at the idea.

"Nothing. My hip just isn't sure it can take all this strain we've been putting on it. It'll be fine after a hot shower." Or so she hoped.

His eyes darkened. "I hurt you."

"No. A bomb in Sierra Leone hurt me. You made me feel terrific, and helped me exercise some muscles that haven't gotten much of a workout lately."

If possible, his look turned even more grim. "A bomb? That's what caused all those injuries?"

"Yeah," she shrugged as if the moment the bomb went off—and those seconds after it—hadn't been the most terrifying of her life. "I was in the wrong place at the wrong time."

"That seems to happen to you a lot."

"Now, see, that's where we'll have to agree to disagree." She reached up and carelessly patted his cheek in an effort to keep things light and easy. "Because I happen to think that last night I was in exactly the right place at exactly the right time."

It didn't work. There was absolutely nothing light or easy about Quinn's expression. "Yeah, which is why you snuck out in the middle of the night."

Jasmine felt a surge of guilt, which made her only more determined not to get drawn into an argument. "Are you back to that?" she asked with a roll of her eyes. "I told you, it was nothing personal. I needed to get on the road."

"Why is it so hard for you to be honest with me?" he demanded, reaching out to grab her elbow.

She shrugged him off. "Why are you so determined to make this into a big deal? We like having sex together, cool. But that doesn't mean I owe you an explanation for everything I do."

"Yeah, because that's what I'm demanding. An accounting of every decision you make." He thrust a hand through his hair, and she got the impression that if he was alone he would have roared in frustration. "You walked out on me."

"I walked out on a guy I met in a bar in Fort Stockton, Texas! We had a great time, but since I live in Atlanta and was on my way to New Mexico, it wasn't like I figured we were in it for the long term. You need to get over it."

"And you need to stop lying to yourself," he growled.

"Don't flatter yourself," she said, exasperated. "Just because you don't like what I have to say doesn't mean I'm lying to myself or to you." She said the last with a toss of her head and a deliberately challenging look in her eyes. If he thought she was going to back down just because he beat his chest and grumbled a little, he was in for a hell of a disappointment. The fact that a little voice in the back of her head whispered that he might be right only made her more determined to stand her ground.

Her defiance obviously got to him, and for a second Quinn looked ready to continue the argument, but he must have thought better of it because he suddenly snapped his teeth together so sharply that she was afraid he might break a molar—or three.

Instead, he cupped her elbow with his hand and started propelling her slowly toward the door. "Come on. You must be exhausted after everything you've done today. Let me get you to Phoebe and Dylan's house, so you can rest."

His solicitous behavior drained the fight right out of her, and as she settled down, Jasmine realized that he was right. She should be a walking zombie by now. Instead, she felt strangely exhilarated, like jolt after jolt of electricity was working its way through her body. She didn't know if it was from the sex or the fighting, but something about being around Quinn lit her up in a way nothing had in a very long time.

As her second—or maybe it was her third—wind swept through her, she glanced back at the computer Quinn had shut off so abruptly a little while before and wondered if she could do some more work before calling it a night. She really did want to get up to speed on each of the cases—particularly the most recent ones—as soon as possible. She wouldn't be able to start taking the virus apart until she'd looked at it from all sides.

Quinn misunderstood her reluctance, and he dropped her arm abruptly. "How badly did I hurt you?"

Annoyance brushed through her again, and she wondered what it was about Quinn that made her feel so many conflicting emotions at the same time. "I already told you, I'm fine."

"You're having trouble walking. That's not fine."

Before she could say anything else, he swept her up into his arms and started for the door.

"Hey, what are you doing? Put me down!" she demanded, shoving against his chest. He didn't even bother to glance down, and the only clue that he'd even heard—or felt—her protests was the way his arms tightened around her.

"Quinn, I'm serious. I want to walk."

He still didn't answer, his long legs beating a path to the door, and her annoyance escalated into anger. Who the hell did he think he was? She wasn't some simpering little girl who needed to be carted around like a piece of luggage, and she sure as hell didn't appreciate him ignoring her.

She shoved against him again, much harder this time. It still didn't faze him—damn stubborn dragon—and that shot her anger to the boiling point. She began to struggle against him in earnest. "Damn it! Let me go!"

"You're just going to make it worse," he said through gritted teeth. "Let me get you to Phoebe's, and then I'll examine you."

"I don't need you to examine me."

"Jasmine, be reasonable. You're obviously hurt and—"

"I am not hurt."

He ignored her, shifting so that he could push against the lab's outer door with his shoulder. "If I'm the cause of it, I need to make sure you're okay. I can heal you—"

"Yeah, and wipe yourself out like you did earlier? No, thank you. You're the one who needs to rest."

"What I need to do is take care of you."

"Actually, what you need to do is listen to me. And put me *down*."

He stopped abruptly, sliding her slowly down his body until her feet hit the ground. Thinking he was finally listening, her anger abated, but it came roaring back when she realized they were standing outside her car. He must have used that crazy speed of his to carry her through the entire lab despite her protests. He had released her only because they'd gotten to their destination. Scratch that—they'd gotten to his destination, which was the passenger side of her car.

The big jerk.

"Give me your keys." He held out his hand as if he actually expected her to turn them over. If so, he had a long wait coming.

Shoving away from him, she headed around to the driver's side, pulling her keys out of her back pocket. "You don't need my keys." She slid the key into the lock and opened the door.

Quinn was around the car in a flash, his eyes spitting fire. "I'll drive you home, Jasmine."

"Good luck with that. Atlanta's about twenty-two hours in that direction."

"You know what I mean."

She did, and it would be a cold day in hell before she let him drive her like some helpless little girl who couldn't take care of herself. She'd lived that life once, in her parents' house, and she never would again. She wasn't that kind of woman.

"I can get myself to Phoebe's," she said, as she slid into the driver's seat. "I have a GPS and directions. Go home and get some rest. I'll see you tomorrow."

"I told you, I'll take you." His eyes glittered with menace, the bright green of the dragon more intimidating in that moment than she liked to admit. All the more reason to stand her ground.

"And I told you, I don't need a babysitter. But thanks for the sex. It was fun." She yanked the car door shut, slamming the lock down before she slid the key into the ignition. Quinn looked like he was going to explode, and she didn't want to take any chances. She wasn't flame-proof, after all.

"Jazz!" His hands came down on the hood of her car, hard, and she jumped a little at the impact. Which only made her angrier. She didn't appreciate scare tactics from men.

She programmed Phoebe's address into her GPS, started the car and began pulling forward. Quinn tried to block her way with his massive body, and she rolled her eyes—hadn't she just done this? Nice of him to remind her that all men were the same, even those who were dragons underneath.

Completely pissed off, she handled him the same way she'd handled the other guys—by hitting the gas and waiting for him to jump out of the way. Only, unlike the two assholes in Fort Stockton, she really didn't want to hurt Quinn. At the last second, when he didn't move, she swerved to miss him. Then drove to the edge of the parking lot and hung a left without so much as a backward glance.

As she sped away from the lab, she couldn't resist rolling her window down and flipping him off. Bastard. If he really thought he was going to tell her what to do, he was in for a shock. Dragon or no dragon, Jasmine Kane bowed to no man. Better Quinn learn that now.

CHAPTER EIGHTEEN

Quinn watched in shock as Jasmine flipped him the bird right before she turned the corner and drove out of sight. *What the hell set her off?* he wondered, still too startled to be angry. He'd been trying to help. She was obviously tired, obviously injured, and he'd wanted to take care of her. To make things easy on her. What was so bad about that? In his world that was what a good mate did. Took care of his female when she was too weak or too tired to take care of herself.

Besides, he'd spent the last year standing by helplessly while people he cared about died, one after the other. It had felt good to be able to do something for Jasmine, even if it was a little thing like carrying her to her car when it obviously hurt her to walk. There'd been no reason for her to go off the deep end like that, let alone try to run him over. For the first time, he had a little sympathy for the guys who'd hassled her in Fort Stockton. Jasmine was a lot tougher—a lot harder—than she looked. It made her pretty much the exact opposite of the kind of mate he'd ever thought of ending up with.

Yet, he wasn't ready to walk away from her. Even though he knew he probably should for a lot of reasons, including the fact that the last thing he needed in his life right now was a woman—a human woman—who thought running him over was an acceptable way to settle their differences. Again, was it the mating bond that made him feel this way about her, or was it Jasmine herself? Certainly he liked those glimpses of her he got when she was relaxed or comfortable enough to lower her guard.

But was that enough, he wondered, to build a lifetime on? He didn't know. Normally, his people only became mates after both had chosen to do so. This whole mate at first meeting thing was the stuff of legends, but he'd never met anyone it had actually happened to.

Wasn't that just typical? His whole life he'd been doing things just a little differently from everyone else. It figured that he would be odd man out when it came to this, too.

Still, this isn't what he'd wanted—a mate who was volatile and prickly and so independent that she would rather suffer than let him help her. His entire life was spent fighting—from the battles he waged to heal badly injured clan members to the war against the Wyvernmoons. The last thing he wanted was a personal life as volatile as his professional one, no matter how fleeting the relationship was.

And yet he couldn't just leave Jazz out there alone, he thought, and he started to undress. He hadn't been joking when he'd told her that Dylan had marked her as being under the protection of the Dragonstar clan. The mark gave her a certain amount of protection— more, certainly, than she would have without it—but it also made her a target for their enemies. Letting her wander around a town she didn't know, especially with a traitor on the loose and the Wyvernmoons doing everything they could to hurt the clan, was asking for trouble.

When he was naked, his clothes safely stowed away in the pouch around his neck, he started to shift. It took a little longer than normal— he'd shifted too many times in the last twenty-four hours for it to be quick and easy. He ignored the additional pain, and as soon as he was able he launched himself straight into the air and took off after Jasmine. The fact that he knew where she was going, and that she had to obey traffic laws, gave him the advantage, and within a couple of minutes he'd caught up to her.

Part of him wanted to land right on the top of her damn car, and say to hell with the whole invisibility thing while he was at it, but four centuries of caution made such behavior anathema.

Still, it was surprisingly tempting. The way she'd sped away from him aroused his predatory instincts. While he prided himself on his ability to reason his way through even his most animalistic instincts, something about this whole situation was fucking with his head in a big way.

Unable to stop himself, he swooped down next to the driver's window and dropped the spell he used to make himself invisible—just for a moment. Partly, he wanted to let her know she wasn't alone, and partly he just wanted to mess with her the way she was messing with him. He wanted to show her that it would take a lot more than trying to hit him with a car to scare him off.

She did a double take, hitting her brakes hard, and he couldn't deny the surge of satisfaction he felt. Was it juvenile? Absolutely. Mean-spirited? Probably. But it was also amusing as hell, especially when she started mouthing curses at him like a drunken sailor. He couldn't hear what she was saying, but he read lips well enough to know that Jasmine had a talent for stringing words together in the most uncomplimentary manner possible.

He backed off, content to follow her for the next few blocks until she turned into the driveway of the house Dylan and Phoebe kept for visitors. Most of the time they lived deep in the cave he'd spent most of his day in, which was a few miles from his own, but while Jasmine was in town he was pretty sure they would stay at the house. Very few people who weren't true clan members were ever invited into Dylan's private cave. This was as it should be.

Still, he was almost disappointed when Phoebe came out of the house before Jasmine had even managed to turn her headlights off. He'd been looking forward to escorting her to the door and listening to her berate him as he did. It was sick and twisted, particularly for a man who wanted peace more than he wanted his next breath, but something about Jasmine brought out the masochist in him.

He watched from on top of the roof as Jasmine grabbed her suit-case and a small, black medical bag from her trunk, then followed Phoebe toward the house. At the last second Jasmine glanced up at the roof and glared. It was a definite fuck-you, and it surprised him so much he almost lost his perch on the slanting tiles.

How had she known where he was when he was invisible? Phoebe could have sensed him—dragons usually could sense other dragons, invisible or not—but she was new to their world, still learning their ways. She'd given no indication that she'd known he was there, and surely she would have waved if she had noticed him.

No, somehow Jasmine had figured out where he was without Phoebe tipping her off. Maybe she'd just been guessing. After all, the roof was the best place for a very large dragon to land. It wasn't as if there were tons of places to hang out where he wouldn't be in the way, since even though he was invisible, his bulk still took up space. People could still walk into him if he was blocking the sidewalk and cars could still hit him in the street.

That had to be it, he decided uneasily, as he heard the front door close. She hadn't known he was on the roof—she'd just been playing the odds. Yeah, right. And if he believed that, someone probably had a bridge they wanted to sell him.

God, mating had more nuances than he had ever imagined—and he hadn't even told Jasmine they were mated. Considering her reac-tion to his attempt to heal her, he didn't even want to imagine what she'd say about the whole bound for eternity thing.

Deep in thought, he took the long way back to his own cave. He was tired, exhausted really, yet for the first time in a long time he was enjoying the night. The stars looked brighter than usual, the desert less stark and lonely. The night air felt great brushing against his face, his scales, and he closed his eyes, reveling in the beauty all around him.

As he flew, he paid attention to his surroundings, to the night animals whirling through the sky below him and scampering across the dark desert sand. More than once he found himself wishing he could show Jasmine something amusing, only to remember that it was impossible. She wasn't dragon. She couldn't fly with him, and even if he carried her, her human eyes would never be able to see what his could.

The dragon didn't care about any of that. He just wanted her next to him as he flew, wanted her under him while he did all kinds of wicked things to her body. And he had to admit, the beast had a point. Jasmine was completely unsuitable for him and everything he didn't want in a mate, but she sure as hell got his blood pumping.

What he was supposed to do with her beyond that was anybody's guess.

The markers leading up to his cave—invisible to all but him— appeared below, and Quinn plunged downward. He loved this part, loved the feel of the wind as it rushed past his face. Loved the way the ground rushed up to meet him. Loved the pounding of his heart as he waited until the last second to pull up.

The ground was looming closer and closer. He knew he should pull up. He was getting too close. But he just tucked his wings in and arrowed straight at the ground.

Suddenly a huge red and bronze dragon came out of nowhere and knocked into him, hard. Quinn went spinning backward through the air. After a few hundred yards, he got his equilibrium back. When he finally managed to stop somersaulting, he dropped to the ground. He'd started shifting before his feet touched the ground.

"What the hell was that!" he yelled, striding back to where the dragon was standing, watching him with fiery eyes. "You could have killed both of us."

The other dragon finally started to shift and Quinn waited impatiently as its wings folded against its back, compressing until they became muscle again. Next were the talons, followed by a shift in skin color and texture, the reshaping of the skeletal structure and finally, the rehumanization of the features.

"I was trying to save your sorry ass!" Logan yelled back, completely unconcerned that they were both naked. It was hard to maintain any modesty among shifters. "What the fuck were you thinking?"

"I was thinking that I like freedom and speed. I wasn't going to do anything stupid."

"Yeah, well, too late. That was the dumbest stunt I've ever seen. There was no way you were going to pull up before you hit the ground, and we both know it."

"Do we?" baited Quinn. "I've done it before."

"Really? That means you're even stupider than I thought. And I didn't think that was possible."

"Careful. You've already hit me once tonight. Keep pushing and I'll start pushing back."

"Well, that would be an improvement, wouldn't it?"

"What's that supposed to mean?"

"You think I don't know you well enough to see what you're going through?" Logan demanded. "You're off your game, Quinn, and more fucked up than I've ever seen you."

"You're exaggerating."

"Bullshit. You just don't know when to ask for help. You've had a crap year, man. A crap few years. No one's denying that. But you can't do this."

Quinn's fingers wanted to curl into fists, but he kept them relaxed with an effort. "Can't do what?"

"Can't go getting all self-destructive, you know? Things are going to get better."

"Are they? Really?"

"Of course they are!" Logan clapped him on the back. "It just takes time."

The slap on the back turned his tolerance to impatience. A man could be expected to take only so much feel-good bullshit, especially from another naked man. "Wow, you're pulling out all the stops tonight. Where did you get that—a Hallmark card?"

Logan's eyes narrowed when he realized Quinn was messing with him. "Fuck you. I'm worried about you."

"Awww, that's so sweet. Now I feel all warm and fuzzy inside." He reached out and shoved Logan hard enough that his friend stumbled back a good five yards.

"Shit." Logan caught himself before his bare ass hit the desert sand, but it was damn close. Quinn couldn't help being a little disappointed. Maybe he could get another shot in.

"Don't even try it, asshole." Logan shoved past him and headed for Quinn's cave. "And don't ever say 'warm and fuzzy' again. It makes you sound like an idiot—especially when you're naked."

For the first time in longer than he could remember, Quinn really laughed. It felt good. "Well, isn't that the pot calling the kettle black. What the hell was all that 'Things will get better' bullshit, anyway?"

"Excuse me for being concerned. I wasn't going to watch you commit suicide—I was trying to be all sensitive and shit." With the ease of long friendship, Logan strode straight through the outer chambers of the cave into the back section Quinn used as a bedroom. He yanked a couple pairs of jeans out of a drawer, followed by a couple of T-shirts, then fired one of each at Quinn.

"I wasn't trying to kill myself, you moron." Quinn quickly slipped into the clothes before heading back down the long and twisting passageway toward the refrigerator he kept in the front chamber. He didn't light the way—let Logan do it himself or chance running into the sharp stalactites and stalagmites that protruded from the ceilings and floors.

Once Quinn reached the front chamber that served as his living room, he grabbed a couple of beers from the cavern he had used magic to transform into a makeshift refrigerator and tossed one to Logan before settling himself on the long couch that stretched the length of his living room. Sometimes being able to wield dragon magic really paid off—especially if it meant you had a cold beer waiting for you in the middle of a cave.

"Oh, really? Then what were you doing? Practicing for your next stint at the circus?" Logan eased onto a large gypsum formation that looked like a giant balloon chair and stretched his long legs out in front of him.

Quinn flipped him off. As he did, he remembered Jasmine doing the same to him. What was she doing now? Was she in the shower? Climbing into bed? For a moment, he tormented himself with images of his mate in a skimpy pair of pajamas.

He felt himself grow hard and forced himself to banish the picture. Focusing on Logan again, he said, "I was just letting off some steam. Things have been tense around here for a while."

"There are better ways to do that than trying to break every bone in your body," Logan answered with a really big grin.

Quinn snorted as he kicked his feet up on the stalagmite formation that doubled as his coffee table. He wondered again about Jasmine.

"I could set you up on a date, you know. There are a lot of women—"

"I don't need your pimping services."

"Not *that* kind of date. But now that you mention it . . ." Logan looked thoughtful. "When *was* the last time you got laid?"

"About an hour and a half ago, thanks," Quinn answered, and he had the satisfaction of watching Logan choke on his beer.

"Well, hell. Maybe I should be asking you to set me up."

"Trust me. You couldn't handle her."

"Oh, yeah?" Logan drained his beer, then went for another one. "Now I'm intrigued. Spill."

Quinn pretended to consider it for a second, then said, "No."

"Now that's not right—you gotta let a guy live vicariously."

"Not after he knocked me out of the sky at two hundred miles an hour."

"God, you've gotten wimpy. It was more like a hundred and seventy-five. And I was trying to save your life."

"So you said. But since I wasn't trying to die . . ."

"Well, I didn't know you'd just gotten laid. If I had, I would have left you alone. No guy kills himself after good sex." He paused. "It was good sex, right?"

"That seems like faulty logic," Quinn commented, ignoring Logan's question. "What if I'd just wanted one last before-I-die lay?"

"Did you?"

"No."

"Well, then, the logic stands. And don't think I haven't realized that you dodged my question."

"Wow, nothing gets by you."

It was Logan's turn to flip him the bird. "Well, if you won't give me any of the details—which really sucks, by the way—can you at least tell me who it is?"

"What is this, junior high? Make me up a list and I'll put an X in the box next to the right name."

Logan laughed, but let the matter drop. They sat in companionable silence for a while, drinking their beers and thinking.

Quinn's mind wandered to Jasmine and then to his own parents' mating. Theirs had been a powerful connection—instantaneous, his father once told him. Much like Quinn's and Jasmine's. And like Jasmine, his mother had been a strong, powerful woman. It was her strength that had gotten her killed, leaving his father alone—and lonely—for much of his adult life.

Was he destined to repeat his father's mistakes? Waiting at home, healing, while Jasmine was out fighting battles she couldn't hope to win? He didn't want it to be like that, couldn't stand the thought of following in his parents' footsteps, but he was realistic enough to know that that was probably exactly where he was headed.

He was so lost in thought, so worried about what the future might bring for him and Jasmine, that he was barely paying attention when Logan asked, "So, if you can't tell me who she is, at least tell me what she's like."

"Complicated." The word popped out of his mouth before he even realized he was going to say it. "She's very complicated."

"Come on, really? How complicated could she possibly be?"

"You have no idea." And in what was turning out to be his modus operandi these days—offering way too much information without thinking it through—Quinn lifted up his sleeve and showed Logan his recently altered tattoo.

It took the other man a few seconds to understand what he was seeing, but when he did, his mouth dropped wide-open. "Jesus Christ! Is that what I think it is?"

Quinn didn't bother to answer, just let the arm of his shirt fall back where it belonged.

"You're mated, man? You're fucking mated, and you didn't bother to tell any of us?"

"Yeah, well, it was a sudden kind of thing."

"How sudden could it be? *You're mated.*"

"You can stop saying that."

"I could, but then I'd lose any chance of wrapping my head around it. How could you be *mated*? Who is she—and don't even bother with any of that keeping quiet bullshit. This is your mate. *Your mate*. Congratulations, by the way. That's awesome."

"I don't know if I'd go that far," Quinn snapped. "I'm still getting used to the idea."

"You keep saying that, but I don't get it. You have to have been seeing her for a while—the mating thing doesn't just occur randomly. Both of you have to decide—"

"That's not what happened."

Logan shifted forward in his chair, staring at him. "What does that mean?"

"It means the band just showed up, the morning after we first had sex. I don't know how or why—it just did."

"And what does she say about it?"

"She's not dragon—she doesn't know what it means. Besides, she was long gone before the thing even appeared."

"Well, shit." Logan shook his head, as if trying to clear it. "You mean, she's gone?" The look of horror on his face underscored just how serious the situation was. Like Quinn needed someone to point it out for him. If Jasmine left him, he'd never find another mate, not while she was alive. He'd never be able to have children, never be able to form any kind of connection to another woman beyond the most basic, sexual one.

Quinn had never been that guy. It wasn't like he'd spent his life searching for his mate the way Dylan had, but that didn't mean he liked one-night stands. He liked being in a relationship, liked caring about the woman he was sleeping with. If his mate rejected him, he'd never have that again.

Not that he was exactly thinking about sleeping with another woman right then. Shit, all he could think about was Jasmine and how it felt to be inside her. How it felt to be held and kissed and touched by her. No, he wasn't interested in another woman and doubted that he ever would be. Much as it was a huge pain in the ass, the universe had obviously known exactly what it was doing when it had paired the two of them up. At least on his side.

"Wait a minute. You said you were with her tonight. How could she—"

"It's Jasmine Kane."

"Who?"

"*Jasmine Kane*. The hematologist Phoebe called in."

"The blond hottie from the lab this afternoon?" Logan's eyes nearly bugged out of his head. "You're mated to *her*?"

"Yes."

"When did this happen?" Logan sputtered.

"I met her in a bar the night after Michael died. I didn't know who she was."

"And she's human?"

"Yep."

"Are you sure? She took the dragon thing pretty well."

"I'm sure."

"Huh." Logan stared at him for a second before adding, "And here I thought you were depressed enough to kill yourself."

"Depending on how this thing ends up, don't rule it out."

"I guess." Logan rolled his empty beer bottle between his hands. "Fate can be a real bitch."

Quinn lifted his beer to his mouth, drained it. "*You* have no fucking idea."

"So what are you going to do about it?"

He shook his head. "*I* have no fucking idea."

"Well, as long as you have a plan."

"Damn straight."

CHAPTER NINETEEN

He'd fucked the bitch. Right there in the laboratory like an animal in heat. It was disgusting. She'd been in the room right next to Quinn's lab and had heard the whole thing. It had taken every ounce of self-control she had not to "accidentally" bust in on them.

Shaking her head, she turned up her iPod and tried to lose herself in the music as she walked to work. It was getting harder and harder to do the deeper she got into this thing.

Oh, she wasn't afraid of being caught—she was too good for that and the rest of them were too stupid. Even Quinn and Dylan didn't have a clue what it was she was doing, and they were two of the smartest dragons the clan had. As long as she could keep them in the dark, she was home free.

She slammed open the door to the Dragonstar clinic and every head in the place came up. One quick glance at her and they went back to their business. Idiots. Sheep. They deserved what they were getting.

Rage ate at her, making her movements jerky and uncoordinated. She told herself to calm down—the last thing she needed was for someone to remember her acting oddly. Not that it really mattered, she was totally covered. Totally safe. But still, it never hurt to be on the cautious side.

She walked to the back room, where she stored her purse in her locker before heading up to the front to sign in. The head nurse wanted to chat a little, and though it was the absolute last thing she felt like doing, she stayed and spoke with her. After all, she still had a few minutes before she officially had to clock in, and it would look odd if she was the first one at her station, ready to go. She'd never been that employee.

Finally, the clock wound down and she wandered up the hall to where she would spend the next nine hours, minus two coffee breaks and a lunch break. Lucky, lucky her.

Except she was lucky, wasn't she? If she didn't have this job and the ability to float between the clinic and the lab, how many opportunities would have passed her by? And if she hadn't had those opportunities, then Brock would have gotten rid of her a long time before. So maybe she'd lay off the complaining—at least until Brock made good on his promise to get her out of here.

It had been days since Michael had died and Quinn still wasn't showing any signs of being sick. Sure, he had all but shut down emotionally—which was a plus, as she figured it was only a matter of time before he offed himself.

But Brock didn't want to wait for him to commit suicide, especially not if it meant his little virus wasn't as foolproof as he'd thought. These new batches were supposed to mutate—infect one person and then anyone with similar DNA would be susceptible to the virus. It was a genius idea, especially considering how hard it was to get close to Dylan and his sentries. They were too strong, too aware, too fucking paranoid to ever let someone sneak up on them and inject them. But most of their family members weren't.

Look at Marta, Dylan's sister. It had been pathetically easy to inject her and the virus had done its job very nicely. Her funeral pyre had barely been cold when her daughter got sick. Sure, Dylan hadn't contracted the virus as they'd planned, which was a total bummer. Brock had been furious; he had taken the virus back to his scientists so they could be certain all the kinks had been worked out.

But they'd been wrong, obviously, as Quinn was showing no signs of getting ill. It was freaking out Brock—and his little scientist dudes. Making them think that they weren't as smart as they thought they were, that the virus wasn't as all-consuming as it should be. She was determined to prove that the plan would still work, and she knew just how to do it.

Once at her station, she triple checked the list of appointments for the day, as if she didn't have the damn register memorized. But still, better to be safe . . . and yes, there he was, fourth on the list. Brian Alexander. Ten a.m. She could hardly wait.

The first hour passed a little slowly, though she knew it would pick up later in the day. She rushed through the first few people who ended up in her chair, wanting to make sure she was free when Brian walked in. If she wasn't, if she missed this opportunity, it would be another two weeks before she got the chance again. This would make Brock very unhappy, and after his last temper tantrum, she was going to try very, very hard to keep him in a good mood.

She was just finishing up with her latest walk-in when Brian showed up, all smiles and upbeat attitude. His brown hair was a little long, a little shaggy, and his blue eyes gleamed brightly, despite the fact that he'd been sick for the last year with one of the few diseases natural to dragon shifters. It was in remission, but the clan doctors had him coming in for twice-monthly blood tests.

"Hey you," she said with a grin, as she finished the paperwork on the previous patient. "Come on over here and tell me what you've been up to these last couple of weeks."

He smiled at her. "Not a lot. Just finishing up a big project at work and hanging with the family. The baby took her first steps the other day—do you want to see her latest picture?"

No. She recoiled at the thought, horrified at the idea of looking into his daughter's face. Brian didn't notice her reaction; he pulled out his wallet and opened it up to a photo of a beautiful baby with big blue eyes, a wide, toothless smile and chubby pink cheeks. Her golden blond ringlets were pulled up with heart-shaped barrettes, and she was wearing a turquoise-and-yellow sun suit that left her plump legs bare.

"Isn't she a beauty?" he asked.

"Definitely," she answered, trying to pull her gaze away from the picture. But she was spellbound by it, hypnotized by the sight of the pretty little girl on wobbly legs. "How old is she now?" The question spilled from her before she could stop it.

"Ten months. Melinda is already planning her first birthday party. It's crazy how fast they grow up. Jake is already seven."

"Oh, yeah?" she said, as she signed her initials on the bottom of his slip, then pulled out the five test tubes she needed for his blood. "That does seem awfully quick. It seems like it wasn't very long ago that he was tottering down the halls here in search of the candy machine."

"No joke." He sighed. "And then they grow up."

"That they do." She reached for the elastic band she needed to wrap around his upper bicep. "Which arm are we doing today?"

"The left, I think. It hasn't seen half the action the right has lately."

"The left it is." She secured the band. "Pump your fist a few times for me."

"You're such a slave driver," he answered, but did as she told him.

"Someone has to be." She cleaned his arm with alcohol, then picked up the needle and test tube. At the same time, she palmed the syringe she'd been carrying around for nearly a week for just this purpose.

After surreptitiously popping the cap off, she turned to him. "You might want to look away this time. We don't want you passing out or anything."

"That happened one time, while I was in treatment, and you've never let me live it down."

"Yeah, well, a girl's got to get her fun somewhere."

"I personally think you're a closet sadist," he teased, but at the last minute he looked away, just as she'd known he would.

And then she was doing it, sliding the needle to take blood from his vein at the exact same time she slid the syringe's needle into his arm about two centimeters away. Sometimes it was really nice to be a dragon. The big hands so often paid off.

"Ouch!" He jumped, and she angled her body so that she blocked his view of his arm as she slowly lowered the plunger on the syringe. "That hurts more than usual—are you sure you got the vein?"

"I did. See?" She held up the first test tube so he could see that it was filling with blood. "Sorry, I used a bigger gauge this time. There's more blood to take because it's your six-month checkup, so I thought it might speed the process along. Next time I'll use the smaller needle."

She finished administering the shot and pulled the needle out quickly, dropping it into the trash can by the side of her workstation. There was no way she was risking leaving the thing in the Sharps disposal case for them to find later. She'd just have to remember to take the trash out during her first break.

"It's no problem. It doesn't hurt anymore."

She switched test tubes, continuing to banter with him as she did. A cold drop of sweat rolled slowly down her back, and she wasn't sure if it was because she was relieved it was done—or because she couldn't believe she'd gotten away with it again.

In the end, it didn't really matter. Brian was infected. The rest was only a matter of time.

CHAPTER TWENTY

Jasmine stared down at the latest viral sample—the one taken from the most recent victim—with something very akin to awe. It was a little thing, as all viruses were, but amazingly wily and sophisticated. Certainly, it was more sophisticated than anything else she'd seen, and that was saying something, as she'd spent nearly every waking moment of the last ten years studying blood-borne viruses and bacteria.

This one was something special. If it wasn't causing so much damage, she'd have to admire it—and the people who created it. And it had very definitely been created. Phoebe and Quinn were dead right about that. Nowhere in nature, or the CDC's research banks, which she had spent most of the night combing, did anything exist with this genetic makeup or combination of symptoms. It was impossible to imagine that the structure of the virus could even cause the range of symptoms that it did, but somehow its engineer had packed everything he could into the thing.

Neural damage combined with liquefaction of organs.

Sky-high temperatures with rapid decay of lower extremity flesh.

Brain damage with quick, severe bleed-outs.

It was the stuff sci-fi horror movies were made of, and yet here it was right in front of her. A biological weapon so deadly, so devastating, that it made her uneasy just to be looking at it.

176 • TESSA ADAMS

It was just one more oddity in the weirdness that had suddenly taken over her life. Her best friend was a dragon. Her lover—or soon-to-be ex-lover, as she was still furious with Quinn—was a dragon. Why should one little virus, even one that could do all this, make her nervous? Especially now that she was pretty much living in the middle of an entire coven of dragons?

She paused for a moment, turned the word over in her mind. Was coven the right word, or did that apply only to witches? What did one call a community of dragons? Was there even a name for it?

"Crazy, isn't it?"

Phoebe's voice came from right over her shoulder, so close that it made Jasmine jump, yanking her attention from her random musings back to the work in the laboratory.

"What's crazy?" she asked.

"That such an innocuous looking virus could cause such damage—and so quickly."

"I was just thinking that. I was really surprised when I was looking through the slides yesterday. I was expecting something more complex than this typical icosahedron structure. Especially considering the damage it wreaks."

"I know." Phoebe scooted a rolling stool next to Jasmine and traced her finger over a few of the straight sides of the nearly-spherical-shaped virus reflected on the computer screen. "I'm still not sure how they managed to engineer it this way, so that all the different strains managed to fit inside these twenty sharp-edged sides. Especially since this thing is so much smaller than the typical HIV virus, but much more potent and fast acting."

"Yet it reproduces like HIV." Jasmine clicked a few keys and pulled up Quinn's exhaustive lab notes.

"It does. Its reproduction is atypical, which is just one of the major problems we have. We have to immunize against it because it's a virus, but we have to do that while dealing with the fact that instead of creating RNA, it actually creates DNA and maps that DNA to the host cells."

"DNA immunization is pretty cutting edge, but it has been done."

"Yeah," Phoebe said, "in a *laboratory*, not in real-life situations on any kind of reasonable scale. But that's not the only problem—this thing has so many different strains, and those strains mutate so fast, it's impossible to get a handle on it for long. We can trigger an immune system response to the foreign DNA—for a short time—but once the virus mutates, that reaction is almost useless.

"Plus this damn thing actually alters its host's DNA within hours of infection, so that even if you can get the immune system to fight it, it's actually killing off the host at the same time it kills off the virus."

"This isn't the first virus in history to do that, Phoebe. We've managed to at least partially immunize against some of them."

"That's what I thought. I told Dylan weeks ago, when I first realized what was going on, that I could tear this thing apart, get inside it, and do exactly that. But I forgot that we're not dealing with human DNA, and dragon DNA doesn't do well with any kind of alteration."

Jasmine looked sharply toward her friend. "You know this for a fact?"

"Quinn does. There's a whole section in his notes on it. This isn't the first time that someone's thought about it." She scrolled through Quinn's notes until she got to a section title, Deviations to DNA. "Dragon doctors started messing with genetic engineering about the same time human doctors did—but the results are much more frightening for us."

"'Us' meaning dragons?"

"Yeah." Phoebe flushed. "Sorry. I know it's weird for you."

"Not really," Jasmine lied. "I just wanted to be sure I understood what you were saying."

"I think that's why this disease spreads so quickly. Once dragon DNA is severely altered, dragons lose the power to cloak themselves within a couple of weeks. Their ability to shift quickly becomes unpredictable or nonexistent and their control over the elements—over fire—is destroyed. Those that don't burn to death are locked inside human bodies with no way out, and the beast goes insane. Annihilates itself and its human side in the process."

Jasmine recoiled in horror, especially as she imagined her friend or Quinn suffering the symptoms Phoebe had just described. Even worse, the doctor in her was devastated by the loss of the best shot they had at defeating the disease.

She didn't voice her thoughts to Phoebe—they'd been friends long enough that she didn't have to—and they worked in silence for more than an hour, the quiet broken only when Jasmine paused to ask the other doctor a question about something that she'd read in Quinn's notes. When she finally got to the end of the third section of notes, she pushed away from the desk and rubbed her eyes wearily.

"I know it's a lot of information to take in at once. I'm sorry about that." Phoebe was watching her with concerned eyes. "I haven't even asked how you're doing."

"I'm fine."

"No, you're not. You're limping and favoring both your left side and your right arm."

"It's no big deal."

"You were blown up! That's a pretty huge deal in my mind."

"Well, I survived." Jasmine shifted uncomfortably, wondered how she could move the conversation back to the virus. She hated talking about her injuries, and she sure as hell didn't want to do it here, in the middle of Quinn's lab. Maybe it was stupid, but after their argument the night before, the last thing she wanted was for him to know just how badly she'd been hurting. "I'm just a little tired."

"Well, then, it's break time," Phoebe said decisively, glancing at her watch. "Come on, it's almost two. I'll treat you to a late lunch."

"I had a carton of yogurt from the fridge in the break room a couple of hours ago. I'm good for a little longer." But she stood up and stretched anyway.

"Getting stiff?"

She gritted her teeth, told herself not to snap. Phoebe was just being a good friend, she reminded herself. It wasn't her friend's fault that her concern felt as heavy and smothering as a wool blanket in the middle of the desert in July.

"No more than usual."

"Still, it will probably do you good to relax a little. You should—"

"It will do me good to work." She didn't snap, but the words came out a lot more clipped and abrupt than usual.

Phoebe didn't say anything for a minute, and Jasmine felt like a total jerk. Just because she couldn't stand sympathy was no reason to take it out on her friend. She opened her mouth to apologize, when Phoebe laughed.

"I'm sorry. I'm hovering when I swore I wouldn't. But new habits are hard to break."

Jasmine raised an eyebrow. "You make a habit of hovering around Dylan these days, huh?"

"I do. I swear that man is always injured. And if it's not him, then it's one of his sentries. These dragons are powerful and have extreme longevity, but they're nowhere near as careful as they should be. They think they're invincible when they're clearly not. They can get hurt as easily as anyone else—more so, because they're always fighting." She shook her head. "Dylan's one of the worst, but Quinn and Logan aren't much better."

Jasmine's entire body tightened at the mention of the other doctor. "Quinn?" she asked as casually as she could manage. "I thought he was the clan's healer?"

"Oh, he is. But he's also usually right in the middle of the fight. I swear, that man's been injured five or six times just since I've been here."

"He has? He certainly doesn't look it." She hadn't seen any evidence of new injuries the one night she'd spent in his bed—in fact, she'd only seen a couple of scars on him at all, and they had looked decades old. But she couldn't exactly say that to Phoebe, not without admitting what the two of them had been up to.

"They never do. They heal super fast and only scar if it's a pretty big injury, or if Quinn can't get to them in time to do his thing." She wiggled her fingers like a magician.

Jasmine opened her mouth to ask exactly what Quinn's thing was—she'd been looking for just such an opportunity since she'd seen him heal Tyler the day before. But she hesitated, not wanting to sound like an idiot. She didn't know what to ask, or how to put her questions into words. For a woman who prided herself on both her directness and her eloquence, it was a strange feeling—one she didn't care for at all.

At a loss for words, Jasmine did the only thing she could reasonably do under the circumstances; she dove back into Quinn's notes like they were the most interesting things she'd ever seen.

To a certain extent, they were. She was fascinated by this virus, even as she was repulsed by it. She felt the same way toward Ebola, only magnified about a hundred times. Especially since she knew how Ebola was transmitted—and how to prevent it. While the vaccine for the virus was still in test trials, good hygiene and medical practices usually kept it from spreading. But with this thing . . . She shook her head. Nothing seemed to work with this virus, including top-of-the-line medical care and prevention.

In some cases they had clear injection sites or documentation that someone had been infected during a fight with the Wyvernmoons. But in still others, no matter how hard Phoebe and Quinn worked to trace it, they couldn't find the point of origin for the virus. Was it from close contact, as they were often in close proximity to other victims? But then, why didn't all the dragons close to the infected dragons contract the disease?

She went round and round in her head, trying to find an answer, but it eluded her. After reexamining a number of cases where the infection route was ambiguous, she was more certain than ever that those victims had also been deliberately infected. But no injection site wound had been found, and from what she could tell, they had been meticulous in searching for it. Still, it had to happen somehow . . .

Oral ingestion, she wondered, making a note to herself. Was intestinal absorption even possible with this virus? And if it wasn't, what the hell were they missing?

The whole thing was perplexing, and a little frightening if she allowed herself to think of Phoebe contracting it—or Quinn. She wouldn't wish this thing on her worst enemy, let alone people she cared about. She hadn't been sure how to classify Quinn, even before their fight the night before, and she sure as hell didn't know now, but she knew he didn't fall into enemy territory.

One touch from him turned her inside out, and the times she'd been with him had been more powerful than anything she'd ever experienced. And yet, it hadn't been all about sex—at least not after the very first time. She enjoyed talking to him, listening to him, and when he'd been hurt, vulnerable, she'd wanted nothing more than to take care of him. She tried to tell herself the reaction stemmed from her medical training, but she'd never been very good at lying to herself. What she felt for Quinn—after two short days—had nothing to do with her being a doctor and everything to do with being a woman.

It was annoying, infuriating. Confusing. While she didn't mind the first two, she hated the hell out of the third. She'd gone into their one-night stand with her eyes wide-open—or at least as wide-open as they could be, considering the fact that she hadn't had a clue Quinn was anything but a very sexy man when she'd seen him at the bar.

Still, she'd done it for the sex. For the fun. For the one night of companionship. But now that they were working together, everything was complicated. She wasn't supposed to think about him when he wasn't with her. Or worry about how he was feeling when he extended himself too far. Or wonder whether she'd hurt his feelings with her display of temper.

But she was thinking, wondering, and worrying. And it was driving her insane. On the surface he might be a good match for her—a brilliant doctor whose research was both solid and cutting edge, not to mention a handsome, sexy man who played her body like a maestro on his favorite instrument.

But underneath it all, he was tormented by demons she couldn't even imagine, a member of a community that thought nothing of draining him dry again and again and forcing her to watch. And he was very, very, very used to getting his own way. Whether it was with women or work or his relationships with the men around him, Quinn commanded respect—and obedience. She was okay with the first but the second sucked ass.

Yet when she compared herself to him on those fronts, she had to admit he seemed better adjusted than she did. Though she'd put her own demons behind her a long time ago, she still had a hard time letting people get close to her and settling down. She admired the roots he had here and the importance of his role in the Dragonstar community, but the thought of staying in one place for longer than a few months gave her hives. She could not, absolutely could not, imagine building a place for herself here, or anywhere else for that matter. Not a solid place, like Quinn had. Not a place that mattered.

As for the obedience thing, she could barely restrain a laugh. Her father had beat the hell out of her throughout her entire childhood in an effort to knock the willfulness out of her, as he had her mother. It hadn't worked and she didn't relish spending years of her life struggling with a dominant male animal for supremacy. She had better things to do with her time.

Since she couldn't remember one of those things at the moment, Jasmine did what she did best. She buried herself in her research until she couldn't think of anything—or anyone—else.

CHAPTER TWENTY-ONE

Quinn strode down the clinic hallway, deliberately blocking out everything around him as he made a beeline for his office. He'd been at the clinic for more than eight hours, since he'd stopped in at six a.m. on his way to the lab. He'd planned to take care of his duties early in the morning, before anyone was around. But then the doctor who worked the first shift at the clinic had called in sick, and Quinn got stuck doing his rounds.

Working an extra shift normally wouldn't have bothered him, but today it was the last thing he wanted to do. He was dying to get to the lab—and Jasmine. He wanted to hear her thoughts on the virus, and he also just wanted to see her. To smooth things over from the night before. To listen to her snipe at him in that sexy voice of hers. To see her mischievous grin when she got the better of him and smell the tart sweetness that was so much a part of her.

He wished she was with him now. Not because he needed anyone to hold his hand while he did his duty but because . . . He sighed. Just because. He really didn't want to do this alone. Though he had friends who would be happy to step in, she was the one he wanted by his side when he completed this most unpleasant of tasks.

Hell, he didn't want to do it at all, but it couldn't be put off anymore. It had been almost three full days since Michael had died, and he still hadn't made arrangements for laying him to rest.

Logan had asked him about it the night before, and Quinn had known, then, that he was being selfish. He hadn't forgotten Michael's death, or the arrangements—how could he when his brother's loss was an ache inside him so large that he was almost swamped with despair? He'd been unable to face it. So he had left him in the cold, forbidding morgue for over two days now. He had failed to make arrangements for his funeral. He had failed Michael—in life and in death.

It would stop now, today, even though the thought of looking at another funeral pyre was enough to make him sick. He'd already watched Cecily burn this year, and his brother Liam, and so many more of his friends and patients. Attending one more funeral, one more torch bearing, one more fire, was more than he could bear—especially when, this time, it would be Michael turning to ash.

Born in fire, die in fire, reclaimed in fire. Never had it been a more bitter pill to swallow.

As he neared his office, he became aware of the nurses and other clinic personnel staring at him, and he couldn't help but read censure in their gazes. What kind of brother was he?

What kind of brother concentrated on his own pain instead of taking care of the last needs of his baby brother?

It wasn't like he was inexperienced at this, after all. He'd arranged the funerals for his parents, for each of his other brothers, for Cecily. He'd never dropped the ball with them. How he could have done so now was completely beyond him.

Furious with himself, he slammed his office door behind him and went straight to the file cabinet to get the forms necessary to release the body. Phoebe was the doctor on record, but he'd told her he would handle it.

He glanced down at the desk and saw that the forms had been neatly filled in, Phoebe's signature at the bottom of each one. She'd done it for him, after all. Had stayed here the night Michael had died and taken care of it, long after Quinn had fled like a coward, which he was very much afraid he was turning into.

If the forms were done, the only thing left was deciding when and where the funeral would be held. Like he gave a shit. Picking up a pen, he jotted off a short obituary containing the highlights of Michael's life, then wrote another note to the morgue supervisor, telling him when and where Michael's body should be delivered.

These instructions could just as easily have been given in person. He knew David was downstairs even now. But the lump in his throat made the idea of talking impossible, and if he had to listen to any more expressions of sympathy, he would probably lose it completely. He'd been overwhelmed when he'd first arrived back at the lab yesterday, with one person after another telling him how sorry they were about Michael. He'd wanted to scream, to roar, to lash out at them— to tell them that they were nowhere near as sorry as he was.

He hadn't, of course. He couldn't—not when everyone was being so nice to him, tiptoeing around him like he was the one who had died instead of his youngest brother. But God, the pain and the anger had grown until he'd wanted to tell them all to go to hell. That they didn't have a clue what he was feeling.

Instead, he'd accepted their condolences, and then he'd turned around and had sex with Jasmine on top of one of the lab tables. Because wasn't that what you did less than forty-eight hours after your brother died?

Goddamn this mating thing. Like he wasn't already fucked up enough, this had to be thrown into the mix, too? Thinking was hard enough without Jasmine messing with his head.

Miserable, aching, he laid his head down on the cool marble top of his desk and closed his eyes. He was tired, so tired. He wanted to say to hell with everything, to walk out into the desert and never come back.

If it weren't for Jasmine, he might actually do it.

He laughed bitterly at the thought. Right, like he would actually do that now, when his clan needed him more than ever. He might like to pretend he'd walk out, but he knew he wouldn't. He couldn't. His duty was too important. There were too many people relying on him, too many responsibilities he couldn't walk away from. But that only made him feel more trapped, and he didn't think he could take one more thing going wrong.

He thought back to the night before, to the way Jasmine had flown off the handle when he'd been trying to help her. He wanted to blame her—had spent most of the night doing just that—but what if it hadn't been her fault? What if he'd really been the cause of the whole thing, as she asserted, and he'd just been too stupid to know it? These insecurities weren't like him, but shit, his whole world was falling down around his ears, and it seemed pretty damn stupid to set himself up for more failure.

Was it possible to walk away from a mate? He'd never seen it happen, not in the more than four hundred years of his existence, but that didn't mean it wasn't possible. Jasmine wasn't dragon, after all—maybe that meant she didn't have the same ties to him that he had to her. God knew, she didn't have any trouble driving away from him the night before, even as his body still hummed from the satisfaction she'd given him.

Pushing away from the desk, he started to pace, barely aware that he was doing it. He couldn't take one more loss, one more failure. Maybe he kept making the same mistake of caring for people who couldn't be saved, but he wasn't a masochist. Not by a long shot. In fact, he was ready to do just about anything to make the agony clawing at his insides stop.

Leaving himself open to more pain, allowing Jasmine to hurt him and walk away, as she kept doing, seemed singularly stupid. Especially when one more loss would shatter him completely.

No, whatever was going on between them had to stop. He didn't have the emotional capacity to have a simple affair with her right now, and anything else was out of the question.

His dragon snapped at the thought, but Quinn pushed it back, told himself that leaving Jasmine alone was the best thing he could do under the circumstances. The only thing he could do. She was human and transitory and more fearless and foolish than he could tolerate. Better to lose her now, before he'd ever really had her, than to lose her later when she'd become everything to him.

No, things with Jasmine had to end, he told himself again, as he dropped Michael's paperwork on his secretary's desk. Linda would take care of it, make sure everything was perfect for Michael. Because while he knew the funeral was his responsibility, Quinn also knew that he couldn't do any more. Not if he wanted to hold on to his last thread of sanity. Just as he knew, instinctively, that spending any more time with Jasmine would snap his control as easily as a hurricane did a tree branch.

He couldn't let that happen. Not now—he had too much work left to do.

She knew the second he entered the lab, which drove her nuts because it meant on some level she was waiting and listening for him when normally her work made her oblivious to the world. Feeling foolish— and more than a little annoyed—Jasmine forced herself not to turn toward him when he gave a general, "Hello."

"Hi, Quinn," Phoebe answered. "I was about to give up on you making it in today."

"Gerald called in sick—I stayed to cover the clinic."

Jasmine could feel the tension go through the room. "Sick?" Phoebe demanded, her voice tightening. "He doesn't have—"

"What he has is a hangover," Quinn said dryly. "His brother's bachelor party was last night."

"Oh, well. That's good."

"Yeah, just peachy. I love it when one of my doctors gets so blitzed he can't make it to work. It's not like I had planned on doing anything today."

"Poor baby. It must be so hard to be in such high demand." Phoebe's voice was low and teasing.

"Well, you should know. When's the last time Dylan got a full night's sleep?"

Phoebe groaned. "Don't even ask. Not since before that whole thing with the Wyvernmoons a couple months back. I swear he spends twenty out of every twenty-four hours trying to figure out how to end this." She glanced at Quinn. "Kind of like you, only from a different angle."

"I hope he's having better luck."

"Don't count on it."

"How about you?" he asked, and the only reason Jasmine knew he was talking to her was that his voice got about ten degrees cooler. "Do you have any brilliant ideas about this virus that Phoebe and I haven't thought of?"

"Not yet. But I'm not even halfway through your notes. They're incredibly thorough, by the way."

"Is that a compliment I hear, or are my ears deceiving me?"

She didn't like his mocking tone, or the look in his eyes that was one shade away from obnoxious. She obviously wasn't the only one who hadn't gotten over the night before, but at least she was being civil about it.

Then again, she had been the one to flip him off. Judging from the look on his face, that wasn't something alpha he-man dragons took in stride.

Not that she cared. The last thing she needed was a man hovering over her telling her what to do every second of every day. She'd gotten more than enough of that from her father when she was growing up, thank you very much. Never again would a man have that kind of control over her.

"It's a fact." She kept her voice a shade warmer than his. Professional, she liked to call it. Though it was a far cry from the husky tone she'd used to whisper naughty words to him the day before in this very lab. *Too bad, so sad.* They both would have to get over it.

"What's your gut tell you, Jasmine?" Phoebe jumped in after a long look at both of them. "I know you're too thorough of a researcher to really voice an opinion yet, but forget that for a second and just go with what you've got."

"I don't think—"

"Oh, come on, enlighten us." Quinn's tone was even more mocking. "You're the world-famous hematologist and infectious disease doctor. Surely you have an opinion on what you're seeing."

Jasmine's eyes narrowed even as she told herself not to rise to the bait. Quinn was in a mood, and was clearly happy to play games with her. She very definitely was not joining in.

"My opinion is inconclusive at this point."

"Screw inconclusive!" he snarled. Before she could so much as blink, Quinn was across the room and in her face. "You think I give a shit about your policies and procedures when my people are dying? Tell me what the hell you think is going on. I promise, we won't hold you to it."

"Quinn, she's only been looking at the evidence for twenty-four hours. Cut her a little slack," Phoebe cut in, putting a restraining hand on his arm.

For a second, he was about to shake her off, but then he relented. With a grimace, he took two large steps back from Jasmine.

"Sorry," he said. "I guess I'm a little punchier than I thought. I was up most of the night."

"It's okay. You've been through a lot. No one expects—" Phoebe broke off at the searing look Quinn sent Jasmine's way. Jasmine's eyes widened. She suddenly remembered what he'd told her in the hotel room that first night. She hadn't actually forgotten it, but with all the work on the virus and all the commotion over her feelings for Quinn, she hadn't given it much thought. He was alone. Sad and suffering and desperate to connect to another person.

God, she really was a bitch.

She suddenly realized that Michael—the brother he'd said he'd lost—had been one of the dragons to die from this virus. She looked at Quinn and understood the desperation behind his kisses, the way he had tried to bury himself in her, in their pleasure, so he didn't have to think about or feel anything else.

He blamed himself for his brother's death. God knew, he shouldn't—his research showed just how long and hard he'd fought to find a cure—but Quinn was the kind of man who believed he was responsible for everyone around him. She already knew that his belief that he was failing his clan was killing him, but believing he failed Michael must be the last straw. For a man who kept such tight control over himself and his world, this had to be a nightmare.

She wanted to say something to him, wanted to help ease his pain somehow. Before she could, Quinn crossed to his desk and started fiddling with his computer. Within seconds, he gave every appearance of being completely absorbed in work, but she knew he was as attuned to her as she was to him. She wondered if she'd been wrong the night before. Maybe he'd had some reason, besides wanting to be Mr. Macho, to insist on taking her to Phoebe's house. Maybe she shouldn't have fought him so hard. Maybe he had just been trying to protect her—and protect himself from losing someone else.

The thought freaked her out, and her self-preservation instincts kicked into overdrive. She wasn't that woman, she reminded herself frantically, the one who worried about why her man did what he did or how her words and actions affected him. She didn't pull punches, didn't try to fit into the boxes men tried to put her into.

And yet, as she glanced over at Quinn, he looked so alone. So desperately, completely alone, despite the fact that Phoebe was perched beside him on the desk, filling him in on the discussion they'd had before he'd shown up.

Suddenly, she felt churlish, even though she knew she'd been right not to give her opinion on the virus. He didn't look like he could take another disappointment, yet disappointment was all she had to offer. Because her gut opinion was that, in terms of this damn virus, the entire Dragonstar clan was completely screwed.

CHAPTER TWENTY-TWO

She'd been having little pangs of guilt all day, and she really didn't like the feeling. He wasn't the first dragon she'd infected by a long shot, but he was bothering her the most. Maybe it was the pictures of his children that were causing her all this grief.

What choice did she have? She was doing what she had to do to survive, she told herself firmly, ignoring the fact that she'd been surviving just fine before she met Brock.

Surviving, she thought, but not thriving. Here, she had to work for a living. She had to fight, if the need arose. She had to be ordinary.

But with Brock she wouldn't have to do anything she didn't want to, and ordinary wouldn't even enter her vocabulary. He'd promised to marry her, to make her the next queen of the Wyvernmoons when this whole thing was all over. She'd seen how the last queen lived and couldn't wait to get started.

She still had a few more things to do, one of which included dealing with the problem she was staring at on the closed-circuit television—as soon as possible. How to do it was the million-dollar question.

It was a shame the original plan hadn't worked. After all, working as closely as he had with Michael, Quinn should have contracted the virus. The fact that he hadn't astounded her and Brock, who wanted to step up the campaign. But she needed to get Quinn's DNA

192 • TESSA ADAMS

before they could move forward—as well as come up with a plan to
infect Quinn. He was entirely too strong, too suspicious. This was not
exactly helpful.

She studied the television, looking for a weakness. Looking for
anything she might be able to use against him. Brock was getting
worried about the medical team Dylan had assembled.

It was only a matter of time, the Wyvernmoon had said, until
they hit on a way to neutralize the virus. She didn't agree. They looked
like bumbling idiots to her.

Still, it was interesting to watch them, the three people Dylan had
placed all his hopes in. *The moron.* As if two human doctors—Phoebe
would always be human in her mind—and a healer who was so burnt
out he practically sizzled when he walked could make a dent in the
problem.

It would make her laugh if it wasn't so pathetic. Especially considering how angry Quinn looked right now. What she wouldn't give
to hear what they were saying. It must be a huge deal because Phoebe
looked pretty panicked. *What a wimp.* It galled her, bitterly, that after
almost half a millennium, Dylan had chosen that milquetoast to be
their queen.

She leaned forward, watched the screen intently, trying to read
their lips. But Quinn had his back to her now, and neither of the
females were talking. *Damn it.* She'd blown it when she'd installed
the camera earlier that week; she hadn't had time to hide the bug as
well before Quinn had come in.

If she'd stuck around a few minutes more, she could have slipped
it somewhere discreet, but he'd surprised her. She'd had to cut and
run and hope to slip in some other time and finish the job. But after
Michael got sick, security tightened, and her plan had gone to hell.
It was almost impossible to be in the lab alone. Too much work was
going on right now.

She enjoyed watching them scramble around like insects—
or would, if it wasn't for the new woman. She looked like a real

hard-ass, completely different from cream puff Phoebe, and so she stayed in front of the screen, watching, long after she should have.

The new doctor probably wouldn't find a cure for the disease—what did she know of dragons, after all—but she looked like she wouldn't go down without a fight, either. Plus, everyone said she was some bigwig from the CDC, as if that made her their salvation or something.

As if.

Then again, it would really suck if she were wrong and that woman *could* figure something out. Though it pained her to admit it, Dr. Jasmine Kane looked absolutely competent.

Her phone rang, and she ignored it. It wasn't the Dragonstar clan phone, but the one Brock had given her months ago. For the first few weeks, she'd jumped every time it rang, but then she'd figured out that was exactly what Brock wanted. It made him feel powerful, and the more powerful he felt, the more powerless he tried to make her. This was completely unacceptable—especially for a future queen. If she didn't hold her own now, she never would.

She glanced at the clock. She knew why he was calling. She was late for their meeting. She didn't want to go empty-handed, especially as the risks had tripled since Dylan and the other sentries had changed the safeguards. Of course, no one was supposed to know that, but she had her ways. Still, they hadn't given anyone the incantation to dissipate them, which meant that while she could get through them—all of the Dragonstars could—she would leave a record.

By itself it was no big deal. After all, they weren't prisoners. At the same time, she didn't want anyone knowing her comings and goings. It was a risk, and an unnecessary one if she didn't have anything to give Brock. This was a problem in and of itself. His goodwill—and interest in her body—only went so far. If she ceased being useful to him, she knew he wouldn't hesitate to find someone else to help him. This would leave her with nothing.

She shook her head. There was no help for it. She'd just have to find a way to get back in the lab and place the bug. The camera wasn't good enough, not at this juncture of the game. She needed to hear what they said, too.

She looked back at the camera just in time to see Quinn stare at the good Dr. Kane as if she were a banana split and he was a starving man. Kane didn't notice, but she didn't have the camera's bird's-eye view.

She'd thought the thing between them had just been two people blowing off a little steam, but now she wondered if she'd misread the situation. She'd known Quinn for a lot of years and had never seen him look like that.

Interesting. Maybe she wouldn't be going to the meeting empty-handed after all.

CHAPTER TWENTY-THREE

"Come on, I'll buy you dinner."

Quinn started at the sound of Jasmine's husky voice right behind him. She'd done it again—snuck up on him when the dragon usually issued a warning when anyone got so close. Stupid beast. It was as infatuated with Jasmine as Quinn was, and in the end it would probably be to their detriment.

"You want to buy me dinner?" He sounded like a damn parrot, but she was flip-flopping so much it was a miracle he didn't have whiplash.

"I do. Surely there's someplace to eat around here that stays open until ten at night?"

"Yeah, of course." He rubbed a hand over his tired eyes and tried his damnedest not to notice how good she smelled. Already, the dragon was scratching at him, wanting a repeat of the night before. But he was hyperaware of how gingerly Jasmine had been moving all evening. The fact that he'd done that to her, leaving her aching and angry, tore him up inside in a way the dragon couldn't hope to match.

"There's a twenty-four-hour diner a couple of blocks up. They make great pie."

She widened her eyes in fake surprise. "You want pie for dinner? I thought doctors were supposed to know better than that."

"And I suppose you plan on eating healthy?"

"Absolutely. I'll add ice cream to my apple pie. That covers three of the four food groups."

He laughed, then quickly straightened up his workstation. He was putting a couple of pens back in their spot in his top drawer when he realized Jasmine was watching him with a big grin. "What's so funny?"

"Nothing. I'm just surprised at the fact that you're a little OCD."

"A little?" He snorted. "When I was a kid, my oldest brother used to sneak into my room and move things around while I was out with my friends, then hang around and see if I noticed."

"Did you?"

"Always. I got my revenge though."

"Oh yeah?" She grabbed her keys from her workstation and headed for the door. "And what was that?"

"I filed his arrow blades down right before a big archery competition, then replaced them with hollow tipped ones I'd spent weeks working on. Every arrow he shot that day went spinning straight into the dust and he couldn't figure out why."

"That's ingenious!"

"I thought so. It was even worth the beating he gave me when he finally figured out what I'd done."

"I bet."

They let themselves out of the lab, and slowly worked their way down the hallway. He noticed that Jasmine smiled at both of the security guards they ran into, calling each by name as she said good night. He wasn't sure what it meant or even why he noticed, but he found it interesting.

"So, how far away is this diner?" she asked, as they walked into the night.

"A couple blocks east of here. Why?"

"Do you mind walking? I've been cooped up all day and would love a chance to stretch my legs."

"Sounds like a good idea to me. I've been inside all day as well."

Not to mention the fact that a walk would give him more time to talk to Jasmine, to get to know her.

He put his hand on the small of her back and guided her through the parking lot and onto the sidewalk. She stiffened at the first touch of his hand, but didn't say anything. He hoped that meant he was making a little progress, even as he reminded himself that he wasn't going to do this anymore.

One slice of pie never hurt anyone, a little voice inside of him whispered, and he decided to listen to it, even as his better judgment told him not to.

"I do have one question," she said, as they strolled down the street. "I thought the arrows used in archery competitions had plastic tips. How did you manage to file that down?"

He stopped for a second, staring down at her. "Phoebe didn't tell you?"

"Tell me what?" She looked wary, and a little intrigued.

"I'm four hundred and seventy-one years old, Jasmine. When I was a child, the only kind of arrows we had were tipped in iron."

"Yeah, right." She laughed and shoved at his shoulder.

"I'm serious."

She looked completely incredulous. "That's not possible."

"Why? Because humans have a much more finite lifespan? You took biology. You should know that different species have different life spans."

"But you're talking about living nearly half a millennium!"

"I am. Surely you read in my notes about our longevity."

"Yeah, but I was thinking more along the lines of a hundred years, not . . . I don't even know how long." She looked him over from head to toe. "It's not like you look like you're on death's door or anything."

He laughed. "I've got a few good years left in me."

"How many?"

"I don't know. Provided I don't catch this damn disease or go down in battle, maybe five or six hundred more."

Her mouth dropped open. "I just can't—that doesn't make any sense to me. You're four hundred years old?"

"Four hundred and seventy-one, give or take a few months."

"Right, of course. Because those few months are critical when it comes to being accurate." She shook her head. "And you'll live to be a thousand or so?"

"Probably."

"Wow. That's unbelievable." Then she did the damnedest thing. She stopped in her tracks, reached up and rested her palm against his cheek, while her thumb tenderly stroked over his skin. "No wonder you look so tired. Four hundred years is a long time to carry the kind of responsibilities that you do."

The defenses he'd spent all afternoon building against her crumbled like a sandcastle in a windstorm. He covered her hand with his own, then closed his eyes for a minute and just savored the feel of her against him. His destined mate. After all this time.

He could barely take it in.

The sense of peace was incredible—even his dragon was calm, quiet, its fire banked. He'd never felt anything like it.

Quinn wasn't sure how long they stood there—he could have remained, just like that, forever—but eventually Jasmine grew restless. She pulled her hand away, and he let it go, reluctantly.

They started walking again, without the light conversation of before. Instead, they continued in silence until Quinn finally decided to stop beating around the bush.

"So, Jazz, are you going to tell me why you invited me to dinner? Seeing as how last night I was pretty sure you never wanted to talk to me again."

Jasmine ducked her head at Quinn's words, more than a little shocked at the remorse that swept through her. Last night she'd been so sure that she was right, and now . . . now she wasn't sure of anything at all. If Quinn was really as old as he said he was—and she saw no reason for him to lie—then he was pretty damn progressive. He never questioned her worth as a doctor. In fact, he took seriously everything she and Phoebe discussed in the lab.

Plus, when Phoebe had started for her car about an hour before they'd left, Quinn had made sure to walk her out as well, even though, as a dragon, Phoebe was more than capable of taking care of herself. Maybe Quinn's behavior the night before was only half as objectionable as she had thought. Maybe what she'd seen as controlling had only been courtesy.

That's why she'd invited him to dinner—to see if maybe she was mistaken about him. Well, that and because working in the lab with him all evening had turned her on, big time. She'd spent half her time trying to concentrate on the data in front of her and the other half trying to keep her eyes off Quinn.

There was something about him—the way he moved, the way he held his body, the way he smelled like sex and sand and the wild desert wind that really rang her bell. After Phoebe left, it had taken all Jasmine's self-control not to jump him right there, as he had done to her the night before.

Turning to him, she said softly, "I invited you because I like you."

"You *like* me?"

The way he said it made the word sound boring and insipid, when she'd meant it as neither. "Don't look so offended. Being liked is a good thing."

He snorted. "I have to admit I was hoping for something more. Seeing as how we've had incredible sex several times now."

"I wasn't talking about the sex. I meant—" She paused, tried to put her scattered thoughts in order. "I like talking to you, when you're not being all overbearing and macho. I like bouncing ideas off of you and listening while you do the same with me. I like the way you give everything you have to your clan—how you never say no, no matter how tired you are." She smiled, warming to her subject. "I like the way you take meticulous notes and always put the cap back on your pens. How you hold onto your temper long after I've lost mine. And I really like how you do tequila shots."

"Oh." He stared at her for a few long seconds, then his lips tilted up in the lopsided grin she was beginning to love. "In that case, I like you, too."

She cracked up. "I'm glad to hear that. Now, are you ready to go get some pie, or what?"

"The restaurant's right across the street." His hand reached for hers, and he tangled their fingers together as he led her across the street.

Within minutes they were seated at a cozy booth in the back of the diner. It was a cool little place, done in retro black and white with touches of yellow, red and blue that made the dining room pop. The walls were decorated with oil paintings, which surprised her, as she would have expected art deco prints instead. They were desert scenes and absolutely gorgeous; starkly simple but with a sophisticated use of color.

As she studied the one above their booth, Jasmine felt a surge of longing well up inside her. She wanted to possess it. It felt strange, as she rarely needed to own anything, but something about this scene—the desert just as daylight broke through the horizon—pulled at her.

The sky was painted a fiery orange as far as the eye could see, and small clouds in shades of red and purple hung over a silver desert with huge rock formations in the distance. Everything about the scene seemed to shimmer with life and intensity and magic. Unable to resist, she reached a finger out and traced it over the bottom of the canvas.

"Do you like it?" Quinn asked, his voice low and intense.

"What's not to like? It's one of the most beautiful landscapes I've ever seen."

"It's Michael's."

Acute disappointment filled her. "You mean the paintings aren't for sale?"

His mouth was grim. "Oh, they're for sale. Or at least they were. My brother painted all of them."

"Your—" Her breath left her in a huge sigh. "Oh, Quinn, I'm sorry. I wouldn't have—"

He shook his head. "Don't worry about it. I'm glad you like them." That crooked grin of his flashed again. "He was really talented, wasn't he?"

"Incredibly talented. He makes me long to see this piece of desert, to watch the sun come up over the rocks. I've been all over the world, seen sunrises and sunsets in some of the most exotic places on earth, but I swear, I've never seen anything like this. It's absolutely awe-inspiring."

He nodded, but didn't say anything. Though his face was blank, his body language stoic, she could feel the waves of pain rolling off of him. They arrowed straight into her, making her wince with the overwhelming strength of Quinn's sorrow.

"I'm so sorry, Quinn." She could barely get the words past her closed up throat. She'd looked at Phoebe's notes on Michael's case right before she'd shut down for the night. It was the most recent and most awful of all the cases she'd read about so far. The idea of Quinn having to stand by and watch as his brother was systematically destroyed by the damn virus made her physically ill.

"It's not your fault."

"And it's not yours, either." She repeated the words she'd told him two nights before. "You didn't make this disease, Quinn. You can't hold yourself responsible for it."

"I feel responsible." His eyes roamed over the diner, searching every nook and cranny of the place instead of risking meeting hers. "I've never not been able to fix something before."

"Maybe you weren't meant to fix this." She reached for his hand, squeezed it. "You aren't Superman, you know."

"Oh, believe me. I know exactly what I'm not."

"I didn't mean it like that."

"I miss him, you know. It's only been a couple of days and already I miss talking to him. He used to tell the best jokes."

"Really? That surprises me."

"I bet." His smile was self-deprecating. "But he wasn't anything like me. Or Liam, our other brother. Life was one big party to him. He always had a million things going on—and he was always smiling."

"He sounds great."

"He was." His eyes grew distant and blank, and she knew he was tormenting himself again. Amazing how quickly she'd learned to read his expressions, especially when she hadn't even known she was studying him.

"Tell me a joke."

"What?" He pulled his gaze back to hers, looking confused.

"Tell me one of Michael's jokes. I think we both could use a laugh, don't you?"

For long moments, he just stared at her until she was certain he was going to refuse. And then, as if a switch had been flipped inside of him, Quinn started talking. And talking. And talking.

He told her Michael's jokes, one after another, pausing to interject a comment about his brother or to tell a funny story of some trouble they'd gotten into as kids, so many years before.

When the waitress came, they ordered huge slices of pie with ice cream and coffee, which they ate in between jokes. Jasmine laughed until tears rolled down her cheeks, wishing desperately that Quinn could do the same. Though he looked relaxed, she knew he was holding himself together by a thread, and she worried that with one wrong move he'd shatter into a thousand pieces.

When the last bit of pie was eaten, Quinn reached for her hand and squeezed it so hard she was afraid her bones would break. "Thank you," he said.

"For what?"

"For knowing I needed to talk about him when I didn't have a clue. For listening while I did."

"I enjoyed every second of it. Your brother sounds like he was an incredible person."

"He was. And he didn't deserve to die like that, Jazz. He really didn't."

"I know. I'm so sorry."

He reached for his wallet, threw some money down on the table. "Come on, let's get out of here." He held out a hand to her.

"Where are we going?"

The look he gave her was so full of pain and vulnerability that she knew, whatever his answer, she'd be going with him. Something inside of her literally ached with the need to soothe him, deep down in a place she'd never known existed inside of her.

"My place." He crooked an eyebrow, daring her to refuse.

The thought didn't even occur to her. Tonight she wouldn't worry about protecting herself, about whether she was going to get hurt. After everything he'd been through—everything he'd done for his clan—he deserved to be put first.

She grabbed his hand with an encouraging smile and let him pull her out of the booth. "Let's go."

CHAPTER TWENTY-FOUR

They were barely out of the restaurant and around the corner before Quinn was on her. Pulling her hard against him, he lowered his mouth to hers and kissed her like a man on the brink of madness.

His lips devoured hers, biting, sucking, licking at her until need was a fiery maelstrom within her. Moaning, Jasmine opened herself to him. She thrust her hands into his hair and gave him everything he demanded.

His response was electric. With one hand on her ass and the other tangled in her hair, he walked her backward into the small alley between two buildings. He moved them until her back was up against the wall and his lower body—hot, hard, and aroused—was pressing into her.

Then, in a move that was as shocking as it was titillating, he reached between them, fastened his hand on the collar of her simple cotton tank top and yanked, his large, powerful fist ripping through the material like it was so much fluff.

She gasped in surprise, her body shuddering as excitement ricocheted through her. She'd never had a man rip her clothes off before, had never driven one to such a state before. It was thrilling and tantalizing and oh-so-amazing. She opened her mouth to tell him so, but he was already pushing her bra out of the way, drawing her nipple into his mouth with a suction so strong she couldn't think, couldn't breathe, couldn't move. She was drowning in pleasure, drowning in the feeling of belonging to him. It was better than anything she'd ever imagined, better even than the times he had already made love to her.

Arching her back, she whimpered, begged for more. Begged for everything she could take, everything he wanted to give her.

Quinn lifted his head for a moment, looked at her in the dim light with eyes that had turned almost completely dragon. She shivered, but instead of scaring her as before, the look ratcheted up her arousal to the boiling point. It was unbelievable, especially considering he'd barely even touched her.

"We should stop," he said, and even his voice was different. Lower, more gravelly. Lust slammed through her like a lightning storm.

"Don't," she whimpered, arching her back in an effort to press herself even more firmly against him. "Please, don't stop."

"We can go to my place."

"I can't wait that long." Her body was wigging out. She wanted him, needed him with an intensity that bordered on insanity.

"You deserve better than this."

"There is nothing better. Quinn, please. I need you."

They must have been the words he was waiting for, since Quinn stopped protesting—instead lowering his mouth to bite down gently on her nipple. She nearly came unglued, her body bucking violently against him as she gave a strangled scream.

"We're in public," he growled against her breast. "If you don't want to get arrested, you should probably work on being quiet."

"Then you should make it easier on me," she gasped between breaths.

His laugh was wicked. "Oh, sweetheart, you're not the take-it-easy type." And then he stopped talking altogether, as his tongue licked around her areola, again and again.

Jasmine sighed, tried to bring him closer. Tried to deepen his caress so she wouldn't go insane right in the middle of the alley. But it was no use and she knew it; Quinn wasn't going to let her rush him.

She'd thought tonight would be about him, but here he was again, making sure her pleasure came before his own.

It bothered her because he was the one in need of loving—the one in need of care and affection—and she wanted to give it to him. Needed to give it to him.

"Quinn," she murmured, stroking her hands down his chest and stomach to the waistband of his jeans. "Let me love you."

"Later," he said, grabbing her wrists in one of his big hands and anchoring them against the wall above her head.

"But I don't want—" He chose that moment to suck her nipple deeply into his mouth, and she forgot all her concerns, forgot everything but the need to orgasm, which rose sharply with each pull of his mouth on her breast. Her body spun out of control, her need for him overwhelming everything else.

Moaning, sighing, she pressed her breast more firmly against his mouth, relishing the feel of his tongue around her areola. Loving the occasional nip of his teeth against her rock-hard nipple.

"Quinn, please," she begged, spreading her legs and pressing her lower body against the hardness of his thigh. She needed him against her, inside her, like she'd never imagined needing anything.

With a groan, he gave her just a little of what she craved. Sliding his thigh between hers, he let her ride him until she was nearly insane with the need to come. She was wet—hot and aching—and so ready for him that one touch of his finger on her clit would send her soaring into the stratosphere.

But he was so much better at holding off than she, and he pulled away from her just as the climax started swelling within. Just as her body was one thrust away from ecstasy.

Jasmine whimpered, tried to follow him, but he held her in place with one hand against her stomach while the other anchored her wrists. "What are you . . . ?" She couldn't finish the question, her need ruining any hope for coherent thought.

"Say you belong to me." Quinn whispered the words as he licked from the valley between her breasts to the hollow of her throat.

"What?" she asked, her entire body straining for completion.

"Tell me that you belong to me. That you're mine." His teeth sunk into her shoulder, hard, and she screamed as pleasure shot through her. "That no other man will touch you while you belong to me."

"Quinn!"

"Jasmine," he prompted, his tongue tenderly licking away the bite marks. "If you want to come, you know what you need to say."

"Fuck you!"

"You wish." He nibbled his way down her throat, licked along her collarbone.

"Come on," she pleaded. "Don't make me say it."

His eyes met hers, and once again she saw the dragon in him. The beast was wild. "I need this, Jasmine." His voice was barely human. "I need to hear you say it, if only for tonight."

Hearing him admit that, listening to him expose his own vulnerabilities, made it so much easier for her to admit her own. "You do things to me no one else ever has or ever will," she whispered. "I belong to you, Quinn."

Abruptly, he lifted his head, stared at her with eyes that glowed electric green. "Thank you."

Before she could figure out how to answer, the hand resting on her stomach moved. Slid inside the waistband of her yoga pants and found her sex warm and ready for him.

"Fuck, sweetheart." He slipped one long finger inside her, curved it so he touched her G-spot with the first stroke. Then pulled back and did it again. And again. On the third stroke of his finger she started to come, wave after wave of sensation swamping her.

He moved his thumb, circled it around her throbbing clit. Once, twice. She glanced up and into his dragon eyes and shot over a higher, steeper edge, her body completely out of her control as ecstasy whipped through her nerve endings. Her muscles spasmed, clutched at him, wanting to take him deeper and deeper inside her until the pleasure was all-consuming, never-ending.

Quinn held her through it, swallowing her cries with his mouth as his fingers continued to stroke her, prolonging her climax. Taking her higher. When she couldn't take it anymore, when her body was so sensitive that she was almost at the breaking point, Jasmine yanked her mouth from his. She rested her forehead on his broad chest and pleaded, "Stop, Quinn. Please stop. I can't take any more."

"There's always more, Jasmine." But he slid his finger slowly out of her, pausing to stroke her labia once, twice. She whimpered, arched against him, so exhausted and shaken that she could barely move. Had she really pleaded with him to take her? Had she really told him, of all people, that she belonged to him? She could barely wrap her head around it.

And yet the panic she expected didn't set in. Maybe she was too relaxed, too satisfied. She didn't know, and for the moment, she didn't care. There would be time enough later to worry and wonder about this night. For now, she just wanted to enjoy it. To enjoy Quinn.

As if he could read her mind, Quinn murmured, "Don't worry, sweetheart. I've got you."

A part of her wanted to argue, to say that she didn't need his help, but any protest she made would sound pretty hollow as his arms were the only things keeping her ass from hitting the ground. God knew her legs didn't stand a chance of supporting her.

"Let's go," he whispered, running a hand across the back of her neck. "Let me love you."

A million arguments entered her mind, a million reasons why going home with him was a bad idea. But she had already made her decision, and there was no use second-guessing herself now. Quinn deserved better than that—and so did she.

"How far away is your place?" she finally answered.

He could have taken her to his house and probably should have. Only a few blocks from the lab, it was close, convenient, and human-friendly.

Quinn knew it was the right choice even as he steered her back to the lab parking lot and into the SUV he kept in the corner of the lot. Knew it was the right choice even as he passed his housing complex and headed out of town. Knew it was the right choice even as he turned off the highway and onto the black desert sand. And still he didn't make it.

He glanced at Jasmine out of the corner of his eye, expecting her to protest—or at least to ask where they were going. In the few days he'd known her, he'd learned that curiosity was definitely her middle name, and it seemed completely out of character that she was so passive now.

He wasn't sure he liked it. Sure, when he'd been younger, he'd always assumed his future mate would trust him to do what was right for her. He'd wanted that, wanted a woman who was content to let him take care of her. Not an automaton, certainly, but not a woman who went haring off into the back of beyond to chase contagious diseases either. Not a woman who risked her life on a daily basis in countries that were politically and economically unstable, not to mention deathtraps of famine and disease.

That was before he'd met Jasmine. Before he'd held her in his arms. Before he'd seen her reach, without hesitation, into his friend's broken body and do her best to heal him. To think about his ideal mate now that he had Jasmine, now that he'd made love to her and listened to her unravel some of the mysteries of the disease that was ravaging his people, seemed not just wrong but blasphemous. She deserved so much better than that.

He reached over and brushed a lock of hair off her forehead so he could get a better look at those crazy purple eyes of hers. "Hey, you doing all right?"

Her smile was relaxed and dreamy. "I'm doing just fine. Why?"

"You're awfully quiet."

She laughed. "And that's not like me?"

"Not really, no."

"I was just looking out at the sky and thinking how incredibly beautiful it is out here. I've been all over the world, and I don't think I've ever felt about another place the way I feel about this desert."

His heart pounded a little more quickly at that revelation. "How do you feel about it?"

"It feels like home. Isn't that strange? I've never really had a home, never had a place where I felt completely safe or comfortable. And yet—"

"Not even as a child?" he interrupted.

"God, no. Especially not then." She sighed, laid her head on his shoulder. "My dad wasn't exactly the nurturing sort."

Quinn's whole body went rigid at the studied casualness in her voice. "Did he hurt you?"

"I survived."

"That's not what I asked." His hands clenched the steering wheel.

"He controlled me—and my mother. Every little thing we did, from what clothes we wore to what we ate to what time I was allowed to take a shower. His word was law and his punishments when I messed up were . . . creative."

Quinn felt his dragon awaken, the beast raising its head as much because of what she'd left unsaid. "Did your mother leave him?" he asked.

"Not quite." Jasmine laughed, but the sound lacked the warm humor he was used to hearing from her. He tensed, anger welling up inside.

"My mom isn't exactly what you'd call a liberated woman. She spent her entire life trying to please my dad, trying to be perfect so he wouldn't beat her. It didn't work, of course. Because no matter how perfect she was, there was always something that set him off.

Something she didn't do right. Potatoes for dinner when he wanted rice. Ivory soap in the bathroom instead of Dial. Buying the wrong kind of beer, even if it was the same beer he'd been drinking for years. She should have known without him having to tell her that he wanted a change."

She turned and looked out the window, but not before he glimpsed the sorrow and shame she was trying so hard to hide. "I'm sorry. I don't know why I'm telling you this."

"It's okay." His voice was lower, darker than usual, but he couldn't stop it. Not when his head was filled with images of Jasmine and her mother at the mercy of a monster. "God knows, I've dumped on you since we met."

"It's not the same."

"Sure it is." He paused, tried to figure out what to say to make her pain better. The scent of it permeated the car, and it was driving both his dragon and his human half crazy. "How did you get out? College?"

"Something like that." Her tone said there was a lot more to it.

"Come on, Jazz. Talk to me."

She shrugged, and the silence stretched between them as he took the SUV deeper and deeper into the desert. Each second that passed stretched his control, so that he was hanging by a thread—imagining all kinds of atrocities—by the time she finally started to speak.

"By the time I was a teenager, my mom was completely worn out. My father broke her bones so often he took her to different hospitals to throw suspicion away from himself.

"I hated seeing her like that, scared and in pain all the time. I started provoking him so he'd take his temper out on me instead. I was faster, so he didn't get as many licks in, and healthier, so my bones didn't break as easily. One day he came home from work and I wasn't around—I was at school working on some biology project or something. He'd spent all afternoon drinking at the corner bar and had worked himself into a hell of a rage by the time he got home.

212 · TESSA ADAMS

"She told me later that he started on her as soon as he'd walked through the door. She didn't tell me what he did, but then, she didn't have to. By the time I got home she was half dead, crumpled on the kitchen floor in the fetal position, unable to get away as he whaled on her. I tried to stop him, tried to help her, and he turned on me. Broke my arm and four of my ribs."

Quinn's world exploded. Pure, unadulterated rage flashed through him like a lightning strike as his talons pushed at his fingertips. His wings started to punch through the muscles of his back, and the only thing that kept him from relinquishing control to the beast was the fact that he would scare Jasmine to death if he did.

Even knowing that, it was a close thing and he clung to control with battered, bloody fingertips. The idea that Jasmine had been hurt by some sadistic asshole was almost more than he could bear. The fact that it had happened while he was alive and more than capable of stopping it—if only he'd known it was going on—was somehow a million times worse.

He gritted his teeth, forced himself to keep it together as Jasmine's voice broke. She swallowed convulsively, struggling to push the rest of the words out. "Anyway, by the time we'd started to heal up—it took a few weeks—I knew I had to get us out of there or we'd both end up dead. I'd been saving money up for college from my afternoon job—I had about six thousand dollars hidden at the back of my closet. Anyway, I waited for him to leave for work one day, and I packed a bag for both of us. Begged her to get in her car and leave with me.

"She wouldn't do it. No matter what I said, she wouldn't leave him. I knew if I stayed he'd end up killing me—I wasn't very good at keeping my mouth shut even then—so I took off. Walked to the nearest bus station and caught a bus to the nearest college town. The rest is history."

But it wasn't. He could see that much in her unbending spine, in the hand that was trembling slightly against her thigh. He stared straight ahead, tried to concentrate on driving, but all the time he was wondering what he'd been doing as Jasmine was being tortured. What problems had he been trying to solve for his clan while his mate made her way in the world, young and battered and alone?

Nothing came to mind, except the knowledge that he'd failed her. He'd failed his mate as surely as he had failed his brothers, his parents, his clan. Goddamnit! He wanted to throw his head back and roar. Someone had hurt her and he had done nothing to stop it!

"Hey." As she finished the story, she realized she'd pressed herself up against the car door in an effort to make herself as small as possible. She straightened up, not wanting to look vulnerable. "It's not a big deal anymore.

"It still hurts you." It was a growl, low and inhuman.

"Yeah, but not in the same way."

"It never should have happened." His shirt ripped as his back rippled with the need to change.

"Quinn, stop it. I'm fine. It was a long time ago."

Not so long ago to him—less than one-twenty-fifth of his lifetime.

His talons shredded his shoes as they poked through the leather. Shit, he was losing it.

"I mean it, Quinn. Stop!"

It was too late—he was too far gone. His vision changed, became so much sharper, keener than it was while he was in human form. He slowed the car.

"Damn it, you're scaring me!" Jasmine fumbled for the door.

He slammed on the brakes and reached over her to pull the door closed. Then laid his head against the seat, closed his eyes, and reached for his dragon. Second by second, breath by breath, he pulled the beast back in—conscious of Jasmine staring at him as he did.

It took longer than it should have, and with every moment that passed he felt more and more guilty. She'd told him about her father, and instead of supporting her he'd gone all crazy alpha male animal on her. What was he going to do for an encore? Beat his chest? Find a small puppy to kick? Beat up on his mate?

Shit. He dropped his head onto the steering wheel and wondered where to start. "I'm sorry. I—the idea of someone or something hurting you . . . upsets me."

"Yeah, I got that impression." It was a typical, smart-ass Jasmine retort, and it might have reassured him if her voice hadn't been so faint.

"Right." He nodded. Then started driving again, making a U-turn as he did.

She didn't say anything for a few seconds, just looked out the window at the blackness of the night. Just when he'd decided she didn't have anything left to say to him, she asked, "Where are we going?"

He turned his head to stare at her incredulously. "Now you ask me that?"

"Well, it seemed obvious before you turned around. Now I'm not so sure."

"I'm taking you home. This was a really bad idea."

"Why?"

"Are you kidding me? I figured after that display you wouldn't exactly be up to coming to my lair."

"Is that what you call it? Your lair? That sounds like a bad porn movie. Next thing you know, you'll be inviting me to see your etchings." Her hand crept onto his thigh.

"I don't have any etchings."

"I'm glad to hear that."

"I frightened you, Jasmine, and believe me, that's the last thing I want to do."

"I was frightened because you were hurting yourself, not because you were shifting."

He stopped the car a second time, turned to her. "Are you lying to me?"

"Why would I do that?"

"I don't know. To spare my feelings?"

She laughed, and this time there was nothing forced or unhappy about it. The sound skittered down his spine and made him shiver. "Did you forget who you were talking to? What makes you think I'd want to spare your feelings to begin with?"

"Could you just stop for a second?" He knew he sounded as frustrated as he felt, but there was nothing he could do about it. The woman was driving him insane. "Stop with the smart-ass remarks and just be straight with me."

"I am being straight with you, Quinn." She brought his hand to her mouth, brushed her lips over the fingertips that had so recently shifted into claws. "I swear I'm not afraid of you shifting. In fact, I've been dying to see one of you guys turn into a dragon since you told me what you were."

The dragon came roaring back. "You want to *see* one of us change?"

She grinned. "Well, preferably you. And preferably not right now."

"Oh, yeah?" He lifted an eyebrow inquisitively. "What's wrong with right now?"

"Absolutely nothing—except that I've got plans for tonight that definitely don't involve you being a dragon."

CHAPTER TWENTY-FIVE

Jasmine nearly laughed as Quinn whipped his SUV around so fast she nearly got whiplash. Nice to know, after everything, he was still as desperate to be inside her as she was to have him there.

She wasn't sure how she felt about his reaction to her revelation about her childhood. Perhaps she should be upset that it had become about him, not her. But she wasn't. Instead, she was kind of awed that she had such power over him—that something that had happened to her so long ago could break through the iron fist of his meticulous control.

It was also nice to know she wasn't the only one going off the deep end in this relationship, that Quinn was somehow as screwed up and uneasy as she was.

Emboldened by the realization, and by the strange intensity of the feelings she had for him despite her better judgment, Jasmine began rubbing his thigh, soft little circles that had his muscles hardening and his breath catching in his throat.

She liked the reaction, wanted more. How far could she push him, she wondered. How high could she take him before he lost control again? She suddenly wanted desperately to find out.

Sliding her hand a little farther up his thigh, she was rewarded when she finally reached his zipper. He was as hard as a rock, and her mouth watered at the thought of what he would taste like. She began to stroke him through the denim—lightly to begin with and then with a firmer touch when his breathing became strangled.

"What are you doing?" he asked, his voice dark and a little dangerous, just the way she liked it. Was that the dragon rising, she wondered. Or was she simply pushing the man to the limits of his control?

There's only one way to find out. She eased the top button of his jeans open and then pulled his zipper slowly down. Slipping her hand inside, she felt his hot, silky flesh. He didn't even try to stifle a groan.

"You'll get us into an accident," he warned, and her nipples peaked at the warning in his voice.

"There's nothing out here to crash into," she answered. "Besides, don't you have great night vision?"

"Not when my eyes are crossed."

She laughed, and his erection jumped beneath her fingers—responding, she assumed, to the sound of her happiness. She grew wet at the thought, a little more proof that he cared about her for something more than getting off. Although she very definitely intended to take care of that for him. After she'd tortured him a little bit.

"I love that you don't wear underwear," she murmured, easing him out of the jeans, then leaning down so that her breath drifted over his cock while she spoke.

"It's easier not to have too many clothes . . . to deal with . . . when I shift." His breath was coming faster now, his hips arching a little off the seat as if he were seeking the warmth of her mouth.

Smiling to herself, Jasmine stroked her hand down him from tip to balls. He shuddered, and one of his hands left the steering wheel to clench in her hair.

"Do it!" he ordered from between clenched teeth.

"Do what?" she asked, right before she pumped her hand up and down him for a second time. "Do this?"

"Jasmine . . ." It was a command, and they both knew it.

The warning almost made her want to torture him more, but she wanted to know what he tasted like as much as he wanted her to take him in her mouth. So, with a sigh of acquiescence, she bent lower and delivered one leisurely lick down the length of his cock.

Quinn's body jerked convulsively, the fingers in her hair tightening almost to the point of pain. "Again."

She rubbed her cheek along his hard, silky length before turning her head and softly kissing just the tip. It wasn't nearly enough—for either of them—but he needed to learn that he didn't dictate everything. Here, now, in this moment, she was the one in control, and she would take him as slowly as she wanted to.

His thigh trembled beneath her head but he didn't say anything, didn't try to force her to go down on him, so she rewarded him with another long, slow lick, then swirled her tongue around and around the head.

He groaned, his hips arching involuntarily off the car seat but, still, he didn't try to take over. She smiled, then gave him exactly what he wanted. Sucking him deep into her mouth, she licked him up and down before pulling back until only the tip was between her lips.

She sucked at him gently, her tongue flicking over the sensitive bundle of nerves centered at the bottom of the head. His fingers tightened in her hair then, but she was too far gone to care. Her pussy was wet, aching, and she wanted nothing more than to take him inside her. But at the same time, she didn't want to let him go. She wanted to keep loving him like this forever.

Quinn tried to keep his eyes on the road, tried to keep going through the desert until he got to his cave, where he could take her any and every way that he wanted to. But the deeper his cock slid inside her beautiful mouth, the more certain he became that he wasn't going to make it that far.

Pulling the SUV to yet another stop, he leaned his seat back so that he could watch her take him. Never had he been so grateful for his dragon vision and the ability to see clearly in the dark. He couldn't remember the last time he'd seen something as arousing as watching Jasmine take him into her gorgeous mouth.

He thrust against her, fascinated by the sight of himself sliding in and out of her cherry-colored lips. He wanted her to continue, wanted to come in her mouth with a need so intense it was painful. But he wanted to hold her, too, wanted to pleasure her again and hear her call his name. Hear her say that she belonged to him, even if she didn't mean it. Even if it was just for tonight.

"Sweetheart, stop," he whispered, forcing the words from a throat that felt like sandpaper. "I don't want to come yet."

She stopped, and he nearly groaned in disappointment. "I want you to come," she answered softly, then ran her tongue up and down his length again.

Her lips closed over him again, her tongue continuing to slide back and forth as she pushed up his shirt and scraped her fingernails softly down his abdomen. It was too much—too much sensation, too much stimulus, too much everything. He tried one last desperate time to pull away from her.

Jasmine refused to relinquish her control. Pulling him tightly against her, she slid his entire length into her mouth and down her throat. Her tongue stroked the underside of his cock, while her fingers snuck inside his jeans to run along his balls and her mouth continued the sucking motion that was driving him out of his mind.

He tried to hang on, tried to fight against the orgasm that was starting at his spine and arrowing straight up his dick, but she hummed sexily and the vibrations sent him right over the edge. He came with a growl, emptying himself into her mouth in an orgasm so intense it left him shaken and a little shocky.

Closing his eyes, he relaxed back against the seat and tried to regain his equilibrium. It was difficult, as Jasmine hadn't stopped touching him.

She ran her fingers lightly over his stomach, brought her hand up to caress his cheek and push an errant lock of hair out of his eyes. She lifted his hand to her lips and put a kiss right in the center of his palm, her tongue dancing over his heart line and down his head line as he tried to catch enough breath to speak.

He'd almost managed it when she sat up, and every thought he had flew right out of his head. Her lips were shiny as she leaned forward and ran them over his cheek, down his jaw. Her hair was tousled from his fingers running through it, and her eyes glistened and glowed in the dim light of the moon. Her breasts were swollen and gleaming, overfilling the cups of her bra.

Never in his entire life had he seen a more beautiful woman—inside and out. This sweet and sexy and sarcastic doctor who had crashed into his life and turned everything upside down.

Just the thought of her walking away made him break out in a cold sweat, not just because he might lose his mate but because he might lose her. In three short days she'd insinuated her way into his life and made him fall for her. Now, he wasn't sure what he would do without her.

His cock hardened at the thought of losing her, his dragon biting and scratching in an effort to get to her. To make her his. To keep her for however many years she lived.

The urge to be inside her rose until he could barely think, barely breathe. Lifting her up, he pushed her bra out of the way, then turned her so that she was straddling him, her beautiful breasts brushing against his cheek.

He paused for a moment and just looked at her, shocked anew at how gorgeous and giving she was. But she grew impatient and squirmed against his already hard cock and Quinn knew he couldn't hold out any longer. Leaning forward, he captured a taut, pouting nipple in his mouth even as he shoved her soft cotton pants down her thighs. He rolled the nipple between his lips, pinching softly, loving how it tightened for him even more.

And still it wasn't close to being enough.

Resting one hand on her back to anchor her to him, he slipped his other hand between Jasmine's legs. She was wet, hot—scorching— and he groaned as he slid one finger inside of her, followed closely by a second. He worked them back and forth, his thumb rubbing against her clit as she rode his hand. Her scent—sweet blackberries and jasmine—rose up, set the dragon inside him to whimpering.

Jasmine was just as far gone. Wanting to see Quinn, needing to watch him take her, she fumbled for the overhead light, punched it on. Then bent her head so she could look between their bodies and see all of the crazy, beautiful things Quinn was doing to her body.

His fingers were deep inside her, his fully aroused cock nestled between the cheeks of her ass as she rode him, slow and easy. His free hand tightened on her hip while his fingers moved harder and faster inside of her, rubbing against her G-spot and making her whimper. At the same time, he lifted his hips and his cock rubbed against her anus. That was all it took—orgasm flooded her, tightening every muscle in her body as she came, screaming his name.

He reached for his jeans and drew a condom from the back pocket, slipping it over his pulsing erection and sliding home as contractions continued to rock her. Jasmine rose onto her knees, riding his cock much harder and faster than she had his fingers.

Their eyes met in the soft light of the car, held, as need arced between them. For a moment she thought of turning away, but she couldn't. She didn't even want to, no matter how intense the feelings racing between them were.

As if he knew what she was thinking, Quinn reached up and grabbed her chin, holding her face steady with his elegant surgeon's hands. His eyes blazed, burned, promised things she didn't want to think about, things she couldn't name. And still she didn't look away. Another release was close, beckoning, growing stronger with each lift and fall of her hips against him.

At the last minute, he slipped his other hand between them, his thumb stroking firmly over her clit. She closed her eyes, but his fingers tightened on her chin. "Look at me," he demanded hoarsely. "I want to see your eyes when you come."

She lifted her lids just as her body convulsed, his words sending satisfaction streaming through her. His eyes glimmered in the light, the look in them intensifying her climax as his own roared through him.

She'd never felt more exposed, more open, more connected to another person in her entire life. And though every instinct she had screamed at her to pull away, to *look* away, she stayed where she was, reveling in this one, perfect moment.

It wasn't enough, but it was all she had and she grabbed on to it with both hands. She would take it, and him, for as long as she could—and to hell with the consequences.

CHAPTER TWENTY-SIX

Despite the late night, Jasmine woke at dawn feeling like something was out of place. She fumbled for the bedside light, but her hand only met air—and that's when it occurred to her that the thing out of place was her. She wasn't in Phoebe's luxuriously appointed guest room. Instead, she was in Quinn's underground cavern. There was no bedside lamp because there was no electricity.

Of course, he didn't need it. He'd said a few words while they'd been walking into the cave last night—after their marathon sex session in the car—and light had suddenly bloomed all around them.

She'd been astounded, and impressed, with his magic, for lack of a better word, and with the gorgeous cave he inhabited when he wasn't crashing in town. The cavern was huge, with stalactites hanging from the ceiling and beautiful, colorful helictites blooming everywhere she looked.

Despite her tiredness, she'd wanted to explore, to follow the sound of the waterfall echoing off the walls. Quinn had laughed and swept her into his arms, convincing her that there was another, more pressing exploration that needed to be done. She hadn't been sorry, but now that it was morning, she was itching to learn more about his home.

Lying there against Quinn, she felt more at peace than she had for a long, long time. For once, her body didn't hurt—not one of her injuries so much as twinged, and she knew he was responsible.

Yesterday, she had ached in every bone in her body, and now she felt ready to hike ten miles through the desert—or to make love to Quinn again. Snuggled up as she was against his strong, hard body, the second option definitely held more appeal.

Yet something was not quite right. When she lifted her head to look around, she finally realized what it was. Both of their cell phones, which were resting on the small carved table on Quinn's side of the bed, were going crazy.

Rolling over Quinn, she ignored his sleepy sigh of satisfaction and the hands that settled on her hips, and reached for her phone.

"Hello?" she mumbled, after punching the accept call button.

"Jazz?" Phoebe's frantic voice came through loud and clear despite the fact that Jasmine and her phone were several dozen feet underground. "Where are you?"

"I'm, uh, with, umm . . ." Pushing her hair out of the way, Jasmine struggled into a sitting position and tried not to feel like she'd just been caught with her hand in the cookie jar. "I'm with Quinn."

"Oh. Oookay." There was a strange tone in her friend's voice, one Jasmine couldn't help thinking sounded like censure. But she didn't know who it was directed at—Quinn or her.

"I'm sorry I didn't call. I wasn't—"

"I'm not worried about that. I called because I'm at the clinic. We've got another case of the virus, and I thought you might like to see it at work, in a living organism."

She shoved herself off Quinn in a hurry, stumbling around in the dark as she searched for her clothes. "You're right. I do."

She found her pants, scrambled into them. "Who's the patient?"

"Male dragon, six foot four, two hundred pounds. He's been sick with another disease that is normal in the dragon world, but it's currently in remission. Like in the other cases, this thing just seemed to sprout from nowhere."

Phoebe paused. "Is Quinn awake?"

"Not yet." She pulled on her bra and went searching for her shirt, only to remember that Quinn had shredded it the night before. "I'm about to wake him."

"He's awake," Quinn mumbled from the bed, his voice husky with sleep. "What's wrong?"

"There's another case of the virus. Phoebe—"

He was out of bed before she could finish the sentence, ripping the phone from her hand. "Who is it?" he demanded. Then, a few seconds later, "Shit. I can't believe this. Can't the guy get a fucking break?"

Another pause, followed by a flick of his wrist that had light flooding the bedroom. Jasmine squawked in alarm, clapping her hand over her eyes. "Tell him to hang in there. I'll be there in ten minutes."

He hung up the phone and tossed it to Jasmine as he reached for the jeans he'd thrown on the floor the night before. "I don't suppose there's any way I can convince you to stay away from the clinic today?" he asked almost conversationally. Only the fine trembling in his hands as he neatly folded the jeans betrayed just how much he wanted her to agree to his request.

"Not a chance. I've been waiting for an opportunity to see how this baby works in action."

Quinn's head came up, and he shot her a reproachful look. Suddenly she realized how insensitive she sounded. "I'm sorry," she said, fumbling awkwardly for a way to make him understand that she meant no harm. "I wasn't celebrating the fact that there was another case. I just need to be able to see—"

"I know what you mean." He crossed to the dresser, pulled out a navy T-shirt and fired it straight at her, before pulling out another one and dropping it—still folded—on the jeans. "It's a little big, but I figure it's probably better than the bra look. At least in public."

"I'm forced to agree," she said, then thought about changing her mind after she put the shirt on and it fell almost to her knees. And she was six feet! She'd hate to see what the shirt looked like on a normal-sized woman.

"You ready?" he asked impatiently.

"*I* am." She eyed him dubiously, as she knotted the shirt at her waist. "But I think you forgot something."

He smiled at her for the first time that morning, and despite the sorrow in his eyes, the grin was just a little bit wicked. "It'll take at least half an hour to get into town by car."

"As opposed to hiking naked through the desert?"

"As opposed to flying," he answered, shoving the clothes into a backpack and then slinging it over his shoulder. "Come on. Let's get out of here."

He grabbed her hand and started through the cave, moving so fast she had to run to keep up. "I'm sorry. Did you say *flying*?"

"I did."

"But I can't fly."

"Good thing I can."

They burst out of the cave and into a desert just coming to life as dawn rolled slowly over the horizon. Despite the urgency of the situation, she paused for a moment, spellbound. "It was here. That picture at the restaurant last night. Michael painted it standing right here."

"He did."

"My God." She shook her head. "It's the most beautiful thing I've ever seen."

"You haven't seen anything yet."

"What's that supposed to mean?"

"Here, hold this." He tossed her the backpack.

She caught it, then started to ask him what was going on. But it was too late—he'd started shifting. She watched, captivated, as Quinn disappeared body part by body part. It was nothing like what had happened in the car the night before, when he'd been fighting the change with everything inside of him.

This was something else entirely, something beautiful and joyous and absolutely fascinating.

It was over too quickly, and then she was staring at a huge, gorgeous dragon with skin the same deep emerald as Quinn's eyes. She'd never seen anything like it, never imagined that such a thing could even exist. And yet she was enchanted, mesmerized, completely transfixed by the creature in front of her.

Reaching out a tentative hand, Jasmine waited for him to rebuff her. But he didn't. Instead, he lowered his head so that she could rub him on the long bridge of his nose. She was shocked at how warm he was, how silky smooth his scales were when she'd braced herself for something cold, and maybe even a bit slimy.

She might have stood there all day, petting him—admiring him—but he snorted impatiently. It was amazing how much the dragon Quinn looked and sounded like the human one.

Slinging the backpack with his clothes over her back, she said, "All right, all right. Don't get your scales all bunched up. What should I do?"

The dragon bent forward, extending its long regal neck, and she blinked at him for a second before it sunk in that he expected her to swing onto his back, much like she would a horse. Excitement burst through her, wiping away any worries she might have had about the dragon not knowing her, and she grabbed onto his neck.

Within seconds he'd lifted his head, flinging her up and onto his back in one fluid movement. Then with a snort that sounded very much like a warning, he took off—soaring straight up and into the purple and red sky that stretched before them like a promise.

It was the ride of her life, the experience of her life—and that was saying something, as she'd ridden just about everything there was to ride in the last few years. Except, of course, for a dragon.

Quinn was in a hurry to get to town, and not in the mood to fool around for her amusement. But still, he managed to thrill her with his headlong flight across the desert. The ground rushed by at an amazingly quick rate, and she hugged his neck more tightly, pressing her body against him so that she could hold on with her knees as well.

He bellowed at the move—a sound of approval that whipped through her like lightning. And then he was spinning, around and around and around, never once slowing his speed as they whirled through the sky.

She held on tight, laughing a little more with each twirl. Too soon, the town came into view, followed by the large, imposing structures of the lab and Quinn's clinic. With a growl of warning, he arrowed straight toward the ground, flying so fast that she was sure there was no chance he could avoid crashing.

She braced herself, but Quinn was a lot more flexible than the average airplane, and he managed to pull up at the last second. Within moments they were on the ground, and he was shifting back to his human form.

Jasmine watched him again, just as fascinated by the process in reverse. As soon as he was human again, she unzipped the backpack and threw him his jeans and T-shirt. He donned them quickly, then took the clinic stairs three at a time, leaving her to trail behind him.

She didn't mind, as it gave her time to brace herself for whatever she would run into inside. She'd read the case notes, seen the samples, but when it came to diseases like this, no file in the world could compare to seeing how the disease actually worked as it attacked its human host.

One look at the room Quinn led her to, one look at the patient laying in the middle of the bed, reinforced that opinion. Because even knowing how the virus worked, even thinking that she was ready for whatever she found, even having spent years in the field dealing with the worst hemorrhagic viruses on the planet, nothing on earth could have prepared her for this scene.

CHAPTER TWENTY-SEVEN

Inside Room 124 of the clinic, Brian Alexander was dying in the most atrocious, undignified manner possible. The second Jasmine saw him, her professional detachment went out the window. She watched the man struggle into a sitting position, his body shaking wildly from the effort.

"Quinn," he whispered, in a voice rife with knowledge. "It looks like I've reached the end of my time limit, after all."

Jasmine was standing near the door and didn't catch Quinn's answer, but the healer was devastated. That much was obvious.

Whatever he'd said must have been amusing because Brian threw back his head and laughed, a full-on belly laugh that shook his entire body and caused blood to leak from his nose and ears.

Jasmine pulled his chart from where it rested on the inside of the door, wanting to know the timeline for the patient's deterioration. What she saw there chilled her to the bone. He'd been fully mobile when he walked in three hours before, suffering from chills, vomiting and a strange tingling in his hands and feet. The day before that, yesterday, he'd been in the clinic for a quick blood draw and he'd been perfectly healthy—as had the blood.

Now, less than twenty-four hours since his routine check-up, Brian was running a sky-high fever, even for a dragon. He was bleeding from every orifice in his body, and his legs were completely paralyzed. All this within five hours of his noticing the first symptom.

She remembered the timeline Phoebe and Quinn had made up and was amazed at how much faster the disease was progressing in Brian than it had in anyone else—even Michael, whose case was the fastest so far on record. If things kept up at this rate, Brian would be dead within fifteen hours. Perhaps sooner.

She glanced around the room, noted the number of machines and other pieces of equipment that he was hooked up to—and the fact that he had no family members in the room. His chart said he was married, that he had children, yet none of them were with him. She wasn't sure she blamed his wife. Brian's toes were slowly turning black, rotting, and the bleeding had increased even in the short time since she'd gotten in the room. This was no place for kids.

Brian and Quinn were still talking, and Jasmine noticed that the sick man kept licking his lips, as if they were very dry—which wouldn't be unusual with this kind of bleeding, even with the IV hooked into his hand.

Slipping out of the room, she went in search of a water pitcher and some ice chips. She found both in the supply room in the middle of the hallway, and filled up the pitcher and then grabbed a plastic cup and a straw. As far as medical offerings went, it was pretty lame, but it was the best she could do. The best any of them could do, short of shooting Brian up with painkillers—which they were already doing.

She was halfway down the hall when a woman came running into the clinic, screaming at the top of her lungs. "Help me! Please help me." In her arms was a beautiful baby girl, no more than a year old and probably less. A steady stream of blood was dripping from her nose.

Jasmine dropped the water on one of the counters next to the nurse's station and ran, reaching the woman just as a nurse did. "What happened to her?" she asked, as she gently took the baby from her mother's arms. Touching the little girl's skin, Jasmine's blood ran cold. She was burning up, her temperature so high brain damage was imminent.

Shooting into action, Jasmine headed down the hall at a run. She glanced in each open doorway until she found an unused exam room. Plopping the little girl down on the bed, she shouted for ice packs even as she began stripping her.

She turned to the nurse next to her. "What works on dragon fevers?" she demanded.

"We don't normally get fevers, so it's pretty much anyone's guess," she answered, full of worry. "We can try ibuprofen—that's what Quinn has been treating the fever with for other patients who contract the virus."

"The virus?" she demanded, ignoring the gasp of the trembling mother who was standing next to her, on the other side of the child's bed. "What makes you think this is it? There's never been a patient anywhere close to this young before."

At that moment, the little girl's body convulsed, her eyes rolling up in her head as she began to vomit. Jasmine turned her over, so that she didn't aspirate, and snapped out, "Get Quinn. I want his opinion."

The nurse's eyes were horrified as she went to do Jasmine's bidding. "Check in the drawers behind you," Jasmine told the mother as she continued to hold the baby. "See if there's a stethoscope in there. I need to listen to her heart."

The woman didn't move, just swayed on her feet with blank eyes. Jasmine realized the woman was going into shock. Of course—as if they needed any more trouble.

"What's her name?" she asked, trying to get the woman's attention and head off yet another disaster.

"Rose." It was the barest of whispers.

"That's a beautiful name," Jasmine told her, internally cursing her lack of familiarity with the room—and the clinic. When this nightmare was over, she swore she would familiarize herself with every room in the clinic, so she was never at this same disadvantage again.

The nurse came back with a bunch of temperature-lowering ice kits, a stethoscope and two syringes. Quinn was right behind her, and Jasmine swore he moved so fast she didn't see his feet touch the ground between the doorway and little Rose's bed, where the baby continued to convulse and vomit, vomit and convulse.

He closed his eyes and ran his hand lightly over the baby's stomach and head. Within seconds the vomiting stopped and the crying began—a high-pitched wail that no one could ever mistake for normal. The baby was in serious distress, and if they didn't get her temperature down, now, they wouldn't have to worry about the progression of the disease.

"Save my baby," the woman chanted, as she stared at Quinn with pleading eyes. "Please, Quinn, save my child."

"I'm trying, Melinda. I promise you, I'm trying. Why don't you go down the hall and check on Brian while I examine her?"

Jasmine realized with dawning horror—this was Brian's baby. Somehow he had managed to infect the baby, probably within an hour or so of getting infected himself, judging from the symptoms.

The nurse took Melinda out of the room—presumably to visit her dying husband and deliver the news that their child was dying with him—and for the first time, Jasmine noticed the little boy trailing after her. He couldn't be more than six or seven, with bright blue eyes and an adorable mane of blond hair.

She closed her eyes and muttered a swift prayer that he too wasn't infected. Surely, God, fate, the universe couldn't be that cruel.

She turned back to Quinn, who was working feverishly over the patient, packing the little girl in ice despite the violent trembling of her body. "What can I do?" Jasmine demanded. She didn't know much about dragon anatomy yet, but she was a quick learner.

"Not a damn thing," Quinn growled, his green eyes all but destroyed as they met hers over the little girl's shaking form. "The fever's too high—her internal organs have already begun to fry."

"Surely there's something we can do? She's just—"

"Besides making her more comfortable, I don't know what to do. At this rate, she'll be dead before her father."

His face was grimmer than she'd ever seen it, and Jasmine knew he was suffering right alongside his pint-sized patient. But when he closed his eyes and held his hands a few inches off Rose's skin, Jasmine jumped toward him. "Quinn, no! Don't. If she has the virus, you can't heal this."

He didn't answer her, didn't so much as acknowledge that he'd heard her. Jasmine cursed as she watched him risk himself for a child who was destined to die, as her father was.

It angered her to see him use his gift with so little regard for himself, but at the same time, could she really blame him? He wouldn't be the man she had fallen for if he wasn't willing to risk himself to try to save a child.

The nurse stood by with a shot of painkillers, waiting for Quinn's or Jasmine's order to deliver the opiate. Jasmine started to tell her to go ahead, but under Quinn's healing focus, baby Rose's skin was losing its dangerous scarlet color and her little body stopped trembling altogether.

Jasmine couldn't tell if he was actually healing her or simply reducing the symptoms. She prayed it was the former, but she was pretty sure it was the latter. Nothing Quinn had been able to do for any patient so far had managed to prolong his or her life, at least not according to the extensive case studies.

Just then, a shrill scream rang through the clinic. Jasmine was out the door in a matter of seconds, tearing down the hall toward the sound at top speed. She froze when she realized the sound had come from Brian's room, that the woman screaming was Melinda.

Has Brian died already? she wondered frantically, slipping into the room. But Phoebe wasn't standing near Brian, who had a look of abject horror on his face. No, she was standing near the cute little boy with the big blue eyes, and Jasmine saw the line of blood leaking from his nose and trailing down his face.

At that moment, it really hit her, the hopelessness and helplessness of this virus that Phoebe and Quinn were fighting. In Africa, she faced incurable diseases every day, but at least she could fight them with education and preventative measures that stopped them from spreading.

This disease, this virus, came out of nowhere. There were no preventative measures to take, no steps to lesson the impact or bolster the survival rate. Anyone who got it—whether by injection or simple communicable contact, as this strain appeared to have been spread—was dead, and there was nothing any of them could do.

The thought was absolutely devastating, particularly as she looked at the utter hopelessness on Brian and Melinda's faces, the fear on their son's face and the agony on their daughter's. This disease was a nightmare of epic proportions.

The next couple of hours passed in a blur as Jasmine assisted Quinn and Phoebe in whatever ways she could—which weren't nearly as many as she would have liked, but then she was still learning the ropes when it came to dragon anatomy and how to treat this disease.

Not that they were actually treating the disease, but simply prolonging the inevitable. Even Quinn, who tried so hard to heal his patients that he was literally gray with exhaustion, couldn't do anything but try to make them comfortable as he ordered their entire wing of the clinic to be locked down and quarantine measures put into place.

No strain of the virus had ever been this contagious before, and he wasn't taking any chances with it spreading, even though only Brian and his children seemed to be affected by it. Melinda was showing no symptoms, and neither were his nurses, Phoebe or himself, though they'd been in contact with Brian for hours. While he'd demanded that Jasmine put on protective gear, she didn't really expect to contract the virus; she wasn't a dragon.

They moved Brian to the biggest room in the wing, so they could move in two other beds for Rose and her big brother, Jake. This way the family could be together and Melinda could tend to all three. After her initial shock, Melinda proved to be a trouper, moving between her husband and sick children as needed—hugging, kissing, soothing. Jasmine wasn't sure she could have stood up under the strain nearly half as well.

Through it all, Quinn and Phoebe worked tirelessly, trying a long list of treatments. Jasmine hung back, taking notes and blood samples, her brain working a mile a minute. She ran through every possible scenario regarding the spread of this disease, which had affected the father and his two kids but not the mother. If it spread by contact, whether by air or fluid, surely the mother would have caught it, too. But she still showed no symptoms of the disease, even hours after her children had fallen prey to it.

Did that mean that all three of the sick patients had been injected with the virus? Or was there a way to spread it that they had not managed to think of yet? She needed to get to the laboratory, needed to look at the blood samples, if she was to even hazard a guess.

Yet an idea hovered in her brain, nebulous and not quite formed, but there nonetheless. She knew it would come when it was ready, perhaps when she stopped trying so hard to catch hold of it.

Baby Rose was the first to go, a little after noon. Her father cried silent tears, which were pitiful to see—particularly as he was almost fully paralyzed by that point. She was followed three hours later by Jake and Brian, within minutes of each other. Afterward, Melinda, healthy and shell-shocked, simply sat in a chair against the wall and stared out the opposite window.

Jasmine's heart broke for the woman. If she'd had to go through what Melinda just had, she'd probably be a blathering idiot.

Quinn called a family member to pick her up—it turned out he'd known Brian and his family quite well, as he'd been treating him for a number of years, off and on, for the genetic disease that had struck him nearly ten years before. Jasmine made a note of the disease off his chart and made a mental note to look it up at the soonest opportunity.

Maybe there was a connection between it and the virus, though she wasn't sure what the connection could possibly be. But she wasn't ruling anything out, not until she'd followed each path as far as she could. Quinn deserved that from her, as did his people.

After Melinda left, the bodies were taken to a special, contained portion of the morgue for immediate autopsy, with cremation soon to follow. Quinn was taking no chances with the contagiousness of the disease. Eventually, the quarantine was lifted, as no one else contracted the disease; the paperwork was completed, and Quinn made his usual rounds. Jasmine was aching to get to the lab, to see what the blood samples she'd drawn showed under the microscope, but Quinn was so exhausted, so damaged by this latest battle, that she knew everything else was going to have to wait.

She found she didn't mind, when usually she resented anything that got in the way of her finding an answer she was looking for. But with Quinn, it came naturally. Maybe because, in his own way, he was what she'd spent her life looking for all along.

CHAPTER TWENTY-EIGHT

Quinn was exhausted, his entire body drained from the healing energy he'd given to Brian and Rose and Jake. It hadn't been enough. But then, with this virus—with him—it was never enough.

Despair swamped him as he followed Jasmine out of the clinic and into the night. He wanted nothing more than to return to his cave to lick his wounds, but he knew they needed to head to the lab despite the late hour. There were blood samples to look at, and they needed to finish their notes while the incident was still fresh in their minds. God knew, he'd been fighting this damn disease for years, and never before had he seen it wipe out a family like this.

He hoped never to see it work this way again, though he had a sick feeling that wasn't going to be the case. Every time this damn virus made an evolutionary leap—such as crossing from a father to his two kids in under three hours—it had a tendency never to go back. The clan might very well be stuck like this for the rest of their lives.

It was a despicable thought.

Jasmine looped her hand through his arm and started pulling him down the street, in the direction opposite from the lab.

"Hey, the lab's that way." He motioned to their left.

"We're not going to the lab. We're going to your house. Phoebe tells me it's just a block or so down this way. Do you think you can make it?"

He shot her an insulted look. "What do I look like? Some candy ass?"

"You don't want to know what you look like right now," she answered tartly, continuing to drag him along.

"We have work to do."

"Believe me, I know. And if it wasn't for you, I'd be in the lab already—deep into the new research samples. But here you are, gray and swaying and looking like one wrong move will have you laid out on the sidewalk. We're going to your place."

"I actually feel pretty okay, all things considered." And he did feel much better than he usually did after something like that. It must be Jasmine again, providing some kind of buffer between him and the pain and exhaustion that had threatened to swamp him in the clinic. He grinned, even as his eyes nearly drifted shut. He could get used to this.

"Yeah," she muttered sarcastically. "You feel great—ready to take on the world. That is, if you don't fall asleep on your feet."

"Med school was worse than this."

"Like that's a recommendation for the state you're in? I remember being a zombie for at least two years there." She eyed him curiously. "You went to medical school?"

"Three times. Things kept changing, and I wanted to keep up."

"Of course you did." She pulled them to a stop in front of a small cul-de-sac. "Now, which one is yours?"

He gave her directions, then let her guide him down the street to his place. He was so wiped out that he floated along in a mix of euphoria and sorrow. Once he got some rest, he knew the anger and sadness would take precedence, but right now he almost enjoyed the strange high that came from being this exhausted.

Within minutes Jasmine had him inside his house and stretched out on the large king-sized bed in the middle of his bedroom. She stood up, as if to move away, but he grabbed her hand. "Stay with me," he said, shocked at how vulnerable it made him feel to ask.

"I'm not going anywhere," she answered, slipping his shoes and jeans off before doing the same to her own. Then she climbed into the bed beside him, her long, lean body fitting against his like she was made for him.

She was made for him, Quinn reminded himself, draping his arm around her waist and pulling her even more closely against him. The last thing he remembered before falling into a deep, dreamless sleep was his mate stroking his hair and whispering soft, sweet words of comfort. Nothing had ever felt so good.

Quinn woke up in a maelstrom of need, his body on fire, aching, burning with the need to be inside Jasmine. His cock was so hard it felt like it would explode, and every muscle in his body was tense to the point of pain.

She was stretched out beside him and her shirt had risen up to the middle of her stomach, leaving the entire lower half of her glorious body bare. His mouth watered with the need to taste her.

Rolling over on top of her, he settled himself between her legs and trailed soft, warm kisses down her jaw, over her forehead, across her cheek. She tasted delicious—like sweet honey and blackberries and sexy, willing woman.

Memories from the day before bombarded his mind, but he shoved them away as he concentrated on Jasmine. He would have to deal with the impact of yesterday soon enough. For now he was going to steal a few moments for himself. For Jasmine.

He let his lips drift over her mouth and Jasmine's eyes slowly blinked open. He wasn't sure what he expected to see there—bewilderment, caution, heat. But he saw none of that, only an open, honest warmth that arrowed straight to his heart—and cock—as well as enough concern for him to drown out all the months and years and decades of loneliness that came before her. No one had ever gotten inside him like she did. No friend or lover or family member had been able to thaw the frigidity that had been growing in him for centuries.

"Good morning," she whispered, reaching a hand out and trailing it over the two days' worth of stubble that decorated his chin.

"I know how to make it a better morning," he answered with a small smile.

"I just bet you do." Her legs slid open wider, making a cradle for him between her thighs even as her eyes drifted shut and she turned her head to the left.

He froze for long seconds, incapable of movement, barely capable of thought as he tried to absorb what she'd done. He told himself it didn't matter, that she didn't know, that humans didn't follow the same rules that shifters did. But those arguments hardly mattered—not to his human side or to the dragon that was even now trying to get out.

Jazz trusted him not to hurt her so completely that she had exposed her jugular to him—something no dragon would ever do unless she felt very, very confident with her mate. And she had closed her eyes while she'd done it. The trust implicit in the action shot right through him, overwhelmed him, made him want to love her and cuddle her and cherish her all at the same time. That it didn't have the same significance to her didn't matter. All that mattered was that she was his.

"Quinn?" Her sleepy, sexy voice rumbled its way through him. "Are you okay?"

He didn't know how to answer. On one hand, he felt better than he had ever imagined he could. On the other, he was on wild, uncharted ground. He didn't know what to say, how to act, what to do to show her just how much she meant to him.

But when her eyes opened and he could see her need for him—a need combined with affection that somehow exactly mirrored his own feelings—it melted him completely.

Leaning forward, he took her mouth with his own, using his lips and tongue to arouse her—to soothe her—in a way he never had before, not even with Jasmine. He wanted her, God did he want her, but even more overwhelming than the desire was the tenderness he felt for her. The softness she brought to him when he was used to being the strong one, the tough one.

He nipped at her lower lip, reveling in the sexy moan she didn't try to stop. Sucked it into his mouth in an effort to ease the confusing rush of feelings tearing at his insides.

She went wild, her strong warrior's body bucking against him. She wrenched her mouth from his, skimmed her mouth down his neck and over his shoulder, and he shuddered with the effort it took to restrain himself. To hold the beast back when it wanted nothing more than to lose itself in her.

But this moment, this morning after one of the worst days of his professional life, meant more to him than a desperate drive for satisfaction. Jasmine was his, and he wanted to show her that being with him didn't always have to be flash and fire, didn't always have to be a struggle for control.

Reaching up, he cupped her face in one of his hands and just looked at her. From the little lines just starting at the corners of her glorious eyes to the small scar that ran along the edge of her jaw to the random scattering of freckles that decorated her nose, he memorized her. Pulled her face, pulled *her*, deep inside of himself, where he could hold on to her whenever his fucked-up life started crashing in on him. And she let him. Instead of struggling against him or trying to move things along faster, Jasmine just lay there and let him look. Lay there and watched him as intently as he was watching her.

When he couldn't take it any longer, when his need to be inside her was nearly overwhelming, he moved so that he covered her. So that every part of her body was covered by every part of his. Not domination, but protection. Not control, but adoration. Bending forward, he kissed the softness of her lips, the corners of her mouth. Traced his tongue along her full bottom lip, lingering at the cute little indention in the center of her lopsided upper lip. She was like the richest, smoothest velvet, so much softer than she looked on the outside. So much hotter than he had dreamed his mate could be.

He wanted to be gentle this time, to give her the tenderness she deserved. But the second her tongue tangled with his, he was lost. Lust rose, sharp and terrible and all-consuming. He ignored it, beat it down, kissed her some more. He was unwilling to give up her lips, unable to break the connection when everything inside of him clamored to be a part of her. To make her a part of him.

He didn't lift his mouth until she whimpered, gasped for air. Only then did he relinquish her lips, skimming his own down her cheek and over the long, graceful curve of her neck to the delicate bones of her shoulders. How could she be so fragile and yet so strong?

Using his free hand, he pushed her shirt up, baring her beautiful breasts. Then he slowly pulled it over her head, fully exposing her round breasts and beautiful, dusky rose nipples. She was amazing, glorious, and as he ran his tongue around her areola, he had only one thought: to worship her, to pleasure her, to make her his, once and for all.

Then he forgot everything but the ecstasy of being with her as he licked and kissed his way over every inch of her body. He explored the curve of her shoulder, the bend in her elbow, the back of her knee. Then tickled her ribs with his tongue before moving between her legs and tasting her. Feasting on her. Claiming her.

He slid his tongue over her labia, once, twice, loving the spicy scent and taste of her. Slipped inside of her and stroked her from the inside as her hands clutched at his hair, his shoulders.

Ran his tongue over and around the hard button of her clit as she sighed and moaned.

And then, with a quick flick of his tongue and a stroke of his fingers, he brought her to climax. Pulling back, desperate to see her, he stroked his thumb over her, intensifying Jasmine's orgasm even as he watched her take her pleasure. Her back bowed, her hips moved languorously against his thumb, and her skin flushed a pretty pink that called to him, urging him to take her. To take all of her.

His cock twitched, but he wasn't ready to give up the view quite yet. Not when she was spread before him like a feast, like a banquet. Not when she was so completely open and vulnerable to him, and he felt like he was the same to her.

When she finally stopped coming, he spread her legs a little wider, then simply looked at her soft, pink pussy.

He trailed a finger over the warm, slick folds, reveling in the feel of her desire for him. Slid a finger between her labia and deep inside her.

"Quinn!" It was a plea and they both knew it. "I want you."

"You have me," he murmured, sliding first one finger and then another into her, nearly losing it at the unbelievable perfection of her body. She was tight, hot, her muscles clenching in a rhythm he could feel resonating all the way to his dick.

Suddenly, he couldn't take it anymore. Rolling onto his back, he reached into the nightstand by his bed and pulled out a condom. After rolling it quickly down his cock, he pulled Jasmine over him and, with his hands on her hips, gently guided her onto him.

She cried out as he sank into her, arched her back and clutched at his hands until he twined his fingers with hers. Something about that connection, that joining of Jasmine's hands with his own as she rode him, sent him right up to the edge of his control.

Fighting to hang on, never wanting the feelings to end—never wanting the closeness between them to dissipate—he clung to sanity even as her breath grew quicker and her movements more frantic. He reveled in the feel of her pussy around him, rejoiced in the slight pressure of her warm weight on his stomach as she slowly moved herself up and down his cock.

"Quinn," she moaned breathlessly, another plea. He knew she was close to shattering again. And he loved it. How could he not when he was the one benefiting from her glorious, unselfish passion?

Slipping his hands around her hips, he cupped her gorgeous, round ass in his hands. He kneaded it for a moment, before slipping a finger into the seam of her ass and pressing against her anus.

She gasped, arched, but she didn't deny him, and as he slid his finger inside of her, he whispered, "Let it take you, my sweet Jazz. Let it have you."

And she did, her back arching above him like a bow as the waves exploded through her. Her sex clenched around his cock again and again, pulling him deeper. Taking him home.

At the last minute she leaned down and brushed her lips over his as her crazy violet eyes looked deep into his own. That was all it took, those moments of connection so deep and profound that he couldn't help feeling like they would be tangled together forever.

With a moan, he let himself go, and the release that swept through him was so strong, so powerful, that for a moment it was like death itself.

"I love you, Jasmine," he said, as the orgasm swamped him. "I love you."

She didn't answer him, didn't proclaim her love back to him. But that was okay. Until she was ready to embrace what was between them, he would love her enough for both of them.

CHAPTER TWENTY-NINE

Minutes later—or maybe it was hours, she couldn't be sure—Jasmine felt Quinn stir against her. How he could be moving she didn't know, not when her body and emotions were so used up she was contemplating staying in this bed forever. There was nothing outside of it that she wanted more than she wanted Quinn.

That thought—on top of the words he'd whispered at the end of their lovemaking—suddenly rang alarm bells deep inside of her. She'd never wanted a man to love her, had never wanted to love a man. With her parents' marriage, she'd seen firsthand how destructive love could be. And yet here she was, in the arms of a man she cared deeply for, reimagining the life she'd had mapped out for herself since she'd gotten into college with a GED.

Since when was she the kind of woman who fell for a few sweet words? she wondered frantically as she struggled to get her heartbeat under control. Since when did she fancy herself caring deeply for a man, so deeply that he could wound her with a stray word or a careless flick of his hand?

Since Quinn, she realized, feeling a little sick, as she pushed against his chest. She was suddenly having trouble breathing, the walls—and Quinn—closing around her until she felt claustrophobic for the first time since she'd walked out of her father's house more than a decade and a half before.

"Hey. Are you okay?" Quinn lifted his head to look at her.

"Yeah, fine." She pushed him off of her and slid out of bed, searching frantically for the T-shirt he'd discarded a little while before. "But it occurs to me that I should probably get going. I need to stop at Phoebe's house before heading into the lab. I've been wearing the same pants for two days now. Any longer and they'll be able to stand up on their own. But I'll see you later at the lab."

She thought she'd managed to cover the panic in her voice pretty well, but Quinn must have picked up on something because he rolled over until he was sitting on the side of the bed. Catching her hand in one of his huge ones, he pulled her between the V of his legs.

"Come on, Jazz. Talk to me."

"I am talking to you." She slipped his T-shirt back over her head and did everything in her power not to make eye contact with him. "But I need to get going. I have some ideas about the virus that I want to check out, and I need to get to the lab to do that."

"The virus can wait."

"I never thought I'd hear you say that."

"Well, you did. You're my mate, Jasmine. Nothing's more important to me than making sure that you are safe and happy."

She reared back, stumbling away from him as his words burned a path through her brain. Had he just called her his mate? *Like, partner? Like, wife?* Surely that wasn't what he was talking about. Surely he wasn't—

"Damn. I didn't mean to blurt it out like that."

"Blurt what out?" Her voice was shaky and way too high, but it was the best she could do under the circumstances.

He shook his head. "We can talk about it later. I—"

"Don't do that to me! Don't spring words like *mate* on me and then pat me on the head and send me on my way. What are you talking about?"

"Look, it's complicated."

"Try me. I'm pretty sure I can keep up." She narrowed her eyes at his very guilty-looking face.

"I know you don't know much about shifters . . ."

"I can guess that when they use the word *mate* it's pretty serious."

"Yes." He nodded.

"Then why are you throwing words like that around? We barely know each other."

He gestured to the bed. "Did that feel like we barely knew each other?"

"That was sex."

"Bullshit." He sprung to his feet, stalked across the room toward her. As she watched him move, his body loose and flowing and yet vaguely threatening, she realized again just how predatory he could be.

"That was a hell of a lot more than just a biological urge. You let me deep inside you, past all those barriers and 'no trespassing' signs you have posted, and I did the same."

"It wasn't like that," she protested, as panic assailed her. "It was nothing."

"It was everything. You're mine, Jasmine."

"Actually, I'm *mine*. I don't belong to any man and I never will."

He growled, deep in his throat, and he advanced, forcing her to back up or get run over. They both stopped when her back hit the wall.

"You told me you were mine when we made love the other night. You said you belonged to me." His voice was low, distorted, much more dragon than human.

"That was during sex. It doesn't mean I want to mate with you. How could you think that?" she demanded. "We've known each other all of four days."

"And we bonded after all of twelve hours. You can't tell me you don't feel it."

"Feel what?" she said, panic turning to terror in the blink of an eye. She was suddenly very aware of the heat deep down inside of her, a fire that had been there from the first moment Quinn had opened his mouth to speak to her.

She had ignored it that night at the bar, but it had burned so hot and bright when she'd been driving away from him the next morning that for a while she'd been sure she was getting sick. She had put it down to too much tequila, but it didn't go away as the day progressed. It had only gotten worse until she'd seen Quinn again. Then the fire had quieted—not going away, but turning into a soft glow that comforted her instead of making her feel like she was being burned alive.

He studied her with eyes the color of the storm-tossed Atlantic. "You know exactly what I'm talking about. I know you do. You have to."

"I don't have to do anything." It was an instinctive protest, one that laid all of her insecurities—all her baggage— out in plain view, and she kicked herself as soon as she said it.

"Yeah, Jazz, sometimes you do." Quinn shook his head. "There's only so much you can control in the universe. Sometimes fate gives you a kick in the ass that you can't ignore."

"You're calling me a kick in your ass?"

"Actually, I was talking about me, but, yeah. It works both ways. I was miserable, self-destructive, flirting with suicide when I ran into you at that bar. Believe me, I wasn't looking for you, either."

She was shocked at the hurt his words caused, especially when they were damn close to the ones she'd just hurled at him. The idea that she had caused him pain bothered her, even when she was so furious with him she could barely see. The feeling only made the fear she felt deeper, more intense.

"If you feel that way, why did you bond with me?" she asked.

Quinn backed away then, thrusting a hand through his hair as he turned from her. And suddenly she knew the truth. "You didn't do it on purpose. You had no intention of mating with me."

He didn't say anything, just stood with his back turned to her. His gorgeous dragon tattoo—an exact replica of what he looked like in dragon form—seemed to be staring out at her, its eyes nearly alive. She shuddered under the perceived scrutiny, felt her heart break wide-open—which was ridiculous. It wasn't like she'd wanted anything more than a casual affair, anyway.

"Well, okay, this is good then," she said, running her suddenly damp palms down the sides of her pants. "You don't want to be mated to me, and I don't want to be mated to you. Surely, there's some way to undo this thing."

"I never said I didn't want you for a mate." Quinn's voice was even more gravelly now, and the eyes he turned to her were pure dragon.

"You just admitted that you didn't choose me. It's the same thing."

"No. It's not." He gestured to his arm, to the three tribal bands encircling his bicep. She was fascinated by them, particularly the deep purple one that had been done in such a way that it seemed woven into the ink of the other two. "Do you think this can just be undone?" he demanded.

"What?" she asked. "Your tattoos?"

He tapped the purple bond. "This isn't a tattoo. It's a tangible representation of my feelings for you, of the commitment we have for each other. It burned itself into my skin that first morning, after we were together."

"That's absurd!" she said, panic choking her so that she could barely get the words out. "Stuff like that doesn't happen."

Quinn just lifted one imperious brow. " 'There are more things in heaven and earth than are dreamt of in your philosophy.' "

"That's Shakespeare, not real life!"

"And you're not Horatio. But the sentiment still stands, Jasmine." He crossed back to her, reached for her with hands that were trembling just a little. "No, I didn't consciously choose you to be my mate any more than you did me. But there's something there—there has to be or we never would have bonded as we have."

He lowered his mouth until it was only inches from her own. "There has to be or I wouldn't feel the way I do about you."

She couldn't catch her breath. "You said you loved me, but you can't. The whole idea is ridiculous."

He looked at her reproachfully. "How can you believe that? How can you not feel what you do to me in every brush of my lips over your body, every touch of my hand against yours?"

"You feel desire."

"I feel love. I love you, Jasmine. Even knowing that you aren't ready for this—ready for me—I love you. Enough to wait until you are ready."

Her knees gave out from under her, and if she hadn't been leaning against the wall, she would have fallen. "You can't say things like that."

"I can't not say them, Jasmine."

The fire inside of her exploded, went from a nice safe little flame to a raging inferno in the space of one breath to the next. Still she doubted it, doubted him, doubted this whole mating scenario. Who had ever heard of two people bonding like this without being aware of it?

Except Quinn had been aware of it, the small part of her brain that was still functioning reminded her. Maybe not immediately, but very soon afterward. And he hadn't told her anything about it.

It bothered her that he'd kept it to himself and then jumped back into bed with her. Maybe there'd been an escape clause, maybe they'd had a chance to turn it around. That he hadn't even brought it up with her didn't bode well for how he viewed their relationship—and her place in it.

"So, if you love me, shouldn't you have told me about this mating thing? Didn't you think I had the right to know?"

He winced. "Of course I did. But when I woke up the next morning, you were gone, and I was sure I'd never see you again. Believe me, you didn't want to be around me then. I was convinced I was totally fucked, mated to a woman I would never see again. It wasn't a pretty picture."

"But you did see me again. Why didn't you tell me then?"

"What was I supposed to say, Jasmine? Thanks for the great sex last night. And by the way, we're bound together for eternity? You would have freaked."

Just hearing the words now, four days later, nearly made her break out in hives, so maybe he had a point. And yet . . . "I'm not a child, Quinn. I don't need to be controlled, steered in the right direction. You had no right to treat me like one."

"And I'm not your father, Jasmine. I'll never treat you like a possession, never try to make you feel like less than you are. I'll never hurt you like he did, and you have no right to treat me like I would."

She gasped, feeling like he'd slapped her. Wishing that he had because it would hurt so much less than the callous way he'd thrown her past back at her. She'd told him that in confidence and never dreamed that he would use it against her.

Tears flooded her eyes, clogged her throat for the first time in longer than she could remember. Frantic, she glanced around for her shoes, her purse. She grabbed them and hit the door at a dead run.

Quinn was quicker and blocked her way. "I'm sorry, Jazz. I didn't mean that."

"Get the hell out of my way!"

"Come on, don't leave like this. Not until we've sorted this thing out."

"Quinn, if you ever have any hope of having a relationship with me in the future, you'll get the hell away from that door. I will not be kept prisoner here."

He looked stricken. "I wasn't trying to do any such thing," he said, moving to the side. "I swear. Jasmine, please, stay and talk to me."

"I can't talk to you now," she said on her way out the door. "I can't even look at you."

She closed the door softly behind her, refusing to give in to the urge to slam it. He didn't deserve the satisfaction.

CHAPTER THIRTY

Hours later, Jasmine was still reeling from the fight she'd had with Quinn—and from the realization that they were bonded. *Mated—whatever*. How was it even possible, when she'd never imagined falling in love, never imagined settling down with any man? She'd never wanted to give one that much power over her. Look at what Quinn had done—deliberately lying to her, and then lashing out at her with the one thing guaranteed to hurt her. Was it any wonder she'd planned to go it alone?

She wondered if this whole thing was just some strange dream or hallucination. It wasn't like she was in love with Quinn, anyway. They'd just been having fun together, enjoying each other's bodies and minds.

Sighing, she dropped her head down onto her workstation. She didn't really think she was going to convince herself to believe that, did she? Not when she could remember so clearly what it felt like to be held in his arms. Or how her heart had nearly broken with the pain she knew Quinn kept bottled up inside of him. Their relationship was a lot of things—wrenching, intense, emotional. Fun and games barely scratched the surface.

Frustrated, furious and completely fed up, Jasmine very deliberately buried her thoughts about Quinn. She had a job to do that in no way revolved around him, and she was going to do it, damn it. The sooner she found the key to unraveling this damn virus, the sooner she could get the hell out of Dodge. And with the way things were going around here, she was more than ready to be on her way.

Liar, the little voice in the back of her head taunted. *You don't want to leave any more than he wants you to.* She shut it down, refusing to listen. The last thing she needed was to break down in tears in the middle of the lab. Phoebe might have a heart attack if she did.

In the meantime, the tension in the laboratory was so thick that Jasmine swore if she tried to walk around, she'd slam straight into an invisible brick wall. Quinn was over in his section, looking at the results of Brian's autopsy report. Except for his regular blood draw, the coroner hadn't found any evidence of injection—which was the number one thing they'd all been waiting to hear about—and Quinn wasn't taking the news well. The idea that this might be an airborne strain was enough to make them all crazy.

She glanced at Phoebe, who was working diligently over a set of petri dishes, while Jasmine was following up on the hunch she'd had the day before, as she'd watched Brian and his children slowly die.

She looked at the strain that had infected Brian, then popped up the blood samples from his two children side by side with it. The strain was the same in all three of them—no mutations, no changes. They were identical, something they hadn't seen in consecutive cases of the disease in a number of months now.

What was particularly interesting about this strain was the way it had invaded the three hosts' DNA so quickly, without the body even having a chance to fight it off—almost as if it had been manufactured specifically for Brian and his children. Which was absurd. Except . . .

She clicked a few keys, separated the virus's RNA from Brian's DNA and compared the two. Her heart started to beat a little faster, excitement thrumming in her bloodstream even as she forced herself to remain calm and focused. She could still be wrong. There was no use getting excited until she knew for sure.

Punching up the viral infection pattern from Rose and Jake, she had the computer separate it out in the same way. As she looked at it, everything snapped into place with an almost audible click.

Still, she wasn't ready to say anything. She needed more evidence, needed to see how this worked with another family. Something Quinn had said jogged her memory, and she pulled up the list of case files, scanning through until she found the two that belonged to Dylan's sister and niece, Marta and Lana. She did the same thing to their samples as she'd done to the others—and came up with the exact same response, despite the fact that the virus was very different from the one that attacked Brian and his family.

On a hunch, she pulled up Michael's sample, looked at it. It was a different mutation from Brian's as well, though no less sophisticated. Pulling it apart yielded the same results she'd seen with the previous two mutations. And yet, if what she was thinking was the case, shouldn't Quinn have been infected?

She pushed away from her workstation and bounded across the lab to where they kept the medical supplies. Picking up a slide, a needle and an alcohol swab, she called out, "Quinn, I need you over here for a second. I want to look at something."

The urgency in her tone caused both Quinn and Phoebe's heads to snap up. "What's wrong?" Quinn demanded, as he made his way across the lab entirely too quickly for her peace of mind. The fact that Phoebe beat him didn't escape her notice.

"I need some blood."

"Whose blood?" he asked.

"Yours, Quinn! Whose do you think? Actually," she turned to Phoebe. "Can you call Dylan? I'd really like to take a sample of his blood as well."

"Of course. But where are you going with this?" Phoebe eyed her intently.

"I'm not exactly sure yet."

"But you *are* on to something. I can tell," Phoebe said with a dawning excitement.

"I think I am. I do want the coroner to take another look at Brian's body, however. I'm pretty sure he missed the injection site."

Quinn held his arm out to her, and Jasmine swabbed it quickly with alcohol, doing her best not to touch him any more than she absolutely had to. She could tell that he noticed by the darkening of his eyes, but he didn't say anything, and she was grateful for that. Her emotions had had more than enough for the day.

She did the blood draw quickly, taking two tubes of blood, then left him to deal with the bandage in her rush to look at the sample. Thank God for Quinn's supercomputer—as she worked, she was aware that Quinn and Phoebe were hanging over her shoulder.

She smeared a little of his blood on a slide, then spun the rest out. She wanted to look at his DNA, which she could only do when she'd separated the white blood cells from the red.

While she waited for everything else to be ready, she took the slide over to the high-powered electron microscope, photographed it, then pulled the photo up on the left side of her computer monitor. She made sure Michael's was on the right, and she studied both of them for long minutes, her eyes going back and forth between the two.

"What are we looking for?" demanded Phoebe, leaning over her shoulder.

"I'm not sure."

"Well, what are you sure of?"

"Nothing yet. That's the whole point of this exercise."

The supercomputer stopped working, so she switched screens, pulling up the DNA information from Quinn and once again comparing it to Michael's. What she saw in the string of code had her heart beating faster.

She could see it there. God, she could actually see it there.

"Jasmine." Quinn's voice was a low warning—a sure sign that he was running out of patience.

She looked at the numbers one more time, then turned to Phoebe.

"Can you help me harvest the DNA from Quinn's blood sample? I want to pull the actual strands out and look at them as well."

"Of course. But could you at least give us some idea of what you're doing? You're driving me nuts!"

"First, did you ever spin Michael's blood out like this—look at his DNA?"

"No," Quinn answered. "It never occurred to us that we would need to."

"Which means you didn't do it for anyone else either, right? Not Lana or Marta?"

Phoebe's eyes narrowed, even as she got out the detergent and alcohol they were going to need to separate the DNA. "What are you getting at, Jasmine? What does DNA at its molecular level have to do with this? And why are we talking siblings and relatives here?" She gestured to the computer screen. "What am I not seeing here?"

"I'd really rather look at everything—"

"Come on! We're not going to hold you to it, whatever it is. Just give us something."

The urgency in Phoebe's voice broke through the excited hum working its way through Jasmine. A quick glance at Quinn showed that he was dying a thousand deaths waiting for her answer, and she knew she couldn't hold out on them any longer, even if she didn't yet have proof to back up her theory.

Turning back to the computer screen, she pulled up Quinn's results. "Do you see this?" she said, pointing to the healthy red blood cells that were magnified and shown in 3-D on her monitor. Then she pointed to a few of the round, spiky things weaving their way through his bloodstream.

"That's Michael's blood, right? After he was infected with the virus." Phoebe bent down to get a closer look. "It looks like everyone else's that we've seen in here."

"Except this isn't Michael's blood. This is Quinn's. I—"

"What?" Phoebe gasped, her hands going to her mouth. "He's infected? Oh my God!"

"He's fine!" Jasmine snapped out, yanking her friend onto one of the nearby chairs before she fell down. "You're fine," she repeated, glancing up at Quinn, whose skin had taken on a decidedly gray tinge. "This is why I didn't want to say anything before I had all my ducks in a row."

"What are you saying? That Quinn's infected but he isn't going to catch the disease?"

"That's exactly what I'm saying. Look at this." She put a finger on the computer screen and traced the virus. "It's breaking down, getting weaker—not stronger."

"How do you know? Maybe this is just another mutation. Maybe it's changed since he caught it from Brian."

"Oh, it's a mutation, all right, but he didn't catch it from Brian. He caught it from Michael." She pulled Michael's blood sample up on the left of the screen again. "See what I'm talking about?" Again, she traced over the enlarged virus cells, only this time they were a lot healthier than the ones in Quinn's system. "See the differences?" she said. "This is the same incarnation of the virus, but it's one where the immune system didn't fight back. It just allowed it in."

She went back to Quinn's blood. "It's a marked contrast to this sample, where Quinn's immune system has almost completely obliterated the virus."

"So, what are you saying? That I have some weird antibodies that prevent me from catching this thing?"

"That's exactly what I'm saying. And I don't think it's just you. I think it's Dylan as well."

Both Quinn and Phoebe went rigid. "You think Dylan's infected?" Quinn demanded, as Phoebe reached for her cell phone.

"I don't know. But I'm guessing he might have been infected three months ago by Marta—" Jasmine clicked the mouse a few times and pulled up Marta's blood sample. The virus bore marked differences to the one that had killed Michael. "But I don't know how long the virus takes to break down. Quinn's immune system has almost obliterated it in five days. Dylan's probably did the same thing, but even so, there should be a trace of it left behind."

"So why do some people infected with the virus get sick and not others?" demanded Phoebe, hanging up the phone after all but ordering her mate to get to the lab.

"That's how all viruses work," Quinn answered. "We've just been so used to thinking of this thing as having a one hundred percent mortality rate that we forgot how likely it was for some people to be infected without developing symptoms."

"Do you think I've been infected?" Phoebe asked. Typical of the scientist, her voice held only mild curiosity, as opposed to the panic that had been there when she'd thought of Dylan or Quinn having contracted the virus.

"Actually, I don't. But we can take some blood and find out right now."

"Yeah. Let's do that." Quinn's voice was tense. "Dylan will lose it if you don't have the answer to that question by the time we explain this to him."

Jasmine spent the next few minutes taking Phoebe's blood and repeating the same steps she'd just gone through with Quinn. But when they pulled up Phoebe's blood sample, it was perfectly clean— no trace of the virus.

Jasmine grinned, excited to have more proof that she was finally on the right trail.

Quinn was watching her with eyes turned nearly black in their intensity. "She's been exposed as much as I have, but she hasn't contracted anything. Why?"

"Because none of the people who have contracted the disease share Phoebe's DNA."

Total and complete silence met her announcement, and for long seconds nobody moved. Then both Quinn and Phoebe started talking at once.

"You can't be saying that this spreads on a DNA level?" asked Phoebe.

"Is that what the mutations are?" Quinn demanded. "Changes in the virus meant to make it more compatible with the victim's DNA?"

Jasmine smiled, thrilled that someone else was now thinking along the same lines she was. "That's exactly what I'm saying. All along, you've been bamboozled as to how this thing spreads. Sometimes it's been injected by a Wyvernmoon, and sometimes it just seems to spread."

She pulled up the samples from Brian and his family again. "This is why it spreads. Look at this mutation—it's different from what killed Michael or Lana and Marta. But it is exactly the same as what killed both of his children."

"So, one family member gets injected with the disease that is somehow modified to their DNA—and then spreads it to the rest of their blood relations?" Phoebe sounded both horrified and fascinated. "By what? Physical contact?"

"I don't know," Quinn said, looking shell-shocked. "But that would explain why Brian's wife didn't get sick. The virus was formulated to break down Brian's DNA, not hers."

"Exactly!" Jasmine told him. "Each mutation we're seeing is actually the virus being mapped genetically to best attack an individual's DNA. Or at least that's my theory."

She pulled up Michael's DNA map, which she'd had the supercomputer start on when she first got there, figuring it would be interesting to see if the virus actually made any significant changes in the host's DNA—which, it turned out, it had.

She showed the proof to Quinn and Phoebe, and Phoebe cursed, very loudly and creatively. "If this is the case, we really do have a traitor in the clan. How else could the Wyvernmoons be getting DNA samples?"

"Absolutely," agreed Quinn, and Jasmine could see that he'd reached the same unsavory conclusion she had. "But it's worse than that, Phoebe. If what Jasmine suspects is true, then when Marta was infected a few months ago, it was a direct assassination attempt on Dylan."

"Just as Michael's death a few days ago was an assassination attempt on you." Jasmine hadn't wanted to say it, knowing how the words were going to hit Quinn, but the scientist in her wouldn't let her leave out any pertinent facts.

Quinn reeled, as if he hadn't seen his own situation as clearly, but that only made it more important to bring the connection to light. It stood to reason that if the Wyvernmoons had tried to kill him once, they would do so again.

Quinn stumbled backward a few steps, turned away, and Jasmine popped up to follow him. She might still be furious at him, but she could see the guilt all over his face and knew it would eat him alive if she left him alone to deal with it.

"It isn't your fault, Quinn."

"They killed him to get to me. How much more my fault can it be?"

"They killed him, not you. And if it wasn't with this virus, it would have been with something else designed to make you vulnerable. Their fault, not yours."

"No."

"Yes!" Phoebe's voice rang out across the lab. "This is no different than when they kidnapped me to set that trap for Dylan, Quinn. Was it Dylan's fault that you were injured in that fight or that I was at Silus's mercy for hours?"

"It's not the same thing."

"It's exactly the same thing," Dylan's voice came from the back of the lab, where he'd entered unbeknownst to them. "You convinced me to stop blaming myself for what happened to Phoebe. If what you said then was the truth, then you can't blame yourself for this. No matter how much it hurts to think that Michael was turned into a weapon to hurt you. It wasn't his fault and it wasn't yours."

Quinn nodded, but Jasmine could tell by the look on his face that it was going to be a long time before he would start to believe what they were saying. If he ever did.

The thought made her ache, as Quinn had spent far too long holding himself responsible for every bad thing that happened in his world. She couldn't help wondering how many more hits he could take before going down, once and for all.

CHAPTER THIRTY-ONE

It was time. After nearly two years of waiting, of laying the trap, it was finally time to spring it shut. If things went as planned, Quinn, Dylan, Phoebe—as well as a number of Dylan's sentries—would be eliminated, once and for all. And as for Dr. Jasmine Kane, well, it would be a pleasure to ensure that she would be taken out of the equation as well.

They'd had to move up the timetable thanks to her. Maybe it would have been okay, maybe things could have waited another week as they had planned, but she hadn't liked the way Jasmine, Quinn and Phoebe had huddled over the computer monitors all morning. She didn't know what they had found—she'd been flawless in disposing the evidence—but still, better to move things along before they discovered the weakness in the Wyvernmoon virus.

Once Dylan and his highest-ranking officials were out of the way, there would be nothing to stop the Wyvernmoons from taking over. Then they could kill any Dragonstar who would not swear allegiance to them—they could, as long as a cure to the virus was not found. If those three damn doctors managed to figure out how to get around the virus—and as the Wyvernmoons had recently learned themselves, there was a way—then there was a chance the takeover would not go as smoothly as they had planned. And that was not acceptable—not to Brock and not to her. The Dragonstars were too big a threat.

Her Dragonstar cell phone started ringing. She answered it with a cautious "Hello," then did her best to sound normal as Gabe, one of Dylan's two second-in-commands, spewed orders for her to get to the lab, ASAP.

She agreed. What else could she do? She couldn't afford to make them suspicious this close to the end. But her skin itched at the thought of being so close to the enemy if something went wrong.

She'd have no means of escape.

She shuddered at the thought of what Dylan would do to her if he found out about her duplicity, but when she closed her eyes, it wasn't their king she saw exacting his revenge. It was Quinn and Gabe, the fires of hell burning in their eyes as they avenged the deaths of their loved ones. Dylan wasn't known for his mercy, but she'd been around him long enough to know that it was there. Gabe had none, and as for Quinn, well, she didn't want to test him. Too many times lately she'd seen his thirst for vengeance.

She would just have to be even more cautious than usual, make sure that she could not be traced to anything. It would be difficult, but not impossible. She couldn't let them find out she was the one who had snuck into Marta's and Michael's houses to steal a few strands of their hair.

But on the off chance—the very off chance—that the plan it had taken Brock and her two years to put together failed, she wanted to make sure she was covered. Because the only thing worse than being a dragon who had betrayed her clan was one who had no clan. It was not a position she ever wanted to be in.

CHAPTER THIRTY-TWO

J asmine laid her head down on her lab station with a grimace. Her back was aching, her eyes burning and her head felt like it was going to explode. And yet, even with all that, she felt better than she had in a long, long time.

They didn't have a cure for the disease—probably wouldn't have one for weeks, if not months—but they had a really sound starting point on which to formulate a vaccine. That was something, not to mention the fact that they now knew that the point of origin for any new familial-based infections was, indeed, an injection.

They still hadn't found an unexplained injection site on Brian, but that didn't mean they wouldn't. In the meantime, Dylan had three of his sentries tracing every step Brian had made in the forty-eight hours before his death. They'd find the moment when he was injected—and when they did, they'd know exactly who to blame.

God knew, Jasmine wasn't the only one who was energized. The lab had enough electricity whipping through it to power a small city for a year. After Dylan had shown up, they had done the same comparison on his blood, and eventually on his DNA. Everyone had breathed a huge sigh of relief that the point of infection had indeed been isolated—and that Dylan had the same antibodies, strangely, that Quinn did. Soon after, the lab had filled up quickly with sentries who wanted to be part of the action, and Jasmine had spent the afternoon working with fifteen different people leaning over her shoulder.

It had been a pain, but the good side of it was that it had kept her from ever being alone with Quinn. From the moment she'd dropped her theory on him and Phoebe, they had all been so busy that she didn't have to worry about him trying to talk to her about being mates.

Not that she figured she should be worried about that—after all, he hadn't felt any need to talk to her about it to begin with.

Now, however, the lab was mostly cleared out—only Dylan, Quinn, Phoebe, Gabe and Callie remained, though Callie had left for a while to run a few errands. Jasmine's stomach growled like it had been twelve days, not twelve hours, since she'd last eaten, and she figured that leaving now was definitely the better part of valor—and discretion, for that matter.

Pushing away from the lab table where she'd been working for the last few hours, she stretched and then snapped off her gloves. She debated telling the others where she was going, but their discussion looked so intent that she hesitated to interrupt them. They could be discussing the weather for all she knew, but it looked much more like they were planning clan strategy—maybe even world domination, she thought with a grin. Better to leave them to it.

She'd bring them something back to eat. There were a few fast-food places within walking distance of the lab, which was perfect since she didn't have her car, as she'd ridden in with Phoebe after she'd gone back to her friend's house to change clothes that morning.

After grabbing her purse from the bottom drawer of her desk, Jasmine swiped her ID card at the door—Quinn had instituted the highest security measures in the last few days and that included an ID check before entering any part of the lab—and listened for the telltale click of the lock disengaging. A quick trip down the long, dimly lit hallway, a small wave to Denny, the night security guard, another swipe of her card, and she was finally outside.

Her first breath of desert air relaxed her muscles one by one as a quiet peace invaded her consciousness. She'd thought she was relaxed, that she hadn't allowed herself to stress over the big fight they'd had that morning, but the second her tense muscles started to let go, she admitted to herself that she wasn't handling it nearly as well as she thought.

Compartmentalizing, yes, but she wasn't actually handling the situation—not by a long shot. Being out here—unwinding for the first time since he'd walked into the lab so many hours before—proved that much to her.

Glancing down the main road, she spotted a submarine sandwich restaurant a few blocks down to the left and headed toward it. At the moment, she was so hungry she was pretty sure she could eat a foot-long sandwich in a couple of bites. But how much food to get for Quinn, Dylan and Gabe? They looked like they could each put away a grocery store, easy.

As she walked, Jasmine looked around the sleepy little town for the first time, although she supposed it really wasn't all that little. Phoebe had told her last night that the population was close to twenty thousand and that just about everyone was a member of the Dragonstar clan. Which was pretty cool, except that Dylan and Quinn feared that all twenty thousand people might become infected by the virus from hell.

What a nightmare Quinn had been living the past few years. She couldn't imagine what it felt like to be a healer of his caliber and watching his clan members die, one after the other. Maybe that's why she hadn't told him to get the hell out of her life that morning during their huge fight. Usually, she would have been out the door before the first accusations started flying.

She shook her head. She didn't have a clue what to do about the whole Quinn situation. On one hand, she had a ton of respect for him—as a doctor and as a person. On the other hand, there was no way she was going to be able to put up with him trying to handle her, either directly bossing her around or keeping information from her that she needed to know.

Like being his mate. How could he have thought it was a good idea not to tell her about that? Even if the idea made her break out in a cold sweat, she still had the right to know.

Deep in thought about Quinn and their future together—if they even had a future, which was doubtful in her mind—Jasmine was almost to the restaurant before she realized someone was following her. Cursing Quinn for distracting her, she reached into her pocket for her omnipresent pepper spray and came up empty-handed. She'd been so frazzled that morning that she'd left her keys—along with the spray—sitting on Phoebe's counter, figuring she wouldn't need them since she was hitching a ride to work with her friend.

Yet another big mistake. It seemed since she'd gotten to New Mexico she'd been doing nothing but making them. For a woman who prided herself on her competence and ability to think clearly under stress, it was a huge blow.

She walked faster. Perhaps she was being paranoid—living in some of the most savage places in the world could do that to a woman.

The footsteps behind her picked up, her pursuer closing ground, and Jasmine's heartbeat raced. What should she do? she wondered frantically. Make a run for it and hope she made it? Confront the bastard?

The only problem with those scenarios was that she'd seen the dragons move, and she didn't stand a chance, either way. If she ran, he could catch her without breaking a sweat. If she fought, she had no doubt he could crush her without a second thought.

She had just made up her mind to flee—she had to try—when a hand fastened on her elbow from behind. Heart pounding, she whirled around with her fists flying. The element of surprise was the only weapon she had.

But the man wasn't surprised—he was completely ready for her and caught the fist easily. "Whoa, Dr. Kane, don't worry. I'm not going to hurt you." He smiled in a way he no doubt thought was charming, but it made her blood run cold.

"Who are you?" she demanded, looking up at his face. Was she ever going to get used to how tall these dragons were? This one was almost as tall as Dylan, which meant he stood a good seven or eight inches above her own six foot frame. It was insane.

Plus, he was built like Quinn, with huge shoulders and heavily muscled biceps that strained against the sleeves of his white T-shirt. She was so screwed.

"I just want to walk with you. Quinn and Dylan are tied up, and they take your protection very seriously."

She paused for a moment, considering. Sending someone to watch her back was exactly something Quinn would do—if he'd noticed she was gone. But he had been so absorbed in his discussion with Dylan that she wasn't sure he had. Still, if this guy was one of Dylan's sentries, she didn't want to offend him. And if he wasn't— well, then, pretending that she trusted him would buy her more time. Maybe she could get closer to the group of people eating on the restaurant patio about a block and a half up.

She turned and started walking toward them without another word.

He fell into step beside her, and after a second she turned and squinted up at him, trying to figure out if he was one of the shifters she'd met at the lab that afternoon, or if he was at Dylan and Phoebe's house the night she'd first arrived. He didn't look familiar, but then she'd met a lot of people, so maybe her memory was faulty.

But she didn't think so, especially since she didn't get the same vibe from him that she got from the other sentries she'd met so far. Despite the huge dragon tattoo on his arm, there didn't seem to be an ounce of warmth radiating from the guy—and that, more than anything else, convinced her that her first instincts were correct. Dylan's dragons were tough, but they had also been nothing but extremely nice to her. This guy looked like he ate live animals for breakfast. Slowly.

She started to ease away from him a little, but he gripped her elbow again, refusing to let her get more than a step or two ahead. His grip wasn't painful, but the look in his eyes had shifted from simply cold to obviously warning. In a flash, Jasmine went from freaked-out to frightened. She could handle herself with men, but dragons weren't technically men. She remembered how strong Quinn was, how easily he had lifted her while making love, and felt more than a frisson of unease run down her spine.

Her fight with Quinn came back to her, his warning that there were things a lot scarier than him in the dark. She was ready to believe it with this behemoth towering over her. What a way to find out that she really had acted like a total ass.

Still, there was no use panicking—or at least, alerting him to her panic—if she could help it. So, not knowing what else to do, she kept walking, her only goal to get within shouting distance of the people up ahead.

As they walked, Jasmine pasted what she hoped was a convincing grin on her face and said, "I'm sorry. Have we met before? I've been introduced to so many people these last few days."

"No problem. Dylan does have a lot of sentries, doesn't he?"

"Is that who I've been meeting? His . . ." She paused, as if considering his words for a few seconds. "His sentries? I'm not exactly sure what that means, but it sounds important."

"Oh, it is. Most clan leaders don't have nearly as many sentries as Dylan does, but then, Dragonstar is the biggest dragon clan."

"I didn't know that." Would he even feel it if she punched him? she wondered. Kicked him? Or would he merely laugh—then snap her neck in two? No, her best bet was to continue stringing him along. It might be suicidal, but she didn't have many options.

Except for the people at the restaurant and the occasional passing car, the street was pretty much empty. She had to keep him going for another couple of minutes, just until she got to the restaurant. Surely she'd be able to find someone in that crowd willing to help her.

"Are you one of Dylan's sentries?" she asked, trying to buy some time. Maybe if he thought she hadn't picked up on the danger he'd be less likely to turn confrontational.

His laugh, when it came, was ice cold and vicious. "Dylan's a lousy king. There's no way I'd work for him."

So much for stringing him along. "Well, if you aren't a Dragonstar, then who are you?" she asked, making sure her voice was as frigid—and as tough—as his had been. Her hand curled into a fist in her pocket.

He bent down so they were almost face to face, and she steeled herself not to react to the changes in his face. Gone was the man who had first approached her and in his place was someone who looked almost reptilian—as if he were so close to the dragon that his features were almost indistinguishable from it. This didn't bother her when it happened to Quinn—but this guy's dragon was as cold and ugly looking as his human form.

"I'm someone who has a lot invested in watching the Dragonstars fail, and I don't appreciate some little CDC doctor sticking her nose in where she doesn't belong."

Fury whipped through her at his words and their implicit threat. It made her incautious when she should have tread lightly. But just the thought that his man was involved in the virus made her crazy. "Are you responsible for killing all those people?" she demanded fiercely. "Are you the one manufacturing that damned virus?"

His eyes changed, grew unfocused for a moment, and then he blinked, long and slow. When he opened his eyes again she knew, for certain, that she was no longer talking to the man. The dragon was in full control, and he was about a hundred times more frightening than his human side.

"That's none of your business," he hissed, low and mean.

"You made it my business the second you grabbed me, so spare me the bad action movie dialogue. I've seen them all." She yanked on her elbow in an effort to free herself, so angry at the thought of this man playing with so many lives that she no longer cared what happened next.

His hand shifted on her arm, his grip tightening until his fingers dug into the muscles of her upper arm. "So you know how this ends. You come with me or I kill you."

"I'd rather you killed me." She did her best to hold her ground.

"Oh, you'll get that wish soon enough—just not now. Not yet."

She glanced up the block to where a couple of people were watching her dilemma with interest. "Help!" she shouted. "Somebody help me!"

They must have heard her, as a couple of them got up and headed her way. The man holding her didn't seem upset, however, and the closer they got, the more she began to realize why. They looked just like him—cold and flat and reptilian. Her chances for escape had just gone from almost zero to well into the negative numbers.

And isn't that just fantastic?

"Hey, Brock, having trouble with the human?" snickered one of them.

"Not at all. I was just explaining to her—"

He never got to finish the statement. Instead, he went flying about ten feet into the street, propelled by an invisible force. Unfortunately, his grip on her arm never loosened, and she went flying with him.

Brock was off balance now, looking for whatever had dealt the blow, and she took advantage, bringing her knee up between his legs as hard as she could. He screamed and his grip loosened for a second as he fell to his knees. It was all she needed to yank her arm away and deliver a fast, powerful kick to the side of his head.

Then she ran, heading for the lab as fast as she could go—which was pretty fast, if she did say so herself, considering her just-healed ankle, still-sore ribs and assorted other injuries.

But she was no match for the dragons. With a roar, one of the men she'd called to for help—stupid her—landed directly in her path. She tried to hit him like she had Brock, but he sent her flying against the building with one careless swipe of his fist.

272 • TESSA ADAMS

She hit hard—harder than she thought possible from one punch. Her ears were ringing as she tried to right herself, to stagger forward. But he was already there, one huge hand closing around her neck as he slammed her into the building a second time. His fingers tightened around her throat and the world started going gray. She fought him violently, kicking and struggling as she tried desperately to pry his fingers away from her windpipe.

Her back was flush against the building, and she felt a weird stinging in her arm from where she must have scraped against a piece of wood or a nail. Her ribs ached, her head felt like it was going to explode. She was only seconds from blacking out. She fought it— fought him—knowing that the second she lost consciousness she was dead.

In a last ditch effort for freedom, Jasmine dug her fingernails into the hand holding her throat, but while the jerk grunted in pain, he didn't loosen his grip by so much as a millimeter. Not knowing what else to do, she used her last burst of strength to reach upward and rake her nails down the side of his face, digging as deep as she could.

He howled, dropping her as his hand automatically went to his cheek. She hit the ground hard, her legs too shaky to support her.

"You bitch! You'll pay for that!"

She braced herself for a kick, but only one landed—square in her injured ribs—before the man flew backward. She watched in shock as his head twisted violently, his neck broken in one quick snap. But no one was there.

Come on! She heard a voice in her head—dark and sexy and completely male. *There are ten of them left—I can't take them all on. We need to get out of here.*

She scrambled to her feet, looking around wildly, trying to figure out where the voice was coming from.

Jasmine, move it! Then a man was shimmering into solidity right in front of her. He reached for her hand and she recoiled, before realizing that she'd been introduced to him earlier. He was a friend of Quinn's—and a sentry.

"Logan?" she asked faintly.

"Who did you expect, Santa Claus?" And then he picked her up and raced down the street to Quinn's lab, ten dragon shifters in close pursuit.

CHAPTER THIRTY-THREE

*G*oddamnit, Quinn, Dylan! I need you! Now!

The frantic shout slammed through Quinn's concentration like a sledgehammer. He reared up from his desk and headed for the laboratory door without a backward glance. Dylan was right behind him.

Where are you? Quinn demanded of Logan.

A couple of blocks north, with ten pissed-off Wyvernmoons on my ass. What the hell were you thinking letting your mate wander around town without protection? They damn near killed her.

Quinn's dragon leaped forward, breaking the choke chain of control he normally kept on it.

"Mate?" Dylan demanded, as the two of them all but flew down the hall to the front door, ignoring the security measures in their haste to get to the battle. "Is there something you forgot to tell me?"

"Later," he growled, shifting as soon as he hit the nighttime air. Dylan did the same.

"At least tell me who she is," Dylan said, as wings burst through his back and scales rippled across his skin.

"Jasmine."

"And Logan knew this before I did?"

Quinn didn't answer, he couldn't, as the shift completed. He launched himself into the air, screaming for Logan. *Where are you?*

Quinn demanded, never in his life more grateful for Logan's odd psychic power, which enabled him to speak telepathically.

Next to the library and moving fast.

We'll be there in a second, Dylan said. *Call for reinforcements.*

Callie, Caitlyn, Travis and Gabe are on their way.

Good.

Quinn was barely aware of the conversation, barely aware of anything but the driving need to find Jasmine, to protect her. Terror was a frantic nightmare within him, the fear that he would be too late to save her. He pushed himself—and his dragon—faster than he had ever gone before. In some small part of his mind, he registered that Dylan was struggling to keep up, but it never occurred to him to slow down.

I see you! Logan yelled, as he came around the corner and Quinn nearly shuddered with relief as he saw Jasmine, safe and alive, in his friend's arms. Then a lightning bolt flew straight at Logan, followed by a second and a third.

Quinn dove, heading straight for the ground at top speed, but he knew he wouldn't get there in time. Sure enough, Logan managed to dodge the first two bolts, but the third caught him in the upper thigh.

He stumbled, went down hard, and just that easily the first two Wyvernmoons in pursuit were on him. Quinn screamed. Then he pulled out of the dive, picked up the two dragons—who were still in their human form—in his claws and threw them against the nearest building as hard as he could.

Both hit with a satisfying crunch. *Are you okay?* he demanded of Logan, as he stalked toward the two dragons who had dared to touch his mate.

Fine, his friend answered. Quinn was conscious of his rolling to his feet behind him. Dylan was half a block away, taking on the other eight Wyvernmoons as they tried to shift and fight at the same time.

The fact that they were shifting would give Dylan a minute or two advantage, but then he would be in serious trouble. King or no king, he couldn't take on eight fully grown dragons in their prime alone—not if he wanted to live.

Get Jasmine back to the lab! he ordered Logan, advancing on the two shifters he already had in his sights. One shot a lightning bolt at him, which he easily dodged. Then he was on them, ripping them apart with his sharp talons and razorlike teeth.

He didn't take his time, didn't make it pretty. Just got in, got the job done, before racing down the street to Dylan's side. As he did, he realized that Logan hadn't followed his orders, but was guarding Jasmine in an alley between two buildings; Jasmine must have seen him savagely kill the two men without a qualm.

He wondered what that would do to her already bad image of him, but he didn't have time to worry about it now. As he reached Dylan, he saw two Wyvernmoons dead on the ground, trapped halfway between human and dragon, proof that Dylan had managed to hold his own so far. Still, Dylan was surrounded by six fully shifted dragons, all of whom were bearing down on him with blood in their eyes.

Damn it, Logan! Quinn roared as he charged into battle beside his king. *Don't you leave her. She needs to be protected.*

One of the Wyvernmoons swiped at Quinn, who barely managed to dodge a full set of talons in the chest. As it was, he was distracted enough that he caught them on his shoulder.

Fire exploded through the right side of his body.

I got this, Logan yelled frantically. *Keep your mind on what you're doing, asshole!*

With a dragon's scream of fury, Quinn turned toward the dragon who had wounded him and went straight for the jugular. He took him down fast and hard, ripping the other shifter's throat out without a second of remorse, then turned to deal with the next two who were coming at him.

———

"Go help him!" Jasmine screamed at Logan, as she watched two evil-looking dragons bear down on Quinn. Both were pitch black and huge, their monstrous eyes glowing with flames while their fangs dripped with saliva. She'd never seen a rabid animal up close, but those two seemed as close to rabid as dragons could get.

"I'm supposed to protect you. Quinn will kill me if anything happens to you."

"I'm fine! Besides, who's going to protect me if the Wyvernmoons get through Dylan and Quinn?"

"Good point." He turned and glared sternly at her, his amber eyes glowing with his own dragon. "You stay here or Quinn will kill both of us."

"I won't move. I swear—just go!"

Logan shifted into his dragon on the run, a huge, red beast with a spiky tail and enormous wings and claws. Grabbing one of three dragons that was currently attacking Dylan, he ripped the thing apart with his bare hands. Jasmine gasped, looked away. Then she nearly cheered when she saw four more Dragonstar sentries landing next to their king.

The battle was over in a matter of seconds, as the seven Dragonstars ripped the remaining Wyvernmoons to shreds. One took off, trying to flee, she assumed, and Logan sent a fireball straight at him. It caught him in the tail, and he dropped about ten yards toward the ground before managing to right himself.

Dylan sent a huge ball of flames straight at him, but he managed to dodge it, heading straight up into the clouds. Quinn took off after him, followed by two Dragonstar sentries she didn't know. They caught up to the injured dragon quickly, but the next thing she knew a smaller, light blue dragon backed off.

Instead of chasing after the Wyvernmoon, she—at least Jasmine assumed the dragon was a she, based on her size and looks—did the strangest thing Jasmine had ever seen. With a high-pitched scream that raised the hair on the back of Jasmine's neck, the dragon raked her claws straight down the sky.

Under Jasmine's horrified and disbelieving gaze, the sky seemed to split in two—and out of the new portal poured too many of the pitch-black dragons to count. The first casualty was a golden brown Dragonstar sentry, who went careening to the ground after one of the Wyvernmoons raked his claws straight down the other dragon's belly.

All hell broke loose, as the black dragons swarmed Dylan and his sentries. Jasmine tried desperately to see Quinn in the melee, but there was too much fighting—and too many black dragons—to find him.

She spotted the golden brown dragon, which had fallen a few feet away and was shifting slowly back to human form. She ran for him, once again cursing her missing medical bag. If by some miracle she managed to get out of this nightmare alive, she was going to transfer the supplies to a backpack—and make damn sure she never went anywhere without it.

As she ran, she caught a glimpse of bright green scales out of the corner of her eye and whirled just in time to see Quinn punch one huge claw into an enemy's chest and rip its heart out. The thing was dead before it ever hit the ground, but three more dragons bore down on him.

"Quinn! Look out!" she screamed, but he was already shooting fire from his palms in a long stream that took out one dragon and seriously singed a second.

At her feet, the injured Dragonstar groaned weakly, and Jasmine forced herself to look away from Quinn and do the job she was trained for. He could take care of himself, she told herself, even against an entire clan of pissed-off dragons. She only wished she believed it.

"What's your name?" she asked the injured man, as she fell to her knees beside him.

"Shawn." His voice was barely audible, and when she went to take his pulse it was weak and fluttery.

"Okay, Shawn. I'm going to help you until Quinn can get over here. I'm not a healer, so it's probably going to hurt a lot more than when Quinn does it, but I don't think I have a choice." She looked down at his stomach, which had been ripped open in much the same way Tyler's had been a few days before. *Damn these Wyvernmoons and their killer talons.*

She looked at Shawn's stomach, which was gushing blood. She needed her bag, an operating room, something! How the hell was she supposed to stop the bleeding if—

A thought occurred to her—a terrible thought that was probably going to hurt Shawn like hell, but one that just might save his life. Reaching into her hair, she pulled out one of the sparkly bobby pins she used to keep her bangs out of her eyes when she was working. Then muttering a prayer for this to work, she shoved her hand deep into Shawn's pelvis, searching for the vein that was gushing so much blood.

Unlike with Tyler, she found it on the first try—*thank God*—and managed to clamp it with the bobby pin. It was a desperate measure— a field surgeon's stopgap—but it would keep him from bleeding out until they could get him moved. If—and it was a big *if*—the fight ended in the next few minutes, he'd survive, though the extended lack of blood supply to his leg might mean amputation was the only option.

Shawn grew pale, his lips pressed tightly together in agony. "I'm sorry," she whispered to him. "I know it hurts. Just bear with me until Quinn gets here."

"I'm fine," he said through gritted teeth, a blatant lie. He had a hole the size of a cantaloupe in his stomach and bone-deep cuts in his shoulder and chest; he was shivering violently despite the early summer heat. Fine was not quite how she would describe him.

Whipping off her shirt, she tried to wipe some of the blood away so she could see how much damage had been done to his chest, but every time she got it clear, more blood welled up. Finally, she just gave up and rubbed him soothingly, praying that the battle being waged in front of them would end soon—and that the Dragonstars would win it. But frankly, she couldn't see how that was possible.

Animalistic cries and screams filled the air, along with the heavy thud of bodies colliding with each other. Lightning and fire whizzed in all directions, coming dangerously close to them on numerous occasions.

Biting her lip as one of Dylan's dragons sent flame streaming way too close to Shawn for comfort, Jasmine climbed to her feet and began dragging the six-foot-six, two-hundred-and-seventy-pound man back into the alley where Logan had stashed her. Moving him went against all her training as a doctor, but leaving him out there—exposed—seemed like an even worse idea.

Shawn passed out about a hundred feet before their destination, which was a blessing, since she didn't have to worry about causing him more pain as she dragged him. When they were finally in the relative safety of the alley, she checked his pulse and breathing—both of which were weak, but present—and then looked around for a weapon.

There wasn't much to work with, but she finally found a plastic beach umbrella that had been discarded near the Dumpster all the way at the back. It wasn't the best weapon, by any means, but after quickly unscrewing the pole from the umbrella, she had a long, hollow stick with a very sharp tip. With enough force it might be able to do some damage—not enough to actually kill a dragon, but maybe enough to buy them time for more help to arrive.

Carrying her prize, along with a few empty glass beer bottles, to the front of the alley, she laid them down next to Shawn, then broke the bottles against the wall, like she'd seen them do in movies. It wasn't as easy as it looked on TV, but she finally got two with wicked edges. Of course, if the Wyvernmoons got close enough for her to be able to use the bottles, she pretty much figured she'd be dead, but it made her feel a little better to have them.

A huge series of battle screams came from outside the alley. After checking to make sure Shawn was still stable—or as stable as he could be—she ran to the opening to see what was going on.

A whole other group of dragons was arriving, whose colors ranged from purples and golds to blues and reds. Dylan's other sentries had finally arrived.

Jasmine's shoulders slumped in relief, even though she could see they were still outnumbered two to one—thanks to the light blue dragon who had let the bastards in. The new dragons headed straight for Dylan, who was fighting back to back with Quinn and a huge blue dragon that she assumed was Gabe, as the three fought off what looked like eight black dragons.

While she watched, one of the Wyvernmoons wielded a lightning bolt like a sword. More than once it landed on Quinn, sizzling across the skin of his chest and arms and leaving black marks in its wake.

She wanted to go to him, wanted to help as she normally would, but in this situation she was seriously outgunned and she knew it. She would only be a liability. The knowledge stung.

The new dragons ripped through the group surrounding the Dragonstar king, and soon all eight of the enemies lay dead and dying on the street. Dylan and his sentries turned their attention to the other Wyvernmoons, who were locked in battle with Logan and a female dragon.

Jasmine winced as she realized how badly the two dragons were injured, guilt assailing her as she realized she'd sent Logan out into that mess. But without him, the purple female dragon—one who had arrived with the first group of reinforcements—would have been dead by now. She looked close to death as it was.

"What's going on out there?" Shawn whispered. "How bad is it?"

"Nine other Dragonstars arrived and it's helping. Dylan is okay and so are the others. They're all injured, but they're all still flying—which means they're in better shape than you are."

"Where's Callie?" he demanded.

"Which one is she?" she asked. She'd met all the sentries in their human forms, but unless she'd seen them shift, she didn't have a clue who was who.

"The light blue one that caused all this," he muttered, and for the first time, his voice had a bit of strength to it. "Traitorous bitch."

"That was Callie?" Jasmine hadn't gotten much of an impression of the woman the one time they'd met at the lab, but she'd seemed nice enough. Talk about looks being deceiving.

"Yeah."

"I don't see her now."

"Probably ran away like the fucking coward she is." Shawn tried to struggle into a sitting position, but he wasn't strong enough, and he fell back to the dirty street. She checked his pulse—at his wrist and in his leg—and didn't like what she found. She needed Quinn and needed him now, or she wasn't sure Shawn was going to make it.

Picking up her makeshift weapon, pathetic as it was, she told Shawn, "I'm going to try to get Quinn. I'll be right back."

"Jasmine, no!" He snagged her wrist as she was standing up, and though he was in bad shape, he was still incredibly strong. "You can't go out there."

"If I don't get Quinn, you'll die."

"He'll kill me, anyway, if I let you go into the middle of that. Just stay here. It'll be okay."

"No, it won't. You don't have much time left, Shawn." She tried to twist her wrist away from him, but he was too strong. "Come on, let go."

"No."

Gritting her teeth, knowing that every second that passed was precious, she finally did the only thing she could think of. She dropped the umbrella pole and with her now-free hand hit Shawn hard in his leg wound, with all of her body weight behind it.

He didn't make a sound, but his eyes rolled up into the back of his head as he passed out. "I'm sorry," she whispered, grabbing up the meager weapon and running for the opening at the front of the alley.

She'd barely taken two steps onto the sidewalk when the light blue dragon—Callie—landed in front of her. Unsure of what to do, knowing only that she was in seriously deep shit judging by the red haze in Callie's eyes, Jasmine started sidling toward where the other dragons were fighting. Surely, if she got close enough, one of the Dragonstar sentries would notice her being stalked by a rabid, pissed off dragon. If she was really lucky, maybe Quinn would notice, and she could kill two birds with one stone.

But with her third step, Callie let out a horrendous screech and came straight at her—razor-sharp talons raised to do as much damage as possible.

Jasmine clutched her umbrella pole, pointing the sharp tip straight at the dragon, who barely seemed to notice the weapon. This was completely understandable, as the metal was no match for her claws, her teeth or the fireballs Jasmine knew she possessed.

Still, standing and taking it wouldn't do any good. Jasmine stepped forward as Callie got closer, raising the pole straight up and shoving with every ounce of strength she had.

It went straight into the dragon's sensitive underbelly, impaling her. Callie screamed, loud and long, and still Jasmine pushed, afraid to stop. Callie's eyes glowed feverishly and, even wounded, she lifted her talons to strike her attacker. Jasmine braced for it, knowing it would be a killing blow. Knowing there was no escape.

The claw came down and Jasmine gritted her teeth, preparing for the pain—but the blow never landed. In the blink of an eye, Quinn was there, grabbing Callie's talons in his teeth and crunching down. Jasmine heard the bones break even over Callie's screams, and then even the shrieks were silent as Quinn sliced her neck open, from one side to the other.

Callie was dead before she even hit the ground.

Quinn shifted quickly. "Jasmine, what—"

She pointed to the alley. "Shawn's dying. You have to help him. He won't make it much longer."

284 • TESSA ADAMS

Quinn didn't argue, just picked Jasmine up and ran with her back to the alley. Quinn started cursing as soon as he saw Shawn, but he was incredibly gentle when he set Jasmine back on her feet. Jasmine watched him run to the other male. Wanting to help as well, she started to follow, but with the first step her legs went out from under her.

She hit the ground hard, then didn't even try to fight it as she passed out for the first—and hopefully last—time in her life.

CHAPTER THIRTY-FOUR

Hours later, Jasmine stood in a hot shower at Phoebe's house, washing blood and grime and God only knew what off of herself. She knew her friend was doing the same, as were Dylan and Quinn and a number of the other sentries. It was a good thing the house had a lot of bathrooms.

She still couldn't believe the fight was over—and that Callie was the only Dragonstar to die, despite the Wyvernmoons best efforts. Shawn had been badly injured, as had Jase and Riley, and it would take time for them to recover, despite Quinn's healing powers. But the others had been in pretty decent shape, and she, Phoebe, and the clan's other doctor, Gerald, had been able to patch them up without Quinn's help.

This was a good thing, as Quinn was still pissed at her for passing out. Like she'd had any control over it. Hell, she was pissed enough at herself for both of them. She still couldn't believe she'd keeled over like a total candy ass. She'd been through civil wars, bomb blasts, firefights and the worst viruses on the planet and never lost her cool. But one fight with a bunch of dragons, and she face planted at the first opportunity. It was humiliating.

Feeling dirtier than she could ever remember, Jasmine scrubbed and scrubbed at her skin, ignoring the pain in her ribs where Brock had cheap-shotted her, as well as the large, very painful bruise on her shoulder. She had bigger things to worry about.

She told herself it wasn't her fault. Callie had attacked her first, and she hadn't even been the one to kill the dragon, but it didn't matter. She couldn't forget driving that pole into Callie's belly, punching through skin and muscle and internal organs.

It wasn't like cutting a person with a scalpel, and she prayed that she'd never have to do it again. Having a hand in taking Callie's life—even in self-defense—was the worst thing she'd ever done.

A wave of dizziness hit her, sharper and more severe than back in the alley. She almost lost her footing. Bracing a hand against the shower wall, Jasmine slowly lowered herself to the floor, keeping her back braced against the wall as she waited for the world around her to stop spinning.

It finally did, but it took a long time. The water went cold around her; she shivered, still not well enough to stand. Finally she attempted to get up, lost her balance and banged her sore shoulder against the shower wall. She saw stars.

Shutting off the water, she dried herself quickly, then took a minute to poke at her shoulder. The pain was getting worse, not better, and as she ran a gentle finger over it, she could tell why. The bruise was on fire, and under the surface was a giant knot. The softest touch made her wince. If she hadn't known better, she would have sworn it was an—

Oh shit. Jasmine's heart pounded faster as she went over to the mirror to get a better look at it.

Oh shit, she thought again. There it was, in the center of the knot.

Another wave of dizziness swamped her, the feeling having nothing to do with Callie and everything to do with the terror sweeping through her.

Sinking down on the bed, Jasmine buried her head in her hands. Now she was well and truly fucked.

Quinn waited impatiently for Jasmine to join him and the other dragons in Dylan's very large family room. He didn't know what was taking her so long, but if she didn't show up in the next five minutes, he was going to go up to her room and drag her ass down here if necessary.

He wanted to see her, to touch her, to make sure she was okay after everything she had seen and done that day. Phoebe, sitting on Dylan's lap, looked shaken, and she'd been around the dragons a hell of a lot longer than Jasmine had. Was it any wonder his mate was hiding in her room? She was probably wondering the best way to get the hell out of there, and he didn't blame her a bit.

The only thing that kept him from storming up to her room and demanding that she let him in was their fight that morning. He couldn't believe less than twenty-four hours had passed—so much had happened it felt like a week. She'd basically told him she didn't want him for a mate, and it hurt to remember her words.

Her breakthrough earlier at the lab had boggled his mind, and she'd discovered it after only four days. He had been working on a solution for years. Phoebe had been damned right when she'd said that Jasmine was brilliant at what she did. As he'd worked with Dylan yesterday—breaking down the antibodies they'd developed against the virus in an effort to formulate a vaccine—he'd been overwhelmed by his feelings for her.

Gratitude, awe, desire, need—all had combined inside of him, mingling with love, until all he could think about was how lucky he was to have *her* for a mate. How he would do anything and everything to keep her safe, to keep her with him and to let her know how much she meant to him—if she let him.

Then all hell had broken loose. He'd never in his life felt the kind of terror he'd experienced when Logan had told him he was on the run with Jasmine. His entire world had narrowed to that one thing, that one moment, the desire to do and sacrifice anything to save her. Himself, Logan, even Dylan, when he had spent the last four hundred years ensuring that his king was safe. It was a horrifying feeling, and an awe-inspiring one.

What it meant—what it boiled down to—was that he wasn't going to let her go. She could call him whatever she wanted, accuse him of being a Neanderthal, throw the biggest hissy fit imaginable, and it wouldn't matter. She was his, and he would ensure she stayed with him.

There was no other option.

Quinn glanced up at a sudden commotion at the door. Jasmine stood there, looking even paler and weaker than before—as though she was on the verge of collapse. He was across the room before he was even conscious that he had moved.

Tyler beat him there. Quinn stiffened as the other man held out a hand to her. What was Tyler doing? The traitor Callie had been Tyler's sister—Quinn had known her since she was a little girl. He still couldn't believe that she had betrayed them—and that Quinn had been the one who killed her, with help from Jasmine. Ty looked absolutely sick, but he hadn't spoken about it yet, and Quinn wanted to make sure he didn't take his sorrow out on Jasmine. He put a hand on the small of her back to offer support—and to ensure Ty knew she belonged to him.

He didn't have to worry. Ty bowed his head and slumped his shoulders, as if ready to offer an apology, but Jasmine spoke first.

"I'm sorry, Ty. I wish there was something else I could have done—anything else."

Ty shook his head. "I've known something wasn't right with her for a long time. It's my fault that I never saw how far wrong things had gone. I'm glad you're okay, Jasmine."

Her smile was pained. "I'm glad we're all okay."

Ty nodded, then headed for the front door, as if just being in the same room with the other dragons hurt. Maybe it did. Quinn tried to imagine what it would feel like if one of his brothers had betrayed the clan, and he blanched. Yeah, it would be too painful.

Then Jasmine looked up at him and smiled, a small, painful twisting of her lips that twisted Quinn's insides as well. "Come on over here, sweetheart," he murmured, grabbing her hand and hoping she wouldn't reject him. "Dylan has food prepared."

She followed him quietly, which itself surprised him. He half expected her to hit him with the nearest blunt object—after all, he hadn't been exactly courteous to her since the fight. The sight of her taking on a fully grown, raging dragon with nothing but a plastic pipe was going to stay with him for a long time, and not in a good way. He blamed himself for letting her get in that situation, but that didn't make her close call any easier for him—or his beast—to deal with emotionally.

About halfway across the room, Jasmine's knees gave out and she stumbled. She would have gone down hard if Quinn hadn't caught her and swept her into his arms. He carried her over to his spot in one of the wingback chairs near the window and cuddled her on his lap. Fight or no fight, she could damn well let him take care of her when she needed it.

"Are you okay, Jazz?" He spoke softly, not wanting to spook her. "I can take you back upstairs to rest. Or to my place." His gaze swept over her body, which was clad in the ubiquitous yoga pants and tank top, this time with a jacket thrown over them.

She didn't answer, just buried her face in his chest and breathed him in. He knew exactly how she felt. He wanted nothing more than to suck in great gulps of air himself, to absorb the sweet, wild scent of her so deeply into himself that he would never get it out.

After a minute, she raised her head and looked straight at him, as if she were bracing herself. Then she said, "I want nothing more than to go back upstairs and sleep. But—" She held up a hand to stop him as he started to get to his feet. "I think you should probably take me to the clinic."

"The clinic? Why?" He glanced over her, looking for a wound he'd missed on his first inspection of her after the fight. "Do your ribs hurt?"

"It's not my ribs I'm worried about."

"Then what?"

She took a deep breath and slid her sweat suit jacket off her shoulder. "I'm pretty sure that Brock or Callie got me at some time during the fight."

"Got you?" he demanded, his brain absolutely unwilling to comprehend what she was saying. "What does that mean?"

She pointed at her shoulder, where a large, red welt had formed. "Someone injected me with something, Quinn. And judging from the way I'm feeling, I think we both know exactly what it is."

CHAPTER THIRTY-FIVE

There was a roaring in his ears, a flame in his belly, a rage deep inside that grew with each second Quinn stared at Jasmine in the goddamned hospital bed. He felt on fire, like his skin was too tight and his body too fragile. He felt ready to explode, and there was nothing anyone could do to stop it.

She was sleeping, her face pale and wan, her body trembling under the thick blankets, despite the fact that her temperature was dangerously high. Phoebe had already given her a mixture of Tylenol and Advil—human medicines—to bring her fever down, but they had barely touched it. They were waiting on a nurse to bring the cooling packs, but Quinn didn't hold out much hope.

Phoebe didn't either. Jasmine was dying, and there was nothing they could do about it. He'd spent the last few hours frantically reviewing his notes from the day before, as had Phoebe, both of them searching for a way to cure this. But it would take weeks, months to grow a vaccine based on their ideas—and that wouldn't help Jasmine. She was already infected.

His beast raged at his inability to do anything, clawed at him in an effort to get out. In an effort to help its mate. But there was nothing he could do but stand and watch as Jasmine's temperature spiked, as her legs and hands went numb.

All they could do was wait for the worst to happen. Wait for her to die the same terrible death the others had.

Quinn fell to his knees, hitting the floor by her bed hard. Tremors ripped through him as he buried his face in her bed sheets, trying to absorb her scent. Trying to hold her inside him. It didn't work. All he could smell was the hospital disinfectant, the sickness, the pain that surrounded her.

He wanted to rage, wanted to scream, but doing so would only wake her up. Only make her pain more intense. So he kneeled, tears streaming down his face for the first time in hundreds of years, and prayed like he had never prayed before.

He needed an idea, needed a cure, needed something to help her. He'd give himself up, take her place, do anything, he bargained—if only she would get better. It should be him lying on that bed, him shaking and suffering from this damn disease. Not Jasmine. Never Jasmine.

Phoebe came closer, rested a hand against his shoulder, and he nearly bit it off, though he knew she was only trying to comfort him. But he was beyond comforting.

He was nearly rabid with pain, nearly blind with it.

He couldn't lose her.

He couldn't lose his mate.

Not Jasmine.

Not Jasmine.

Not Jasmine.

The words were his mantra, a refrain in his mind that played over and over as he fought for control.

It was a long time coming, and the only way he managed to achieve even a semblance of calm was to remind himself that this wasn't about him. It was about Jasmine, and she deserved more than to wake up to a wild, rampaging dragon who was more problem than comfort.

There would be time for his fury later. Right now, he needed to take care of her.

The nurse came in with the ice packs, and he placed them around her body. Phoebe tried to help and the dragon snarled at her. Jasmine was his mate—he would take care of her.

She woke up when the ice packs touched her, her body shivering so violently that her teeth knocked together. "Qu-Qu-Quinn," she gasped, reaching for him.

"I'm here, sweetheart. I'm right here, Jasmine."

She grabbed on to his hand with her trembling one, and he was horrified at how weak she was. The disease was progressing faster now—faster even than it had with Brian and his family. Was it because she was human, the doctor in him wondered, or just because that was the new nature of this beast?

Not that it mattered. Either way, she was dying and there was nothing he could do about it, nothing.

"I'm c-c-cold," she choked out. "So cold."

"I know, sweetheart. But we have to get your fever down."

"Please. Please." The words came out on a small sob, the best that Jasmine could do in her weakened state, and they nearly killed him as he finished putting the ice packs around her.

"Baby, I have to. We have to get your fever down."

She moved her head back and forth on the pillow, softly, carefully, but even that movement hurt. He could see it in her eyes, in the way she clenched her teeth to keep from crying out.

Goddamnit! The beast grabbed hold of him by the throat, frustration and fury riding him hard as his talons punched through the tips of his fingers. He fought it back, tried to stay focused, tried to stay centered, but it was almost impossible. His mate was dying and he was causing her more pain.

He could barely breathe with the agony ripping apart his insides.

"Quinn." Dylan's voice came from the doorway—cool, concerned. "Maybe you should go for a little while. Take a walk, get some fresh air."

He turned on his king, had him up against the wall in a heartbeat, his hand around his best friend's throat. "How dare you?" His voice was barely human. "That's my mate. My *mate*. You want me to leave her? Just walk away from her while she suffers?"

Dylan didn't move, didn't try to defend himself. He just met Quinn's eyes, reflecting his own hell right back at him.

"Fuck." Quinn pulled away, thrust a hand through his hair. "Sorry, Dylan. I didn't mean—"

Dylan shook his head, then draped an arm around Quinn's shoulders. "My fault. It was a stupid thing to say. I would never leave Phoebe."

"Quinn!" Jasmine called his name, and he was back at her bed in a heartbeat.

"What, sweetheart?" It was his turn to take her hand. He lifted it to his lips, kissed the center of her palm.

"Stop it! You're acting—" Her breathing was labored. "You're acting like a Neanderthal."

"I am a Neanderthal, Jazz. I thought you knew that."

She smiled through the pain. "There's a lot I never got to learn about you." She stifled a sob. "I'm sorry I was such a bitch yesterday."

He brought her hand to his chest, held it tightly against his heart. "Don't be."

"Maybe this sick thing isn't so bad after all," she said with a weak laugh. "It gets you out of all kinds of shit."

She started to cough, turning her head away from him and fumbling for the basin sitting on the table next to her bed. He watched in horror as she spit up blood, again and again. Copious amounts. His heart squeezed so tightly in his chest that he feared it might explode.

He rubbed the back of her head while she coughed, then handed her a small cup of water to rinse out her mouth. The disease was shifting, progressing, moving to the next stage as the virus ravaged her lungs and started in on her other organs.

He couldn't stand it any longer.

Closing his eyes, Quinn tried to center himself, but it was hard.

Jasmine's pain dragged at him, nearly took him under, but he forced himself to step back. To pull inside himself.

He placed his hands on her stomach, and the familiar warmth that came when he healed someone flowed through him.

"Quinn, no!" She grabbed his hand, tried to push it away. "Don't do this to yourself."

He opened his eyes, pinned her with a look that brooked no argument. "Relax, Jasmine."

"I've seen you after you do this. It won't help. I'm going to die anyway. Please don't do this." Her voice cracked, then broke altogether. "I don't want to think that I hurt you, too," she whispered. "I don't want your last memories of me to be of the pain I caused you."

"It's not you that's hurting me," he hissed, bending close to her so that she could see the sincerity in his eyes, feel it in the way he touched her face. "If I don't at least try to ease your pain, it will kill me. Can't you see that?"

"Quinn!"

"Sssh." He rested his forehead against hers and used every ounce of strength he had to will her to calm down. "I love you, Jasmine. Let me do this for you."

She sobbed, shaking her head back and forth against the bed pillow. But she made no other move to stop him, and Quinn quickly took advantage of her compliance.

Placing his hands over her belly once more, he centered himself, opened himself. And let all of her pain come into him.

The first wave nearly brought him to his knees. It was more intense, more powerful than anything he had ever felt before. Was it because she was his mate, he wondered, or was her pain just that powerful? That intense? For her sake, he prayed it was the former.

As he worked his way through her body, shoring up her internal organs, trying to lower her fever, working to reduce the paralysis in her legs, the agony was excruciating. She was fully human, without the dragon's strength and power, and the disease was ravaging her much faster than normal—at least at this stage. It was as if everything had been accelerated by a good six to eight hours.

Fuck! The realization slammed him out of her body and back into his own. He tried to get back to her, to heal her a little more, but she shut him out before he could go back in, locking barriers in place that he didn't think she knew existed.

"That's enough, Quinn." Her voice was steadier, stronger than it had been in hours. "You did too much." She reached out a hand to him, and he took it, sinking gratefully into the chair Phoebe shoved next to the bed.

"Look at you. You look like hell again."

"I'm fine."

"No, you're not." She sighed, burrowed against him. "But thank you for what you did. I wasn't ready to leave you yet."

Her words had him choking on his own emotions, and he looked away, not wanting her to see him tear up. But she only laughed and said, "Come on, Quinn. If this is the last time I have to spend with you, I don't want it to be miserable. We deserve better than that, don't you think?"

He nodded. "Yeah. Of course." Neither noticed as Dylan and Phoebe slipped quietly from the room.

"Okay, then." She cuddled even closer. "Tell me something I don't know about you."

He laughed. "What do you know about me? We've known each other only five days."

"And yet it feels a whole lot longer, doesn't it?"

He nodded again, not trusting his voice.

"All right. I know that you're brilliant and talented and an incredible healer. You're generous, you work too hard, you give too much. You also have a terrible temper and a jealous streak a mile wide—which is a little surprising in a man of your intellect, I must admit."

"I was never jealous before you came along."

She grinned. "I don't know if that's a compliment or not."

"Oh, it's definitely a compliment. Before you, I never felt for a woman enough to care whether another man wanted her, would try to take her from me. But with you, I can't even think about you with someone else."

"It doesn't look like you have to worry about that now, does it? Interesting little side benefit of this damn virus, don't you think?"

"Shut up," he growled. "Don't joke about this."

"It's joke or cry, and I don't want to spend my last hours with you with tears rolling down my face. So . . ." She took a deep breath. "I've told you what I know. Now tell me what I don't."

She patted the bed next to where she was laying. "But do it from up here. I don't want to waste a chance to touch you."

"Okay." He settled himself gingerly on the bed, pulling her more firmly into his arms. "I love to watch the desert at sunrise, when the sun is just beginning to peek over the mountains. I hate that I'm the last of my family, that the line will die out with me because the Wyvernmoons killed my brothers and I couldn't stop them."

"It's not your fault."

"No, it's the Wyvernmoons'. And I swear I will destroy them for what they've done to my family. What they've done to you."

"Quinn, don't say that. You can't spend your life avenging the past."

He didn't answer; there was nothing he could say that wouldn't upset her. Because the one thing he knew, beyond a shadow of a doubt, was that after she died he would do whatever it took to ruin the Wyvernmoons once and for all. She deserved that much, and so did all of the other people who'd died at those bastards' hands throughout the years.

He didn't want to think about that now, didn't want to imagine his life without Jasmine. So he let it go, choosing instead to regale her with tales of his childhood and growing up the middle of three brothers.

They talked for hours, about little things and important things, about themselves and who they'd once been. With each hour that passed, Jasmine got weaker—her temperature spiking again, her body trembling, her lower body becoming completely paralyzed. He held her through it all, and as she drifted into an uneasy sleep, Quinn let the pain move through him. He embraced it, wrapped it around himself. He wanted to suffer as Jasmine did, to feel what she felt.

It was only fitting.

She was his—even if it was only for this very short time. It was his duty, his right, and his privilege to carry her burdens. She was his mate. They were one. They were—

He froze as a thought so outlandish, so bizarre, so medically questionable occurred to him that normally he would have discounted it completely. But he was desperate to save her, so desperate that he was willing to consider a treatment he would have laughed at the day before.

It wasn't going to work, he told himself, even as he eased himself off the bed. Jasmine whimpered in her sleep, and he comforted her absently, his mind already on the logistics of the task.

It couldn't work, he told himself, even as he rummaged through the cabinets gathering supplies.

In fact, it might even kill her. Yet he still went out into the hall to search for Phoebe. *But she's dying anyway.* At least she'd die knowing they did everything they could to save her. *Absolutely everything.*

He broke into a jog, yelling for Phoebe as he looked into every room he passed.

She came out of the lounge at a run. "Is it time?" she asked, following him down the hallway. "Is she—" Her voice broke.

"I have an idea," he answered. "It's crazy and it probably won't work, but it's an idea."

"What is it?" she demanded, her hands clutching at his arm, and he remembered, for the first time, that he wasn't the only one losing Jasmine. She was Phoebe's best friend, and her death wouldn't be easy on the future queen.

He explained his idea. Though Phoebe looked doubtful—really doubtful—she never said a word. Just helped him ready everything they needed.

When everything was assembled and Quinn was sitting next to Jasmine, Phoebe looked him in the eye and said, "Are you sure you want to do this? You know as well as I do that it could kill her faster than the virus."

He glanced at his mate, pale, paralyzed, already starting to bleed out. "If we leave her like this, she'll die in excruciating pain. Fast, slow. What's the difference? Dead is dead. Besides, I know she'd want us to try this. She wouldn't want to give up, even if the cure is fatal."

"I know. I just wanted to make sure you understand, in case things don't go as you hope."

Quinn nodded. "I do."

"All right, then. Let's do this thing."

Phoebe swabbed the inside of Jasmine's elbow, put in a small port for the blood transfusion, before turning to him and cleaning his arm as well. Then she inserted the needle into his arm, which would draw his blood out and into the tubing that was hooked up to Jasmine.

Before, they'd briefly debated the merits of collecting his blood and then transfusing it into Jasmine in the normal way, but Quinn was adamant that it not happen that way. They were one—his heart was hers, as was his body and his soul. His blood, with its virus-resistant antibodies, needed to be hers as well. And it needed to flow directly from his body to hers.

There were risks—of course, there were risks. He was dragon, she was human. Pumping his blood into her, with its very different DNA, might very well kill Jasmine. Her body might be too far gone, too inundated with the virus to fight to accept the antibodies in his blood. She might—

He cut his thoughts off as the blood started to flow from his arm into hers. Praying the entire time, Quinn watched, fascinated, as the dark red liquid worked its way through the tube and into her.

Praying that he wouldn't make her worse.

Praying that his blood wouldn't hurt her.

Praying that it would bring about the miracle he was so desperate for.

Phoebe kept the machine running and the blood pumping until he'd given Jasmine well over a liter. Then she shut it off. He objected that Jasmine needed more.

"We'll see what happens," Phoebe answered, unmoved by his pleas. "She's taken plenty, and you need to hang on to the rest of your blood. You might need it, you know."

He wanted to fight her: he had no need of his blood, no need of anything, if Jasmine died. But in the end, he kept his mouth shut, determined to save his arguments in case he needed to convince Phoebe to let him try it again.

The next hour and a half was the most excruciating of Quinn's life. He watched Jasmine—and the clock—with an intense obsession, waiting for signs that the blood transfusion was either helping her or killing her.

For the longest time, nothing happened. Then her temperature gradually got worse. The trembling started again, and her nose started bleeding.

"Shit, fuck, damn," Quinn cursed. He buried his head in Jasmine's stomach while Phoebe wiped the blood away.

"I'm sorry, Quinn."

"We need to try again." He lifted his sleeve feverishly, holding his arm out to her. "Come on. We need to do it again."

"It's not working. We knew it was a long shot."

"Bullshit. We haven't given it enough of a chance. She needs more of my blood."

"She needs to be left alone, to die with a little dignity."

"No!" He grabbed another kit, ripped it open. "She needs another transfusion." He tried to hand it to her.

Phoebe shook her head, stepped back. "I'm sorry, Quinn. I can't."

"Goddamnit! I know this is the right thing to do. I know it, Phoebe." Something inside was driving him, something more primal than his dragon. Something more instinctual. "Let me try one more time."

When she didn't move to help, he swore again. Then he slammed the needle into his own vein with all the finesse of a berserker.

"Quinn, what are you doing?" Phoebe rushed forward.

"I'm saving my mate." He reconnected Jasmine's port, then flipped the switch on the machine. Within seconds, his blood was pumping into Jasmine again. It wasn't as pretty as when Phoebe had done it, but the job was getting done, and that was all that mattered.

He gave blood until he felt light-headed, until his heart started stuttering in his chest, until Phoebe was screaming at him to stop. He ignored her and kept pumping his blood into Jasmine.

"Damn it, Quinn!" Phoebe yelled. "You're killing yourself." She stepped forward to turn the machine off, and he snarled at her, more beast than man.

"Fine. I'm going to get Dylan—and a sedative. If you haven't turned that thing off by the time we get back, I'm knocking you out."

"You can try." It was the dragon's voice, low and gravelly and dark.

Phoebe left in a huff, and Quinn closed his eyes, resting his head against the wall as weakness swept through him. He wasn't stupid. He knew he was giving Jasmine too much of his blood—he could feel the weakness weighing him down, the dangerous lethargy invading his mind.

But he didn't stop. He couldn't. He would rather die here, now, giving Jasmine a chance to live than to spend one day of his life without her. She was his mate, his everything, and giving his life for hers was no sacrifice.

Phoebe burst back through the door with Dylan on her heels and a syringe in her hand.

"Come on, man." Dylan laid a hand on his shoulder. "This is madness."

"It's not madness."

"Quinn, please." Phoebe took a step toward the machine, and he knocked Dylan out of the way, adrenaline surging through him.

"Don't touch it."

"We have to—"

He locked eyes with her, bared his teeth in a move no one—least of all Dylan—could mistake. "Don't. Touch. It."

Dylan stepped in front of his mate. "Phoebe, I want you to go back outside. Quinn is—"

"Stubborn as hell and mean to boot."

They all froze at the voice coming from the bed, then turned as one to stare at Jasmine, who was awake and struggling to sit up. "But he's mine and I would really appreciate it if you didn't kill him just yet." She eyed the blood-filled tube that ran from his arm to hers. "Or let him kill himself."

"Jasmine!" He was out of his seat in a heartbeat, reaching for the thermometer and blood pressure cuff. "You're awake."

"Now, can I take this damn thing off?" Phoebe muttered, but she was blinking back tears.

Quinn barely noticed as she turned the machine off and unhooked Jasmine. He was too busy staring at his mate's clear violet eyes, too busy taking in the healthy rosiness of her cheeks.

Ten minutes later, Jasmine continued to improve. Her blood pressure was normal, and she seemed perfectly coherent, but her temperature remained elevated. "How do you feel?" Quinn demanded.

"I feel good," she answered, moving her legs beneath the covers just to prove she could. "Better than I ever have."

She glanced at Dylan and Phoebe. "Is this energy running right under my skin what it feels like to be a dragon? Like your heart could burst right through your chest? Like you could take on the world and win?"

Dylan laughed. "That's exactly what it feels like."

She grinned. "I like it."

Phoebe checked her pulse and her responses to cold, heat and pain against the bottom of her foot, then retook her temperature. "I'm glad to hear that. Because it looks to me like Quinn gave you more than just his blood."

"What does that mean?" Quinn demanded. "Is she all right?"

"I think she's fine. But I also think she's got an awful lot of dragon characteristics all of a sudden, characteristics that weren't there before you did your little reverse vampire number."

"Dragon characteristics?" Jasmine repeated. "What's that mean?"

"I can't be sure without a blood test, but I'm thinking that Quinn's blood did something to you. Changed you," she added, at Jasmine's blank look. "Your temperature is elevated, and your pulse is much quicker. Your grip is a lot stronger than it's ever been. Quinn made you, if not a dragon, then the closest thing to it." Phoebe leaned over and hugged her. "Welcome to the clan."

CHAPTER THIRTY-SIX

Two days later, Quinn brought Jasmine home to the house he kept in town. The dragon wanted him to take her to his cave, wanted him to claim her there, where the rules of society had little impact.

But the man still remembered her so close to death, and he wasn't all that keen on being so far from the clinic, just in case she had a relapse.

"I'm perfectly capable of walking," Jasmine protested, laughing as he carried her through the house to his master bedroom.

"I know you are," he said, humoring her, even as he laid her in the center of the big bed. "This is for me."

"I bet," she snorted. She held her arms out to him and cuddled close as he settled on the bed next to her—which was all that mattered.

They lay like that for a long time, her fingers tangling in his hair as he rested his ear against her chest, listening to her heartbeat. It was dragon fast now, and his beast preened with the knowledge that he had done that to her. That his blood was running in her, changing her, making her Dragonstar. Phoebe didn't think she'd ever be able to shift because she didn't have an actual beast inside of her as the others did, but Quinn didn't care. All he cared about was that she was whole and healthy and now able to live as long as he could.

She was his mate, in every sense of the word.

"I love you, you know. And not just because you saved my life."
She whispered the words against the top of his head.

"I know that. I love you, too."

"Really?" she demanded, rolling with him so that he was on his
back and she was above him. "Then make love to me."

He shook his head. "I don't think you're ready yet. You nearly
died two days ago."

"But I didn't, thanks to you and your weird medicine." She
grabbed his hand, slid it inside the low-cut waistband of her yoga
pants. "I want to celebrate the fact that I'm alive, and I can't think of a
better way of doing that than making love with my mate."

His cock hardened at her words, and the easy way she called him
her mate. Rolling back over, he trapped her beneath him, reveling in
the soft heat of her as she tangled her legs in his.

"If we do this—"

"Oh, we're doing it," she said, licking her way down his throat.

"If we do this," he repeated, "we do it my way."

"Don't we always?"

"I don't want you to hurt yourself."

"Then hurry up and get inside me. I'm dying here."

"Don't joke about that!"

"God, you're bossy. Give it a rest."

"Why don't you give me a rest?"

Her hand slipped between them, massaged his cock. "I'd rather
give you a ride."

Quinn gave up, letting his absolute joy in his mate—his beautiful, healthy, alive mate—swell through him. Then he pulled her hand
back up to his mouth, where he used his tongue to stroke from her
wrist to the top of her palm, lingering for long moments over her
chained and broken life line.

She'd had a rough time, this mate of his, but now she was his to
protect. His to care for, and he would do whatever it took to make
sure that she had what she needed to be safe—and happy.

Jasmine gasped at the feel of his tongue on her, going perfectly still. And for a moment—just a moment—she was soft and pliant, her body his to command.

He pressed himself against her, savoring the feel of her soft, lush curves against the hard planes of his own body even as he made sure not to rest his weight on her injured ribs. Then her arms were around him, pulling him down to her, and everything he wanted to say to her, everything he wanted to promise, simply faded away as desire—harsh and all-consuming—took over.

Jasmine sighed as Quinn pulled her even more tightly against him, until she could feel every part of him pressed to every part of her. His arousal was hard as a brick between her thighs and she delighted in it. She moved restlessly in an effort to feel him more fully against her.

He accommodated her, shifted his strong hands until they were cupping her ass. Then he was lifting her, shaping her, molding her body to his as he thrust against her.

"Put your legs around me," he growled against her lips, and she did. The pleasure—the sweet, soft, incredible pleasure that came from the movement—made her gasp in delight.

He took instant advantage, his tongue slipping between her parted lips with all the subtlety of a conquering army. But as he stroked it against the top of her mouth, ran it in one glancing caress over her own tongue, Jasmine couldn't bring herself to care. Not when his invasion sent frissons of delight through her whole being. Not when she'd been so certain that she would never feel him like this again.

The thought sent need spiraling through her, and she rocked against Quinn, desperate to have him inside her where he belonged. Desperate to feel him anywhere and everywhere as he claimed her.

It was a strange feeling for a woman who had spent her life running from emotional entanglements—and from alpha males who expected her to bend to their every whim. But she didn't mind

Quinn's dominance anymore, not when she knew she was more than capable of standing up to him.

Not when she knew that he would never force or bully her into doing anything she didn't want to do.

And not when she knew how very much he loved her—enough to give up his life for her. It was the same way she loved him.

As she pulled him down to her for a kiss that went from sweet to wild to hotter than hell, she thanked God for giving her this beautiful man. For showing her a way to have him and be true to herself as well. It was more than she had ever guessed was possible.

"Jasmine, baby, you're killing me."

"I'm not doing anything," she answered, even as she nipped at his full, gorgeous lips.

"Fuck," he whispered. It was a curse, a prayer, a statement of intent, and she was more than willing to go along with him for the ride.

"Quinn," she gasped, his name suddenly the only word she knew.

He bucked against her, his cock growing harder still. Then he was kissing the corners of her mouth. She waited, lungs burning, body on the brink of an explosion, for him to continue.

But suddenly he was the one moving slowly, his tongue tracing every curve of her lips before he nibbled his way across her cheek, down her chin to her throat. She arched, tilting her head to the side to give him better access, moaned as he licked at the pulse beating crazily at the hollow of her throat.

Heat sizzled along her nerve endings, burst into flames that seared her from the inside out. She pulled him closer, so close that she could feel his heart beating wildly beneath the firm muscles of his chest. So close that the fine sheen of sweat coating his neck mingled with her own.

Pushing against him, she rolled them over yet again, so that she was once more on top. She ran her hands over his pecs, toyed with his nipples through his T-shirt, reveled in the involuntary surge of his hips against her own. She lifted and lowered herself, riding the hard ridge of his erection as she would if there were no clothes between them.

He groaned deep in his chest and went from teasing to dominating in an instant. Claiming her, he bit her lower lip, sucked it between his teeth and brushed against it with his tongue. He delved deeply into her mouth, so deeply that she couldn't remember what it was like to breathe without him there.

His tongue caressed hers, circling, playing, turning her inside out with each touch. He tasted so good—of limes and the desert and hot, burning passion—that she knew she'd crave the taste of him for the rest of her days.

"Quinn," she moaned again, sliding her hands up to the cool, wet silk of his hair. Tightening her fingers until she knew there was a pinprick of pain. Tightening them more until he erupted with a growl.

Then he was devouring her, his hands squeezing her ass while his denim-clad cock slid back and forth between her thighs. His mouth was everywhere, *everywhere*, moving down her throat to nudge aside the neckline of her tank top so he could trace his tongue over the swell of her breasts. Nuzzling the curve of her breast as his tongue swept over her lace-covered nipple with small, velvet strokes that had her burning hotter than ever.

She was on fire, her body aching and heavy and desperate for the feel of him within her. His fingers dipped beneath the waistband of her pants, stroked her skin until all she could feel was him, all she could think of was him.

Once she would have regretted this, would have hated letting him see her so vulnerable and needy. But none of that mattered now, nothing mattered but him and having him inside her now and for the rest of her life.

Then Quinn's teeth scraped against her nipple and she forgot her own name, let alone any reservations she once had about being with him. She had never wanted anything the way she wanted him, her entire body tightening until the need to come was a screaming agony within her.

Her hands clutched at his hips and urged him closer. Urged him to take them all the way. His laugh, low and seductive, brushed against her painfully hard nipple right before he pulled it into his mouth and began to suck.

She moaned, arched her back, pressed her breast more firmly against his mouth.

"Take me," she murmured, as he skimmed light hands up her arms, over her back. She was adrift, all of her concentration focused on this man and his carefully controlled caresses. "Please take me."

The words were out before she could stop them, a plea she hadn't known she was going to utter.

"I will," he answered, sliding his lips along her throat, and she didn't know if she should be relieved or disappointed at his easy acceptance of the physical meaning behind her words.

Then her gaze met his and she knew he hadn't taken anything lightly. His eyes glowed electric green, and they were filled with so much love and desire and possessiveness that she felt her own fill with tears.

This is what it is like to be loved, she thought, as he licked his way down her neck and shoulder.

This is what it is like to be wanted, she realized, as he nipped at her breasts and arms.

Then suddenly, he picked her up, shifted her so that her back was against his chest, and walked her slowly across the room. "What are you—"

"Trust me," he said, his mouth hot against the curve where her shoulder met her neck.

"I do." She was exactly where she wanted to be—in Quinn's hands, and she wasn't ever going to take that for granted.

Before she knew what was happening, Quinn positioned them in front of the mirror. She waited for the nervousness to come, but felt only need. For her lover. For her mate. She was in Quinn's hands and she knew he would never hurt her.

"What do you see?" he murmured, as he slipped her shirt over her head, then did the same to his own. His hands went to her breasts, cupped them from behind, and his thumbs played gently over her nipples.

"I see you," she answered, and it was no less than the truth. Here in the dim light of his bedroom, she did see him—all of him. The strong, powerful body. The wary eyes. The gentle heart that beat beneath the rough, domineering exterior. She saw the man who would walk through hell to keep her safe and who would expect her to do the same for him. It was more than she had ever dreamed possible.

"You are so unbelievably beautiful," he whispered into her ear. "I can't believe how beautiful you are."

She tried to turn, wanting to wrap her arms around him, but he held her fast, one large hand splaying across her pelvis to lock her in place.

"I want you to watch me take you," he murmured. "I want you to see everything I do to you as you feel it. I want you to watch as my hands and lips and body take yours."

Heat spiraled through her, had her pushing her back more firmly against his chest. His muscles rippled at the strong contact, his cock growing even harder and longer against her back. She reached behind her, cupped his ass through his sodden jeans and held him tightly against her. She needed to feel him, to anchor herself in the press of him against her—otherwise she would simply spin away, her body and heart and soul no longer hers to control.

Nothing in her whole life had ever felt as good as Quinn did at that moment. The feel of his body behind her, the touch of his hands as they glanced over her body again and again. She grew wetter, hotter, lust building with each touch of his fingertips.

She moaned, her hands clenching on his ass as she demanded more from him. But he merely laughed. "Don't be so impatient, sweetheart," he murmured against her ear, as he slowly slipped her wet pants down her legs. "We'll get there eventually."

"I need you now!" It was a whimper, a plea for mercy.

But Quinn had no mercy, and as she watched his eyes darken to forest green, she knew she was in for it. Today, this moment, Quinn would be satisfied with nothing but everything she had to give.

He groaned, his breath coming in hot pants against her cheek for long seconds before he pulled away to yank off his own clothes. "I need to make you crazy, need to hear you scream my name as you come. I came too close to losing you. I need to know that you're safe and healthy and here with me. Forever."

Her legs trembled, but she locked her knees in place, determined to give Quinn everything he asked.

He caught her eyes in the mirror and for endless seconds there was nothing else—just that one hot, elemental connection. For a moment she wanted to jerk away, wanted to close her eyes. It was too personal, everything she felt laid open to him in one blinding instant. But his eyes held her, trapped her, made her spellbound, and all she could see was him. All she wanted was him—and the life they could build together.

Then he was moving, his hard fingers cupping her aching breast. She jerked, arched into the sensation, melting as his fingertips swirled around and around her nipple, each circle bringing him closer to the aching bud, though he never touched it.

It was a double shot of sensation, to watch and feel those long, elegant hands touching her. Heat, rapid and all-consuming, built in her, raced down her nerve endings into every part of her body.

"You have the most beautiful breasts," he said softly, as he raised his left hand and cupped her other breast. "Look how pretty they are, Jasmine."

"Quinn." It was a protest, one he had no trouble ignoring.

"Your skin is such a gorgeous shade of ivory, with just the barest touch of rose. And so soft—you're so incredibly soft here, like the most expensive silk. And these—"

Finally, his hand glanced across her nipples and she moaned, arching into the contact, every cell in her body focused on that one brief touch.

"These are incredible. Sweet, responsive—" Again he ran a finger across her nipple; again she arched against the contact, seeking more. "And so damn sexy I could spend my life right here, loving them. Can I do that, Jasmine?" His breath was hot against her cheek, his words even hotter. "Can I suck these gorgeous nipples for hours? Can I slide my cock between your breasts and into that hot little mouth of yours? Can I come in your mouth, on your breasts? On your stomach? In that hot little ass of yours?"

"Quinn!"

His breathing was coming heavier, his big body shuddering against hers as his words wound their way around them both, chaining them more tightly together. "Can I, Jasmine? I need to be in every part of you, need to know that I've marked you, branded you. Claimed this hot little body of yours until all you feel is me."

His fingers tugged on her nipples and she screamed as fire whipped through her. "Until all you know is me. You're mine and I'm never giving you up."

"Yes," she gasped, her head thrashing back and forth against his chest as she tried to get closer to him. She wanted to take him every way she could, needed him in every part of her.

He leaned down, bit her neck, and she whimpered, her body going into sensory overload. But he didn't give her time to process her feelings. Instead, he kept moving, his tongue and lips and teeth trailing hot kisses over her shoulders and upper back even as his fingers continued to squeeze and flick and rub against her sensitized nipples.

It was too much, the heat rushing through her body. The lust clenching at her womb. Her eyes drifted closed as she savored everything Quinn could do to her body with such little effort.

"Look at me!" he barked, and her eyes flew open, electricity sizzling along her nerve endings.

He laughed at the heat in her eyes, sliding a hand down her stomach to her sex, shoving two long fingers roughly inside of her.

She cried out, her body bucking wildly against his as need—raw and overwhelming—stripped away everything but the desire to be underneath this man as he took her any and every way he wanted to.

"I want everything you are, Jasmine." He circled his thumb around her clit and hurtled her into an orgasm so intense her knees collapsed beneath her. He caught her, held her up with one powerful arm against her belly. "Everything you'll ever be."

"You have it." Once again, she met his eyes in the mirror, saw the heat and lust reflected in his.

"And will you take me in exchange?" His teeth sank into her shoulder and she shuddered, her body erupting again. "Take everything I am? Everything I want to give you."

"Yes!"

"There's no more running now, Jasmine. No more backing away from me. From what's between us." His fingers twisted inside of her. "You're my mate and this is forever."

"Yes!" she sobbed, riding his hands as need for him exploded within her. She couldn't take the pleasure, the torture. It was too much. Watching him and hearing him and feeling him—she couldn't think, couldn't catch her breath, couldn't do anything but experience.

Ripping herself out of his arms, she turned and sank to her knees in front of him. "Jasmine!" Quinn's voice was low, warning, but she paid no attention. She couldn't; all her concentration suddenly focused on the long, hard cock in front of her. She worked at his zipper frantically, yanking his pants down and off, then leaning forward until she could stroke her tongue up and around his huge length.

Quinn's breath slammed out of him, his hands tangling in Jasmine's hair of their own volition. This wasn't how it was supposed to go, wasn't how he'd planned it. But it felt so good, so fucking good, as she ran her tongue over his testicles before taking them into her mouth and sucking gently.

"Fuck, Jasmine." His hands tightened in her hair and he tried to pull her away, but she wrapped her arms around his upper thighs and hung on. Then he couldn't fight anymore, didn't want to fight, as the most incredible pleasure of his life slammed through him.

He glanced into the mirror and nearly came at his first sight of Jasmine's naked back. It was incredible, intense, more arousing than he thought possible to watch her from the back *and* the front as she took him.

When she finally pulled back, giving his balls one last kiss, he didn't know whether to give thanks or howl in disappointment. But she wasn't done—not by a long shot. Now her hot, gorgeous mouth was swallowing him whole.

Fuck, he was going to lose it, his cum boiling up inside of him as his mate claimed him as surely as he was claiming her. His control was in shreds, his body completely in her thrall, and he didn't care. He was hers to do with as she wished.

His teeth clenched, his jaw locked as the moist, sexy heat of her mouth drew him in deep. Her tongue ran in circles around his throbbing cock—up and down and around until he was clinging to control by his fingertips.

He looked down, watched as she slid him back and forth between those cherry-red lips of hers. Her eyes were closed, her long, golden lashes resting on her cheeks as she tucked the head of his cock against the roof of her mouth and slid him down her throat.

"Look at me!" His voice was low, guttural, more animal than human. But she understood what he was saying and those beautiful purple eyes flew open. He stared into their violet depths as she took him—as he fucked her mouth and she fucked him up—and wondered if he would ever be the same.

Then the pleasure exploded through him, sweeping up from his balls to the base of his cock, taking him by surprise as she sucked a little harder, her tongue wiggling over the sensitive spot on the underside of his cock.

"Fuck!" It was a groan, a plea, a prayer, but his mate had no mercy in her soul. She took him deeper, her hands clenching on his ass as she worked her throat convulsively.

And then he was coming, spurting inside of her, his cum jetting furiously into her mouth. She took it all, swallowed it down, consumed him and left him so damned shaky he nearly fell on her.

And still he burned.

Pulling her up by the hair, he spun her around, shoved her—stomach down—onto the bed. She moved to her knees, wiggling that sweet ass of hers, and it was as if his orgasm of a moment before had never happened.

With a growl, he launched himself at her, slamming himself into her hot pussy again and again. She screamed, pushed back against him. Her fingers tangled in the pillows, her head thrashed from side to side and her vaginal muscles gripped him in fits and spasms that had him seeing stars.

"Jasmine!" He called her name as the orgasm rose sharply in him. He wanted her with him, *needed* her with him with an intensity that was overwhelming.

And then she was screaming his name, her pussy clenching around him as her climax hit, the waves milking him despite his best efforts to hold on.

With a cry—of thanks, of need, of bone-wrenching fear—he came, emptying himself inside of her. Giving her everything he had in one bone-crushing, mind-numbing, soul-searing orgasm.

When it was done, when he could finally move without landing on his ass, he picked Jasmine up and carried her into the bathroom. He set her on the edge of the tub, then started the bathwater for her.

"I'm sorry. I wasn't planning on being that rough."

She wrapped her arms around his legs, rested her head on his stomach. "I'm not. I love it when you're like that."

"Yeah, but you just got out of the clinic—"

"Which I could have left yesterday, if my mate wasn't so overly protective."

"You nearly died," he growled, tilting her head up so that she had to look at him.

"But I didn't, thanks to you. And I was more than ready to begin our life together with a bang." She grinned at her deliberately bad pun.

"Are you sure?" he asked, the urge to know what she was thinking suddenly overwhelming. "A few days ago you stood here and told me you'd never be my mate."

"I was wrong."

"Yes, you were." He ignored her eye roll. "But I need to know what changed your mind. I need to make sure that you're not just here out of—" He broke off, unable to even say the word.

"Out of gratitude?" she asked archly.

He nodded.

"Oh, Quinn, how a man like you could be so insecure, I have no idea." She pulled him down next to her so that they were almost on eye level. "I'm here because there is nowhere else in the whole world that I would rather be—and no one I would rather be with. I fought against caring about you, against loving you, not because there's anything wrong with you but because I knew there was something wrong with me."

She paused, tried to look away but he wouldn't let her. "There's nothing wrong with you," he said.

"Let's see if you say that after living with me for a couple of weeks. I'm grumpy, mean-tempered, and often suspicious as hell. My family life wasn't the best—I told you that—and I've spent years running from my past. I didn't want to love you because I was afraid I would cave to your domination like my mother did to my father, like I did to him."

"You were a child and I would never hurt you. I would never expect you to bend to my will just because—"

She laid her fingers on his lips, stopping him abruptly. "I know that now. And I love you more because you would never force me to do something I didn't want to do. You might yell and bluster and use those fabulous eyes of yours to intimidate me—"

"You think my eyes are fabulous?"

She laughed. "You know they are. But you would never make me do something I didn't want to do. That's enough for me. More than enough for me."

"What about your job?"

"I think there's more than enough to keep me busy right here for now, don't you? And when my feet get restless, I figure we can take off together for a while. You wouldn't mind seeing the world with me, would you?"

"There is absolutely nothing I would like more."

"Good." She kissed him, hard. "Then what do you say? Do you think you can handle me?"

"I don't know." He stood up and lifted her against his chest before stepping into the bathtub. "But I'm willing to spend the rest of my very long life finding out."

"That's good enough for me."

"For me, too," he said, and for the first time in a very long time, his future was something to look forward to instead of dread.

It was more than enough.

Read on for an excerpt from

Tessa Adams's next Dragon's Heat novel,

FORBIDDEN EMBERS

Coming soon from Heat

He knew what he had to do.

Even as the words came to him—even as the *idea* came to him—Logan Kelly searched for a way around them. A way around *it*.

But there was none. He knew there wouldn't be. Better minds than his had been working on this for months now. Years. All to no avail. The thought that had snuck up on him as he'd been drifting off to sleep really was the only rational solution.

That didn't mean he had to like it.

The walls of the cave seemed to close in on him, the stalagmites a crowd of upturned daggers. Without conscious thought, he broke off the sharp tip of one and shoved it in his pocket before using a burst of preternatural speed to get outside.

Under the stars.

Amidst the cacti.

In the middle of the desert that had become more of a home to him than the rolling green hills of Ireland had ever been.

The thought destroyed him, made him dizzy. Nauseous. Not having forsaken Ireland, but having to soon forsake the endless caves and deserts of New Mexico as well. And with it the only men and women he'd ever considered friends. Family.

Bending over, he braced his hands on his knees and sucked huge, gulping breaths of air deep into his lungs. One after another, until the world around him stopped spinning. One after another, until the panic receded. *I'll do this for them*, he told himself, *because I'm the only one who can*. The realization steadied him, when just moments before he'd been certain that nothing could.

Unable to bear his thoughts—his own stillness—for one more second, he walked. Around him, the desert teemed with life. Night predators searched out prey. Prey scrambled for new and better hiding spots. In the distance, an owl swept down toward the still-warm sand at amazing speed. Seconds later, a small animal squealed in pain.

He refused to let it get to him. Predator, prey. It was the way of the world. Certainly, the way of *his* world. After a decade of watching his clan mates living in fear, he was sick of being the quarry. Sick to death of hanging around and waiting for the next attack, the next wave of sickness, the next horrifying death of someone he loved and was sworn to protect.

He was ready to strike. It was the nature of the beast, after all. The nature of *his* beast and those of his closest friends. He would find their weak spot, hit fast and hard. Whatever damage he sustained—even if it was absolute—would be worth it if he could finally find a way to neutralize the enemy.

He snarled at the thought of the Wyvernmoons, and his long legs ate up the miles, walking off his frustration, his pain. Inside, his beast thrashed and snarled in an effort to get out, but Logan kept him on a very short leash. One slip and the dragon would burst free. He couldn't afford that, not now, when logic and reason were everything.

The hot-tempered screams of the animal would not advance the case he knew he had to make.

As he walked, he memorized the feel of the desert at night. After living here more than two hundred years, he could call it up at will, but he wasn't taking any chances. South Dakota in winter was as different from New Mexico as one could get and still be in America. God only knew how many winters he would have to endure in that hellhole compound before he would once again find his way back here.

If he ever did.

The pragmatist in him knew that there was a good chance that he would die on this latest quest, knew that he might never see his beloved stretch of desert again. He didn't fear death—at three hundred and ninety-seven years old, he had faced that enemy many times before—but he did regret that he might never again enjoy the peaceful solitude of a walk over the land, his land, while a blanket of stars carpeted the sky.

He broke into a run, all but flying across the forty or so miles that separated him from the small house he kept in town. The closer he got to town, the more the telepathic voices and thoughts of the other Dragonstars crowded in on him. They pressed down from every side, nearly blinding him. Almost making him insane with the fear and worry and pain that threaded through so many of his fellow dragons.

It was exactly what he needed to cement his resolve. Usually his psychic abilities drove him nuts. Though they made things easier in battle, the rest of the time they were nothing but a pain in the ass.

An ability to eavesdrop on thoughts and conversations that were never meant to be public.

An invasion of privacy that, even after close to four centuries, he sometimes couldn't block.

His psychic ability was one of the reasons he spent so much of his free time deep in the desert, away from the other dragon shifters. It was often the only way he could give the civilian dragons of the clan any privacy. The only way he could quiet the nonstop chatter in his head.

He slipped silently into town, nodding to his friend and fellow sentry, Ty, as they crossed on the street. It was Ty's turn to patrol the town boundaries, and though Ty looked like he wanted to talk, Logan didn't stop. He couldn't afford to. His plan was only half-formed, and he didn't want to talk to anyone until he could back up his resolve with action.

No, he would wait until the council meeting in the morning, a gathering of the other sentries like himself, to reveal his plan. Till then, he had to prepare himself. He must be resolute, unshakable—otherwise, his king would never go along with what he wanted to do.

Dylan had to go along with it, a voice inside his head whispered. They were running out of time. Even with the new advances Quinn, Jasmine, and Phoebe were making against the virus that was killing his people, it was only a matter of time before the Wyvernmoons trotted out some new version of the disease. Even though their last attack was decimated, the Wyvernmoons would soon be back, looking to wipe out the Dragonstars once and for all.

He wouldn't let that happen. He couldn't. Not when this clan, *his* clan, was the only one who had taken him in after long centuries of searching. Not when these people, *his* people, had given him the only home he'd ever known.

This was one of the many reasons it was so difficult to contemplate leaving, and one of the main reasons he had to.

After looking around his house for signs of disturbances, he opened the door and let his senses flood the place—searching for the thoughts, the presence, of any intruders. He found none, but he still checked every room to make sure no enemies lay in wait. As he did, he cursed the Wyvernmoons and the fact that such hypervigilance was even necessary.

It wouldn't be for long, not if he had anything to say about it.

When he was convinced his house was clear, Logan strode into the kitchen and yanked a scissors out of one of the drawers. Then he went into the bathroom and, without remorse, cut off the long, flowing hair that had all but been his trademark for centuries. Amidst the Dragonstars, almost all of whom were dark, his long blond hair and red eyes were legendary.

With his hair was gone, he barely recognized himself. Then Logan reached into his pocket and pulled out the stalagmite he'd shoved in there earlier. He studied it for a moment. It seemed strong enough and sharp enough.

Then he reached up and raked the hard tip down the right side of his face, from his eye to the corner of his mouth.

He knew what he had to do. As his blood flowed freely down his face and neck, he also knew he had reached the point of no return.

He would do whatever it took to keep his clan mates safe.

ABOUT THE AUTHOR

Tessa Adams lives in Texas and teaches writing at her local community college. She is married and the mother of three young sons.